## "He'd be nothing without his daddy's money."

Gabby snorted and pushed the stroller to the trail once more. The words stabbed Dylan's heart. She could have been talking about him.

"Has he bothered you?"

"His attitude bothers me. Other than that, he's harmless." Her footstep faltered, but she adjusted her balance.

He'd have to take her word for it. But it was obvious she wasn't telling him the whole story. His spirits sank. Why *would* she confide in him?

He was merely the uncle she was being forced to deal with.

When they reached the end of the paved portion of the trail, they turned back. Gabby didn't want to tell him about her personal life. He got it.

Loneliness smacked him square in the middle.

He finally had a life worth sharing but no one to share it with.

He was playing at being an uncle, playing at being a cowboy, playing at being part of a small town. Something told him he was going to walk away from Rendezvous disappointed if he played at being important to Gabby.

**Jill Kemerer** writes novels with love, humor and faith. Besides spoiling her mini dachshund and keeping up with her busy kids, Jill reads stacks of books, lives for her morning coffee and gushes over fluffy animals. She resides in Ohio with her husband and two children. Jill loves connecting with readers, so please visit her website, jillkemerer.com, or contact her at PO Box 2802, Whitehouse, OH 43571.

**Laurel Blount** lives on a small farm in Middle Georgia with her husband, David, their four children, a milk cow, dairy goats, assorted chickens, an enormous dog, three spoiled cats and one extremely bossy goose with boundary issues. She divides her time between farm chores, homeschooling and writing, and she's happiest with a cup of steaming tea at her elbow and a good book in her hand.

# The Cowboy's Secret

## Jill Kemerer

## &

# A Rancher to Trust

## Laurel Blount

## LOVE INSPIRED
### INSPIRATIONAL ROMANCE

# LOVE INSPIRED®

INSPIRATIONAL ROMANCE

Recycling programs for this product may not exist in your area.

ISBN-13: 978-1-335-46278-7

The Cowboy's Secret and A Rancher to Trust

Copyright © 2021 by Harlequin Books S.A.

The Cowboy's Secret
First published in 2020. This edition published in 2021.
Copyright © 2020 by Ripple Effect Press, LLC

A Rancher to Trust
First published in 2019. This edition published in 2021.
Copyright © 2019 by Laurel Blount

All rights reserved. No part of this book may be used or reproduced in any manner whatsoever without written permission except in the case of brief quotations embodied in critical articles and reviews.

This is a work of fiction. Names, characters, places and incidents are either the product of the author's imagination or are used fictitiously. Any resemblance to actual persons, living or dead, businesses, companies, events or locales is entirely coincidental.

This edition published by arrangement with Harlequin Books S.A.

For questions and comments about the quality of this book, please contact us at CustomerService@Harlequin.com.

Love Inspired
22 Adelaide St. West, 40th Floor
Toronto, Ontario M5H 4E3, Canada
www.Harlequin.com

**Printed in U.S.A.**

# CONTENTS

# THE COWBOY'S SECRET

## Jill Kemerer

To Debbie Hanna and Ronda Gieskin
for your friendship and laughter. Love you both!

Peace I leave with you, my peace I give unto you:
not as the world giveth, give I unto you.
Let not your heart be troubled, neither let it be afraid.
—*John* 14:27

# Chapter One

"**Y**ou can't trust a cowboy." Gabby Stover typed instructions for housekeeping at the front desk of Mountain View Inn, the premier—and only—hotel in Rendezvous, Wyoming. Bright June sunshine streamed in through the large windows near the counter, but she kept her focus on the computer where it belonged. Her shift as the day manager would be over soon, and she still needed to check tomorrow's reservations and review her daily checklist.

"I'd give the cowboy outside a shot." Stella Boone, the new reception clerk, pretended to brush off her shoulder. "That hottie is definitely not from around here."

Gabby scrolled through the reservations, not bothering to glance out the window to catch a glimpse of the guy. She did *not* have time to indulge in Stella's uncanny radar for spotting attractive men. There was enough to deal with at the moment, especially since Babs O'Rourke, the inn's owner and Gabby's friend, had thrown down a bombshell this morning.

Was Babs really selling the place?

Gabby took a deep breath to relieve the sudden tightness in her chest. If the inn transferred to new owners, she'd more than likely no longer have a job. And she loved her job. She'd been working at the inn since she was nineteen years old. She was good at managing it—enjoyed meeting new people and sharing her enthusiasm about Rendezvous with them. It gave her pleasure to make sure they were comfortable. Plus it paid better than most jobs around here.

With the baby to think about, she needed every penny. Her niece, Phoebe, deserved a stable home and wonderful childhood—the opposite of what she and her sister, Allison, had endured.

"Do you think he's staying here?" Stella asked. "Maybe I can be his personal tour guide."

"I wouldn't get your hopes up." Gabby forced herself to speak in a pleasant tone. "Take it from me, cowboys are liars."

"That's a rotten thing to say, considering you're such good friends with Mason Fanning." Stella pulled a compact out of her purse and checked her appearance in the small mirror.

"First of all, this isn't the place to check your makeup. It's unprofessional." She tried to inject as much sternness as possible into her glare. "Second, Mason is a rancher, not a cowboy. There's a big difference."

"Sure. Big difference. Whatever you say." Stella fluffed her hair. "Does this mean Judd Wilson made it on your hot list, or is he more cowboy than rancher?"

Hot list? Gabby's eye began twitching uncontrollably. She'd hired Stella as a favor to the girl's sister, Nicole, who'd recently joined her support group and was due this summer with triplets. But Gabby's goodwill was quickly running out. As for Judd Wilson...the successful rancher was a looker, no denying it, but she had no romantic feelings for the man.

A shame. Judd was a good guy. But she was always attracted to the bad boys—the charmers in Stetsons with a twinkle in their eyes and snake oil on their tongues. Thankfully, she'd come a long way since the Carl debacle, and she had no intention of making a mistake of that magnitude again.

"Steer clear of cowboys, okay, Stella? It's for your own good."

"You sound as uptight as my sister. Ooh, he's coming in!" She tossed her blond hair over her shoulder and flashed her biggest smile.

Gabby had to refrain from rolling her eyes. Only then did she catch a glimpse of the man.

*Oh my.* Hottie didn't do him justice.

Her heartbeat thumped as her living, breathing cowboy fantasy-nightmare strode her way. He took off his hat, revealing short, messy black hair. She tried not to stare at his full lips, dark eyebrows and brown eyes. His shoulders were wide, hips slim, legs long. He wore jeans, cowboy boots and a black T-shirt. Flawless. Her knees trembled. She firmed her muscles.

This one was going to be trouble.

He stopped at the counter and exhaled as if something heavy was on his mind.

"May I help you?" Stella batted her eyelashes.

"I'm looking for Gabrielle Stover." Even his voice was perfection. Low with a slight rasp—a shiver rushed over her skin.

"You're looking at her." Gabby pasted on her most professional smile. "What can I help you with today?"

He frowned, pulling out a piece of paper from his

back pocket. She forced herself to look away from his sinewy fingers to check the clock. In another hour she'd pick up Phoebe from Eden's place and kick off her Friday night with a pizza. Maybe this would be the weekend she'd coax her niece to crawl. At nine months old, Phoebe was scooting and pulling herself up to a standing position with help from the furniture, but she'd yet to crawl. If only Allison could see her daughter... Sudden emotion clogged Gabby's throat. Her little sister would have been a great mommy if she'd lived.

The cowboy handed her the paper he'd smoothed out. She began to read. Her stomach dropped, leaving her nauseous, reeling.

*Oh, please, no. No...*

The man standing before her was Phoebe's father!

"Stella, keep an eye on the front desk." Gabby rounded the counter and curtly motioned for the man to follow her. She led him down the hall to her private office and offered him a seat before practically collapsing into her own chair.

"You're here for the baby." Saying the words out loud ripped something from her soul. He was here to claim Phoebe. He was going to take her niece—Gabby's whole world, the baby she'd been raising as her own ever since Allison's heart attack.

"Are you okay?" He tilted his head, those brown eyes darkening with concern. "You look...ill."

Ill? Of course she was ill! This was what she'd feared from the day Allison first tried to contact him. Her sister's poor judgment had led to a one-night stand during a trip to Texas. Allison had tracked down the guy, Sam Pine, and had written several emails to let him know she was pregnant and keeping the baby. He'd never responded, nor did he seem to be on any social media sites. After Allison died, Gabby had tried to contact him, too. As a last resort, she'd mailed a letter to the only address she could find linked to his name, although she'd doubted it was current. That had been six months ago.

Unfortunately, a father had rights, and there was nothing she could do about it. He was the dad. She was merely the aunt.

"I'm…fine." She tried to compose herself. "So, Sam, I—"

"Sam?" It was his turn to look green. "I'm not Sam. Sam died. I thought you knew."

Sam died? Relief swept in. This guy wasn't the father! He wasn't taking Phoebe away!

Shame brought her back to the situation at hand. She couldn't celebrate the sad fact Phoebe's father was dead. The baby truly was an orphan. How horrible.

"No, I had no idea." She shook her head. "He never responded to any of Allison's emails or mine, after—" she licked her lips and pressed them together, willing her emotions back in place "—after Allison died."

"I'm sorry about your loss." He averted his eyes, then glanced up at her once more. "What happened?"

She opened her mouth to speak, but the words jammed in her throat. *Come on. Tell him the facts. Don't get emotional. You've gotten good at it.*

"Twelve hours after giving birth to Phoebe, Allison was asleep in her hospital room and had a heart attack."

His exhalation came out in a whoosh. "A heart attack?" He rubbed his cheek. "In the hospital? And she died? How could that have happened?"

The same questions she'd asked herself countless times since getting the call from the hospital telling her that her sister was gone. A fresh gush of pain spilled down to her gut.

"The doctor told me her death was caused by a spontaneous coronary artery dissection." Her tone was brisk and no-nonsense, nothing like her current emotional state.

"What does that mean?" He looked genuinely distressed, and her outward calm faltered a bit at the sympathy in his expression.

"A tear formed in her heart. The flow of blood was blocked. They told me she passed quickly."

"And she had no prior heart problems?"

Gabby shook her head.

"So you're raising the baby."

"Yes." She lifted her chin, daring him to question her authority where Phoebe was concerned. Then it hit her— if this guy wasn't Sam… "Exactly who are you?"

"Dylan Kingsley. Sam's stepbrother." He extended his hand. She reluctantly shook it, and he could read every question running through her beautiful slate-gray eyes. Why was he here and how would his showing up affect her life? He'd prepared answers for both questions before arriving.

He wasn't going to lie to her—not exactly. He simply couldn't tell her the whole truth. Not until he was reasonably sure she was raising his niece with love and stability. Two things he'd been deprived of as a child.

Gabrielle Stover sure wasn't what he'd expected— but then, he hadn't known what to expect. The internet search he'd done on her hadn't given him much to go on besides age—twenty-seven, four years younger than him. She had no social media profiles. Neither did he.

First impressions? She was professional and not happy to see him. But why would she be? She didn't know him.

"You're Phoebe's uncle." She leaned back in her chair, eyeing him with suspicion. Her chestnut brown hair rippled over her shoulders in soft waves. The white blouse and crisp black pants she wore hugged a curvy but trim figure, and gave her the authority of someone in charge.

"Yes." The instant he'd seen her in the hotel lobby, he'd been drawn to her. The blonde next to her with come-hither eyes had been safe, but Gabrielle? Not safe at all. She was his type, which meant she was all wrong for him. A beautiful, confident girl like her would want someone dependable, a man she could rely on. No one had depended on him in a long time. Not even his own father. Dad wouldn't have sold his company, King Energy, without a word to him if he had. Worst of all, though, Dylan had failed the one person who once upon a time *had* relied on him—Sam.

"Why are you here?" Gabrielle pierced him with a laser-like stare. He tried not to squirm.

"I want to meet my niece." Dylan planned on more than meeting the child. He intended to set up a trust fund for Phoebe and monthly child support, too. He could afford it. It was the least he could do for Sam's little girl. But he wasn't doing either until he knew for sure Gabrielle was raising the baby with love. And that meant keeping the fact he was a multimillionaire a secret.

What advice would his late father give in this situation? Dad would probably tell him not to screw it up.

Money had only bought him and his father trouble when it came to women.

At least Gabrielle would have to dig deep to find out Dylan was rich. He'd always gone by his middle name, and his father had been private to the point of almost being reclusive. The man never mentioned his son in the rare interviews he'd given. The first fifteen pages of results for Dylan Kingsley in any search engine displayed articles by an astrophysicist with the same name.

"Why now?" Cocking her head, she narrowed her eyes. "She's nine months old. Allison and I repeatedly tried to contact him until six months ago. Why are you showing up here after all this time?"

"I didn't know about the baby until last week." It was the truth. But at the skeptical gleam in her eyes, he continued. "Sam died over a year ago. My father had a stroke and passed not long after. I hit the road. When I came back to Texas last week, it was the first I knew of the baby. Your letter had been sent to my address. Sam lived with me briefly before moving to Austin."

"I'm sorry about your family." She had the grace to appear contrite. "How did Sam die?"

He flexed his jaw. Thinking about his brother always ripped him up inside. Almost nine years younger than Dylan, Sam had come into his life as a happy five-year-old when Dylan's mother married husband number three. Despite the age gap, Dylan and Sam had been close. And he'd let his little brother down. "Does it matter?"

Her eyes widened, lips parted to ask a question. He braced himself. But she didn't speak.

"He's gone, and he's not coming back." Dylan couldn't bring himself to tell a stranger that Sam had died of a drug overdose. He wouldn't let her think the worst about his brother. He still couldn't believe his brother had been messing around with heroin. Worse, Dylan had been wallowing in his own problems and hadn't taken Sam's call the week he'd died. Could he have stopped him from overdosing?

He'd always regret it.

"It matters to me." She leaned forward with her hands clasped on the desk. "I need to know Phoebe's health history. If he had cancer or diabetes or heart problems…"

Fair enough. She had a point.

"It was an overdose—an accidental overdose."

"Oh."

Right about now would be when he'd expect her to ask about Sam's estate—find out if Phoebe had inherited anything. His own mother would have dollar signs in her eyes in this situation. She'd used him to squeeze money out of his father countless times. And then there was Dylan's ex-girlfriend. Robin not only dumped him when his dad sold King Energy, but she'd also had the nerve to try to get back together after finding out he'd inherited Dad's fortune.

His niece would never be used as a pawn for money if he had anything to say about it.

"Were you close to him?" Gabrielle's tone softened, and sympathy brightened her face.

"Yes, I was." He hadn't expected sympathy.

"I was close to Allison, too." Her words broke at the end. "I miss her."

The naked emotion touched him. He missed Sam, too. To distract himself, he studied her office. Paneled walls, jewel-toned carpet, an oak desk and two typical conference room chairs. A file cabinet stood to the side, and a potted tree was in the corner. The walls had two framed paintings of mountain scenes. No personal photos he could see.

Doting moms usually splattered pictures of their kids

all over their offices. Why weren't there any photos of the baby?

"So you work here, huh?" he said.

"I do. I'm the day manager." It was as though an iron curtain fell over her earlier vulnerability. She straightened, all brisk and no-nonsense. "What did you say you'd been doing for the past year?"

*Be careful what you say.* "Moving around. This and that…"

"I see." Disapproval radiated loud and clear through her pursed lips.

He doubted she did. Three days after his father's funeral, he'd packed his bags and flown to France. Two weeks later, he'd moved on to Italy, then Germany, the Alps, Finland and wherever the wind had taken him. He wished he could say he'd enjoyed the traveling, but it had underscored his new reality.

He was alone. He had no purpose. And no amount of money or traveling would change it.

"Can I see the baby?" he asked.

"My shift ends soon." She stood with her head high. "You can come over to my apartment around six to meet Phoebe."

Surprised, he rose. He hadn't expected her to allow him to see the baby so quickly.

"Here's my address. It's not far." She scribbled it on a piece of paper and handed it to him.

"Thanks." He slipped it into his back pocket.

She escorted him to the door, down the hall and back to the front desk. She wasn't short, but he had at least six inches on her. She was a very attractive woman, reminding him of the fact he had to be careful where she was concerned. He couldn't let chemistry affect his ability to size up her parenting skills.

"I'll see you in a little while." He put his cowboy hat back on and nodded to her before exiting. With nothing else to do, he figured he'd drive through the small town. It would be good to get a feel for the community his niece would be growing up in. If all went well, he'd meet the baby tonight and be satisfied she was in good hands.

Since Gabrielle thought he was just some guy off the street, she wouldn't have any reason to put on a false motherly act to press him for money. If he got a sense of peace about her raising Phoebe, in the morning he'd tell her he was directing his attorney to set up the trust fund and child support. Then he'd…

A breeze caressed his face as he strode to the truck he'd rented.

What? What was he going to do next?

He didn't know. He'd been wandering without direction for a long time. A night in Rendezvous, Wyoming, wasn't going to cough up answers for him. He wished he knew what would.

"This visit isn't going to change anything." Gabby took Phoebe out of Eden's arms and kissed the baby's soft cheeks. Her giggles filled the small apartment Gabby called home. Eden Page was one of her best friends as well as Phoebe's babysitter. Gabby usually picked up Phoebe from Eden's, but today she'd asked her friend for a favor. "Thank you so much for bringing her over. I don't have much time to get this place in shape. It was so weird having him show up like that. At first I thought he was the father. But he's not. Sam died. He's Sam's stepbrother."

"He died?" Eden's expressive brown eyes oozed with compassion. "So Phoebe will never meet her daddy. That's so sad."

"I know. It is."

"And this uncle wants to meet her, huh?" Eden set the diaper bag on the foyer floor. "That's it?"

"Yes. At least that's what he said." She bit the right side of her bottom lip. "If he thinks I'm going to share custody with him, he's fooling himself."

"Did he say he wanted to?"

"No, but all the way home, I've been going through worst-case scenarios."

"Remember what Babs always tells you. Don't borrow trouble." Eden scanned the living room and shrugged. "Your place looks good to me. I'll give the kitchen a once-over if you'd like."

"Would you? Oh, you are a lifesaver!" Gabby set Phoebe on the quilted mat in the living room and handed her a toy while Eden crossed over to the kitchen separated from the living room by a counter with bar stools. "How did the week go without having Noah around?"

"I miss him. He's such a sweet little boy. But having all the one-on-one time with Phoebe is making up for it a little bit."

Until last week, Eden had also been babysitting her nephew, Noah. But now that her brother-in-law, Mason, had gotten remarried, he and his new wife, Brittany, were splitting childcare duties and didn't need Eden's services anymore. Gabby envied Mason a tiny bit—he'd found someone to share his life with. Part of her wished she could have a relationship like theirs, too. But it wasn't likely. She'd be the first to admit she had trust issues when it came to men.

"Not having Noah around must be a big change for you." Gabby tossed a few toys into a basket.

"It is, and I hate change. But I can't stop it." Eden rinsed a mug. "By the way, I'm glad you invited this guy—Dylan, right?—over to meet the little sweetie. You wouldn't want to deprive her of an uncle."

"No, I couldn't deprive her of an uncle." A teeny part of her *did* want to deprive Phoebe of this particular one, though. If Dylan was anything like her own father or Carl, she wanted her niece as far from him as possible. At the moment, she didn't see much difference between him and them, but she wasn't being fair. She didn't know him at all. "One thing's for sure—we're going to have a *lot* to talk about at this week's meeting."

"When don't we?" Eden grinned.

Gabby, Eden, Mason and Nicole met every Tuesday at the inn for their support group. They'd all lost loved ones who'd been in the prime of their lives. Mason's first wife, Mia, who was Eden's older sister, had died of cancer six months after Noah was born. Gabby had lost Allison last year and Nicole's husband died unexpectedly on Christmas Day due to complications from muscular dystrophy.

Eden glanced up. "How long did you say he'd be in town?"

"He didn't say. I doubt long." Keeping an eye on Phoebe, Gabby tidied the magazines on the end table. Dylan had drifter written all over him. If he'd been moving around for a year, doing who knew what after his father died…

It didn't take much of a stretch of the imagination to figure out the guy didn't have a job, didn't have roots. Maybe he'd come into a small inheritance and rather than put it toward his future, he was running through it like a fool. Or he could be like her daddy, latching on to a new woman in each town to support him. Both scenarios spelled deadbeat. The muscles in her neck tightened.

"I'm fine with him meeting Phoebe, but I can tell you right now, I'm not going to have her influenced by some charming, shifty cowboy who will only let her down. If he wants to visit now and then, fine, but not unsupervised. And there will be rules."

"Is he charming? What does he look like?" Eden closed the dishwasher door and returned to the living room. She knelt on the floor by Phoebe, who clapped her hands with glee. Gabby said a silent prayer of thanks she'd been blessed to have Eden caring for the baby while she worked. The woman was a gift from the good Lord.

"I don't know. He's…attractive." She made the word sound as bad as an infectious skin disease. Attractive wasn't a good trait on this guy. "The way Stella was flirting, you'd think she'd have accepted a marriage proposal from him on the spot."

"Stella flirts with every guy under forty."

"True." Gabby hustled down the hall, stowed a laundry basket in her bedroom and loped back. "Here, I can take her."

"Why don't you change quick?" Eden said. "You'll feel better in your jeans."

"You don't mind?"

"Why would I mind? You know I could eat this little dumpling up." Eden scrunched her nose at Phoebe and tickled her tummy. Throaty baby laughter filled the air.

"Okay, I'll be right back." She raced to her room and donned her best jeans and a blouse patterned in various shades of red. With a quick brush of her hair and a swipe of tinted lip gloss, she was ready to face whatever came her way. She returned to the living room, and Eden handed her the baby. The air filled with her little gurgles.

"I can tell you're worried about this situation," Eden said. "But there's no reason to get worked up. He's not the father. And you *are* her legal guardian. You call the shots."

"You're right." She shifted Phoebe to her hip. "I guess I've been scared for a long time, always worrying Sam would show up one day and take her from me." She considered herself a rational person. She wasn't gullible—not anymore, anyway—and she tried to do the right thing. Why was she so agitated?

*Something about him reminds me of Daddy. Of Carl. And I don't allow men like them in my life anymore.*

"He's not the enemy." Eden frowned. "Unless… Did you get a weird vibe from him? Do you think he might be shady? Dangerous? We should call my dad to come over and supervise. No one would dare mess with you with Dad scowling at him."

"No, he seemed fine." She let out a little chuckle. "I don't need a chaperone. I can take care of myself." And she could. She'd taken care of herself and Allison all through their teen years and beyond. And now it was her privilege to take care of Phoebe.

"Well, try not to worry, then." Eden hugged her. "You're the most welcoming person I know. You'll get off on the right foot with him for Phoebe's sake. I know you."

"Thanks, Eden."

"If you're sure you don't want me around, I guess I'll take off. Call me the instant he leaves."

"I will." She held Phoebe tightly. "Thanks again."

After seeing Eden to the door, she took the baby to the couch and selected a children's book from the basket below the end table. For now, she'd try to keep things as normal as possible. And that meant concentrating on Phoebe and not worrying about Dylan.

He'd meet the baby and leave.

Life wouldn't change.

If she kept telling herself that, maybe it wouldn't.

Hopefully, this uncle would breeze out of their lives as suddenly as he'd breezed in.

She'd just have to keep a level head until he did.

## Chapter Two

In and out. Nice and easy. Dylan stared at the 3B on the door inside the apartment building. All he had to do was observe Gabrielle interacting with his niece for a while. He'd know the baby was in good hands, and his gut was telling him Gabrielle wasn't like his mother or his ex. For his niece's sake, he hoped she wasn't. Worst-case scenario? He'd stay in Rendezvous through the weekend to make sure.

After two sharp knocks the door opened, and he straightened, raising himself up to full height. The woman before him had shed her no-nonsense manager outfit to wear formfitting jeans and a colorful shirt, revealing toned arms. She looked younger, less closed off than she had at the inn. Her hair still fell loose around her shoulders. He wanted to touch it.

*Touch her hair?* If he'd been worried about chemistry before, he needed to up his composure tenfold.

At the sight of the baby on her hip, his heart hiccupped. Seeing the child in the flesh was a precious gift—a piece of Sam lived in the bouncing baby girl. With dark curls grazing her neck, rosy cheeks and huge dark blue eyes, she looked as healthy and happy as a child could be. She stuck out her tongue and blew bubbles at him.

"Come in. I hope you found my place okay." Gabrielle held the door open, and he took off his hat as he entered. The apartment itself was beige, on the small side and could use some TLC. The red living room furniture added color to the mix, and the dining table held a vase full of daisies. It was welcoming, he'd give her that. She led him to the living room. "Have a seat."

He lowered his frame onto the couch, not sure what to do.

"This is Phoebe Ann Stover." She smiled at the child with so much tenderness, he almost looked away. He'd never been the recipient of that level of affection. What would it be like to have someone adore him? "She's nine months old, sleeps through the night, loves sweet potatoes and scrambled eggs, but then again, she'll eat anything I put in front of her. She's a happy baby. Sweet as can be."

Sleeping through the night was good, right? Were babies supposed to eat eggs and sweet potatoes? He knew nothing about children. He peered at Phoebe, who held her arms out to him, opening and closing her chubby hands. He hadn't held a baby before. Gabrielle wouldn't expect him to pick her up, would she?

"Want to hold her?" Gabrielle's expression held no malice, but he could see she had questions she wasn't asking. That made two of them.

"Umm…"

The baby lunged for him, and Gabrielle laughed. "Well, it looks like you don't have a choice."

Before he knew it, the bundle of energy was in his hands. He held her an arm's length away, then eased her closer until her little bare feet rested on his thighs. Soon she was bouncing, her giggles filling the air. She was strong. Watching her push her little legs up and down with so much gusto made him chuckle. Instinctively, he drew her closer. She pressed her palms against his cheeks, and he pretended to blow out a mouthful of air. She laughed. How could such an itty-bitty thing produce such a hearty sound? Someday he'd have to break it to her he wasn't a great comedian.

Someday? It implied an ongoing relationship, and he hadn't thought that far ahead.

"I think it's safe to say she likes her uncle Dylan." Gabrielle wore a wistful expression. "Do you want something to drink?"

Uncle Dylan. He liked the sound of it.

"No, thanks." He made a silly face, and Phoebe laughed harder. She had Sam's eyes. Everything else must have come from her mother. Had Sam even known he was about to have a baby? If his brother could have seen the little girl, he might have had a reason to say no to drugs.

Dylan handed Phoebe back to Gabrielle. She tucked the child on her lap. The baby squirmed, but Gabrielle kept a firm grip on her, distracting her with a pastel bunny that rattled when shaken.

"Would you mind telling me more about her father?" She licked her lips nervously. "I don't have much to go on at this point. When she's older, she'll want to know about him. All Allison said was she saw him playing guitar with a rock band at a bar in Austin. They both had too much to drink, and a month later, she realized she was pregnant."

He winced. Hearing Sam summed up like that didn't do his brother justice. What could he tell her to give an accurate picture of the funny, sensitive kid he'd known and loved?

"Sam was a great guy. He loved music and practiced guitar constantly. School wasn't his strong suit. He opted not to go to college so he and his band could try to get noticed. He worked hard at it. Moved to Austin after high school and played with anyone who would let him. Music meant a lot to him."

He wasn't going to bring up Sam's drug use. He still struggled to make sense of how his talented brother could have thrown away his life on that junk. If he would have checked on Sam more often, maybe he would have noticed the signs.

"How old was he?" she asked.

"Twenty-one."

"The same age Allison was. Do you have a picture?"

He nodded and took out his phone. He scrolled through until he found one from two Christmases ago. At the sight of Sam's smiling face, his chest tightened uncomfortably. The hardest part of the past year was knowing he couldn't talk to or see his brother. One minute they were celebrating Christmas together, the next he was gone.

"What about your sister?" he asked. "What was she like?"

Her face lit up. "She was special. An absolute sweetheart. She, too, skipped college, and worked at the reception desk of a dental practice here in town. I don't want you to think she went around sleeping with guys all the time. It wasn't her personality at all. She…well, I think she must have felt stifled after high school. The nine-to-five grind and living in a small town got to her. A few of her girlfriends decided to fly down to Texas for a weekend, and that's when she met your brother."

The baby let out a sound he could only describe as the hoot of an owl. He met Gabrielle's eyes. They both started laughing.

"Well, I guess that lightened the moment." She hugged Phoebe and kissed the top of her head. "So, Dylan, I don't mean to be blunt, but what exactly do you want? You came a long way. What are your intentions with Phoebe?"

How to answer? He didn't know. He'd assumed he'd check on his niece, make sure she was being raised with love, do what he could to provide for the girl's future and move on as if he'd never met them. He hadn't even considered being part of her life—in any capacity—until tonight.

Seeing the baby with Sam's eyes altered his view, though. What else did his niece inherit from his brother? His musical talent? His sense of humor? Dylan wanted to find out.

"Gabrielle—"

"Call me Gabby."

"Okay, Gabby." Actually, in her home environment she seemed more like a Gabby than a Gabrielle. He shook his head and shrugged. "I don't know what I want."

"I've raised Phoebe since the second she came home from the hospital. She's like my own child. I'm her legal guardian…"

He inwardly cringed. He hadn't realized she thought he might want to fight for custody or visitation rights or something. In fact, he hadn't considered how his showing up would affect Gabby at all.

*You've been wrapped up in your own world for too long.*

"I'm not here to claim any rights—I know nothing

about raising babies." He held up his hands, palms out. "I just wanted to meet her."

But it wasn't true—not the last part at least. He'd also wanted to check out her living situation and financially support her.

"Well, you met her."

He scanned the room. Tidy. Neat. Although nothing like the luxurious home he grew up in or the high-end condo he owned in Dallas, this apartment felt warm and inviting. The baby seemed to be in good care. He could leave with a clear conscience.

But he didn't want to.

"I loved Sam. Miss him. This is his child. I want to be part of her life." As soon as the words were out of his mouth, his stomach clenched. It was the first commitment he'd made in a long time. Was he up to being part of his niece's life? He quickly added, "You know, visit her at times and send her birthday presents and stuff."

"I see." The muscle in her cheek flexed. "What you're asking for is fair. But I need to know more about you. I have to know you'll be a good influence on her."

He frowned. She didn't think he'd be a good influence on his own niece? She'd deduced this from the short time they'd been together? He wasn't sure what to think about that. Most people fell all over themselves sucking up to him and trying to win his favor.

But that was because they knew he was rich.

And Gabby didn't.

What would she do if he told her how much he was worth? Would she manipulate him to get her hands on some of the money? His own mother had done it many times. His ex, Robin, had tried, too.

On the other hand, if she didn't know his background, would she find him worthy of being in Phoebe's life?

Was he worthy? He ran his finger under his collar.

He'd been having an identity crisis for a year. When had he lost his confidence?

*When Dad sold the company without even considering letting me run it.*

"I'm starving. Why don't I order a pizza and we can discuss this further?" Gabby rose, lifting Phoebe high in the air. Her little legs kicked as she laughed.

Pizza sounded good. After a year of gourmet meals, high-end hotels and surface conversations, talking to Gabby sounded even better. Normal, even.

How long had it been since he'd been treated like any other guy?

Not in grade school. Certainly not running around with other rich kids at prep school. College—nope—still hanging out with wealthy peers. The four years he'd worked in upper management at King Energy had ensured his days were spent in board meetings, on the golf course or reviewing the performance of the managers below him.

His old world no longer existed. For once he wanted to be an average Joe. But he'd have to be careful not to let Gabby guess his true background. He wouldn't outright lie to her, but he'd be stingy with details.

The trust fund, the child support could wait. Just until he knew her better. Then he'd tell her the truth.

Why had she invited him to stay for pizza? Gabby paid the delivery guy and carried the steaming box to the kitchen counter. Her stupid heart had softened when he'd talked about his brother. It hadn't been an act, either.

Sam's death had broken something inside him—just as Allison's death had done to her. Her pity had kicked in, and she'd invited him to stay without thinking it through.

What had Eden said earlier? She was the most welcoming person she knew. Gabby scoffed. Not a good trait in this situation. She really had to put a clamp on her invitation-prone mouth.

"Let me help with that." Dylan held out a twenty-dollar bill.

"No, thanks. I've got it." She shook her head. "I was ordering one tonight no matter what."

"Really, I want to—"

"No, you're my guest." She held out her hand. "I'll grab a few plates."

At least he'd offered to pay. But then, Carl had at first, too.

She might as well figure out Dylan's work situation while she had him here. Phoebe was playing with the toys attached to the tray of the jumper seat near the couch, so Gabby pulled out a stack of paper plates and napkins from the cupboard. After grabbing slices of pizza, they returned to the living room. She sat on the couch, and he took a chair. Even several feet away, his presence filled the room. He seemed bigger, stronger—more appealing in general—here in her apartment than he had at the inn. And he'd been something special there.

This wasn't a good turn of events. She'd already known she was attracted to him, so encouraging more interaction with him wasn't smart.

She bit into her slice, oozing with mozzarella and pepperoni. Maybe he wasn't slathering on the charm like Carl had, but she knew next to nothing about this strapping cowboy. He could be buttering her up for his own purposes. She needed to find out more about him.

"What do you do for a living, Dylan?"

He finished chewing. "I'm not employed at the moment."

*Bingo.* Unemployed. She'd pegged him as a no-good cowboy the instant she'd seen him, and she always trusted her instincts.

"What kind of work did you do in the past?" She tried not to appear too eager for his answer. What had he said he'd been doing for the past year? Something about this and that. Hardly reassuring. He probably went from job to job when he got bored or restless.

"I guess you could say I work for hire."

The cheese stuck in her throat. *Just like Daddy. Just like Carl.* They'd both traveled as cowboys for hire. Her father also occasionally had taken trucking gigs. Knowing Dylan was like the two men who'd let her down put her in a pickle. She had firm rules about cowboys—specifically about not dating them. But how did the rules apply to a relative of Phoebe?

"Is that what you've been doing since your father and Sam died? You mentioned being on the road for the past year."

"Sort of." He took a sip of soda. "I took time off. Needed to work through some stuff."

How was he paying his bills if he'd been taking time off and traveling? If he was like Daddy, he was probably skimming money from a girlfriend or two. She liked her other idea better—that he was blowing through a small inheritance. But then, she couldn't assume he'd inherited anything. His mom might still be alive.

"Did your mother take your father's death hard?"

He choked and thumped his chest a few times. "Sorry. No, I doubt she's given him a second thought."

Her mouth dropped open, and she quickly closed it.

"They divorced when I was a toddler. No love lost there."

"Did he remarry? And Sam came into your life through the new wife?"

"Dad never remarried. I'm his only child. Sam came into the picture with Mom's third husband."

So his mother had married Sam's father. Made sense. Didn't answer her question of how Dylan was supporting himself, though.

"It's awfully hard to take so much time off when you have bills to pay." She tried not to sound judgmental. But seriously, if he was taking time off and wandering around, how was he dealing with his responsibilities? Every adult had those.

His eyes sharpened and narrowed, but he didn't say a word.

"How have you been supporting yourself?" She didn't care if it was forward. She needed to know—for Phoebe's sake. For her own. And she'd see right through him if he lied to her. She'd gotten good at sifting fact from fiction.

"I don't need much."

Hmm…he wanted to play the ambiguous answer game, did he? She wasn't born yesterday.

"That's a nice truck you drove to the inn earlier."

"It's a rental." His eyes were unreadable. Warning flags waved in her brain. This back and forth reminded her of Carl, but back then she'd been a naive teenager. She'd wanted to accept every lie he told her. She'd believed the best in him. And she shouldn't have.

Most welcoming person or not, she wasn't putting up

with any games Dylan wanted to play. Phoebe was too important. Her niece would not grow up being jerked around by some unreliable guy pretending to be something he wasn't. She should know. Until she was eleven years old, she'd thought her father was the greatest man alive. But cold hard facts had shattered her notions about him.

"Look, I know we just met." She set the plate on the end table and locked eyes with his. "In any other circumstances, it would be insulting for me to ask you what I'm about to ask. But this is my niece, and I can't let her be around someone who isn't reliable. Where are you getting your money to live on?"

He blinked once, twice, three times. Then his expression became unreadable. "My dad left me a little something."

Relief spread through her like rain over a dry prairie. She'd been right. He'd come into some cash. Blowing through a small inheritance she could handle. Preying on gullible, lonely women, she could not.

"And you returned home because the money's running out?" She didn't wait for him to answer. "That's fair."

He opened his mouth but didn't say anything.

"What are you going to do next?" She wiped her hands off on a napkin.

"I'm not sure." His face fell.

There was something broken about him. She knew broken. If it wasn't for the baby, she probably would have fallen apart a long time ago. The brittleness edging her curiosity softened.

"You're struggling with their deaths, aren't you?" she asked.

"Yeah." He nodded, setting his plate aside. "I am. No matter where I go, it doesn't change the fact they're gone."

"The traveling… Have you been trying to escape?"

"Maybe." He drew his eyebrows together. "Looking back… I guess I might have been."

"Does anything help you with the grief?" She'd been blessed with her support group—their prayers and meetings each week had gotten her through the toughest of times.

"Somewhat." Their gazes locked, and the connection between them could not be denied. Flutters filled her chest. "My faith helps me hobble through."

"It gets me through, too. I know I'll see Allison someday."

"I'm glad." He sighed, dropping his elbows to his knees. "Faith wasn't part of my life until a few years ago. As for Dad and Sam… I don't know what they believed." He arched his eyebrows.

Her and her big mouth. "I'm sorry. I didn't think before I spoke."

"It's okay." He seemed to see right through her. "You meant well."

Phoebe started to fuss. She was probably hungry. "I'll be right back. I'm going to fix her a bottle."

A few minutes later, she took Phoebe out of the jumper seat and set her on her lap with the bottle. The baby snuggled in her arms as she drank it. This was one of Gabby's favorite parts of the day. There was nothing more relaxing than having Phoebe cradled in her arms.

"Did you grow up around here?" He had an intent gleam in his eye as he watched them.

"No, Allison and I moved here to take care of our grandma after I graduated from high school. Allison was going into eighth grade." She caressed Phoebe's forehead, trying not to dwell on the other reason they'd moved to Rendezvous. She'd finally seen Carl's true colors. The man she'd dated during her senior year of high school had been living a double life. She'd grown up fast after that.

"What happened to your parents?"

"Oh, they're still alive and well. Mama lives down in Laramie with her boyfriend, and Daddy is probably charming some widow in Montana. I don't talk to them much anymore."

"And it's just you and the baby? No husband?" He didn't seem to be fishing about her love life with an ulterior motive, but what did she know?

"No, just us."

"And you plan on staying here?"

She laughed. "Oh, yeah, Rendezvous is home. I can't imagine living anywhere else. I have good friends here, and I love working at the inn…" She proceeded to tell him about her job and how she loved the town. He asked about the area and before she knew it, an hour had passed.

"I should get going." He stood and took his plate into the kitchen. Then he walked over and touched Phoebe's cheek. "You take care now, little one."

"What's next?" Gabby stood, carrying the baby, and followed him to the door.

"I don't know. Let's sleep on it and talk tomorrow."

"Okay." She frowned. "You can stop by after noon."

He put on his hat, tipped it to her and left. After locking the door behind him, Gabby carried Phoebe back to the couch and stretched out on it. Impressions tangled in her mind.

She wasn't sure what to make of him. He was easy to talk to—too easy. In fact, she'd done all the talking. She pressed her hand against her forehead. What was wrong with her? She was supposed to be finding out if he was worthy of being part of Phoebe's life, not gushing about how much she loved Rendezvous.

Still, he *had* shown his vulnerability when it came to the deaths of his brother and father. But as far as his work history, his future plans…she'd completely flaked out on getting any concrete answers.

And once again she'd invited him over.

In all his travels, he hadn't found this.

Dylan drove across Silver Rocks River and turned onto Centennial Street to drive through downtown Rendezvous. After 7:30 p.m., the sun was still out. Families entered and exited the few restaurants along the street, and once he passed the main businesses, a line appeared around an ice cream stand—the Dipping Dream. He slowed and pulled into a spot in front of a park. Green grass was dotted with picnic tables where people were barbecuing. The smell of grilled burgers reminded him summer had arrived. Rendezvous made it look slower, more fun than he was used to.

Little girls and boys stood near the playground equipment taking turns lassoing a fence post. He chuckled as one of the boys stuck out his tongue and a girl threw down her rope and began chasing him. They looked like they were having a good time.

From what he'd seen of the town, it appeared to be a place where everyone knew each other. He got out of the truck and enjoyed the warm breeze. A white gazebo was nestled in the park. Mature pines partially hid a ball diamond from his view, and he could just make out what appeared to be seven-year-old girls playing softball. Shouts erupted. Proud grandparents and parents stood up cheering.

An unexpected longing hit his heart. This was what community meant. Ice cream stands, barbecues with friends, peewee ball games—all things he'd missed out on as a kid. He hadn't realized until this moment that he was still missing out on them.

Would Phoebe play softball? Would Gabby be in the stands jumping up to cheer her on?

Of course, Gabby would cheer the girl on. It was obvious she loved the baby. Who wouldn't love the girl with her chubby cheeks and cheerful smile?

Earlier when he'd watched Gabby holding her and giving her the bottle, something had shifted inside him. The maternal picture they presented had kicked up a longing he'd never had before. For a brief moment, he'd wanted a child and a wife of his own who would love a baby the way Gabby did Phoebe.

"Na na na na na!" Up ahead, two little girls taunted a group of boys. Another round of chasing ensued. He shook his head. Kids being kids.

Gabby had been easy to talk to. The one red flag he'd had about her was when she'd probed into his financial situation. Why did she want to know what he'd been doing and how he'd been supporting himself for the past year? And what had the comment about his nice truck meant? Had she been trying to figure out how much money he had?

"Charlie!" A brunette in her early twenties waved to a couple of guys strolling toward the metal bleachers.

"Hey, Misty," one said without breaking stride. "You watching the game? Emma's playing."

"I was on my way to get a sundae, but I might as well

join you." She jogged over to them, and they all laughed about something. Their camaraderie deepened the stirring he'd been feeling for the past few hours.

Man, he was tired of being alone. He turned in the direction of Dipping Dream.

As he'd listened to Gabby talk about her life and friends here in Rendezvous, he'd found himself wishing she'd keep talking for hours. She seemed so genuine. And when she'd asked, "What next?" he'd had no idea how to respond.

What was next?

He supposed he should return to Dallas to set up the trust fund and child support. It had been a year since he'd checked in with any of his old friends. They'd been growing apart for a long time, though. The only people he'd had contact with at all this year were his lawyer and his financial advisor.

The thought of checking out of Mountain View Inn tomorrow and putting his life back together in Texas weighed on him. He didn't know how to put it together. It all seemed meaningless without…

Maybe it was time to face facts. He'd spent his entire life trying to impress his father and get his attention. Now that Dad was gone, there wasn't anyone to impress.

Dylan slowed as he neared the ice cream stand. He had to figure out what to do with his life. No more traveling around the world, delaying the inevitable.

What would it hurt to spend the rest of the weekend here? He could get to know Phoebe better and find out more information about how Gabby planned on raising her.

Come to think of it, he didn't know much about either of them. He'd gotten so mesmerized listening to Gabby talk about the town, he'd barely asked any questions at all. He didn't know her ideas on school and extracurricular activities. Who babysat his niece while she worked? What church did Gabby attend? Would she spoil the baby or be strict? Did she plan on having fun birthday parties for the girl? How would they celebrate Christmas? Would he be invited?

As he fell into the back of the line, relief mingled with peace.

Yes, he'd stay a few days and gather more info. He'd find out how Gabby intended to raise Phoebe. And if he didn't like what she said, he might have to speak up. In fact, he might have to be more involved with the baby than he originally intended. Money was a poor substitute for a flesh and blood person who cared. He should know.

His niece deserved an uncle she could depend on.

But what if he let her down the way he had his father and Sam?

He firmed his shoulders as Phoebe's smiling face played in his mind. He'd have to be someone she could depend on.

He couldn't live with himself if he let her down, too.

# Chapter Three

⟡

She had to set some ground rules with Dylan. Gabby spooned a bite of mashed carrots into Phoebe's mouth the next day. Half of it dribbled out, and she scooped the orange mush back in. Phoebe clapped her hands, her little mouth working through the bite. Her bib had *She's the Boss* embroidered on it, and the tray of the high chair was smeared with bits of bananas and carrots.

"That's right, peanut, you're the boss, and your uncle better not think he can come and go as he pleases." She scraped the side of the container and fed Phoebe another bite. "You're worth more than that. I know how hard it is to resist a handsome man like Dylan when he breezes into town with a slippery smile and words full of sugar. And I know how much your heart breaks waiting for him to show up on your birthday or to the school play he promised to attend. Don't worry. I will not let him string you along."

She was ridiculously glad she'd told Dylan not to come over until after noon. Saturdays were her one day to be lazy. She'd been relaxing in her pajamas and enjoying every second of cuddly bliss with the baby until she'd finally forced herself to shower and get dressed.

Her clock said it was ten minutes after twelve. Would he stop by? Maybe he'd left town already. *Yeah, right.* Wishful thinking would get her nowhere.

The problem was she'd enjoyed his company a little too much last night.

He seemed less shady than she'd originally pegged him for. But that wasn't saying much. It wasn't as if he'd been in a hurry to cough up answers to the questions she'd presented. The moments when he'd been transparent about struggling with the deaths of Sam and his father had been endearing. But the other moments—the ones where he'd hemmed and hawed about his job and what he'd been doing—had not.

Still, he'd been sweet with Phoebe. Gabby doubted he'd been around many babies, and he hadn't hidden the fact he liked his niece. Then again, Phoebe was adorable—everyone liked her.

The little pumpkin smacked her hands on the tray, her mouth open for another bite.

"Well, excuse me." Gabby gave her another spoonful. "You're hungry today, aren't you?"

A knock on the door caught her attention, and her heart immediately started pounding. It was him. She was sure of it. Number one on her list—find out Dylan's intentions. Number two—set some rules. She'd spell out her expectations for him if he wanted to spend time with Phoebe.

She scrunched her nose at the girl. "I'll be right back."

The high chair was a matter of steps from the door, and she quickly checked the peephole. Dylan. Her pulse went into overdrive. She unlocked the door and let him inside.

"I would have called…" His outfit mimicked yesterday's except he'd swapped out his black T-shirt for a gray one.

"It's fine. Come in." She hustled back to Phoebe and gestured to a dining chair. "Have a seat. We're just finishing up."

He settled into the chair opposite her and glanced around her apartment. Then he tapped his fingers on the table, appearing every bit as uncomfortable as she felt. They hadn't been ill at ease last night. What had changed?

"Did you sleep well?" Gabby finally asked. His name had been on the reservation list at the inn yesterday, but at the time she hadn't realized he was Phoebe's uncle. The reservation had been for one night only.

"I did." He nodded. "My room was quiet and comfortable. The staff was welcoming, too."

She could only assume he meant Stella when he referred to the staff. A flare of jealousy sprang up, but she squashed it.

"I'm glad to hear it." As soon as Phoebe finished the final bite of carrots, Gabby wet a washcloth and began to wipe her face and hands with it. After a bit of fussing, the child was clean. She lifted her out of the high chair and set her on her lap. The previous silence snowballed into awkwardness. She wasn't sure what to say, what to do.

*Get it over with. Find out his intentions and set the rules.*

"So last night we didn't really get around to discussing how to move forward in this new…ah…territory we've found ourselves in." She watched him carefully.

"No, we didn't." He shifted in his seat.

"I want to make sure we're on the same page. Phoebe's needs come first."

"Yes, of course." He sat up straighter.

"I hope I don't come off sounding like a taskmaster, but we need to set some ground rules. You mentioned wanting to be in her life. What specifically did you have in mind? Do you plan on visiting her often? Or would it be easier if you sent her gifts for her birthday and Christmas?"

As he exhaled, his eyebrows drew together. "Umm…"

"And, in the future, I'm really not okay with you showing up unannounced. I'd appreciate having at least a week's notice if you're coming into town."

"Uh-huh." He bit the inside of his cheek, giving him an adorably lost look she hadn't thought possible on such a strapping man.

"It might be tempting for you to try to be the cool uncle, but please don't overdo it. It can be difficult for a little girl without any father figure in her life. I don't want her to get unrealistic expectations about you." Her words came out faster as she brought up each new point.

"I take it that means you're not dating anyone."

"You are correct." Was he fishing? It didn't matter. "Since I'm on a budget, I think it would be inappropriate for you to buy expensive gifts for her, not that you were going to, but it's worth mentioning."

He seemed to consider her words. "What do you have against expensive gifts?"

*Everything if there aren't any feelings behind them.* Her mind flashed back to the necklace Carl had given her before they'd split up. The old ache in her heart flared hot and painful.

She held Phoebe tightly as the girl waved to Dylan and began babbling loudly. His grin was instant, and Gabby's ache was replaced by something new and uncomfortable.

"Children need love. It's easy for them to confuse an expensive gift with emotional closeness." She should know. It wasn't only Carl who'd duped her. Her own father hadn't cared that she and her sister lived in a run-down double-wide trailer and never had enough food. But he always brought a new doll or game after being on the road. New toys didn't keep them warm during long winters. "I don't want her to believe you're something you're not."

"Something I'm not? What do you mean?" His blank stare caught her off guard. Maybe she should have thought this through more before speaking. Sure, men had let her down time and again, but he didn't need to know all that.

She wasn't going to tell him how hurt she'd been by her dad and Carl. She didn't talk about them to anyone.

"She doesn't have a daddy, and if you show up once or twice a year with the latest toy and make a big deal over her, it will be pretty tough for her the rest of the time when you're not around."

"I guess it makes sense." He rubbed his chin. She detected nothing but sincerity from him. "You know better than I do."

"Ba-ba!" Phoebe pointed at him.

He looked at Gabby. "What does ba-ba mean?"

"She calls everything ba-ba at this point."

He made a silly face at Phoebe, who slapped her tiny palms on the table in excitement. Staring at his handsome features, Gabby was tempted to touch the slight cleft in his chin.

Really, she should not be thinking about the cleft or about touching him!

"How do you plan on raising her?" He turned his attention to Gabby and watched her intently.

What was he getting at? Was he concerned she was doing a bad job? Sure, she often worried she wasn't enough for Phoebe. Shouldn't the girl have a mommy *and* a daddy? And sometimes she felt guilty about working all day, but she loved her job, and Eden was a wonderful babysitter.

"She's in good hands."

"I know. I'm not worried about her physical care." He leaned back. "But as she gets older, how do you plan on disciplining her? How important is her education to you? Are you going to sign her up for sports? Will you screen her friends?"

Gabby was speechless. For Mr. Vague-About-Himself, he'd certainly gotten quite detailed about Phoebe's life. Did he think Gabby wasn't up to the task?

Honestly, she hadn't really considered everything he mentioned. She'd been so busy getting through each day trying to move on from Allison's death, that she hadn't given a ton of thought to Phoebe's future. Maybe she should have.

The creases in his forehead clued her in he might be worried based on his own experience. He'd mentioned his parents' divorce. What had happened in his childhood to make him worry about Phoebe's?

"I'll do my best." She attempted to smile. "I haven't thought that far ahead. I take parenting day by day at this point."

The unsettling sensation in her stomach made her want to wrap up this visit as soon as possible.

"Are you leaving this afternoon or waiting until to-morrow?" she asked.

"Yeah, about that…" He turned to Phoebe and continued the goofy faces. "I think I'll stay in Rendezvous for a while."

Her mind froze. She could hear her heartbeat. He was *staying* here longer? Was it because she didn't have a ten-year plan for Phoebe?

"A while? Could you be more specific?" Her voice was squeakier than a mouse's. "How long?"

"It's hard to say." He lifted one shoulder, and his mouth curved into a grin.

"Why?"

His warm brown eyes held something she hadn't detected in them until now. Hope.

"I'd like to get to know my niece better."

It was as if a ticking bomb began to count down in her brain. A bomb to disaster.

This was how it started—the charming smile, the proclamation he was staying for a while, the wriggling into her life, the playing with her emotions.

The inside of her mouth turned to sludge as she remembered the months she'd spent hanging on Carl's every word, dropping everything when he called and hushing the voice in her head whispering he was playing her. Carl wasn't the great guy he'd pretended to be. She'd been a fool.

Not this time.

"Look, it's sweet of you to take an interest in Phoebe, but from what you've told me, I really don't know enough about you to encourage you to stick around."

"What do you mean?" His expression darkened.

"I have no idea what you do for work. You mentioned

living in Texas. Do you still live there? And what exactly have you been doing for the past year? Don't say this and that—it's not a real answer."

His mouth dropped open, but she didn't give him time to speak.

"How do I know you aren't a deadbeat?"

A deadbeat?

This was a new one. Dylan almost laughed out loud, but the worry and sincerity in Gabby's stormy gray eyes held him in check.

Here he'd been worrying she'd asked about his finances yesterday in order to gain something, and in reality, she'd been worried he was a deadbeat. A sobering thought.

"I'm not a deadbeat."

"That's what they all say," she muttered, diverting her attention to Phoebe.

"They? Who?"

"Cowboys." She met his gaze again, and he was struck by the fierceness in them.

She thought he was a cowboy? Maybe his boots and hat made him look like one. Outside of the office, jeans and cowboy boots had always been his style.

The funny thing? As a kid, he'd always wanted to be a cowboy. His friend had grown up on a ranch, and Dylan remembered one summer—he must have been thirteen or fourteen—he'd gone over there often to watch the men working cattle. Cowboys were tough and cool and everything he'd wanted to be. His friend, along with the ranch hands, had kindly taught him how to ride and rope.

Yeah, he would gladly be mistaken for a cowboy any day.

But Gabby said it like it was a bad thing.

"Cowboys aren't deadbeats." He crossed his arms over his chest. "They're strong and dedicated, and they never quit. They'd give their lives for the animals depending on them."

He, on the other hand, was not strong or dedicated, and he had quit more than one thing in his life. Gabby didn't need to know all that, though.

"Yeah, well, I wish they'd think about the people who depend on them, too." Someone must have let her down. She reached over and grabbed a pale blue stuffed dog from the counter and handed it to Phoebe, who gripped it with both fists and pounded it against the tabletop while blowing raspberries. "You didn't answer my question. How long are you planning to stay?"

His mind blanked. How could he possibly answer her when he didn't know? If he said a month, would it be long enough? Or too long? What if he liked it here and wanted to stay through the summer?

"A month. At least." His palms grew clammy as he realized he'd committed to being here for four whole weeks, the longest he'd stayed in one spot for over a year. Every ten days, without fail, he'd get restless, pack up and move on. Was he even capable of staying in one spot for a month anymore?

"Well, where are you going to stay?" She sounded as incredulous as he felt.

"I'm not sure."

"The inn isn't set up for long-term guests. It would be expensive."

His lips twitched in amusement. She didn't want him at the inn, that was for sure. In his experience, any hotel was set up for long-term guests for the right price. But she didn't know his pockets were deep. And if he told her the truth, he wouldn't be a cowboy in her eyes anymore.

"I'll find something." He'd have no problem finding lodging for a month.

"Okay, but what are you going to do while you're here? You can't be hanging around my place all the time. People will talk, and I won't be gossiped about."

"I won't give them anything to gossip about." She brought up an interesting point, though. What was he going to do all day while he was here? He hadn't thought this through. He'd gotten caught up in small-town wishes last night.

The stuffed dog hit him in the face.

He blinked, and Phoebe let out a deep laugh, and it grew and grew until the child was practically hysterical. He couldn't help it; he laughed, too.

"Oh, you think that's pretty funny, Phoebe, hitting your uncle in the face." He pointed to her, keeping a teasing quality to his tone so she wouldn't be scared. He picked up the stuffed dog and pretended to make it dance.

After a while her laughter finally settled down, and, grunting, she pointed to him.

"Do you want the doggy?" he asked.

She bounced on Gabby's lap and clapped her hands. He held it out to her, and she snatched it from him and chewed on its ear.

"Didn't anyone tell you not to eat dogs?" He shook his head as she slobbered all over the poor animal's ear. "I can see I'm needed here."

Gabby's tender smile hit him in the gut.

Maybe he'd better tell her the truth. He was neither a cowboy nor a deadbeat. He was just a lost guy living off his dad's money.

She let out a long sigh. "If you're serious about staying, then I have some rules."

She seemed to be big on rules.

"Supervised visits only with the baby." She lowered her chin and gave him a stern stare.

"I wouldn't know what to do with an unsupervised visit anyway."

"Okay, good." She raised her chin level again. "You can stop by for a little bit after supper on weekdays. Not every weekday, mind you, but once you get settled, we can work out a schedule for once or twice a week. Saturdays are my day to relax, so please don't come over then."

So far, the schedule sounded limiting. An hour or two once or twice a week? Would it be enough?

"What about Sundays?" he asked.

"Phoebe and I go to church." Her shoulders relaxed, and the sideways glance she shot him hinted she wasn't as sure of herself as she was coming across. "You're welcome to come with us."

"I'd like that." And he would. He missed regularly attending a place of worship.

"Good, and one more thing. You need to get a job."

A job? What kind of job? A tornado built in his chest as all the possibilities ricocheted off him. He hadn't had a job in over a year, and he doubted Rendezvous had any need for upper management.

"I'm not sure where to look." Was he even qualified for anything Rendezvous offered?

She averted her eyes. "Talk to Stu Miller. One of his ranch hands quit and moved away last year after getting married, and his right-hand man died a little over a month ago. He could use a cowboy for hire. Tell him I sent you."

Instantly, the storm inside him calmed. He didn't have

to sift through the possibilities. A position was there for the taking—he could literally *be* the cowboy she thought he was.

But his conscience nagged him. From all visible signs, Gabby lived on a budget, and raising a baby couldn't be cheap. He should set up the trust fund and the monthly child support payments. Relieve some of the financial burden of being a single mom.

But if he did… She might flip from being skeptical to having stars in her eyes. Staying in town for a month with a woman who might try to leverage the baby for his money would leave him too vulnerable.

No, he'd do it his way this time.

And that meant taking a shot at the cowboy life he'd always dreamed about.

"Okay." He nodded firmly. His heart felt light—lighter than it had in a long time. "I'll talk to the guy about getting a job."

She visibly relaxed.

"But you've got to do something for me, too."

"What?"

"Let me spend more than a few minutes once or twice a week with Phoebe. And I need to know more about how you plan on raising her."

Oh, chicken and biscuits, the man was staying!

This was a disaster. Why hadn't she been firmer when he'd thrown out he was sticking around for a while? This guy could be as slippery as the stones in Silver Rocks River. And, worse, instead of discouraging him from staying by telling him he had to get a job, she'd gone ahead and handed him one.

What had she been thinking?

Stu *did* need help. Badly. But it didn't mean Dylan had to trot over there and work for the man.

What if Dylan liked it here so much he stayed? For good?

She wasn't one to hyperventilate, but her breathing got distinctively shallow. *Stop being dramatic.* "I don't mind discussing Phoebe's care, but I'm the one raising her so I call the shots."

"I respect that." A sparkle in his eyes appeared that hadn't been there previously. It made him even more attractive. "The baby—she's got my brother's eyes, and I couldn't live with myself if I didn't make sure she grew up with anything less than she deserves."

Less than she deserves? Gabby tried not to bristle. What did he mean by that? He talked as if he had something to offer. She thought back to the expensive rental truck and his admittance he'd gotten a small inheritance. Maybe the money had gone to his head.

"I'll see to it she has everything she needs," she said. Phoebe threw the stuffed toy on the floor, and Gabby bent to pick it up.

He crossed his arms over his chest. "And I'll be here if you need me."

Need him? She almost laughed, but he'd said it with a straight face. She hated to break it to him, but she would never need him. Maybe he'd gotten a false impression from her.

"Look, we hardly know each other," Gabby said. "And no offense, but I've got this. I took care of the baby fine up until now, and I'll continue to do so whether you stay in Rendezvous or not. If you want me to take you seriously, I suggest you talk to Stu and get settled. Leave raising Phoebe to me."

The muscle in his cheek jumped. Good. She'd struck a nerve. Just because he'd decided to live here for a while didn't mean he'd stick around forever. If he wanted to be in Phoebe's life, he had to earn the right. And that meant not only getting a job, but keeping it for as long as he stayed. Abiding by her rules. And not expecting her to bend over backward to make him comfortable.

He wanted to be in Phoebe's life? Well, he'd have to earn her respect.

Gabby had no time for anything less. And her niece deserved the best he had to offer. Come to think of it, they both did. And if Dylan couldn't or wouldn't give Phoebe the attention and devotion she was worthy of, Gabby would send him packing with no regrets.

"No one is questioning your parenting skills," he said. "You said it was tough on a girl not having a father figure in her life. I get that. I'm not asking to be her dad or the fun uncle or whatever you think. I want her to have a good life. The same as you do."

Well, she hadn't been expecting those words to come out of his mouth. A blast of shame heated her neck. Dylan Kingsley was saying all the right things. And she couldn't help thinking he was sincere. Maybe she should put aside her misgivings and give him the benefit of the doubt.

"Okay." She sighed. "If you're serious about staying here for a month or so, I'll meet you halfway on the schedule. I'm also willing to listen to your thoughts on how to raise her. Beyond that, I make no promises."

His slow grin held appreciation and gratitude. And it upped his appeal to a dangerous level.

"Thanks, Gabby. I won't let her down."

She cocked one eyebrow but didn't say a word. He'd better not let Phoebe down. If he did, she'd make sure he regretted it. Only one question lingered—could she remain immune to the handsome cowboy?

The last one had broken her heart, but she was a long way from the gullible eighteen-year-old she'd been back then. She'd learned how to protect herself. No one could break her like Carl had ever again. Not Dylan, not anyone.

# Chapter Four

He could see himself working here.

Stuart Miller's ranch sprawled against the backdrop of blue skies and mountains. Sunday afternoon, Dylan walked past empty corrals toward a weathered red barn. Cattle grazed on a hill in the distance, and everywhere he looked were signs of summer. Green grass and blue and yellow wildflowers covered the prairie. A gurgling river snaked behind the outbuildings. The light swoosh of breeze kept the heat at bay.

The view, the quiet, the vastness of this place filled him with the sensation of coming home. He hoped he'd make a good enough impression to get hired.

He didn't have any real experience with cattle ranching, no references to share. How did a job interview like this work, anyhow?

A tall, older man with a paunch came out of the barn and strode toward him. He looked exactly the way Dylan pictured a seasoned ranch owner would. He wore a cowboy hat, short-sleeved shirt, jeans, leather chaps and cowboy boots. A thick gray mustache covered his tanned, lined face. His piercing blue eyes took in Dylan as he approached.

He squared his shoulders and held out his hand. "Dylan Kingsley. Thanks for agreeing to meet me, sir."

Now that they were face-to-face, Dylan noticed the toothpick he chewed. After a lengthy once-over, the man took his hand, pumped it once and hitched his chin.

"Stu Miller. Coulda used ya last week when we were sorting cattle."

He wasn't sure how to respond, but no response seemed necessary since Stu turned on his heel and strode back toward the barn. Should he follow him? Or was that it? Had he failed some secret test?

"Well, are you gonna saddle up or not?" Stu called over his shoulder, waving for him to join him.

He jogged to catch up with Stu. They strode in silence until they entered the barn. His eyes took a minute to adjust to the dim light. The smell of straw and manure brought him right back to spending summer days at his friend's ranch. He savored the memories of a time when life had kind of made sense.

"Tack room's back there." Stu pointed to the wall beyond the empty stalls. "Grab a saddle, and I'll get your mount. Meet me out front when you're ready."

Didn't Stu want to question him about his experience? Get any info about his previous jobs? Find out if he was qualified?

Was he hired and didn't know it?

He selected his equipment from the orderly tack room, hoisted a saddle off one of the racks and brought it all outside. A pair of quarter horses stood near the fence. Stu was already seated on one.

"You'll be riding Jethro today. This here's Diego."

Dylan made quick work of saddling Jethro, gently patting and murmuring to the beautiful mahogany horse. When he prepared to mount, Jethro's ears angled back as if more than ready to get on with the ride. He patted the horse's neck and kept a loose grip on the reins. It had been a few years since he'd ridden, but it felt natural to be back in the saddle.

Stu gave him a long stare. "Where's your rope?"

He'd forgotten the rope. Of all the dumb moves… A real cowboy would never make such a rookie mistake.

"I'll be right back." Dylan dismounted, secured Jethro's reins to the nearby fence and loped back to the barn to grab a rope. Within minutes he was back on the horse and ready to ride.

Stu urged Diego forward. Dylan rode alongside him. They fell into an easy rhythm. Jethro seemed like a disciplined, smart horse.

"I've split the herd—about 250 head of Black Angus and Hereford cattle—into groups for better grazing rotation. We'll check on the north pasture. Where'd you say you were from?"

"Texas. Dallas area."

"Humph." Stu crossed a bridge over a narrow section of the river and continued on a trail through the prairie grass.

He waited for more questions, but Stu didn't ask any. In fact, he remained silent as they traveled over a ridge, passing a field of tall grass and a small grouping of trees before edging along a creek previously hidden from view. Dylan followed Stu until they climbed another hill, and the rolling pasture spread out before them. Cows—black, brown or tan—and their calves contentedly munched away at the grasses. He and Stu rode along the fence until they reached a gate.

"There's a pond beyond the crest. Let's go have a look-see." They went through the gate and checked cattle as they made their way to the crest. Stu grew more chatty as they neared the herd. "Had to give the 95 blue tag calf a dose of penicillin yesterday. Doing fine this morning. I lost one calf late April. Hate to lose 'em."

Dylan wasn't sure how to respond. His experience as a teen had been limited to riding the horses and learning how to rope. He and his friend hadn't joined the cowboys in working with actual cattle.

"See anything out of the ordinary?" Stu flicked a glance his way.

He straightened in his saddle, looking out over the herd and prairie. What would be out of the ordinary? He had no idea what was normal and what wasn't. All he saw were cattle grazing.

"Looks peaceful to me." He hoped he wasn't missing something obvious.

"Let's get to the pond, then."

Within minutes they'd picked their way over the rockier terrain to the water's edge. Some of the cattle were lying near it. A few were drinking. All seemed calm.

Stu skirted the herd and rode toward a stand of trees. "You see that?"

Dylan peered toward the woods. He saw a black lump moving. "Yeah. Is it a calf?"

"Yep." He signaled Diego in that direction. When they reached the trees, Stu motioned Dylan forward. "Get in there and direct him back. I'll get him back to his mama once you've turned him."

Dylan's palms grew clammy, but he nodded. How was

he supposed to direct him back? What if the calf got hurt or ran in a different direction? He didn't know what to do. *God, I don't have any idea how to get this calf out of here. Will You help me?*

Why would God listen to an imposter like him? He had no business being here.

Maybe he should tell Stu the truth—he had no idea how to make a calf behave. But Stu had already taken off. And the calf was moving deeper into the trees. Dylan couldn't stand the thought of the little guy getting hurt. There was nothing to do but guide Jethro into the woods slowly, carefully. The calf wasn't more than fifteen feet away, and the horse seemed to have homed in on the little guy.

Dylan almost signaled Jethro to get right up on the calf, but the horse clearly had experience with cattle. Jethro seemed to be tracking its movements. Dylan began murmuring to the horse, and to his relief, the closer they got to the calf, the more it appeared whatever the horse was doing was working. The calf slowed.

He tightened the reins, and Jethro shook his head, then stopped. The calf stopped, too.

Now what?

Jethro's ears pricked, and Dylan took it as sign. "Go on."

The horse moved around the calf, causing it to turn. Good. Now he just had to get it out of the woods. He urged Jethro forward, and as soon as he did, the calf took off running in the direction where Stu waited. At the last minute, though, the calf changed direction. Stu snapped into action, cut it off and herded the calf back to the prairie with the rest of the cattle.

Dylan was sweating. Had he messed up? It had all

been going smoothly until the calf got a mind of its own. Maybe he should have taken a different approach. Then the calf would have gone straight to Stu.

"I'm glad to see you kept your trigger finger under wraps in there," Stu said. "Last thing I need is a lassoed calf being injured as he's dragged over branches and stumps." He stopped Diego and took out a handkerchief from his pocket, wiping his forehead. "Jethro's a good cutter. He knows what to do around cattle."

"I can tell he's smart."

Stu nodded. "We'll check fence on the way back."

A while later they rode back to the stables, took care of the horses and then sat in wrought-iron chairs under the barn's awning. Dylan's nerves began to ping-pong. Stu hadn't asked him any questions about his background or experience beyond wanting to know where he came from.

Would this be the interview? He couldn't lie about his experience, but it would be a shame if Stu sent him packing. After spending a few hours out here, he wanted to spend more.

"We're moving cattle again on Monday." Stu's legs were splayed as he watched Dylan's response. The toothpick between his teeth was still working.

He nodded.

"You can get settled in one of the cabins before then."

He tried not to show his surprise. Did this mean he was hired?

"Payday's every other Friday. You're on your own for meals. You have a horse?"

"Um, no," Dylan said, his hope rising. "I can get one, though."

The toothpick bobbed between Stu's teeth. "You can

ride Jethro. He needs to be working. It hasn't been good for him with Josiah gone."

Josiah must have been the man who died. A pang of sympathy hit him. "I appreciate it."

"You know how to operate a tractor?"

"No, sir."

"We'll be baling hay next month. Could use your help with that."

Next month? His conscience dug into his ribs.

"I don't know how long I'll be in town," he said. The split-rail fences around the corrals, the peeling paint of the barn and the worn, if tidy, appearance of the ranch didn't escape him. If he had to guess, he'd say Stu couldn't afford to lose a cent. The man would be better off hiring someone who knew what he was doing. He owed Stu the truth. "I don't have much ranch experience."

"I know." Stu leaned back, eyeing him.

"That obvious, huh?"

"You've got good instincts. You know how to ride and you're strong. You want the job?"

The compliment speared heat through his chest. Stu thought he had good instincts. There was a first time for everything. His father hadn't thought so.

"I do want the job. Are you sure you want to hire me considering I might not stay long?"

"I was born on this ranch. Been at it sixty-seven years. I've seen a lot of restless cowboys. Right now my choice is between you and a couple of fifteen-year-old kids from town. The work's hard. Hours are long. I'll take the help as long as you're willing to stay. But no boozing, no carousing. I've got no use for that on my land."

"You can count on me." He'd gotten the job—he was going to be a real cowboy! Satisfaction filled him as he realized he'd be spending his days in the open air on horseback. Moving cattle—he'd have to figure out how to do that—and checking fence and maybe even driving a tractor to bale hay.

Satisfaction shifted to excitement. "Did you say you have a cabin I can stay in?"

"Sure do." Stu stood. "Come on. I'll take you over there."

They walked past the barn down a dirt lane where he could see weathered wood cabins. Most were tiny. One was larger. And a big log structure was tucked behind them.

"That there used to be the bunkhouse, but about ten years ago, it became more of a meeting place. Two of my ranch hands, Jim and Spud, got married and started families, so they didn't want to bunk together anymore. They live in town. The two-bedroom house was Josiah's before he died. He was my right-hand man for thirty years. His wife died of cancer a few years prior."

Dylan glanced over at Stu. The toothpick moved up and down quickly, and he could see the stress lines around his mouth. It must have been hard on him losing a trusted friend. Then the man pointed to the smaller cabins. "Steer clear of the one on the end. Critters found their way inside. Haven't gotten around to getting rid of 'em yet. This one here's in the best shape. Cade left it clean and tidy before he moved. Got married last month and relocated to Colorado. Why he'd want to live there, I have no idea. Anyway, take your pick."

"The one you mentioned is fine." He wasn't taking the large cabin, not when he'd only be here a month or so. Plus Stu might hire someone long-term, someone with experience who would rightly expect to live there.

The rancher pulled out a full keyring. After finding the correct one, he led the way up the path to the small, covered wooden porch and unlocked the cabin door.

Dylan entered and frowned. His bathroom back in Dallas was bigger than this place. A double bed stood in the corner next to a window. To his right, a row of kitchen cabinets lined the back corner. There was a small stove and a refrigerator, too. A table with two wooden chairs separated the kitchen and the living area, which consisted of an old plaid couch, a rocking chair and an ancient television. Rag rugs covered the wooden floor.

"Is there a bathroom?" He hated even asking the question. What if the answer was no?

"Behind the bed." Stu pointed.

He opened the door and was pleased to see a full bathroom complete with a tub and shower combination. All original with hard-water stains, but at least they were there.

"I'll let you get settled. Take tomorrow off. We meet at the barn at five o'clock sharp Monday morning. If you need me, my house was the one you passed driving in. Here's my cell number." Stu told him the number while Dylan entered it into his phone. He then texted him so he'd have his number, too. "Oh, by the way, you'll want to get some chaps and gloves. If you need an advance, let me know. Rendezvous Outfitters has never let me down."

"Thanks." He shook Stu's hand again. "I appreciate you giving me the job."

"Here's your key." And with that, Stu left.

Dylan looked around the cabin. It was tiny. Ancient. The opposite of luxurious.

And it was the best lodging he'd had in over a year

because he had a job. A purpose. He was officially a cowboy.

Yeehaw!

Gabby could use some motherly advice and a woman to lean on. Sometimes she resented the fact her mother showed no interest in her life and had moved on with a stranger down in Laramie. At least Gabby had Babs O'Rourke. Her redheaded, seventy-one-year-old boss was the closest thing to a mom she had here in Rendezvous, or anywhere for that matter.

Their weekly Monday afternoon business meeting in Babs's office at the inn was almost wrapped up. Yesterday Gabby had filled her in briefly about Dylan coming to town, which meant as soon as the meeting ended, Babs would have a laundry list of questions for her about him. Her boss had been the town busybody for years and wouldn't give up the title anytime soon. Gabby didn't hold her gossipy ways against her. She had a heart of gold.

"Now that we have business out of the way, tell me more about this mystery uncle. Stella told me he's hotter than a batch of fries fresh out of the deep fryer. Is he tempting you to change your mind about cowboys?" Babs leaned forward over the desk with her fingers splayed, revealing long red nails. Her short hair had been curled, teased and sprayed, and she wore heavy eyeliner, thick mascara and crimson lipstick.

"No." Gabby held herself primly.

"Give him time, sugar. So what's he going to do? Just sit around town counting down the minutes until he can see you and the baby?" She tapped one of her red talons on the desk.

"No, and so we're clear, he's here to see the baby. Not

me." She'd been surprised when she'd gotten Dylan's call yesterday afternoon telling her Stu had hired him. She hadn't expected him to talk to Stu so quickly. She'd figured he'd linger around town until he deemed it absolutely necessary to get the job. "Stu Miller hired him."

"Oh, good. That poor man has had tough times lately. Cade getting married and moving out of state was bad enough, but then Josiah dying…well, it's hard to lose your best friend." She made a clicking sound with her tongue and shook her head. "Isn't he down to two ranch hands? I told Jimmy Ball to send over a few of those high school boys, but you know how it is. Jobs, sports and their own chores leave them little time to work for someone else."

"I do know. I hope Dylan will be a help to Stu."

"Why wouldn't he be?" Babs gave her a questioning look. "You don't think too highly of him, do you?"

She sighed. It wasn't fair for her to project her concerns about cowboys onto him. At least not until he proved her correct. "I don't know him. I'm sure Stu will be happy to have an extra set of hands."

"Don't sound so enthusiastic," Babs said almost under her breath. "Okay, so what do you know about him? He's tall, dark and handsome—I got that from Stella. You say he's from Texas, right? And he's been traveling since his daddy and stepbrother died. Sounds like he needs a place to settle. Maybe Rendezvous will feel like home."

"I hope not." An involuntary shudder rippled down her back.

"Gabby." Babs stared at her hard. "You're concerning me. Now tell me the truth. Is this about your grudge against cowboys or is Dylan a risk to the baby? I will not let my little Phoebekins be put in danger, uncle or not."

"I can't imagine he'd be a risk to the baby. He doesn't

seem the type." Guilt nibbled at her. "He wants to get to know her and be part of her life."

"See? That's not so bad. An uncle to dote on her is a good thing."

"I guess."

"When will you see him again?"

"I'm not sure. I expect he'll want to get settled at the ranch. He's staying in one of the cabins there."

"You'll have to let me know next time he comes around. I'll just happen to stop by." Babs raised her eyebrows, her green eyes sparkling. "I need to see this hunk for myself."

Gabby was more than ready to steer the conversation in another direction. "Have you thought more about what you told me on Friday? Are you still set on selling the inn?"

She lost some of her sparkle. "I am. I know you aren't keen on it, but I can't help it. I've unloaded the other properties, and this is the final one."

"But it's your livelihood. Your pride and joy."

Her face fell. "It was. I kept going full-steam ahead after Herb died, but now..."

"I wish you'd reconsider." If she could get Babs to keep the inn, her life wouldn't be so up in the air. "I'll take on more responsibilities—anything."

"You already run the place, Gabby. It's not the money or the work."

"Then what is it?" She hadn't considered there might be a personal reason—a bad reason—for Babs to want to sell the inn. "You're not sick or anything, are you?"

"No, honey." She shook her head. "You don't have to worry about that."

"Then what?"

"I'm ready to retire for good. I might travel or winter down in Florida or… I don't know. I've been feeling it in my bones. I need to be free. And as long as I own this inn, I'm not free."

Gabby wanted to plead with her, tell her she'd run it single-handedly, but she was being selfish. If Babs wanted to retire and be free, Gabby wouldn't be so heartless as to try to stop her. Besides, she probably needed the money from the sale of the inn to do the things she wanted.

Babs sniffed. "I hate to get you worked up, but there's been some interest in it."

"But it's not even on the market yet." Her heart sank. She thought there would be more time—months preferably.

"I know, but I'm partnering with a real estate agent this time instead of selling it on my own, and Dorothy Wendall put the feelers out."

Gabby took a deep breath. Putting out feelers and getting interest might amount to nothing. She shouldn't let herself get all worked up even if Dorothy Wendall was the best real estate agent in town.

"Do you know who's interested in it?" Gabby asked. Maybe this wouldn't be so bad. A local could be buying it—they'd know how hard she worked and want to keep her.

"Nolan Hummel." Babs made a production out of straightening the papers on her desk.

Nolan Hummel? The arrogant jerk who'd asked her out more than once and hadn't taken being rejected well? He always looked her up and down like he was evaluating a porterhouse steak. Gabby would rather scrub toilets than work for him.

"Why would he want an inn?" Gabby tilted her head. "His family specializes in shipping. Didn't he get promoted to vice president last year?"

"He did, and I don't know why he wants it, hon. I'm just trying to keep you in the loop. I guess we can ask him when he tours the place."

"He's touring it. When?" She scooted to the edge of her seat.

"I'm not sure. He'll be in town this week, and I'd imagine he'd want to schedule a visit soon."

She gagged a little. There was no way he was buying the inn. He didn't even live in Rendezvous. As far as she knew, Nolan resided almost an hour south where Hummel Freight's headquarters were located. He came to Rendezvous only every few months to check in with his vendors.

What if Nolan moved here? She'd have to see him all the time. And possibly work for him. A dull ache formed behind her temples.

"You said *some* interest. Is anyone else, by chance, interested in buying the inn at this point?" At Babs's shake of the head, she sighed.

"When Dorothy Wendall lists it next week, I'm sure we'll have more prospects. I'm not a big fan of Nolan, either, sugar. He talks to me like I'm ninety-nine years old and as stupid as a skunk crossing a busy highway. But the Hummels can afford the place, and I know they wouldn't run it into the ground. They know business."

Gabby couldn't argue with that. They did know business, and they'd likely be good owners of the inn.

Too bad she couldn't see herself working for their son. Life was too short to spend it working for someone she loathed. If Nolan Hummel was a serious buyer, she'd have to put feelers around town and find out if anyone was hiring.

But how would she find a job she loved as much as this one? And could she afford to work somewhere else? Good-paying jobs were few and far between in this town.

"Would you at least give me some warning when Nolan schedules his tour?"

"Of course. And don't feel like you need to keep the fact I'm selling the place a secret. The entire town knows. I figured spreading the word might flush out a buyer." Babs pushed her chair back and stood. "Am I still babysitting Phoebe tomorrow night?"

"Yes, please." Tomorrow was Tuesday. Gabby was blessed that Babs loved babysitting Phoebe for her while her support group met in one of the inn's conference rooms. "Thanks for being such a wonderful grandma to her."

"Don't you mean Glam-ma?" Babs preened and laughed. "I'm tickled you let me help out."

She stood and rounded the desk, pulling Babs in for a hug. "I don't know what I'd do without you. I don't blame you for wanting to retire and enjoy life. You deserve it."

Babs gave her a squeeze before stepping back. "I enjoy life plenty. I'm just…well…going through some things. Thanks for understanding. It will all turn out all right. Don't you worry."

"I won't." She pasted on a smile. But the worries were already kicking up in the back of her mind. It hit her that if Babs was retiring and traveling, she wouldn't be around for Gabby or Phoebe. There went Glam-ma…and Gabby's mom away from mom. What would she do without Babs?

He'd never been this sore in his life.

Wincing, Dylan eased his body onto a park bench at

the entrance of Riverwalk Park in downtown Rendezvous Monday evening. When he'd called Gabby this afternoon, she'd tried to blow him off about seeing Phoebe today, but he'd gotten her to agree to a walk on the river trail after she finished supper.

He didn't know what model car she drove, so every now and then, he looked back to scan the narrow parking lot for a pretty brunette.

Today had been exhausting. Draining. Somewhat embarrassing. And absolutely fantastic. He had a whole new respect for the cowboys he'd always admired. Until today, he'd never ridden a horse for more than a couple of hours, and he couldn't remember a time he'd done any hard, manual labor. His parents had hired people to do the heavy lifting. Now he knew why.

A long soak in a Jacuzzi would do him a world of good. But he'd have to settle for another sweltering night in his cabin instead. The place didn't exactly have the amenities he was accustomed to. The shoebox with no air-conditioning felt like a sauna. Maybe he could pick up a fan here in town.

"Hey there," a woman called. Gabby pushed a stroller toward him. Her hair was pulled back into a bouncy ponytail, and she wore black leggings ending at her calves, a long turquoise T-shirt and running shoes. "Hope you haven't been waiting long."

"I haven't." He stood, trying not to flinch. Every nerve ending twitched. Every muscle spasmed.

"What's wrong?" She stopped the stroller as soon as she reached him.

"Nothing." He couldn't help smiling as Phoebe grabbed both her bare feet and grinned at him. He bent his index finger to wave to her. "Hey there, smiley. You sure are happy today, aren't you?"

The baby replied by sticking her toes in her mouth. He wished he was that flexible. It sure would make ranch work easier.

Straightening, he met Gabby's eyes, and a burst of anticipation chased away all thoughts of sore muscles. With her flushed cheeks, she had a glow about her, one he could almost reach out and touch.

"Thanks for meeting me," he said. "I know you're probably tired from work."

"A girl needs to exercise." She raised her eyebrows as she shrugged, smiling.

Her trim figure made no argument with that. He extended his arm for them to start walking. "Which way?"

"Hang a right. We'll take the scenic route."

"Want me to push the princess?" He hoped she'd agree. There was something about watching Phoebe's cute face that melted away his worries.

"Go for it." She took her hands off the handles, and he began pushing. They fell into a brisk pace. The warm, sunny evening lured people outside. Several couples and families were on the paved trail. Gabby glanced his way. "What did you do today?"

Where to begin? It had been the longest day of his life, but the time had passed by as quickly as a blink of an eye.

"I helped Stu feed the cattle, then we moved part of the herd to a new pasture." He hadn't been good at moving cattle. Hadn't been comfortable being around them at all. The other ranch hands, Jim and Spud, were seasoned pros, and even the high school kids, Cody and Austin, had known what to do more than him. He'd kind of lagged along, doing whatever Stu told him to do. He hoped his boss wasn't disappointed.

"Sounds like a typical day on the ranch."

"Yeah, we fixed part of a fence where a bull broke through." At least he'd redeemed himself with the fence. For years he'd been strength-training and running daily. Digging holes, hauling fence posts and pounding them into the ground had been the easiest part of the day.

"I guess you feel right at home, huh?" She made it sound like a statement, but when he glanced her way, he noted the curiosity in her eyes.

"It's day one." He wanted to feel at home, but his lack of skills worried him. Stu could fire him at any minute. It had been obvious he didn't know what he was doing. "We'll see how it goes. What about you? Was everything smooth at the inn?"

Her eyebrows drew together, but then her lips curved upward. "It was fine. We're booked through the first week of July, so that's good. The town has a big celebration for Independence Day every year. It's a lot of fun, and I'm glad we'll be able to draw tourists to it."

"I'm assuming the summer months are busiest at the inn." He glanced at Phoebe, who stared contentedly at him and gurgled, still holding her feet.

"For the most part. We do get some visitors as well as hunters and fishermen in the fall. And we're usually busy during the holidays. January through March are the slow months."

"I can see that." The trail wound along the top of the riverbank, and the water below flowed over rocks, kicking up sprays of waves. Between the river, the blue sky, a hawk flying overhead and the mountains in the distance, a sensation of awe and belonging came over him.

"Oh no," Gabby said under her breath.

"What?" He looked around. Besides a few couples strolling their way, a man wearing athletic shorts and a tight T-shirt was talking on a cell phone while power-walking toward them.

"Nothing." The word was clipped. She pulled her shoulders back and kept her pace. When the man saw her, his gaze took her in from head to toe, then he ended the call and pocketed his phone.

Dylan sensed Gabby would have gladly spun on her heel and sprinted in the other direction, but she stood her ground as he approached.

"Gabrielle." The way her name rolled off his tongue irritated Dylan. There was something oily about this guy. The man locked eyes with Gabby. "Good to see you."

"Nolan." Her tone was no-nonsense. "I heard you were arriving this week."

"Then you must have heard you'll be seeing a lot more of me."

"Rumor has it." She blinked pleasantly.

He noticed Dylan for the first time.

Gabby turned to him. "Nolan, this is Dylan Kingsley. Dylan, Nolan Hummel."

Dylan held out his hand, and Nolan eyed it for a moment before shaking it. What was his problem? Was he not worth a handshake? It was an odd sensation to be looked down on. He couldn't remember it ever happening before.

"I see you're raising Allison's child." Nolan nodded to the stroller.

At her sister's name, Gabby stiffened. Dylan longed to touch her shoulder and tell her it was okay. But he didn't know why she was bothered. Had Gabby dated this guy? Maybe her sister had. Or they could be related somehow.

"Yes, I am," she said.

"Noble." His smile didn't reach his eyes.

"There's nothing noble about it. I love her." She widened her eyes and gestured to the trail. "Well, I won't keep you. Enjoy your walk."

He cocked his head. "I had cleared my schedule to be at the inn all day tomorrow, but something came up. I'll see you Friday instead."

"Great." Her tone could have chipped ice. "See you then."

Dylan took a long stride to catch up to her. She wasn't volunteering any information. He wanted to ask her about Nolan, but it wasn't his place.

"Do you mind if we stop a minute?" she asked after walking in silence several yards. "There's a restroom up ahead."

"Sure." A sidewalk cut into the trail, and he followed her to the small building with restrooms. "I'll wait out here with Phoebe."

"Okay."

When Gabby disappeared into the building, he made funny faces at Phoebe. She kicked her feet and let out a squeal. After a few moments, though, she started to fuss, arching her back. Was she uncomfortable? He wasn't sure what to do. As the fussing turned to a cry, he unhooked the straps and lifted her out of the stroller. She grinned at him, clapping her hands.

"You wanted some sunshine, didn't you?" He sat again, letting her bounce her feet on his thighs as he kept a firm grip under her arms. Funny, how natural holding her felt. And it was only his second time. "Do you know what? Your uncle Dylan has never been this tired and sore in his life. I rode Jethro for hours, and my legs feel like jelly. Watching you bouncing your little knees makes my joints ache."

She giggled, and on impulse, he hugged her to him. Who knew such a tiny baby could erase his troubles? She squirmed, so he moved her back to bounce on his legs. She jammed her fist into her mouth, drooling.

"You know what else, smiley?" The entire day came back to him—the exhilaration of working with the men, the embarrassment of not knowing what he was doing—and he realized he needed to share it with someone, even if it was a baby. He used a gentle, singsong voice. "I was a real cowboy today. I helped move cattle from one pasture to the other. Some of those calves and their mamas were slow. Real slow. So we left them alone. Stu told me we'll move them tomorrow. You know what else? I have my own cabin, and it's teeny. As bitty as you are. In fact, I've never slept in something so small. I kind of like it, even if it is hotter than a furnace."

She let out a happy squeal.

"I know, that's how I feel, too. It's good to be alive, isn't it?" He closed his eyes as the words sank in.

It *was* good to be alive. He wished Sam and Dad could still enjoy a perfect summer day.

"Hey, sorry about that." Gabby loped over to them.

"No problem. Is everything all right?" He stood to set Phoebe back in the stroller. He had no idea how to get her strapped back in.

She took Phoebe from him and kissed her cheek, then she lowered her back into the stroller and secured her. "Yeah, Nolan isn't my favorite person. And unfortunately,

I can't ignore him. My boss might be selling the inn to him, so I have to be on my best behavior."

"Why?" He tucked away the information.

"Why isn't he my favorite person? Or why do I have to be on my best behavior?"

"Both."

She pushed the stroller to the trail once more. "He thinks he's a big shot, but he'd be nothing without his daddy's money."

The words stabbed his heart. She could have been talking about him.

"Anyway, I'll leave it at that." She fell into a fast pace. "How's your cabin? Do you have everything you need?"

"I'm getting there." But he wasn't. The bedding was threadbare, and he didn't have even the basic items needed to live, like more than a day's worth of food and supplies. "Has that guy bothered you?"

"Yes and no. His attitude bothers me. Other than that, he's harmless." Her footstep faltered, but she adjusted her balance. "Don't worry about Nolan. I certainly won't."

He'd have to take her word for it. But it was obvious she wasn't telling him the whole story. His spirits sank. Why *would* she confide in him? He was merely the uncle she was being forced to deal with.

When they reached the end of the paved portion of the trail, they turned back. Gabby began telling him about how the town raised funds three years ago to pave the river trail, and although he enjoyed her enthusiasm, he listened with half an ear.

She didn't want to tell him about her personal life. He got it. The problem was besides Phoebe—who had no idea what he was talking about—Gabby was the only person he even remotely wanted to tell about his.

Loneliness smacked him square in the middle.

He finally had something worth sharing but no one to share it with.

He was playing at being an uncle, playing at being a cowboy, playing at being part of a small town. Something told him he was going to walk away from Rendezvous disappointed if he played at being important to Gabby.

He wasn't important to anyone. The story of his life.

## Chapter Five

❧

"Everything is going off the rails, and I don't know what to do." Gabby hung her head Tuesday night. She'd told herself again and again to stay positive and not to flip out, but as soon as Nicole, Eden and Mason walked into the conference room for their weekly support group meeting, she'd lost it.

"Hey, what's wrong?" Eden immediately sat beside her, putting her arm around Gabby's shoulders.

She looked from one concerned face to another. Mason was frowning, and Nicole was massaging her very pregnant belly.

"Babs is selling the inn, one of the potential buyers is not my favorite person and I've seen Phoebe's uncle three times in four days. It's a bit much."

"I heard Nolan was in town asking about the inn." Eden's lips puckered like she'd sucked on a lemon. "He isn't considering purchasing the place, is he?"

"He might be." She shouldn't have said what she did. It wasn't fair to Babs or Nolan. Her feelings weren't a factor in the deal.

"Are you worried you'll lose your job?" Mason asked.

"Yes." And she was worried about more than that. "If I don't like the owner, I'm even more worried about keeping it."

"I'm sorry, Gabby," Nicole said. "Stella told me it was going up for sale. Thank you for hiring her. I think having a steady job is grounding her."

Gabby doubted it, but she wouldn't disrespect Nicole. "I'm glad to have her at the front desk. Customers like her cheery smile." If only she could inspire some ambition in Stella to want to actually perform her duties without Gabby nagging her.

"You won't move, will you?" Eden chewed the corner of her bottom lip.

"Move? Of course not! Where would I go?"

"To another town where you can manage another hotel. A nicer one." Eden's face fell. "You're really good at it."

"You'd make more money if you moved to Jackson," Nicole said. "Think of the swanky hotels they have."

"My home is here." Gabby glanced at Eden, who looked unusually emotional. "I'll make it work."

"You mentioned the uncle. How is he? What's his name again?" Mason crossed his leg so his ankle rested on his knee.

"Dylan Kingsley. And he's working for Stu."

"He's a ranch hand?" Mason sounded surprised.

"He's a cowboy." She shouldn't sound so disgusted, but she couldn't help it.

"Here we go…" Mason said under his breath as he averted his eyes. Eden actually rolled hers. Gabby didn't care. They had no idea how much pain Carl had put her through, and she wasn't going to enlighten them now.

"What's wrong with a cowboy?" Nicole's cheeks were flushed.

"Nothing." Gabby raised her hands. "Everything."

"Well, which is it?" Nicole looked confused.

"I don't know. My daddy was a cowboy for hire, and let's just say I thought the world of him until I realized he was cheating on my mom with women all over the state."

"Oh, I'm sorry." Nicole winced.

"Don't be."

"Not all cowboys are cheaters." Nicole's tone soothed the tension.

Maybe not, but the ones she'd trusted had been. "I don't have time in my life for a cheater or a liar."

"Let's change the subject," Eden said.

"Sorry, guys, I'm superstressed." Gabby slumped, overwhelmed by all the changes. "With losing Allison and raising the baby and now a mystery uncle and I might lose my job…"

"I get it, Gabby." Nicole's sad eyes met hers. Shame zipped down her core. Her own problems were miniscule compared to Nicole's. How could she complain when Nicole lost her husband and was pregnant with triplets? "I've been struggling, too. There are too many what-ifs for my taste. What if the babies come early? What if they come late? Will I be able to take care of them all? And then there's Mom…she's dating a new guy…not that it matters. Sorry to hijack the conversation. Is there anything we can do to help you?"

"I'll be fine. I have nothing to complain about." Gabby shook her head. She hated indulging in pity parties. "We'll all help with the babies in any way we can, so try not to stress about them too much. And what's going on with your mom? Don't you like the new boyfriend?"

"He's okay. She's head over heels. As usual." Nicole shifted, wincing. "Why don't we get into our Bible reading?"

"I'm dealing with some stuff, too." Eden's eyes had grown round.

"What is it?" Mason leaned forward. "What's going on?"

"It's nothing like what you're all going through." Eden's face crumpled. "It's just that Mom and Dad are making some changes, and I don't know how I fit into them."

"What kind of changes?" Gabby asked. She couldn't imagine the Pages doing anything other than what they'd always done. They owned a large cattle ranch outside Rendezvous, and Eden had gone away to college for a few years before moving back home to be near her sister, Mia—Mason's late wife—while Mia had cancer treatments. After her death six months later, Eden had stayed at the ranch to babysit Noah for Mason. Eden never mentioned wanting to do anything else.

"They're talking about buying an RV and traveling around the country." Her expression gave Gabby the impression of a lost little girl. "It's bizarre."

"Would you go with them?" Nicole asked.

"No." She shook her head as if it was the last thing she'd ever do. "An RV sounds awful. I want to stay on the ranch. It's my home."

"We'll look after you," Mason said.

"Thanks," Eden said. "I've gotten used to life back home. And now it's going to change. Again."

"Well, one thing isn't going to change. You'll always have us." Gabby reached over and squeezed Eden's hand.

"I want to believe you." Eden sighed. "But it's obvious things are changing for all of us. Mason, you're married now. Nicole, you're having triplets and starting over after years away. And, Gabby, the new uncle and possible job loss don't reassure me you'll be staying in town even if you want to."

"Hey, don't get worked up, it will be all right. I'm not going anywhere." Gabby squeezed Eden's hand.

"Remember what you've been telling me for years?" Mason leaned back in his chair. "God's not going to desert us. He's got this."

"I wish my faith was as strong as yours." Nicole shifted in her seat. "Sometimes I feel like my life keeps going from bad to worse. I wish I could get a job. Then I could afford my own place. It's…hard right now, living with Mom and Stella."

Gabby couldn't imagine living with her mom again after so many years of independence.

"We have a lot to pray about tonight," Gabby said. "Where should we start?"

Mason cleared his throat. "If you don't mind, I'd like to share something I came across when I was reading my Bible this week. I think it fits well with what we're talking about. It's from John 14:27. 'Peace I leave with you, my peace I give unto you: not as the world giveth, give I unto you. Let not your heart be troubled, neither let it be afraid.'"

Gabby let the words sink in. The Lord didn't give as the world did. She wanted His peace. But she didn't know if she could prevent her heart from being troubled, not with her personal anxieties mounting. Thinking about her friends' problems wasn't helping, either. But that's what prayer was for. *Father, I need You. Give me Your peace. Help me lean on You. Help my friends, too.*

Dylan came to mind. It had been pleasant to walk with him last night even though they'd crossed paths with Nolan. In a strange way, she'd been glad Dylan had been by her side. His presence had been a buffer between her and the threat to her job Nolan represented. Afterward, she'd wanted to lean on Dylan, to share her worries about her job. But she hadn't, and it was for the best.

"Okay, where did we leave off last week? Philippians?" Gabby shoved everything out of her mind. Sharing with Dylan, opening up to him, would only lead to trouble. She had enough of that right now. Why ask for more?

"Haven't you ever fished before?" Stu took a step back as Dylan held a fly-fishing rod in one hand and an empty spool in the other.

"Can't say that I have." He had no clue what to do with any of the equipment Stu had brought. An hour ago, they'd finished checking the cattle and taking care of the horses, and Stu had told him they were going fishing—they'd earned it. Since Gabby had some meeting on Tuesday nights, Dylan hadn't objected. But his stomach was roiling as once again he looked like a complete fool.

"Don't they have rivers in Texas?" Stu's ever-present toothpick bobbed as he spoke.

"They do. I've just never been fishing."

"Well, come on then. I'll teach you. A man should know how to fish." Stu dug around in his tackle box and tossed a few plastic containers Dylan's way. "Attach the backing to the rod, then you can attach the line and the leader."

He shuffled the plastic containers until he found one with the backing label on it, then he stared at the reel.

How was he supposed to attach this and whatever else Stu mentioned, and why were there so many things involved?

"It snaps off." Stu took the reel out of his hand and lifted one side. "The orange line is the backing. Wrap it around the reel twice, then tie it with an anchor knot. If you move it back and forth a few times, it'll get nice and snug. Then you can attach the line."

Heat rushed up his neck as he tried to process what Stu wanted him to do. What length of backing should he wrap around it? Did he cut it first? And what was an anchor knot?

"Okay, so I gave you a good all-purpose size rod." Stu opened the package and pulled out a few feet of backing. Then he wrapped it around the reel, leaving about three inches dangling. "Here, you can tie the knot now."

Was he sweating bullets? It was bad enough he revealed his ignorance about the ranch on a daily basis—how was he going to explain to Stu he didn't know what an anchor knot was? For the first time in his life, he wished he'd had some wilderness training.

Stu was busy preparing his own rod and reel. He finished attaching everything in what seemed like one minute flat.

"Would you mind demonstrating the anchor knot?" He wanted to crawl under the rocks across the river and never come out. But more than that, he wanted to fish and try everything a ranch in Wyoming offered.

"Didn't your daddy teach you anything, son?" He didn't look mad or even sarcastic. His expression was curious.

Dylan winced. His dad had taught him things—to do his best in school, to not waste time on hobbies, to dominate at football, to network with the right people. Dylan had tried to live up to his standards, but he'd never met his expectations. Even working for Dad's company had been a joke—the man had never seriously considered passing it on to him. He just wished he would have realized it before Dad sold it.

"My father ran his own business and didn't have much time for leisure." The sad truth was, his dad had considered him unworthy to take his place. Why else wouldn't he have had the decency to let him know he'd sold the company? Dad's administrative assistant had told Dylan a solid thirty minutes before the news went public. He could still taste the metallic tang of the emotional sucker punch. His father should have warned him, not misled him into thinking he truly had a shot at running the company someday.

"If you don't have time for leisure, you're not living. Life isn't all work." Stu gestured to the reel. "Hook it over like this…" As Stu demonstrated what to do, Dylan paid close attention to his instructions, and soon his rod was ready for fishing.

"Now you want to get the rod to bend and stop twice. Once behind, once ahead. And you want to keep the tip of your rod straight so you can get your line to follow a nice, straight path. When you bring the rod back, don't go too far. You don't want your line falling behind you in the grass."

It took several tries, but eventually Dylan was casting in a reasonably straight line. He stood on the riverbank and marveled at the clear water running over the rocky bottom.

"Did your father teach you how to fish, Stu?" He glanced over as the man cast his line several feet upstream.

"Yes, he did. I was a little tyke, and I remember tagging along with him everywhere. I might as well have been a burr on his side when I was a young'un. He taught me everything. How to ride my horse, how to rope a cow, how to work cattle, how to repair things around the ranch. Hunting, fishing, you name it, he taught it to me."

A sudden longing pinched his heart. It would have been nice to have had a father like that.

"Do you have siblings?" Dylan asked.

"Two sisters. One's over in Cody, and the other's in Florida. Ma and Pa both passed away."

"My dad died, too. A year ago." The sound of line whizzing through the air mingled with the water rushing over the river rocks.

"I'm sorry to hear that. Your ma?"

"Still alive. I don't see her much."

Stu stared at him but didn't ask questions. They continued fishing. Dylan tried to picture his own father showing him how to fish. The idea made him laugh. Even if Dad had taken him out here, he just would have pinpointed all the ways Dylan was doing it wrong. The only things Dylan had gotten right in his eyes were sports and, well, that was it. His father had been proud of Dylan's high school football days. As a star receiver, his height and athleticism had served him well. He'd even been offered a scholarship to a small university in Arizona, but Dad had scoffed at him getting a degree from there, so he'd passed to attend a more well-known school.

He gripped the rod tightly, casting it again, but the line arched over his head and landed in the water with a plop. Maybe his dad had been right not to consider him to take over the company. If Dylan couldn't even stand up to him about what college he wanted to attend, he doubted he'd have had the steely strength to run the company the way Dad had. Now that he thought about it, King Energy had never quickened his pulse the way ranching with Stu did.

"Get it nice and straight." Stu made a motion with his wrist.

Dylan sighed and forced himself to do it the way he'd been shown. This time the line raced out ahead of him easily. It served no purpose to keep thinking about his late father. Still, he wondered what would Dad think if he could see him today? Fly-fishing. Ranching. Sleeping in a tiny, rustic cabin. Hanging out with his niece and her pretty aunt.

He'd shake his head in disappointment. Manual labor? Not for the Kingsleys. Fishing? A waste of time. And he'd throw in his two cents about being on his guard concerning Gabby. There would be the prenup lecture Dad insisted on giving every time Dylan talked to a woman.

Nothing he did had ever been good enough.

"Hey, you got one!" Stu pointed to where his line disappeared in the water. "Jerk up to set the hook. Don't pull too hard. I'll get the net."

He flicked the rod up and water splashed. Then he reeled in the line, his excitement mounting as the fish on the end battled him.

"You've got it! Keep with him." Stu stood next to him with a large fishing net. "Okay, ready? Raise the rod to get his head above the water, and I'll scoop him in."

Dylan followed his directions, and to his amazement, Stu raised the net high holding a big flopping fish.

"You did it, and on your first try. That there's a beauty, too. Good work." Stu's grin spread from ear to ear, and his toothpick dangled out the side of his mouth as he worked to get the fish unhooked. "Brown trout. See the golden color? The black spots give it away. Hoo-boy, this must be eighteen inches. We're frying him up tonight."

As Dylan listened to Stu explain how they'd fillet the fish and cook it, a surge of appreciation filled him. Stu's dad had taught him what he needed to know, and Stu was passing on the knowledge to him.

"Your father sounded like a good man, Stu."

The rancher paused, his toothpick bobbing, then he nodded. "Every kid should have a father like mine."

The peace of the blue sky and dancing river seeped in, and he began to see his father through a different lens. Dad had never taken the time to teach Dylan life skills or show him how to run the company, but Dylan hadn't asserted himself, either. And he had never been passionate about oil and gas like Dad was. Maybe they'd both been at fault.

It was over. He had to start moving on with his life, not stay stuck in the past.

Dylan helped Stu gather the tackle box and gear. If he ever had a child, he wanted to be the kind of dad Stu's father had been. "Thank you for teaching me today. In fact, thank you for everything."

"Sure thing. Come on, let's go have ourselves a fish fry."

As they headed back, Dylan thought about Phoebe. Who would teach her how to fish? Would Gabby get married? If she did, what kind of man would raise Phoebe? If Gabby didn't marry, would Phoebe learn everything she needed to know?

She should have a good father. One who would teach her things, one who would be there for her. One she could count on.

He wanted to be a man people could count on.

He wasn't there yet, though. When was the last time anyone had been able to count on him? He didn't know, and he didn't care to think about it anymore. His fish was waiting.

She shouldn't have invited him over. The next evening, Gabby, with Phoebe on her hip, escorted Dylan to her kitchen. His hands were full of takeout food from Roscoe's Diner. He set everything on the kitchen counter.

It had been a long day at work. A long, boring day listening to Stella compare and contrast the good points of local cowboys Cash McCoy and Judd Wilson. Honestly, Gabby had strived to be patient at first, but it hadn't taken long before she'd done everything in her power to avoid Stella's mindless chatter. In the end, she'd given up and picked up her phone for a distraction. Dylan was the first person to come to mind. Hence, the invitation for him to come to her place for dinner. The fact he'd immediately offered to pick up burgers from Roscoe's had made it worth it.

"This smells amazing." She peeked into the bags. "Did you order fried pickles, too?"

"And onion rings. I'm starving." He reached beyond her for the plates. His forearm extending in front of her reminded her all too well he was a strong guy. Her stomach flip-flopped. She blamed it on being hungry. Not on him and his muscles.

"Stu taught me how to fly-fish last night." He sounded excited.

"Oh yeah? How'd you do?"

"I caught one. A big one."

"Now you'll be telling this tale until it becomes legendary." She couldn't believe she was teasing him. She'd known him less than a week. Letting down her guard already. Had she learned nothing from her past mistakes?

*Oh, lighten up, already!*

"It was a trout. A brown trout. And it was seventeen and a half inches long." His eyes twinkled.

"Next time you tell it, it will have grown to twenty inches. In ten years, it will be thirty."

"It'll still be seventeen and a half." He unwrapped the burgers and set them on two plates. Phoebe shifted in Gabby's arms and held her arms out to him.

"Looks like she wants you." Gabby was curious to see how he'd respond. The other night on their walk, she'd been surprised to see him holding Phoebe after she finished up in the restroom, especially since he hadn't seemed very comfortable around the baby before.

"Come here." He wiped his hands down his athletic shorts then took Phoebe from her. He lifted her smiling face above his and made silly faces at her. She squealed, kicking her legs. Then he brought her back down, holding her firmly against his side. The picture they presented sent a rush of longing through Gabby's heart. She never let herself play the what-if game, but what if she had a husband, a partner to help raise the baby?

"I'll bring the food over." She took the plates full of burgers and sides to the table. He sat across from her. "Do you want ketchup or ranch dressing to dip?"

"Both. Why not?" He continued with the goofy faces as Gabby left the table to get the condiments. He really was good with the baby. But it didn't change anything. And entertaining her wasn't the same as taking care of her. She returned to the table with ketchup and ranch dressing.

"Here, I'll put her in the high chair so you can eat."

"Thanks." His appreciative smile brought heat to her cheeks. Avoiding touching him, she quickly strapped Phoebe into her high chair and gave her a small handful of puff cereal. Then she sat back down.

"So how is everything going at Stu's? I know he's been shorthanded." She took a bite of the burger. So good.

"It's great. We finished moving cattle, and we've been checking calves, fixing fence and looking over the hay-fields. I guess we'll be baling next month. He's hired a couple of teenagers to work for a few hours every morning, so that's helping a lot."

Next month? Was he planning on staying longer than his original month?

"Stu's a nice man," she said. "Keeps to himself, but he's always willing to help when a neighbor's in trouble."

"He's helped me more than he'll ever know." He bit into his burger and turned his attention to Phoebe.

What did that mean? He'd been working for Stu for a week. What could the man have possibly helped him with in such a short amount of time? She munched on an onion ring. Maybe the money. Had Dylan needed a job more than he'd let on?

A pit formed in her gut, and the onion ring suddenly tasted burnt. Was he smoothing the way to make her feel sorry for him so he could ask her for money?

Carl had done it so deftly, she hadn't known what had hit her until she'd found herself loaning him money for his electric bill, his car repairs—whatever emergency cropped up on a regular basis—and always with the assurance he'd pay her back as soon as possible.

She was still waiting. He'd never repaid her one red cent.

"What do you mean? How has he helped you?" She prepared herself for a sob story about his bills.

His face grew red. "My dad wasn't the outdoors type, and Stu has been teaching me things I never knew how to do."

Relief spilled through her as cool as a morning rain, and it was chased by shame. She had to stop thinking the worst about him. "Like what?"

"Well, fishing the other night, for one thing. And how calves like to hide in ditches. The warning signs of foot rot. Why he rotates the herd so often."

"Is his ranch so different from the ones in Texas?" She glanced at Phoebe who had a piece of cereal stuck to the outside of her fist as she attempted to feed herself another piece.

He finished chewing and his forehead creased. "He's different. He's patient."

She couldn't argue with that. Stu was one of a kind.

"Has that guy, Nolan, been back at the inn?"

"Not yet. He's coming Friday for a tour."

"If he buys the place, how will it affect you?" He finished off the burger as he waited for her to answer.

"I'm not sure. Best-case scenario, I can continue my position as day manager. Worst case? He fires me to run it himself."

"What would you do then?"

Her throat felt clogged all of a sudden. She hadn't done any preparation for the worst-case scenario. If she began talking to the locals about job openings, everyone would assume she didn't want to remain on as the manager—and she did. Very much. But if she didn't find out who was hiring, she might be out of work in the event she did lose her job. It felt like a no-win situation.

"I have options." She kept her voice firm, but inside she quaked. Did she have options? And if so, what were they?

"Are you worried about it?"

She nodded, not trusting herself to speak.

"I can help…" His words trickled off as if he wished he wouldn't have spoken up.

"I don't need help."

"I'd like to contribute financially. For Phoebe."

"No, thank you." She should be touched he offered, but she'd seen too much, been through too much, to take him seriously. "Money always complicates things."

He blinked and averted those gorgeous brown eyes. His expression had been sincere, but he'd clearly thought better of the offer as soon as it was out of his mouth. He was probably relieved she wasn't holding him to it.

Phoebe let out a series of loud noises and slapped her palms on the tray. Gabby was still finishing her final bites, but she moved to get her out of the high chair.

"Let me. Finish eating." He rose, gesturing for her to stay seated. "Is it okay if I get her out and sit her on my lap?"

"You might want to wipe her hands first. There's a box of baby wipes on the counter, or you can wet a washcloth."

He took out a wipe from the container.

"Okay, Phoebe, I see you liked the cereal." He gently wiped her hands, which she tried to keep out of his reach. She grunted in irritation. "But you liked it a little too much, so let's get you cleaned up."

Gabby couldn't get over his patience. He talked in a low, soothing voice as he wiped her hands carefully. Then his face twisted in confusion. "How do I get her out?"

"Press the buttons under the tray." She made a motion with both hands to demonstrate.

"Right." It took him a few moments, but he got the tray off and soon freed Phoebe. As he sat back down with the baby on his lap, Gabby suppressed a longing sigh. She wished Phoebe had a daddy. A real daddy.

But she couldn't let just anyone into her life—their lives. Only the best for her baby niece. Only the best would do.

## Chapter Six

Friday evening as the sun grew hazy on the horizon, Dylan surveyed his cabin and groaned. He had to buy some supplies. New bedding, towels, more food, a coffeemaker—and a fan. Definitely a fan.

In Dallas, he'd spent the hot days in air-conditioning and had relied on restaurants and takeout for meals. Even when traveling he'd never worried about food because he could always order room service. But this week's PB and Js were wearing thin, and all the physical labor was making him hungrier than ever. Earlier he'd driven into town after finishing up his ranch chores to pick up a pizza. He'd called Gabby to see if she wanted to share it, but she'd told him she had plans. He'd wanted to ask what plans and with whom, but he'd ended the call with a *maybe another time* and had been fighting a sense of dejection ever since.

This week had been incredible. His body was adjusting to riding a horse for hours at a time. His palms had grown callused and weren't as tender as they'd been on Monday. Best of all, he'd been able to spend a few evenings with Phoebe and Gabby, and he was starting to feel comfortable with them, too.

But his conscience kept prodding him. Gabby worked hard to provide for herself and the baby. And now she was worried about losing her job. Shouldn't he be getting the child support and trust fund in place for her? Take some of those burdens off her pretty shoulders?

Before he could talk himself out of it, he dialed Edward Brahm, his lawyer. Ed had been his dad's lawyer as well as a close family friend. Dylan trusted him.

"Well, what do you know?" Ed's voice boomed through the line. "You're still alive after all. I thought you'd fallen off the face of the earth."

"You might think I did when you hear where I'm at." He'd always enjoyed bantering with Ed.

"Why? Where'd you land?"

"Wyoming. On a cattle ranch."

"A cattle ranch? Did you buy one or something?"

"No, I'm working on one as a ranch hand. Temporarily."

"A ranch hand?" He guffawed. "Now I've heard everything. You know all you have to do is call Steve if you're having trouble accessing money."

"Haha, funny." Steve Zosar was Dylan's financial advisor, not that he'd ever had trouble accessing his cash. "My money's fine. I'm calling for a different reason. I found out Sam has a child."

"A child? Are you sure about that?"

"Yes, I am." He crossed over to the window where the pastel colors of the sunset spread low in the sky. "I came out here to meet her. Her name's Phoebe. She's nine months old."

"Hmm." Ed took his time before continuing. "That doesn't explain why you're working on a cattle ranch."

"It's complicated, but I'm… Well, I'm happy."

"Good. I know losing Sam and your dad was tough." The teasing was replaced with his business tone. "What can I help you with? I'm assuming this isn't just a friendly call."

"You're right, although, I will admit it's good to hear your voice." Dylan weighed what to say. Maybe he was looking for advice at this point. "I'd like to financially provide for the baby. Set up a trust fund. Monthly child support. That sort of thing."

"Is there something you aren't telling me? You sure this isn't your kid?"

"If it was, I'd have claimed her already." The thought of Phoebe being his own daughter quickened his pulse. It had been a long time since he'd considered being a family man. "How soon could you get something worked out? And what would be involved?"

"It depends. You'll want to spell out precisely what you're providing and the terms of the agreement. Needless to say, your father had his share of women troubles when it came to money, so I suggest extra prudence."

"Yeah, I don't need to be reminded." Gabby's smile came to mind, and her tell-it-like-it-is personality had already convinced him she'd never be like his mom or Robin. But one week wasn't enough to know for sure, was it? He'd thought Robin was perfect until her true colors came out, and that had taken some time.

"First things first," Ed said. "Are you sure the kid is your brother's?"

"She's got his eyes, Ed."

A muffled grunt came through the line. "Do you have

amounts in mind for the child support? And how do you want the trust fund set up?"

They went back and forth on the terms and amounts until Ed had no more questions.

"I'll have my team work on these, and I'll call you when they're ready."

"Don't rush." He hesitated. "I haven't exactly told Gabby who I am or what I'm worth."

"Good. It might be best if she doesn't know at this point. Wait until the papers are drawn up. Then she won't be able to use the knowledge to her advantage."

"She's not like that."

There was a long pause.

"Look, Dylan, I know there are nice girls out there. But until you're sure—and I mean really sure—you can trust her, don't tell her about the money. It's not like you two are dating or getting married and she needs to know. This is a unique situation."

A unique situation. He couldn't argue with that. But his heart kept prodding him about misleading her.

"Thanks, Ed. It's good to hear your voice again."

"Same here. Call me anytime. I'll contact you when everything is ready." He hung up, and Dylan stared at the blank screen for a moment.

Ed's advice was good. It echoed his own thoughts since finding out the baby existed. But he hated lying to Gabby. She was big on truth and trust.

Was it so bad to let her believe he was a cowboy for hire? For a few more weeks?

If he told her now and she started fawning over him because she thought she could profit from it, he didn't know if he could handle being disillusioned again. He couldn't imagine her doing that, but what he could imagine was her reaction if he told her he'd inherited a fortune.

She made no secret of the fact she didn't think much of guys who lived off their daddy's money.

Besides, if he spilled the beans, he would have no reason to be a cowboy. He was working on Stu's ranch because she didn't want Phoebe around a deadbeat. His millions made that point as dead as the deer carcass he'd stumbled across this morning while checking on a few cows.

The charade would have to continue—at least until the trust fund and child support papers were ready. It wasn't really harming anybody, him keeping his wealth a secret. He didn't need to feel guilty.

The longer he stayed, the more he wanted to be a regular part of Phoebe's life. He didn't want to only send gifts and cards occasionally. He wanted to be the uncle she could rely on as she grew older. What that looked like, he couldn't say at this point. Maybe coming into town every three months to visit or…

Images of him living in Rendezvous, riding horseback, fly-fishing, maybe even having a barbecue in the park with a group of friends flitted through his mind.

No, this wasn't a permanent thing. Just because Gabby was softening toward him didn't mean anything. Sure, he was attracted to her and thought she was doing a great job as a mom. But they came from different backgrounds. She was more grounded than he was. What would she think if she knew how aimless his traveling had been all last year? She'd be disappointed in him and think it was a waste of time and money to travel with no purpose. And she'd be right.

"There's no way I can work for Nolan." Gabby tucked her feet under her body on the comfy couch in the screened-in porch off Eden's living room Friday night. She'd always loved the Pages' ranch. The rambling white farmhouse had large windows and gorgeous views of the prairie and mountains. The sun was going out with a bang by streaking pinks and purples throughout the sky. Phoebe played with a toy on a fluffy rug between where Gabby and Eden sat on padded wicker chairs.

"I don't blame you." Eden's glass of iced tea sweated water droplets down its side. "He's always so…"

"Full of himself? Arrogant?" Gabby fluttered her eyelashes innocently.

Eden snickered. "I was going to say clueless, but those fit, too."

"Today I spent eight hours with him questioning my every move." Irritation bubbled up her core. It had been a bad day. "And it wasn't because he genuinely wanted to learn anything. He's convinced he has a better way to do everything. *Everything.*"

"Why would he think that? He's in the shipping business, not hotels." Eden took another sip.

"Exactly. If it wasn't the email system we use, it was the employee uniforms. And he had so many opinions on how the rooms should be organized and how he'd remodel them. Frankly, I agree they need to be remodeled, but the stuff he was suggesting sounded horribly out-of-date. Like, hire a designer already."

Phoebe began to babble. She was trying to stuff a purple plastic cow in her mouth. Every time she squeezed it, the cow made a mooing noise. Gabby returned her attention to Eden.

"If he stayed all day, does that mean he's already negotiating with Babs?" Eden asked.

"I don't know, and I'm too afraid to ask her."

"Well, there must be another job you could do here in town if he does buy the place."

Gabby slumped. "That's the problem—I love my job. And I want to work at the inn. Unless I take a big cut in pay, the only thing I can come up with is getting my insurance license, and it would mean I'd have to take classes and pass exams. But at least I'd have regular hours."

"You sitting behind a desk selling insurance?" Eden made a sour face. "Are there even any openings in town?"

"Who knows? Cathy Davies has worked the front desk forever at Dalton Insurance. She could put in a good word for me."

"Are there any other options?" Eden frowned.

She shrugged. "I'm just telling you what I've come up with, and it isn't much at this point."

"Maybe Nolan wouldn't be around much. It's not like he lives in Rendezvous."

The thought lifted her spirits. "Maybe you're right. He still works for his dad. It's not as if he's quitting his day job. At least, I hope not."

"Ba-ba-ba." Phoebe had shifted to all fours. She reached for a stuffed elephant, but it was too far away. She planted one hand forward.

"Look!" Gabby kept her voice soft. "Do you think she'll crawl?"

"Oh, I hope so!" Eden brought her hands together and watched Phoebe shift one knee ahead.

Gabby quickly got out her phone and scrolled through to take a video. Phoebe moved her other hand, her knee, and repeated the process. She crawled forward until she got to the elephant. And Gabby got it all on video.

"Good job, Phoebe!" Gabby clapped her hands. "You did it. You crawled."

Eden stretched out an open palm to Gabby, and they high-fived.

Phoebe gripped the elephant in one hand and flopped to a seated position. Then she chewed on the elephant's leg. Gabby couldn't help herself—she scooped up the baby and showered her with kisses. Phoebe cooed, then started to fuss, so she put her back on the floor to play with her toy.

"I wish Allison could have been here to see this," Gabby said as she sat back down. Her chest felt tight with emotion. She wanted the baby to reach these milestones, but each milestone hurt, knowing her sister was missing every one of them.

"I wish she could be here, too." Eden grew pensive. "Noah turned four a few months ago, and when he blew out the candles, I almost started crying because Mia will never see him grow up."

"Does it get easier?" She looked into Eden's brown eyes. They'd both lost sisters. Eden had helped raise Noah until Mason remarried a few weeks ago, so she knew what it was like to love her sister's child, too.

"It was easier when I took care of him." Eden turned away abruptly. "I knew life would change—it couldn't stay the way it was forever. Even if Mason hadn't remarried, Noah would continue to get older, go to school—he wouldn't need his auntie Eden anymore."

"He'll always need his auntie Eden."

"Not in the same way. Not like he used to. And that's okay, because he has a wonderful mommy in Brittany."

She'd known Eden was struggling, but her own grief

and being thrown into instant motherhood had prevented her from thinking too much about Eden's pain.

"You know you can have your own family, right?" Gabby watched for her reaction.

"I suppose." Her voice sounded faraway as she gazed out the screened window. "Don't laugh, but I always saw myself being a ranch wife living here in Rendezvous— on this ranch, preferably."

"There are eligible ranchers here, you know." She kept her tone light.

"I know. But I'm not going to kid myself. The guys around here aren't really my type. Judd Wilson is quieter than me, and that's saying something. Cash McCoy is too wild. It would never work."

"Maybe you should get to know them better. They might surprise you."

Phoebe crawled to the side of the couch and pulled herself up to a standing position. Gabby picked her up and set her on her lap. She snuggled into her arms.

"Right back at you." Eden cast her a sly glance.

Her? Date? She shook her head. "I'm too busy. I have a million problems, and I'm not adding a potential boyfriend to the list."

"What about Dylan? He's good-looking. I've seen him a few times in town."

Jealousy flared hot and sudden. Did Eden want to date Dylan? Picturing him with Eden—or anyone else for that matter—brought a sour taste to her mouth. But who was she to object? This was her best friend, and if anyone deserved a great guy, it was Eden.

Was Dylan a great guy?

She hated to admit it, but he was growing on her. He stopped by when he said he would. He'd gotten a job and seemed to really like it. He called or texted to arrange to see the baby, and he hadn't shown up unannounced since moving here.

"You got awfully quiet." With a gleam in her eye, Eden cocked her head.

"So far Dylan has been reliable, and he seems decent. If you want to date him, I can give you his number."

"Me?" Eden's face recoiled in horror. "No, I meant you. You should date Dylan."

At the thought of dating him, hope and anticipation did a happy dance around her heart. He was gorgeous. And easy to be with. And good with the baby.

And a cowboy.

Her number one deal breaker.

Even if she could get past his profession, she hadn't spent enough time with him to deem him worthy.

"No." Gabby shook her head. "Not going to happen."

"It's the cowboy thing, isn't it?" Her face fell.

"Yep."

"Couldn't you make an exception?"

She wouldn't answer. Because part of her wanted to make an exception. The same part of her had wanted to believe the best in her dad and Carl. It was her weakness and had let her down time and again. "No, I don't have room in my life for dating right now."

"I have too much room…for everything." Eden rested her head against the back of the chair. "Maybe you're right and I should get to know the guys around here better. I could even…try dating. I don't think Judd or Cash or any guy in town even knows I exist."

"What are you talking about?" She shook her head. "You're so beautiful and kind. They've noticed."

"Oh yeah? Then why haven't any of them asked me out? The only girls who get noticed around here are Stella Boone and Misty Sandpiper."

"Well…" Her words held a nugget of truth. "It's probably because Stella and Misty are around them more. They make an effort, do things with the guys."

"I don't want to do things with them."

Gabby studied her friend. It would do Eden good to get out and have some fun. She'd been more and more pensive lately.

"Why don't we organize a group outing. A barbecue or something? We can invite a bunch of people. Then it won't be awkward or weird."

"It will still be awkward and weird." Eden grimaced.

"No, it won't. You'll see. We can plan it for next week—Saturday. We'll have a picnic at the city park. Potluck. I'll spread the word." She perked up thinking about it. "Tomorrow at church you can personally invite Judd. I'll tell Stella to invite Cash and Misty and the other guys. Nicole can come. And Brittany and Mason."

"I guess a picnic would be fun." Worry lines creased Eden's forehead. "Could *you* ask Judd, though?"

"I think you should ask him."

"Then you'll have to invite Dylan."

"Fair enough." She instantly pictured Stella flirting with him, and Misty probably would, too. *Yuck.* They'd be all over him. And he'd eat up the attention. Carl always had.

Was it fair to keep comparing Dylan to Carl, though? When she was growing convinced he was nothing like her ex?

So what? It didn't mean he was fair game for her to date him. He was Phoebe's uncle. She'd be dealing with him the rest of her life. A botched romance wouldn't just hurt her, it would hurt Phoebe. She wouldn't do that to the baby.

Dylan may have overdressed for church. He glanced around at the people making their way down the aisle and regretted wearing a button-down shirt and tie. All the other men wore short-sleeved shirts open at the collar or polo-style shirts with jeans. His fitted dark gray dress pants had been overkill, too.

Yesterday, he'd driven to Jackson to buy supplies. He'd wanted to invite Gabby and Phoebe, but she'd made it clear Saturdays were her day to relax. He hadn't wanted to ruffle her feathers. Plus the conversation with Ed had forced him to do some thinking—not only about Gabby, but about his future, too.

Living in Texas didn't make sense if he wanted to see Phoebe on a regular basis. In fact, living in Texas didn't appeal to him at all now that Dad and Sam were gone. With the company sold, he had no place of employment. His friends had moved on without him, and he couldn't think of a reason to go back.

Yesterday, he'd been sure he'd feel in his element in Jackson since it was full of trendy restaurants and upscale shopping. And in some ways he had. He'd been raised to enjoy expensive boutiques and gourmet food; he was used to not checking a price tag and never thought twice about buying items he didn't really need.

But the things he needed the boutiques didn't carry. He was desperate for a fan and a coffeemaker, not the several-hundred-dollar espresso maker the kitchen store carried. He wanted towels strong enough to hold up to the dirt he brought in every night instead of the fluffy white hotel-quality ones he'd briefly considered purchasing.

He'd ended up dropping a lot of money on new clothes, including his current outfit, and now he wished he hadn't. These clothes didn't work in Rendezvous.

He didn't fit into his old life anymore, and he didn't seem to fit into the new one, either.

Maybe he was kidding himself that he could stay here for a month.

Clasping his hands and bowing his head, he tried to push away the feeling of defeat.

*God, what am I doing here? I'm pretending to be something I'm not. But I think I was pretending to be someone else back in Texas, too. What am I supposed to do?*

He straightened as he sensed someone wanting to enter the pew. Glancing up, he did a double take. Gabby smiled at him. Phoebe wore a pink dress and matching headband with an enormous bow. The baby's little nose scrunched as she grinned. He scooted down so they could sit.

"Can I help you with that?" He gestured to the diaper bag slung over her shoulder.

"No, I've got it."

He caught a whiff of her floral perfume. The baby held her hands out to him, and he gladly hauled her onto his lap, facing him. She clapped her palms against his cheeks and giggled. This kid—she brought so much joy to his heart. He puffed up his cheeks and she smacked them, laughing and loving every minute of it.

"You looked lonely over here," Gabby said when she'd gotten settled. "We figured we'd join you."

"I'm glad you did." He didn't care if she'd sat here out of pity or not; he welcomed her friendly face. Her blue sundress brought out her feminine side. She didn't wear much makeup, and she didn't need to. Her natural beauty called to him.

He ran a finger under his collar. What was going on with him? This was Phoebe's aunt, not a potential girlfriend. He had to do a better job of fighting this attraction. At least it seemed to be one-sided on his end at this point. The thought should have relieved him, but instead it was depressing.

Organ music played, and Gabby took Phoebe back into her arms. He followed the service and peeked at his niece and her pretty aunt often throughout. The pastor spoke about temptation. Dylan focused straight ahead. Temptation sat next to him and smelled fantastic.

Soon they were saying the final prayer and being ushered out of church. Gabby dropped her bulletin as they made their way down the aisle, and Dylan bent to pick it up for her. Handing it back, his fingers brushed hers, and his skin heated at the touch.

As they followed the crowd outside and down the sidewalk, he caught himself wanting to take her arm, hold her hand, keep her close to him. But he didn't have that right. So he stayed by her side, his spirits dropping, knowing his time with her today was about to end.

"What are you doing next Saturday?" She kept a tight hold on Phoebe, who was trying to bounce on her hip.

"Nothing, why?"

"Eden and I are organizing a picnic, and we want you to come. It's potluck. At the city park."

"I'd like that." He knew he was grinning like a fool and didn't care. A picnic. He'd been dreaming of one since he'd arrived. And if she was okay with him coming to a picnic, maybe she'd be okay with him asking her to go shopping with him, too. It couldn't hurt to ask, could it? "Can I ask for some advice?"

Her eyes sparkled with curiosity. "Of course."

"I need to buy some supplies, and I'm not sure where to go. I'm talking things like a fan and towels."

"There's a supercenter an hour south of here. It would be your best option."

"Okay. Thanks." If he asked her to come, would she say no?

"When are you going?" She adjusted Phoebe's headband.

"I was thinking today. Why? Do you want to come with me?" He held his breath. He'd never been this insecure around a woman before. What was his problem?

"Yeah, I would. Phoebe is outgrowing her clothes, and I haven't had a chance to get down there to stock up on stuff."

She wanted to come with him. He stood taller. This day was looking up.

"What time do you want to leave?" he asked. The sooner the better in his opinion.

"Well, I'm going to try to spread the word about the picnic now, then I'll go home and change."

"I need to change, too." He stared down at his outfit and shook his head again.

"What was that look for?" Her mischievous smile made his pulse quicken.

"I wasn't sure what to wear." He shrugged.

"You look good to me."

She thought he looked good? His chest expanded. "How about I pick you up in an hour?"

"I'll be ready." She flashed him a grin and disappeared in the crowd.

Rocking back on his heels, he wanted to pump his fist in the air, but instead he shoved his hands in his pockets and strolled toward the parking lot. Score one for team Kingsley. He'd gotten Gabby to agree to spend the entire afternoon with him.

Why was that a good thing? She didn't want to date him. And he couldn't really date her. Not as things stood, at least.

He and Gabby were friends, and outside of Stu, she was the only friend he had at the moment. He'd take whatever time she was willing to give.

As he reached his truck, he thought back to last week when yearning for the simple pleasures of a small town had practically knocked him over.

He was getting what he'd wished for. A community. Barbecues with friends. A purpose working on the ranch.

Sure, none of it would last, but he'd enjoy it while he could. Life had given him enough lemons lately. He'd happily drink the lemonade until it ran out.

## Chapter Seven

Something wasn't adding up about Dylan Kingsley. The man pushing the shopping cart next to her was more complicated than she'd originally thought. Or maybe she was the one complicating things.

On the ride here, they'd enjoyed a pleasant conversation. He'd told her about the summer he'd learned how to ride a horse. She'd filled him in on how she and Allison entertained each other as kids by running through sprinklers in the summer and playing house or Barbies. She'd asked him questions, but he'd been tight-lipped and vague about the rest of his childhood. It reminded her of when she'd first met him—and her suspicions had flared all over again. Had she been wrong about him? Was he hiding something from her? Was he really like Carl and she'd been fooling herself?

If he was like Carl, he'd fill up the cart and pretend he'd lost his wallet.

Phoebe was strapped into the cart and happily gripped the bar, watching everyone who walked by. Several people waved to her and mentioned what a cute baby she was. Their kind words warmed Gabby's heart.

"Where should we head to first?" Dylan asked.

"What do you need?" A blast of air-conditioning, bright fluorescent lights and displays of beach towels and plastic dishes greeted them as they passed the grocery section into a general merchandise area.

He listed the items, and she pointed to the far corner where housewares were located. "This way."

They found the fans. Gabby began checking the prices of each, and Dylan zoomed to a top-of-the-line model and hauled it into the back of the cart.

"Aren't you going to look at all of them?" She pointed to a cheap box fan.

"Why?" His thick eyebrows drew together, giving him an adorably confused look.

"To find the best value."

"This has the features I want." He dusted off his hands and joined her at the front of the cart.

"How do you know the other ones don't?"

"Box fans only blow in one direction." He nodded to the one she'd been looking at.

"It's inexpensive, though." Had he even checked the price?

"I'm sure it is, but it doesn't have what I need." He pointed to the other fans on the shelves. "Those two are basically the same model, and I'd have to buy an end table for them to sit on. The one I'm buying stands up, oscillates and has a remote control."

It sounded fancy and pricey. But she reluctantly conceded his argument made sense.

He resumed pushing the cart until they reached the bedding section.

A fluffy comforter in the palest mint green drew her eye. She sighed longingly. She didn't have the funds to replace her current faded denim coverlet, but if she did, she'd go with the mint-green one. It was light. Feminine.

Dylan, on the other hand, was holding a navy-and-tan bed-in-a-bag set at eye level to read what was in it. She peeked at an identical one sitting on the shelf. The price seemed terribly high. Trying to act nonchalant and staying within reach of Phoebe, she eyeballed the prices of the other comforters and bedspreads. He'd picked the most expensive one. Surely, he'd put it down and find another. But he didn't. He put it in the cart.

Her initial impressions from last weekend roared back. The expensive truck. The small inheritance he seemed to be blowing through like the wind. The way he spent his money wasn't any of her business, but what if it became her business? What if he used his relationship with Phoebe to try to borrow money from her?

She almost snorted. The idea was laughable. He didn't strike her as the type. Really, she had to give him the benefit of the doubt instead of letting her past mistakes color all of her opinions about men.

"You mentioned towels." She used her most pleasant tone. "Do you want to find them next?"

"Yeah." The corner of his mouth twisted. "Wait. The bedding set—I'm not sure if it's the right one."

"Why not?" *Because it's over a hundred dollars!*

"It comes with a bunch of things I don't think I need."

"Like what?" She perked up. Was he asking her opinion?

He picked up the bedding set again and read. "Shams and a bed skirt and a valance. I don't even know what those things are."

"Shams are the fancy pillowcases you cover a pillow with and set on top of your regular pillows, the bed skirt hides what's under the bed and a valance is like a minicurtain."

He grimaced and shoved the bedding set back on the store shelf. "Did you see any other sets without all that stuff? Nothing froufrou. Dark would be best."

"No pink stripes?" She winked as she pointed to a little girl's set a few feet away.

"For Phoebe, yeah. For me? No." His grin sent her heartbeat sprinting. "I'd get it dirty and ruin it."

Phoebe let out a cry and pounded on the bar, so Gabby unstrapped her and carried her down the aisle to check the other sets. "What about this? It comes with a set of sheets, two pillowcases and a lightweight comforter."

"Perfect. Dark gray. No polka dots or flowers. I like it." He stood behind her, looking over her shoulder. His cologne or aftershave reminded her of the mountain air— fresh and clean. If she took the tiniest step back, she'd be touching him.

She stiffened. No need to think about touching him. Instead, she pivoted forward so he could see the package better. "And the price is half the other one."

"Right." He read the description on the package. "But do you think it will hold up?"

"I do. More expensive doesn't always mean better quality."

"I'll take your word for it." He placed the bedding in the cart.

Twenty minutes later they'd added towels, cleaning products and a coffeemaker to the pile. She'd questioned his need for the more expensive coffeemaker, but he'd assured her it was necessary for the early-morning work he did. Did a cheap coffeemaker produce an inferior cup of coffee? She didn't know. She'd only ever had the cheapest model, and her coffee tasted fine.

As she glanced at the cart, she couldn't shake the worry that he was a spendthrift. What would he do when his money ran out?

Her dad had taken to driving a truck and preying on weak women in different towns. Carl had done the same, minus driving big rigs.

She didn't know what Dylan would do, and she really didn't want to find out.

All she knew was a man who wasn't responsible with his money wasn't the man for her.

Dylan couldn't believe how cheap everything was in this store. It was his first time shopping in a supercenter. His watch alone had cost ten times more than the contents of the entire cart. There was an extra spring in his step as they moseyed toward the baby section.

He wanted to buy some things for Phoebe. Spoil his niece a little bit. He got the impression Gabby wouldn't like it, though.

It was strange to have someone judging him for thinking he was spending too much on items he considered practically free. It reinforced his previous misgiving that Gabby had to worry about money in a way he never did. Shouldn't he be fast-tracking the trust fund and child support? For her sake?

She stopped and began browsing through a rack of baby clothes. Bright-eyed and quiet, Phoebe sat on her hip. One by one, Gabby selected sleeveless dress sets with tiny matching shorts ruffled at the legs. And one by one, she set them back after checking the price.

"What about this one?" He held up a baby blue dress

with bows on the back and a matching headband. It was cute. Phoebe would look adorable in it.

"I'm not sure." Gabby flushed, shaking her head. "I want to see what else they have before I make a decision."

He checked the tag. Under twenty bucks. Size 12 months. He furrowed his eyebrows together. Phoebe was nine months old. Would it be too big? "What size is she?"

"She's growing out of her 6-9 months clothes. That's the next size up." She shifted to the next circular rack and browsed through little T-shirts that snapped at the bottom.

"What all does she need?" He tossed the baby blue dress in the cart and reached for one with watermelon slices printed all over it.

"Onesies. A few dresses. Short outfits. Oh, and a hat. I've got to protect her head from the sun."

"I'm on it." He puffed out his chest and searched the area for shorts.

"Um, I've got this." Her eyes flashed with worry.

"I'm getting her some clothes." He wasn't budging. "She's my niece, too."

"Well…" She dragged the word out. "Don't buy much. You already have a lot to pay for." She nodded toward the cart.

He almost laughed. She was worried about him paying for all this stuff? It was a drop in the bucket. Nothing. "Don't worry. I've got it."

"I know it's none of my business but your inheritance… It won't last forever." Her eyes grew wide as if she couldn't believe she'd just said that. "I mean, it's always smart to save for a rainy day. Then if you get the itch to move around again, you won't have to worry about your money running out."

He averted his eyes, overcome with sudden emotion and insight. She wasn't judging him. She was worried. Worried he wouldn't be able to pay for everything, that he'd run out of money if he wasn't careful.

Shame rushed from his head to his toes in a big whoosh. He should tell her he was rich. It was wrong to mislead her and allow her to keep thinking whatever it was she thought.

What did she think?

"Why do you think my money will run out?" He crossed over to where she suddenly grew very interested in those baby T-shirt things.

Her neck grew pink and she didn't meet his eyes. "You've been doing… I don't know…this and that for the past year, and you mentioned a small inheritance. If you didn't have a job, you had to be spending it. And it costs a lot to live. The nest egg won't last forever."

"I was traveling. I went overseas." He couldn't bring himself to admit he'd been hopping from country to country, living in luxury, fine dining every night, watching the sun, moon and stars from expensive balconies and contemplating the meaning of life.

He hadn't figured out the meaning. And those twelve months seemed shamefully indulgent now that he'd met Gabby.

She raised her eyebrows. "Overseas. Traveling. Not cheap."

The truth climbed up his throat, ready to be spoken.

But he already knew how she'd react. And it wouldn't be to fawn over him and try to get money for herself.

She'd be disappointed in him.

Just like his father had always been.

"I never buy anything I can't afford." He tightened his jaw. It was true. And he was buying Phoebe some clothes. He didn't care if Gabby approved or not. She had no right to look down on him for his financial situation—whether she thought he was rich or poor. It was his business. Not hers.

He went back to the display table with itty-bitty shorts and selected half a dozen in various colors. Then he picked out T-shirts to match, threw four more dress sets in for good measure and selected a turquoise one-piece swimsuit with pink flamingos and ruffles.

A touch on his arm made him flinch and turn.

"Hey, I'm sorry." Gabby's pretty gray eyes swam with regret. "You're right. It's none of my business how you spend your money. I shouldn't have said anything."

He blinked twice as his heart swelled. "It's okay."

"No, it's not." Her throat worked as she swallowed. "I had a few complicated relationships. My father, in particular, did things that made me not trust him, and my ex-boyfriend piled onto my trust issues. It was wrong of me to project their mistakes onto you."

He tilted his head, viewing her through new eyes. What had her father done to abuse her trust? And what about the ex? Had he broken her heart?

"I have trust issues, too, Gabby," he said quietly. "Why don't we finish up here and call it even?"

"Sounds good." Her genuine smile could have knocked him over with a feather.

As she walked back to the baby racks, an uncomfortable feeling spread throughout his body.

He cared about her opinion.

He cared about her.

He hadn't cared about anyone since Sam and Dad died. He preferred it that way. Life was safer without responsibilities, but was it better? He wasn't sure he wanted to find out.

* * *

Gabby couldn't stop peeking at Dylan all the way home. They'd finished their shopping—she'd done a double take at his enormous bill but kept her mouth shut—and stopped at a nearby coffee shop for a snack and to give Phoebe her bottle before heading back. At the coffee shop, he'd told her about some of the places he'd visited last year. She hadn't realized he was so adventurous. He made it sound easy, riding a train from Paris to the Alps.

She'd been out of the state only a handful of times. She couldn't imagine traveling around the world, especially by herself the way Dylan had. Hadn't he been scared? Worried about not speaking the language? Lonely? Homesick?

He must have had a larger inheritance than she'd originally assumed. She wanted to tell him to hang on to his money. Invest it. It was nice of him to buy Phoebe some clothes, but she'd rather see him save for his future.

There she went again, assuming she knew everything about him. Who was she to conclude he didn't save? He could have a 401(k) tucked away and everything.

Casting a glance at his tanned arms lightly gripping the wheel, then up to his handsome profile and the T-shirt hugging his biceps, she mentally rolled her eyes at herself. *Sure, he's got a 401(k), a financial advisor and an accountant to boot.* Didn't all cowboys? She smiled at her own joke.

"What's the story on your dad?" He peered at her, keeping one eye on the road. The blue sky and green hills were empty and peaceful. "Or do you not want to talk about it?"

"I don't mind. My heart isn't so sore about it now." She thought back to the last time she'd seen him. Mom had kicked him out, and he'd been hauling his belongings out in trash bags. He'd come inside and reached for the framed family photo of the four of them, and Mom had swiped it out of his hand. *You ruined this family! You can't have the picture. It's mine!* And Gabby had glared at him, hating him for cheating on Mom. After her mother stormed out of the room, Allison had tiptoed to him and handed him the photo. He'd hugged her tightly while Gabby watched, her eyes burning with so much anger.

The anger had faded to a general wariness with time, but there was still a part of her that blamed him for destroying their family. He hadn't only cheated on Mom. He'd cheated on her and Allison, too.

"Dad was, for lack of a better word, charming," she said. "I thought the sun rose and set around him when I was a girl. He was gone a lot—working on local ranches or driving trucks—but whenever he was around, he made us feel special. Bought us toys, took us out for ice cream, that sort of thing."

"But?" He glanced her way, and she was relieved to see compassion in those brown eyes.

"But when he wasn't around, it was if we didn't exist. Mom did her best, but we were poor. It didn't bother me until I turned eleven. That's when I found out about the other women."

"He was cheating on your mom?" He frowned.

"Yes, with more than one lady. And the worst part was he was spending time with their children—more than he spent with us. All his charm and random gifts felt cheap and dirty after I found out."

Her throat felt raw. She'd thought she was over it, but talking about it brought a fresh wave of pain. She took a few deep breaths to calm her nerves. "Mom threw him out. I was angry at him. He came back a few times to visit, and Allison always wanted to see him, but I didn't. I couldn't forgive him for not only neglecting us, but for robbing us of our time with him so he could be with someone else's kids. It hurt."

"I can imagine," he said softly. "Do you ever talk to him?"

"No. And I don't talk much with my mom, either. After the divorce, she flitted from boyfriend to boyfriend like a lovesick teenager. It was as if when Dad left, she decided she no longer had responsibilities. Allison and I were basically raising ourselves."

"Now I know why you're so nurturing and responsible." The cleft in his chin drew her attention. He thought she was nurturing? Responsible? She tried not to let it go to her head.

She stared out the window. "What was your dad like? You must miss him."

"Sometimes I do." His knuckles tightened around the steering wheel. "And sometimes I think I'm looking for closure."

"Why? Weren't you close?"

"I wouldn't say close. I mean, we worked together, but he had high standards. It was difficult to live up to them."

"You worked together?" Finally she was learning something concrete about his life before his brother and dad died.

His face flushed, and he waved like it didn't matter. "He owned a business. I worked for him. Then he sold it."

She had a feeling there were about a million things left unsaid between each short statement. "I take it you didn't want him to sell it?"

He met her eyes then. So much hurt was in them, she

was tempted to reach over and touch his arm to comfort him.

"I didn't even know he wanted to sell it."

"He didn't ask you about it? Warn you in advance?" Her stomach clenched. It sounded mean. Needlessly hurtful.

"No," he said quietly, his gaze focused ahead. "I've blamed him. I've blamed myself. None of it changes anything. He's still gone."

"What type of business was it?"

"Can we not talk about it anymore?"

"Sure." A few miles sped by as questions piled up in her mind. It must have been hard on Dylan to find out secondhand his father was selling the company. Like her, he'd been betrayed by a parent. "What about your mother?"

He let out a half-hearted snort. "She was kind of like yours, except she used me to get back at my father. They divorced when I was three."

"What do you mean she used you?" Gabby knew people who refused to follow visitation schedules and made life as miserable as possible for their ex-spouses at the expense of their kids. One of her high school friends had developed an eating disorder because of her parents' drama.

"She'd fight him about when I could visit and demand more child support. She's had a few husbands since. Nothing really changes. We don't talk anymore."

"I'm sorry. I understand, but I'm still sorry."

"I am, too. I wish people didn't have to be so selfish sometimes. Your parents missed out on you, and it's a shame because you're a really great person."

"Thank you." The compliment warmed her like the summer sun. "It would be great if divorce didn't have to be so messy. I'm twenty-seven and still miss having parents to lean on."

"I know exactly what you mean." His lips curved into a soft smile. "We'll make sure Phoebe never feels like a chess piece or an afterthought."

*We'll?* What did he mean by that?

"Yes, I'll do my best to make her feel loved and important." She watched for his reaction.

"So will I."

"You will? Am I missing something? I thought you were staying here for a month or so." She tried to ignore the anxiety sizzling through her veins. If he'd changed his mind about staying, he could also change his mind about wanting a more active role—a legal role—in Phoebe's life. If he went to the courts, they'd probably agree.

"I am, and I'm not sure what I'm doing next, but I know it won't be in Texas. I'd like to be closer to Rendezvous, at least within driving distance, to see Phoebe more often. I don't want her to only know me through birthday cards and Christmas presents."

On the surface it made sense. He wasn't making demands, just stating he wanted to see the baby on a regular basis. But Gabby had seen too much, had been lied to too many times to take his words at face value.

The words cowboys said sounded good, but their actions never matched up.

She'd been warming up to Dylan. She actually liked spending time with him. But she couldn't forget what was important—loving and protecting Phoebe. And to do that, she'd better start safeguarding her own heart before she went and made another stupid mistake like falling for Dylan Kingsley.

## Chapter Eight

The following Saturday afternoon, Dylan carried a cooler to the pavilion in the city park where a crowd had gathered. A strong wind from last night had mellowed to a gentle breeze, and sunshine made everything bright. Laughter and conversation grew louder as he approached. He couldn't believe two weeks ago he'd been watching other people hang out in this very park, and now here he was—getting ready to hang out with them, too. He might not belong here the way they all did, but he'd been invited. It was enough for now.

Enough for now? He scoffed. It would have to be enough for forever. He had no business making long-term plans here, considering no one knew the truth about him.

He wasn't like them.

He hadn't earned his money. He'd inherited it. And he'd let down the two people he'd loved the most. When Gabby found out the truth, he had a feeling he'd be letting her down, too.

*Stop being negative. What's the big deal? You're rich. Who cares? Enjoy this. For once, just relax and enjoy a simple outing.*

He scanned the crowd for the cute, no-nonsense brunette who'd organized this shindig. There she was. Gabby's dark brown hair was pulled back into a high ponytail. Her white shorts showed off her trim figure, and her brick red tank top draped like a blouse to her hips. She was laughing at something someone said. He frowned when he saw who she was talking to. He'd seen the guy in church last week. Gabby seemed to be very friendly with him.

She turned and stared straight at Dylan. Time seemed to stop as their eyes met. Then hers crinkled in the corners as she grinned and waved him over. "Dylan, come meet everyone."

A flush of adrenaline spiked through his veins. How had he gotten so fortunate to meet this woman? She was going out of her way to make him feel welcome. And she did it without an ulterior motive, unlike some of the women from his past.

He strode under the pavilion and placed the cooler he'd borrowed from Stu in line with the other ones, then he wiped his hands down his shorts and made his way to Gabby's side.

"Dylan, this is my friend Mason Fanning." Gabby shifted to look up at him, then extended her arm to indicate the man she'd been talking to. "He's in my Tuesday night support group. And this is his new bride, Brittany."

Relief spread through his chest, and he probably pumped both Mason's and his beautiful wife's hands a little too hard.

"Gabby told us you lost your brother," Mason said. "I'm sorry. It's terrible losing someone you love when they're so young."

This guy spoke as if he had experience with it. "Thank you, I appreciate it."

"You'll find several people, including myself, around here who have lost special people way too soon. If you need anything, I'm here."

He didn't know what to say. Another stranger going out of his way to welcome him. He didn't deserve this.

"Oh, there's Eden! I've been dying to introduce you." Gabby moved past him to greet her friend. He watched them hug. Gabby dragged her by the hand to him. The petite brunette had an understated beauty. "Dylan, this is Eden Page. She babysits Phoebe for me, and she's my best friend in the whole world."

"It's my pleasure." He smiled at her, wanting to put her at ease. A slight blush rose to her cheeks, and her kind eyes instantly made him like her. She was slightly taller than Gabby, with expressive brown eyes and shiny, dark brown hair that slid over her shoulders.

"It's good to meet you, too. I'm glad you found Gabby and the baby. Phoebe is such a sweet thing. I'm thankful she'll have an uncle."

"Mason, why didn't you tell me Ryder was coming?" Gabby's voice rose with excitement, and once again, she rushed away.

Dylan turned his attention back to Eden, but her face had lost some of its color. He peered into her eyes. "Hey, are you okay?"

"I'm fine." She didn't look fine.

"Why don't you sit down? I'll get you something to drink."

Her eyebrows formed a V, but she let him lead her to a picnic table.

"What can I get you? A Coke? Water?"

She sat on the bench and stared up at him. "Um, I don't need anything."

"There you are." Gabby appeared, dragging someone by the hand behind her. "For a minute I thought you guys ditched me."

Dylan shifted to introduce himself, but his mouth dropped open instead. Wasn't this Mason? The man he'd just met?

"Dylan, this is Ryder Fanning," Gabby said. "He's Mason's identical twin."

"Good to meet you." Ryder thrust out his hand, and Dylan shook it.

"Identical twin. I thought I was seeing double for a minute." He chuckled, shaking his head.

"Trust me, you're not the only one." Ryder grinned. "Mason and I didn't even know each other existed until last Christmas. It took us a while to get used to seeing each other."

"Really? You didn't know each other? I've got to hear this story." He glanced down at Eden quickly to make sure she wasn't going to pass out. Her color had returned, and her lips were pursed. She didn't seem thrilled to have Ryder around, but what did he know?

"Excuse me." Eden stood and gave them both a lukewarm smile. "I see someone I need to talk to."

Dylan stepped aside so she could leave, and then he turned his attention back to Ryder, but Ryder's attention was firmly fixed on Eden as she strode away.

"I'll be right back. I have to do something." Ryder followed Eden.

"That was weird." Gabby wore a thoughtful expression. "Oh, good. She's talking to Judd." She leaned closer to him. "She actually took my advice. I'm floored."

"Where's Phoebe?" It occurred to him he hadn't seen the little ball of cuteness, yet. He'd stopped in at Gabby's a few nights this week. She had even allowed him to give Phoebe her bottle and showed him how to change a diaper. He'd mangled the first one, and the second had fallen off when he'd picked up the baby, but the third had stayed put. It was a start.

"Babs insisted on watching her. She thinks I don't have enough fun, but she's wrong."

He hadn't considered how raising Phoebe had impacted Gabby's life. "Do you miss your life, you know, before raising the baby?"

"Oh no." She laughed, her teeth flashing as she grinned. "Life is much better now, well, except for Allison being gone. She would have loved this party."

He found it difficult to believe being plunged into motherhood with no help or warning would make anyone's life better. But Gabby wasn't the average woman, either.

"Hey, boss, introduce us to your friend." The flirtatious blonde he'd met the day he'd walked into the inn materialized with a tall, curvy girl who had light brown hair and hazel eyes.

Gabby stiffened. Was that a stifled groan? He must have been mistaken, because she smiled brightly. "Dylan, this is Stella Boone, you might remember her from the inn. We work together. And this is Misty Sandpiper."

Stella moved to his right side, and Misty somehow edged to his other side, leaving Gabby standing awkwardly in front of them. Both girls began peppering him with questions, and Gabby raised her eyebrows, gave him a smirk and told him she'd be back in a little while.

Disappointment broke his concentration, but he forced himself to engage with Stella and Misty.

As he answered their questions and admitted he was from Dallas, Stella clung to his arm and raved about how she always wanted to go there and how he'd have to take her sometime. He couldn't picture a scenario where he'd ever take Stella to Dallas, but he nodded politely, all the while keeping an eye on Gabby. A very pregnant woman hugged her, and the cowboy Eden had been chatting with tipped his hat to the pregnant woman. Eden disappeared down a path, and Ryder followed her a few minutes later. Mason had his arm slung over Brittany's shoulders when several guys broke away from the group to grill the burgers.

One of the men stopped to talk to Gabby. Dylan narrowed his eyes. The guy looked to be in his late twenties, and he was handsome, lean and muscular. Dylan could see the appreciative gleam in the guy's gaze clear over here, and the cowboy kept getting closer to Gabby. She laughed at whatever he said, and then he had the audacity to whisper something in her ear.

Dylan clenched his hands into fists.

"Don't you think so, Dylan?" Stella asked.

"What?" He had to pull it together. What was Stella talking about anyhow?

"We should plan a day trip to the hot springs soon."

"Oh, right. Sounds fun." It didn't sound fun, though, not unless Gabby was coming. "I'm real busy at the ranch. I don't know if I'll be able to get away."

"But you *have* to come with us. Stu won't mind if you play hooky one afternoon." She batted her eyelashes at him.

He wouldn't say it out loud, but the only woman he'd

consider skipping out on the ranch for was Gabby. And from the looks of it, he wasn't the only cowboy in town who felt that way.

Where had Eden disappeared to? Gabby barely listened to Cash McCoy's tale of getting bucked off a bull at last weekend's rodeo. Eden was supposed to be making an effort with Judd Wilson, but Judd was standing silently near Nicole, who didn't seem bothered by the lack of conversation. And Eden was nowhere in sight.

How was she going to get Eden on a date if she was never around the guys who would date her?

The one person who would be guaranteed a date after the picnic was Dylan. The way the single ladies were fawning over him was getting annoying. She hadn't invited him here to jump-start his dating life. The only one she wanted to play matchmaker for was Eden.

She discreetly scanned the crowd and caught Dylan laughing at something Stella and Misty said. Those two had latched on to each of his arms like rabid nurses conducting earth's final blood drive. Seriously, didn't they have anyone else to talk to? They acted like he was a celebrity or something.

He was probably lapping up all the female attention. How long would it be before he was too busy to stop by and see Phoebe? She wouldn't think about it. Wasn't this what she wanted, anyhow? For him to get bored and move on so her life could go back to normal?

Well, it *had* been nice of him to bring over dinner Tuesday and Thursday this week. He'd been as excited as she was when Phoebe crawled throughout the living room. And when she'd insisted on teaching him some of the basics of baby care, he'd taken her guidance like a champ. She wished she would have videotaped him changing Phoebe's diaper—it had been hilarious.

She frowned. Would she and Phoebe get shoved aside as afterthoughts when Dylan knew more people? Especially pretty girls like Stella and Misty? Her gaze tracked to where a small crowd of women had gathered around him.

It appeared he'd freed his left arm from Misty's claws and was attempting to loosen Stella's grip, as well. He stepped away from them. She wished she could hear what he'd said. Their disappointed faces soothed her irritation.

"Excuse me, Cash, but I think the guys are done grilling the burgers. I'm going to announce it's time to eat." She was glad to have an excuse to get away from him. Cash was exactly the kind of cowboy she avoided thinking about romantically—he knew he was good-looking, and he charmed every girl he came across.

"Everyone," she yelled, clapping her hands, "the food is done—" No one could hear her.

A high-pitched whistle got everyone's attention. Dylan's index finger and pinky were in his mouth as he whistled again. The pavilion grew quiet.

He approached her and grinned. "Thought you could use some help."

Her heart should *not* be singing a show tune right now.

"Thanks for coming, everyone," she said loudly. "Go ahead and get in line for the food—it's all ready."

"Mind if I say grace, Gabby?" Mason said before the conversations resumed.

"That would be terrific."

They all bowed their heads, and as soon as the short prayer was finished, a line formed at the tables covered

with checkered tablecloths and filled with casseroles, sal-
ads, slices of watermelon and trays of cookies and cakes.

She loved potlucks. And picnics. And sunny days at
the park surrounded by good friends.

"Should we get in line?" Dylan interrupted her reverie.

"Sure, but I understand if you'd rather eat with your
fan club." She kind of hoped he would. Then her suspicions would be confirmed, and she could stifle some of
the tender feelings she'd been having toward him.

"My fan club?" His face grew red. "Please don't ever
leave me alone with them again."

"Why not?" Was he being serious? They fell into the
back of the line.

"I feel more comfortable with you." His brown eyes
gleamed with sincerity.

The compliment rushed through her, blowing down
the house of cards guarding her heart.

Dylan preferred to be with her. He chose to be with
her over younger, prettier women.

*Do you really believe it? It's a classic cowboy move.
Make you think he prefers you to them, then go behind
your back and flirt with them. As soon as we're done eating, he'll find an excuse to talk to them again.*

They filled their plates and took seats at a long picnic
table. Mason and Brittany joined them. Then Ryder and
Nicole, followed by Judd. Eden sat across from Judd.

Gabby bit into her burger. At least one thing was going
right. Eden and Judd were having a conversation. Her
friend even chuckled at something he said.

Gabby relaxed. She didn't need to get all amped up
over nothing. Who cared if Dylan really did prefer her
company to Stella's and Misty's? She had no interest in

being more than friends. She'd be thankful she got along with him…for Phoebe's sake.

The next hour was filled with friendly conversation, way too many desserts, and then some of the guys drifted away to try their hands at horseshoes. The ladies found seats in the shade to chat while they watched.

"That's quite the hunky uncle Phoebe has." Brittany's eyes sparkled as she turned to Gabby. Her tone was all teasing. "Must be terribly hard to spend time with him."

"How long's he staying, Gabby?" Nicole turned to her, curiosity all over her face.

"I don't know." She sounded snippy and knew it. "If you'd like to take him off my hands and spend time with him, you're welcome to it."

They both raised their eyebrows with amused expressions and sat back.

"I thought everything was going okay with him." Eden watched her thoughtfully. "Did something happen?"

Her tension mellowed. What was wrong with her? These were her friends, and they were just having some fun.

"No, nothing happened. I'm sorry. It's just all new." It wasn't. Not really. The past two weeks had allowed her to get to know him better, and her gut was screaming he was a good guy. But was he?

It was too early to tell.

"Well, I give you a lot of credit for accommodating him," Brittany said. "I'm sure it hasn't been easy rearranging your schedule to let him get to know the baby."

Actually, it had been easy. Very easy. He'd made few demands, and had bent over backward to see Phoebe only when convenient to her.

"So you don't know how long he's staying in town?" Nicole asked. "Do you think he'll make it permanent?"

Hope zinged up her spine.

"I don't know. I don't think he knows his plans yet." But if he did stay… She pictured outings together like last week's shopping expedition, and more walks by the river with Phoebe. Friday nights for pizza and catching up.

"Have you heard anything more about the inn?" Eden asked. "Has Nolan been back?"

"No to both." Good, a change in topic was desperately needed. "Apparently Nolan's been away on a business trip, and Babs said she's had a few nibbles but no bites."

"Well, that's good news, right?" Nicole asked.

"Yes, it buys me time."

"Oh, Eden—" Brittany whirled to face Eden "—do you think you'd have time this week to come over to the studio and look at the apartment above it with me? Mason insists it's time to renovate, and I agree, but I want a female opinion."

"I'd love to." Eden's face lit up.

They got out their phones and checked their calendars. As Brittany and Eden discussed the layout of the apartment above Brittany's dance studio, Gabby watched the horseshoe game. Mason and Ryder were partners, and Dylan and Judd were the other team. The clink of metal on metal and a round of female cheers on the other side of the horseshoe pit told her someone had scored.

As Stella and Misty high-fived each other and cheered for Dylan, Gabby tried not to get annoyed. Dylan wasn't hers. Not even close. And she had dating rules.

No cowboys. Especially good-looking ones.

She needed to douse these feelings—the attraction and the jealousy—pronto. Nothing good would come from them.

* * *

Dylan couldn't remember the last time he'd spent an afternoon with such welcoming people. Mason had invited him to stop by the ranch anytime. Judd had been quiet, but he'd mentioned hunting together this fall. And Ryder had peppered him with questions about being a ranch hand after Dylan told him he didn't have a ton of experience and that Stu was teaching him everything he needed to know.

He hauled the cooler to the back of his truck, then returned to the pavilion to help Gabby collect her dishes and the camping chairs she'd brought.

"All set?" He slung the folded chairs in their bags onto his shoulder.

"I can get them. You don't need to help." She carried a casserole dish in one hand and held out the other.

He ignored it. "I want to."

They made their way to her car, and he waited for her to pop the trunk before setting the chairs inside. She stowed the dish in there as well, then straightened and slammed it shut.

"What are you doing now?" he asked.

"Picking up Phoebe from Babs's place." Her gray eyes gleamed with attitude. He wasn't sure why.

"Want some company?" He hoped she understood he meant he wanted to be with her, not just to see the baby.

"Why? Are you lonely? Stella would be happy to hang out with you." A sarcastic smile briefly lifted her lips.

"I would never be that lonely." He couldn't help noticing they were only a few inches apart. He instinctively wanted to close the gap. "I had a good time today, and I don't want to go back to the sauna yet."

"The sauna?"

He chuckled. "Yeah, I've named my cabin the sauna. It's about the same size as one, and it's definitely the same temp."

"Really? Even with the new fan?" She leaned against her car. "I thought you were a big, strong cowboy. Aren't you supposed to be immune to the weather?"

"You're thinking of a Navy SEAL. I'm a mere man."

"I suppose you could come over for a while—to enjoy my air-conditioning." She brought her index finger to her lips, not meeting his eyes. "Give me fifteen minutes to pick up Phoebe and meet at my place."

"Done." He opened her car door and waited for her to slide into the driver's seat. Then he bent slightly and tried to find the words he wanted to say.

She looked up at him with a confused expression.

"Thanks. For inviting me today. For letting me come over now." He straightened and shut her door before she could respond.

*Idiot.* He didn't know what he'd wanted to say, but it wasn't *thanks for inviting me.*

He marched back to his truck, only to be waylaid by Stella and Misty.

"We're going to Rendezvous Saloon tonight." Stella acted coy. "Why don't you join us?"

The last thing he wanted to do was go to some bar with these two. "Uh, no, thanks." He gave them a smile. "I have plans."

And he waved to them, got into his truck and slowly backed out.

He had Gabby to thank for that—he had her to thank for everything. Raising his niece. Getting him a job. Introducing him to her friends. Making him feel like he belonged here.

He'd find a way to repay her.

The trust fund and child support came to mind.

*Not yet.*

But he'd have to do it soon.

# Chapter Nine

She'd messed up. She shouldn't have told Dylan to stop by.

Gabby set the empty casserole dish in her sink and filled it with hot water. Phoebe had fallen asleep on the way home from Babs's place, and Gabby had left her strapped in her car seat on the living room floor. Dylan would be here any minute. What had possessed her to tell him to come over?

Flattery. That's what.

He'd made it clear he preferred her company to Stella's and Misty's, and instead of being rational and reminding herself they were mere words, she'd clung to them. And she shouldn't have. He was her friend. Nothing more. And she'd make doubly sure to keep it that way.

She couldn't rely on Dylan. If she started leaning on him, getting close to him… It would only leave her with hurt feelings or worse.

A knock on the door set her heartbeat off on a mad dash. Taking a deep breath, she forced herself to keep her pace slow as she approached the door and opened it.

Dylan held two iced coffees in his hands. "Thought

you might need one of these. Hope you like caramel macchiatos."

"Ooh, they look great. Thanks." She stepped aside to let him in. His arm brushed her shoulder, and she was all too aware why the ladies had flocked to him at the picnic. He had a presence. He didn't need to flirt for attention. He automatically got it. "Make yourself at home."

"This is *much* better than the lumpy sofa at my place." His knees splayed and legs sprawled as he got comfortable on the couch. He'd taken off his running shoes, and somehow made the shorts and T-shirt look even better than his formal church outfit—and that had been appealing indeed. "Is your coffee okay? I wasn't sure if you liked the sweet stuff."

She'd already slurped a long drink and practically swooned at the frozen deliciousness. She took a seat on the chair near the couch and kicked her feet up on the ottoman.

"I love the sweet stuff." She took a moment to study him. He looked more relaxed here than he had at the picnic, and that was to be expected. Meeting new people could be overwhelming. There was an air of contentment around him as if life didn't get much better than this.

As a matter of fact, she had a little of the same feeling, too.

"You had a good time today, didn't you?" She watched for his reaction.

His smile was instant and genuine. "Yeah, I did. Your friends are nice. I like them."

Pride filled her chest. Who didn't want to hear they had good taste in friends?

"I agree. They're great."

"So what was the deal with Eden and Ryder?" He

sipped his iced coffee and watched her through those curious brown eyes.

"What do you mean?" She didn't think there was a deal between them—had she missed something?

He shrugged. "I don't know. I got the impression she doesn't like him much."

"Really?" She curled her legs to the side. "Why do you say that? She's never said anything to me."

It didn't surprise her Eden hadn't said anything negative about Ryder. She kept her opinions to herself. Gabby, on the other hand, spoke hers loudly and often.

"Maybe I'm wrong. She acted funny when he arrived, and it almost seemed like she was trying to avoid him, but he wasn't taking the hint. He followed her a couple of times."

"He did?" She hadn't considered Ryder and Eden could be on the outs. But why would they be? He wasn't even from around here. He lived in Los Angeles. Just because he'd been visiting more often didn't mean there was something going on between them she didn't know about.

"Yeah. But she was talking to that guy—the one in jeans and a cowboy hat."

He'd just described half a dozen guys there.

"Did he have short black hair? A slight gap in his teeth?"

Dylan lifted one shoulder. "I don't know. I didn't get a good look at him. It wasn't the jokey guy who was all over you. It was the quiet one."

Must have been Judd. And Cash had not been all over her. "Cash is friendly to all the ladies."

"He looked extra friendly when he was with you." The words were low, almost beneath his breath.

"Yeah, well, that's his way." She should be offended

he was judging Cash, but she wasn't—in fact, she felt positively buoyant. Was he jealous?

"I know. I could tell you were trying to get away from him. Some people are hard to shake."

"Like Stella and Misty?" She blinked innocently.

"Yes. They aren't just hard to shake, they need to be professionally removed—like superglue or a termite infestation."

She laughed.

"Are you seeing any of those guys?" The question sounded light, but the gleam in his eyes told her otherwise.

"No."

"Why not?"

She dunked the straw into the coffee a few times. "I'm not into cowboys."

"And why's that?" He sank back into the couch, his expression serious.

Instead of automatically changing the subject, she stared at him. They'd shared personal stories before, but none this close to her heart. Telling him about Carl—not everything, obviously—might not be a bad thing. If he knew why she didn't date cowboys, he'd get the hint and know she wasn't interested.

"I told you about my dad." She set the drink on a coaster on the end table, steepled her fingers and brought them below her chin. "My ex also let me down."

"What did he do?" He leaned forward with his elbows on his knees.

"He wasn't who I thought he was. I was eighteen, a senior in high school, planning a way for Allison and I to move out of Mom's trailer after I graduated, and Carl came along. He was older, tall, good-looking—a cowboy. All the girls crushed on him when he rode into town. And I couldn't believe he noticed me."

Dylan scowled.

"We started dating almost instantly. He said all the right things, and I lapped them up like the naive schoolgirl I was. Of course, I thought I was so smart and cool. I wasn't." She shrugged one shoulder in self-mockery. "I'd had a job at the grocery store since I turned sixteen, and I worked as many hours as possible outside of school to save for Allison and I to live on our own. Within a few weeks, Carl had a funny habit. He always needed me to pay for whatever we were doing. He'd claim he lost his wallet or had lent money to a friend. Soon he needed help paying for his gas or an overdue bill. He'd always look so embarrassed. I would give it to him. In my eyes he was perfect."

Dylan shifted but didn't speak.

"He always assured me he'd pay me back as soon as he got paid. I dated him for six months before I realized he wasn't faithful." She almost choked on the words. He'd been more than unfaithful; he'd been married to someone else. After all these years, the shame of it still felt fresh.

"I never saw a penny of my money again," she said. "It was a hard lesson to learn."

"Did you break up with him?"

"Yeah, but it took me a couple more weeks before I realized he wasn't going to change and he didn't really love me. Allison and I moved to Rendezvous not long after I graduated. We stayed with our grandma. Starting over in a new place helped a lot."

"Do you ever miss him?" Dylan asked gently. "Did you love him?"

The questions surprised her. Previously she would

have said no, she hadn't loved him or missed him, but now that she was older, she could admit the truth. "Yes and yes. But also no and no."

He barked out a laugh and shook his head. "Well, what is it? Yes or no?"

"At first I missed him terribly. I was convinced I loved him. I thought he was the love of my life. I had wedding bells in my head. But after being away for a while, I realized I only missed who I thought he was, and that I'd fallen in love with a mirage, not a real person."

"Hmm…" He sat back again, staring ahead as if contemplating her words. "I never thought of it that way, but I know exactly what you mean."

"You do?" She hadn't expected him to understand. "What happened to you?"

"Robin. She and I met at a party of a mutual friend. She was smart, gorgeous and she wanted to talk to me. Like you, I was surprised she chose me. She was so friendly and outgoing. Soon, we were dating. I worked for my dad at the time."

"What did you do for him?" It was odd he would think a beautiful woman choosing him would be surprising. Didn't he know how handsome he was? And his undemanding personality drew people to him.

"Eh." He shrugged. "Mostly pushed papers around and made sure people were doing what they were supposed to."

"You weren't working on a ranch?" She'd never pictured him pushing papers and managing people.

"No, not at the time."

"What kind of company was it?"

He didn't meet her eyes. "It was in the energy field." He seemed embarrassed. Maybe his dad hadn't been a very good businessman or something. She'd seen plenty of businesses come and go in Rendezvous.

His jaw clenched. "Anyway, Robin and I dated for several months. At first I liked her take-charge attitude. She made the plans. It was nice. Until she decided to take charge of my entire life. Everything was about getting ahead, meeting the right people. No matter what I did, it disappointed her. When I told her Dad sold the company, she left me."

Her spirits sank. She hadn't been the only one used and dumped.

"I tried to get her back, but she was done." His fingertips tapped against his shorts. "After my dad died, she suddenly came back into my life. She wanted to get back together—she was back to happy, friendly Robin. But it was because of the inheritance."

"Oh no, that's terrible!" Gabby pressed a hand over her chest. She thought back to when they'd first met, and she'd been convinced he was just another deadbeat cowboy. All because Carl had hurt her. How had Robin's treatment of him colored his first impression of her?

"I survived." He shrugged.

Phoebe made noises, alerting them she was waking up.

"She'll be hungry." Gabby got to her feet and headed to the kitchen to make a bottle.

"Do you mind if I turn on the Rockies game?" he asked. "If you had plans or something, though…"

"Go ahead. I don't mind. I like to keep up with the scores. People staying at the inn love talking sports." She actually enjoyed watching baseball games in the summer. Plus it seemed something friends would do—not romantic at all. And if he was going to be here, she might as well keep it as far from romance as possible. Now that he'd opened up to her about his ex and his previous job, she felt closer to him. It was fine if they were going to be semirelated through Phoebe, but it wasn't fine at all if she started to fall for him.

The sound of the television clicking on mingled with Phoebe's fussy sounds as Gabby prepared the bottle. Then the baby grew quiet. Gabby peeked around the cupboard, and her heart melted.

Dylan had gotten Phoebe out of the carrier and was cradling her to his chest. He bounced her gently, whispering something in her ear.

There was something about seeing a brawny man tenderly holding a baby that went straight to her heart.

Maybe watching baseball together wasn't a good idea. *You're just lonely. This doesn't mean a thing.*

"Can I feed her?" He met her eyes as she approached him with the bottle.

It seemed a harmless request. Why was her stomach dipping in resistance?

"Sure, why not?"

He settled on the couch with Phoebe in his arms and began feeding her the bottle. Phoebe stared at him with laser-like intensity, and Gabby returned to her chair.

As she watched them, her eyes grew heavy. The crack of the bats and drone of the announcers on television only lulled her more. She tried to stay awake, but it had been a long day. She'd close her eyes. Just for a minute.

The loud ringtone coming from Gabby's phone almost gave him a heart attack. He glanced over at her, curled up in the chair, sleeping. She looked young, beautiful and peaceful. He checked his own phone—after eleven o'clock at night. Should he try to wake her up?

He shifted Phoebe, also sleeping, to his other arm and reached over to shake Gabby's shoulder. "Hey, wake up. Someone is calling you."

She lifted her head, her eyelids trying to open, and gave him the most confused stare he'd seen in a while.

"What? Why are you here? Where am I?" Her voice was muffled as if she chewed on cotton. He tried not to laugh.

"You're at your apartment. You fell asleep."

Her phone blared again.

She bolted upright and swiped the phone. "Hello?"

Expressions of anxiety, then concern, then downright worry tightened her face.

"Okay, calm down. I'll be right there. No, you're not bothering me…Of course not. I'll come to you." She hung up.

"What's wrong?" he asked.

"It's Eden. She had some bad news and is completely freaking out. I've never—not once since I've known her—seen her get hysterical about anything." Gabby got up. Her jerky movements proved she wasn't quite awake all the way. "I have to go out there."

"Want me to go get her?" He stood, keeping Phoebe cradled under his arm.

"No, no. I'll go. You wouldn't know how to find her." She scurried to the kitchen, grabbed her keys and her purse, then smacked her forehead. "The baby."

"I'll take care of her. You go find your friend."

"No. I'll call Babs…" She rubbed her right eyebrow and shook her head. "I can't. I forgot she was going to Jackson after I picked up the baby. No big deal. Phoebe can come with me…" She seemed to be talking to herself.

"Gabby." He put his hand on her shoulder. "I will stay here and take care of Phoebe."

"You?"

Didn't she think he could handle it? Should he be offended? "Yes. After you fell asleep, I changed her diaper and played with her. We were fine then, and we'll be fine now."

"I don't know." She chewed on her fingernail.

"Look, she's sleeping." He nodded to the baby. "Why wake her?"

Her gray eyes softened. "I guess you're right. Her formula is in the kitchen. The bottles are in the cupboard. If she starts fussing, assume she's hungry. Make sure you burp her. And be prepared for a nasty diaper—it could blow right through her pajamas."

Nasty diaper? He did not look forward to that.

"Oh, you need to put her in her pajamas. Come on, I'll show you where everything is." She waved him to follow her, but he caught her hand and stopped her. The touch undid him—he quickly dropped her hand.

"Gabby, I know where you keep everything. You've taught me how to change her. We'll be fine. Now go."

Her worried eyes met his, and he wanted to hug her and assure her everything—her friend and him watching the baby—would be fine. But he couldn't. Couldn't touch her because holding her would be his downfall.

With her lips in a thin line, she nodded. "Call me for any reason. I don't know how long I'll be gone. She's almost half an hour away."

"I can stay all night."

And with that, she nodded, clutching her purse, and left. At the click of the door, he stared down at Phoebe, asleep in his arms. Her hair was sweaty where her cheek rested against his arm. He caressed her little head and sat back down on the couch.

A few minutes later, Phoebe's eyes blinked open, and spotting his face, she instantly let out a wail.

"Hey there, smiley, you don't need to cry," he said softly. "Your mama's helping a friend. She'll be back a little later."

Her lower lip wobbled, her eyes squeezed shut and her mouth opened wide—letting out the loudest cry he'd ever heard.

He'd never been alone with the baby before. Gabby had always supervised them, and if Phoebe cried, Gabby had known what to do.

How was he supposed to handle this? How could he stop the crying?

"What do you need?" He sprang to his feet. "You hungry? Or do you not like my face?"

He shifted her in his arms, her head at his shoulders, and went into the kitchen. Her cries grew more urgent. His insides were winding tighter and tighter with each wail.

Was Phoebe in pain? What had Gabby told him? His glance fell on the clean bottles lined on the counter.

*Assume she's hungry.* Right. He fiddled with the formula and hoped for the best. Had he prepared the bottle correctly? The wails were pounding into his head—he'd try anything to stop them.

"Here you go, here's your bottle." He tried to give it to her, but she turned her head and cried harder. Her face was brick red, and her little body stiff with tension. "Okay, I take it you're not hungry."

The basket of toys stood in the corner, so he went over and took out a stuffed bunny. "Look at Mr. Bunny." He pretended to make it hop. She paused, her lips wobbling, and then resumed crying.

Once more, he tried to give her the bottle, but by the tone of her cries, he might as well have been lighting her favorite toy on fire.

Why had he thought he could take care of a baby by himself? Gabby would know what was wrong. She'd get her to stop. What if she came back and the baby was still hysterical? She'd never let him take care of his niece again.

*God, I don't know what to do. I hate seeing her upset. How do I make it better?*

He stood up. She still cried and twisted to face away from him. Locking her in his grip, he shifted her to face the television. Her tiny legs dangled as he gently bounced her. Slowly, the cries subsided.

"You didn't want to see my ugly mug, did you?" He kept his voice low. "I don't blame you. But I'd never hurt you. I'm only here because your mama had to leave for a little bit. Her friend needs her—and she's the type of person who will drop everything for her friends."

The phone call he'd ignored from Sam bloomed fresh in his mind. Had Sam been calling for help? If he had taken it, would he have prevented Sam from overdosing a few days later?

He'd been wrapped up in his own misery about Dad selling the company and Robin leaving him—he hadn't wanted to talk to anyone. He'd figured Sam called to tell him about his latest gig or something. He'd never dreamed Sam would die within the week.

Gently kissing the top of Phoebe's head, he tried to push away the guilt. Gabby's confession about her ex earlier had bothered him more than he cared to admit. The fact a guy would use her like that... His muscles tensed, and Phoebe twisted to look back at him. Two fat teardrops clung to her lashes, and her lower lip jutted out.

"Come on, let's get you in your pajamas. You'll feel better." He carried her to her bedroom. Maybe he should have told Gabby the truth—the whole truth—tonight. Sure, he'd given her the condensed version of him and Robin and his dad, but there was more to it. Much more to it.

Why was it still important for him to make her believe he didn't have money? When she so obviously never would expect anything from him?

"She doesn't mind me now, but if she knew everything..." He laid Phoebe on the changing table, grabbed the wipes and put on a fresh diaper. Then he put her pajamas on, snapping them incorrectly twice before redoing it right. She made little babbling noises. She was back to her happy self. "Your mama doesn't like rich guys, especially ones who didn't earn their money. And I'm not like her. It's midnight and she's helping her friend. I couldn't even answer a call from my brother."

He scooped her up and carried her to the living room.

He didn't deserve a woman like Gabby.

But he wanted to.

Her mind was racing in opposite directions. One thought dominated—help Eden. The other—had she made a ginormous mistake leaving the baby with Dylan?—chased closely behind. Gabby parked her car behind Eden's on the shoulder of the old two-lane road. Turning on her flashlight, she began making her way across the rocky plain, then up the grassy hill to where a clearing was hidden from the road. She knew the spot because Eden had brought her out here on several occasions, including when they'd camped overnight a few months after Mia died. It had been a cathartic experience with millions of twinkling stars in the black sky and just the two of them talking through the grief.

Tonight was equally as clear, and Gabby had no problem seeing the path ahead of her. A dozen worries circled her brain. Would Dylan be able to handle Phoebe? What if something went wrong and he didn't know what to do? Had she warned him about not letting Phoebe have any pillows in her crib? And what if he tried to feed her something she couldn't handle? Did he know what babies could eat? And what about Eden? Why was she hysterical? What had happened?

When she reached the top of the hill, she scanned the flat clearing until she saw Eden sitting on a blanket, her knees bunched up to her chest.

"Hey," Gabby said, jogging to her side. Eden didn't move, so she clumsily folded her legs to a seated position next to her. "What's going on? Why are you out here all alone?"

"I'm always alone, Gabby." Eden continued to stare ahead, her arms wrapped around her knees. "And I'm about to be even more alone."

"What are you talking about?" Gabby's heart leaped to her throat. Eden's tone set her nerves on edge.

She faced her then. "Dad called me after the picnic. He was all excited. Apparently he and Mom bought an RV and plan on traveling the country sooner rather than later."

Gabby cringed. The past four years had been difficult for the entire family.

"I know how close you are to them." Gabby put her arm around Eden's shoulders.

"That's not the worst part. They don't want to ranch anymore. They're going to sell it." She started crying then.

"Oh no." She rubbed Eden's back as she sobbed. "I don't know what to say. It's your home."

She sniffed. "I always thought I'd get married and bring the kids over to the ranch for Christmas and Sunday dinners and…" She hiccuped and cried at the same time. "All of my memories are there. Mia was there. How can they even consider letting some stranger have it all?"

Now she understood why Eden was so upset. This was about Mia as much as it was about losing her home.

"You'll always have your memories of your sister. They're locked up here—" Gabby pointed to her temple "—not in a house."

Eden sniffled and blew her nose into a tissue. "I know you're right, but it hit me so hard, especially after the picnic."

"What was wrong with the picnic?" She thought about Dylan's observation regarding Eden and Ryder.

"It was so obvious I don't fit in with the guys around here. Judd said two words to me. Cash completely ignored me. And the only guy who made any effort was the one I don't like at all."

"Judd's quiet. The two words he said to you were two more than he said to most of the women there. And you don't want Cash. He's a player." Should she ask about Ryder? "Why don't you like Ryder?"

"I didn't say that," she snapped.

"You weren't talking about Ryder?"

Eden sighed. "It doesn't matter. Let's drop it."

Gabby raised her eyebrows but didn't push it. A shooting star streaked across the sky in front of them. "Did you see that? A shooting star."

"Maybe if I wish on it, my parents won't sell the ranch."

"Maybe." Gabby wanted to give words of comfort, but she couldn't lie to her best friend. "Change can be good sometimes."

"For you." Eden shrugged.

"What do you mean by that?"

"Nothing. I just noticed how Dylan looked at you. He didn't want you out of his sight."

Her heartbeat quickened. Was it true?

"I'm the only one he knows here."

"He wasn't scared, Gabby." Eden blew out a long breath. "He likes you. And I'm glad. I just…well, I want someone to look at me like that. And instead I'm getting kicked out of my house. Maybe Brittany will let me rent the apartment above her studio for a discount."

"It's been a long time since you were on your own. Having your own apartment could be exactly what you need."

"I've never really been on my own. I dormed with three other girls at college, and lived with Mom and Dad during the summers. I like life how it is now."

"Who's to say you won't like it even better a year from now?" Gabby stood and held out a hand to Eden. She took it, stood and Gabby hugged her.

"I can't stand the thought of someone else living in my house, Gabby." Eden turned to head back down the path.

"Understandable."

"I feel like I have no control."

"I know the feeling well." Gabby followed her, shining the flashlight before them.

"Thanks for coming out here. I'm sorry to call so late. I just couldn't process any of this. I felt paralyzed sitting up there, and all I could think to do was call you."

"I'm glad you did. That's what friends are for. You were there for me night and day after Allison died." They reached the bottom of the hill, and Gabby put her hand on Eden's arm to stop her. "You'll always have me. That's one thing that won't change."

"I know. We'll always be friends. I'll get through this. It's not the worst thing in the world. Losing Mia was."

"I wish Mia and Allison were still here."

"Me, too." Eden stared at her with clear eyes. "I think you should get married and have more kids."

"Me?" She forced out a laugh. "I'm not getting married."

"I think you will and sooner than you think." Eden continued walking forward. "You should, you know. Phoebe would get a daddy, and you'd have someone to lean on."

"I don't need anyone to lean on. I have you and the rest of the group."

"It's not the same." Eden headed toward their cars.

She had a point. It wasn't the same, and she knew it. The fact Dylan had been there to watch Phoebe had allowed her to drop everything and come here to help Eden. Without his offer, she would have had to wake someone else, bring the baby or not come at all.

She checked her phone to see if he'd called or texted. Nothing. No news was good news, right?

"Are you going to be okay going home on your own?" Gabby asked as Eden pulled her keys out of her pocket.

"Yeah." Eden hugged her. "Thanks for coming out tonight. I'm sorry to drag you away."

"Don't be sorry. I wanted to come."

"I'll see you tomorrow." Eden got into her car.

"Hey, Eden?"

"Yes?"

"God will get you through this."

Eden nodded. "I hope so, Gabby. I hope so."

Half an hour later, Gabby quietly unlocked her door and tiptoed inside. The television screen glowed, but no sound came from it. Where were Dylan and Phoebe? As stress tightened her lungs, she stepped into the living room. The sight before her drained every ounce of anxiety.

Dylan was sprawled on her couch with Phoebe cuddled up on his chest. Both were sleeping.

It was the most precious sight she could imagine.

Eden's words echoed in her mind. *You should get married and have more kids…sooner than you think.*

At the time, she'd thought it was ridiculous.

Now the idea didn't seem so out there.

"Hey." She tapped the bottom of Dylan's foot. "Wake up. I'm home."

He shifted, curling his arm around Phoebe protectively. *Have mercy.*

"Dylan, wake up." She carefully picked up the baby. Dylan was a heavy sleeper. She carried Phoebe to her room and set her in the crib before returning to the living room.

He'd sat up and was raking his fingers through his hair. She tried not to stare. He looked so sleepy and adorable…and handsome.

"Was she okay for you?" Gabby perched on the edge of the chair.

"What?" He yawned. "Oh, yeah. She was great."

"She didn't cry at all?" Sometimes Gabby got the feeling she was dispensable—that any adult would do in Phoebe's eyes.

"She cried a little after you left." He looked sheepish. "I think she missed you."

"Really?" Her spirits lifted. How messed up was that? She shouldn't be happy the baby cried.

"Yeah, but she settled down." He picked up his shoes and started putting them on. "How is your friend? Everything okay?"

"She'll be fine. She had an unpleasant life surprise."

"I know how that goes." He nodded. "Well, I'll get out of your hair. Thanks for the picnic and letting me come over—by the way, the Rockies won."

He crossed to the front door. She followed him.

"You don't have to thank me. I should be the one thanking you. Thanks for watching the baby for me—and for offering. It helped me out." It was scary to think she could depend on him. The facts were there, though. He'd come through for her in a jam.

"No problem. I'm glad I could help. See you in church tomorrow?"

"Yes."

He opened the door, hitched his chin to her and left.

She stared at the closed door for several moments.

The whole friend thing had flown out the window the instant she'd spotted him cradling Phoebe on the couch.

She could no longer herd him into the same pasture as Judd and Cash and the other cowboys in town.

Dylan Kingsley made her heart beat faster, and she didn't know how to deal with it.

Erasing the cowboy from her mind was her last hope. If she only knew how...

## Chapter Ten

"Refill your vaccination gun." Friday afternoon, Stu wiped his forehead and pointed to the ancient flatbed truck where coolers and supplies were ready. Dylan nodded and loped over there, grabbed the medicine and refilled it the way Stu had shown him earlier that morning.

The sun was scorching. Several local men and women had joined them for a day of branding and vaccinating. Since his lassoing skills weren't on par with Stu's other regulars, he'd gotten the task of giving the calves their shots. He'd been focused on the task for hours, even though thoughts of Gabby kept trying to distract him. She'd let down her guard Saturday night, and he'd actually come through for her. He'd been reliable, dependable.

It had been easy. He'd been in the right spot at the right time. The thing was, he wanted to be in that same spot for a long, long time.

"What are you waiting for?" One of the men yelled to a teen, shaking Dylan from his thoughts.

The pen where he was standing held calves separated from their mamas. Dust, loud mooing and thunderous hoofbeats filled the air whenever one of the crew chased down the next calf. Everyone seemed to be enjoying themselves. The calves appeared no worse for wear, either. As soon as each one was done, it trotted off to join its friends like it hadn't been poked with a needle and had a symbol burned into its flesh.

"We have about ten head left, then we can eat." Stu waited with the branding iron in his hand for the next calf to get dragged over.

Dylan prepared to inject another one. At first it had scared him—what if he poked the wrong spot or the calf kicked him?—but he'd quickly gotten the hang of it. In the three weeks he'd been working for Stu, he'd seen two dead calves out in the wild. He wanted to do whatever he could to make sure the rest of them lived.

They finished taking care of the remaining animals, then opened the pen so they could return to their mamas. Everyone packed up quickly and headed over to the old bunkhouse where a few ladies from church had organized a meal to celebrate the day.

Dylan stopped in at his cabin and washed up before joining the rest of the crew. After filling his plate with pulled pork, cheesy potatoes and cookies, he found an empty table and tore into his food. Stu and two elderly women Dylan had seen in church sat with him.

"How are you liking Rendezvous, Dylan?" The white-haired lady in jeans and a patchwork short-sleeved shirt watched him with an expectant air. "I'm Lois Dern, by the way. I've seen you in church with Gabby."

"Good to meet you, Lois." He nodded. "I like it here a lot."

Stu's toothpick bobbed twice.

"I don't believe we've met. I'm Gretchen Sable." The

brown-haired woman he guessed to be in her late sixties had understanding eyes. "I hear you're Phoebe's uncle."

"Yes, ma'am." He polished off a cookie.

"Gabby is wonderful. A natural with the baby." Lois stared at him as if expecting a reply.

"Um, yes, she is."

"And she's so helpful," Gretchen said. "We think the world of her." Well, that made two of them. He thought she was pretty special, too.

"Do you plan on staying in the area long?" Lois asked.

"Um…" He wanted to say yes, but he couldn't. Not as things stood at the moment.

"I have to warn you, though, Dylan," Gretchen said in between bites of a potato chip, "Gabby refuses to date cowboys. If she'd loosen her stance, I'd set her up with my nephew Judd immediately. Have you met Judd?"

Dylan glanced at Stu for help, but he shrugged, lifting his hands as if to say *you're on your own*.

"Yes, I have met him. He's a good guy."

"He is. The best." Gretchen smiled. "So if she won't consider Judd, she probably won't—"

"Nonsense, Gretch." Lois crumpled her napkin. "Gabby might not be attracted to Judd."

"Not attracted?" Gretchen's cheeks grew pink. "What are you saying? Judd's ugly? Because I know better."

"Don't twist my words. I'm just saying you've had your heart set on Judd and Gabby together, but neither of them seems all that interested in the other. Admit it."

"Only because she refuses to date cowboys."

"If he liked her, he'd ask her out and keep asking her out until she said yes." Lois picked up her napkin once more and dabbed at her lips.

Gretchen glared at Lois, then turned back to Dylan. "Are you enjoying working on the ranch?"

"I love it. Stu's a great boss." At least he could answer one question truthfully.

"You're a good worker." Stu cocked his head. "You should stay on permanently."

Permanently? His chest swelled. He'd like nothing more than to stay here.

"I appreciate it, Stu," Dylan said. Every day on the ranch was like being at the best summer camp imaginable. Sure, it was hard work, long hours and physically demanding. But it was also peaceful. He could hear himself think when he rode out on Jethro. It drove away the sensation of constantly having to move on.

He had a feeling he'd been trying to find an honest day's work his entire life.

And he'd found it.

Here.

"I'll have to think about it." He met his boss's eyes. Stu nodded.

"Are you going to the Fourth of July parade, Stu?" Gretchen asked.

"I don't know."

"Well, I heard through the grapevine you aren't going to be riding in the parade this year." Lois leaned in. "Understandable with Josiah gone. Why don't you watch the parade with us? We get our chairs set up bright and early to get our spots. I'll tell Frank to set up one for you, too."

"You don't need to go to trouble on my account." Stu flicked a glance at Gretchen.

"It's no trouble," Lois said.

"Come with us," Gretchen said. "We know it hasn't been easy losing your best friend."

"You can come, too." Lois turned to Dylan. "Unless you planned on sitting with Gabby."

"Uh…" He didn't know what Gabby's plans were, and he hadn't thought about going to the parade. Hadn't really thought about the Fourth of July Fest at all.

"Well, if you don't, I'm sure Cash McCoy would be happy to sit with her." Lois leaned back and shrugged. "He'd probably be fine taking her to the festival afterward, too."

"I'll take her." The words shot out of his mouth. He did not like the idea of that smarmy Cash guy hanging around Gabby and the baby. "That is, if she wants to go."

"She'll want to go. You know, this town has a lot to offer." Lois stared at him hard. He squirmed. Why was he squirming? "Rendezvous is a nice place to settle down."

"If only Nolan wasn't buying the inn…" Gretchen made a tsk-tsk sound.

"He's not for sure buying the inn," Lois said. "But if he does, my guess is she'll put up with his nonsense for a while…but not forever."

He'd all but forgotten Gabby was worried about her job. He let out a small groan. He'd spent Monday and Wednesday evening with her, and she hadn't mentioned a thing about Nolan.

"Isn't there anyone else who wants to buy it?" Dylan watched the ladies. Both of their faces fell.

"Unfortunately, no. And Gabby would never mention it, but we've done the math, and there aren't many opportunities for her here."

Gabby had said something similar a while back. His nerve endings splintered. It wasn't fair of him to keep her in the dark. He needed to do something.

*Yeah, and that something is to tell her the truth and*

get Phoebe's trust fund and child support set up. Stop being so selfish!

Selfishness had prevented him from taking Sam's calls. And selfishness was stopping him from doing the right thing now. But what was he supposed to do? He couldn't simply hand Gabby some papers with a *don't worry about money.*

He owed it to her to tell her the truth. He just didn't know if he had the courage to go through with it. Not when his life was finally starting to make sense.

"I might have another buyer!" Babs shuffled the papers on her desk as Gabby sat down after her shift ended on Friday.

"Are you serious?" Gabby's heart leaped to her throat. If someone else bought Mountain View Inn, Nolan couldn't, and she wouldn't have to work for the control freak. "Please tell me you're being serious."

"I'm being serious." Babs's green eyes twinkled under her heavily mascaraed lashes. "It's a silent buyer, or I'd tell you who it is."

"A silent buyer?" Was that good or bad? Did it mean she might be able to keep her job? Her palms grew clammy thinking about it.

"Yes. Dorothy called a few minutes ago to let me know."

"What does it mean? Will they send someone out to see it? Will I get to meet them?"

"Wish I could tell you, sugar, but I don't know." She shrugged. "As soon as I hear something, I'll tell you."

Gabby sank back into her chair. It was good news, yes, but new concerns came to mind. "What if Nolan makes an offer first?"

"He might. If he does, the other buyer could put in a counter offer. My gut tells me if Nolan was in a hurry, the papers would already be signed. You know him. He needs to analyze it to death while he throws his weight around for a while."

Unfortunately, she did know and agreed with the assessment.

"Want me to watch Phoebe so you can go to Fourth of July Fest with your hunk?" Babs scribbled something on a paper.

"What?" She should have prepared herself for this. She knew how Babs's mind worked. "He's not my hunk. And I don't know what I'm doing yet."

"He's a hunk. You can admit it."

Gabby rolled her eyes. Dylan was a hunk—but she didn't need to fan the matchmaking flames Babs enjoyed kindling.

"You know I'm right." Babs pulled a tube of lip gloss out of her purse and ran the wand across her lips. "Anyway, I'd love to take the little butterball off your hands on Saturday. Just let me know."

"Thanks, Babs."

"What are you doing tonight?"

Gabby could feel her neck warm. "Oh, the usual. Pizza."

"You're not telling me something." Babs gave her a shrewd look and pointed the tube at her.

"Dylan is coming over to see the baby."

"So it's a date."

"It's not a date."

"It's a pizza date."

"It's *not* a pizza date."

"Gabrielle." Babs gave her a long, intense stare. She

never used her full name. It reminded Gabby of getting scolded. "I had forty-one wonderful years with Herb. We went on adventures together. We bought properties and started businesses. He thought I was the best thing since sliced bread—of course, it helped he was color blind—I don't know many men who could handle my loud style. We were happy. And I miss him more than I ever thought possible."

A lump formed in Gabby's throat. Herb had been a great guy. Babs's bright, over-the-top personality had dimmed in the two years since he'd passed.

"I want you to have the same thing." Her voice softened. "I know you have your whole cowboy rule, but from all accounts, Dylan seems to be a decent guy. At least give him a chance. I want you to find your Herb."

"I want to find my Herb, too, Babs." And she did. "I didn't realize how much until Dylan arrived."

"See?"

"It's not what you think, though." She tried to find the words. "Having him around helping with the baby made me see how nice it could be to have a partner in life. And I would like for Phoebe to have a daddy. But I'm not ready for all that yet."

"Not even with Dylan?"

"Especially not with Dylan." She couldn't go there. It was too scary. She didn't know him well enough. What if he was laying the groundwork to get her to trust him? And then he showed his true colors? If she allowed herself to care about him, her heart could get smashed into bits. "It would be too complicated, with him being Phoebe's uncle."

"I don't know about that. Just be open to the possibilities, okay, hon?"

"Okay." Her heart had been teetering closer and closer to falling for him, but could she risk it?

"Now, let's get out of here." Babs pushed her chair back. "Did you put Stella on the night shift this weekend?"

"I did. She needs the experience."

"I just hope she doesn't flirt too much. It wouldn't do us a lick of good if she starts batting her eyelashes at a married man."

Gabby laughed. "Don't worry, she uses her flirting energy for good-looking younger guys. I think she has a radar for them or something."

"I'll take your word for it." Babs strolled with her down the hall. "Have fun on your pizza date."

"It's not a—"

Babs laughed. "Sure, it isn't."

"Call me as soon as you hear anything from Dorothy." Gabby waved to her as she exited the building.

"Will do."

Would a silent buyer be like a silent partner? Running the inn from afar? Letting her do her thing? She hoped so. It would be a dream come true.

The only thing better would be to own the inn herself, and that wasn't ever going to happen.

Gabby crossed the rear parking lot to her car. After unlocking it, she climbed in and stared at the distant mountains for a few moments.

Babs and Herb had been a power couple, and they'd adored each other. Herb had supported Babs's business ventures. He'd been her emotional rock. Gabby had meant it when she'd told Babs she wanted to find her Herb.

She rubbed her chin. The problem was she needed to be in control—of her job, her life and the baby. Any man who wanted to be with her would have to accept her independent nature.

Did a man exist who could handle the full Gabrielle Stover? Dylan seemed to check all the right boxes. But would he try to change her? Or, worse, find someone on the side to fill in the gaps? She turned the key in the ignition. Her heart was already too drawn to him. Anything other than happily-ever-after would crush her. But life was short, and time was moving fast. Should she take a chance or play it safe? She'd have to figure it out soon.

## Chapter Eleven

"I mixed it up this week." Dylan opened the box of pizza in Gabby's kitchen that evening. He'd had a lot to think about since eating with Stu, Lois and Gretchen earlier. After showering, he'd sat on his front porch and pondered his life. And when Gabby came to mind, which she did almost instantly, he'd wondered if he was putting too much importance on money. Why was he assuming she'd be mad when he told her he was rich? "I swapped the sausage for bacon. What do you think?"

"I think my stomach is growling, and it smells exquisite."

Phoebe was strapped into her high chair and happily working on bites of cantaloupe and tiny pieces of soft bread. Her mouth was a gooey mess as she grinned at him. He patted her head. "Hey, smiley, you're enjoying those, aren't you?"

Gabby yawned, covering her mouth to try to hide it, but failing.

"Long day at the office, huh?" He noticed her eyes weren't as animated as usual, and bags had formed under them.

"Not really." She slid a slice of pizza onto her plate.

"Are you nervous about Nolan buying the inn?" He mimicked her movements and joined her at the table with three slices on his plate.

She'd just taken a big bite, and she nodded as cheese stringed between her mouth and the pizza. Holding up her index finger, she finished chewing.

"Yes, I'm still worried, but I did hear some good news today—well, it might be good news."

"What's that?" He ignored his pizza for the moment to take her in. Her hair fell down her back in messy waves. Her hot-pink T-shirt had a scooped neck, revealing a delicate silver necklace with a circle charm.

"Babs might have another buyer."

His muscles involuntarily tightened. "Oh yeah?"

"I can't say anything beyond that, but anyone would be better than Nolan." She quirked her head to the side. "I'm realistic, though. Even if someone else buys it, my job isn't secure."

Dylan bit into the top slice. He'd never had to worry about job security.

"Do you have a backup plan?" he asked.

"Me?" She touched her chest, grinning. "You clearly don't know who you're dealing with. I have backup plans for my backup plan."

Another thing he admired about her.

"The problem is none of them are all that good."

"Let's hear them."

"I could get my insurance license and work for an agency here in town."

He continued eating as he listened.

"The power company sometimes needs people, but the only jobs that come up on a regular basis are maintenance. It would mean being on the road and a lot of physical labor."

He tried to picture her—strong, yes, but with delicate features and a petite frame—out working on power lines. He didn't see her enjoying it.

"The other option is to move somewhere else and manage another hotel."

Move? Somewhere else? He attacked his food a little too forcefully. He liked it in Rendezvous, and she did too. But if she moved, there would be no point in him living here.

Why had he assumed life could—or would—stay as it was?

If Gabby moved, it meant no more playing with Phoebe. No more Friday night pizzas. No more picnics and Rockies games and all the things he was beginning to look forward to. No more racing pulse whenever Gabby was near. No ranching, no community, no life.

"Moving is my last resort." She picked a piece of pepperoni off the plate and popped it in her mouth. The fact moving wasn't at the top of her list reassured him.

"What would be your first resort—you know, if the sky was the limit?"

"Sky's the limit?" A dreamy smile lit her entire face. "I suppose I'd buy the inn myself. Then I wouldn't have to worry about someone coming in and firing me or making my life miserable."

"Would you want the responsibility that comes with it?" From what he could tell, she'd fit into the role well.

"Yes, I would. I love the place. I would renovate the rooms—you know, freshen it up. Make it as inviting as possible. Babs has given me a lot of freedom, so I already know what works and what doesn't."

"You love your job, don't you?"

"I do. I'd hate to give it up for any reason."

What if he made sure she didn't have to give it up? The inn was getting a new owner, whether Nolan bought it or not. Gabby knew the place inside and out. And Dylan had the funds to make it happen.

He wanted to buy it for her.

He glanced at Phoebe smearing her hands on the tray. "You make it look easy, Gabby."

"What?" She blinked rapidly, and the vulnerability in her expression touched him.

"Being a mother and having a successful career."

"Is that a problem?"

"No, not at all." He shook his head. "I admire it about you. I could have used some of your gumption last year."

"When you were traveling?"

"No." He was ready to show her the side of himself that embarrassed him—the self-centered one who'd let down his brother. "After Dad sold the company and my girlfriend dumped me, I pretty much didn't leave my place for two weeks. I was miserable. And, I can admit it now, I was stuck in a pity party of epic proportions. Sam called and I didn't answer."

"I get it. I can throw myself a mean pity party, too."

"But if I would have taken the call…" He lifted his gaze to the ceiling briefly. "I didn't know he had a drug problem. What if he was reaching out for help? What if I had taken the call and said something that would have stopped him from OD'ing?"

Compassion swam in her gray eyes. "It wasn't your fault, Dylan."

He sucked in a breath. He wanted to believe her. "I don't know."

"I do. Some things are in our control and some things aren't. You no more forced Sam to take drugs than I caused the tear in Allison's heart. I hate that they're gone. Hate that we lost them. But it won't do either of us any good to wallow in regrets."

His chest tightened, and a lump formed in his throat as her words sank in and soothed the deepest part of him. He reached across the table and covered her hand with his. "You really think so?"

"I know so." Her eyes shimmered with appreciation. "This world is full of trouble. But Jesus overcame the world—for you and me and Sam and Allison."

It was as if a heavy, rusty weight lifted off his heart. For the first time since Sam's death, he started to believe he wasn't to blame.

His gaze fell to her lips. Why couldn't he look away?

"Do you want to go to the Fourth of July Fest with me?" he blurted out.

"I planned on going…" She lowered her eyelashes. "Babs offered to watch the baby, but you probably want to spend time with Phoebe, too."

"Babs can watch Phoebe."

"You want to be with me? Just me?" Wariness crept into her features.

"Yes." He braced himself for her rejection.

"Like a date?"

"Yeah, a date."

"I don't date cowboys." The words sounded weak.

The smart thing to do would be to distance himself emotionally, but he wasn't ready to slink away and do everything by her rules. Not anymore. He hadn't asserted himself with his father, and he regretted it. He didn't want to make the same mistake with Gabby.

"Could you make an exception?" he asked. "Just this once?"

Silence filled the room. Then she sighed.

"I don't know, Dylan. I don't think it's smart. I mean, you told me you're going to be here a month, and the month is almost over. You haven't mentioned what you're doing after you leave."

She didn't sugarcoat things, that was for sure.

"Stu told me I could stay on permanently." His chest burned as he thought of making Rendezvous permanent. He wanted it. Badly.

"If you stayed, what would you do? Be Stu's ranch hand indefinitely? Do you have goals? Plans? Dreams?"

Goals. Plans. Dreams. His spirits fell. He wasn't enough for her. Dad hadn't thought he was ambitious enough, either. Nor had Robin.

An apology clung to his lips—the assurance that of course he wanted to be more than a ranch hand—but the words refused to come out.

*God, I'm tired of trying to fit into a mold that isn't me.*

He wasn't going to. Not anymore.

"I like being a ranch hand. It suits me." Had he really said those words? "Riding out, checking fence, moving cattle with Stu is exactly what I'm supposed to be doing."

He might as well head to the door now. She'd never accept a mere ranch hand as suitable dating material. If he told her he wanted to own a ranch, maybe then she'd think he was worthy.

"So you're not chasing the dream of owning your own ranch?"

"No." As much as he wanted to impress her, he wasn't going to. He'd found his authentic self by helping Stu, and he refused to deny it. At this point in his life, owning a ranch would do nothing for him.

"You're not like anyone I've ever met." She framed her chin in the crook between her thumb and index finger. "What if the pay doesn't meet your needs?"

It would be the perfect time to tell her his needs would be met a thousand times over for the rest of his life.

*Tell her the truth. You know you have to.*

A cold sweat broke out on the back of his neck.

He wasn't ready. He needed to prepare—to figure out the right words.

"I don't need much." It was true. But the sinking feeling in his gut proved he shouldn't have taken the easy way out.

Seconds ticked by.

"Okay, I'll go with you to the festival." Her determined chin rose. "Just so we're clear—I will be your date."

He had to be missing something. He'd told her his life goal was to be a ranch hand—a cowboy—and she'd changed her mind about dating him? She'd said yes?

It was his turn to stand. He walked over to her, tipped her chin up and stared into her eyes. Fire, fear and excitement glittered within them.

This woman—he didn't know a woman like her existed. Passionate, selfless, caring, generous. He clenched his jaw.

He loved her.

He was absolutely head over heels in love with this woman.

"I'm going to kiss you." His voice was low as he watched her reaction. It wouldn't do to scare her off, not when she'd finally opened up enough to let him in.

"I'm not going to stop you." Her words were all bravado, and he could see the previous hurts and questions in her eyes.

He slid his palms up her biceps oh so gently and cupped her face. Slowly, he lowered his lips to hers. He sucked in a breath at the sweetness of them. Then he pressed her closer to him, savoring her supple frame in his arms, the softness of her lips, the rightness of them together.

He'd been waiting for this moment his entire life.

Her arms crept around his neck, and her hand caressed the back of it. The kiss ebbed and flowed, and he wanted to convey how much she meant to him.

Gabby Stover was more than he deserved. She was more than any man deserved.

When he finally broke away, he moved his hands down to her slim waist.

"Well, then…" Her cheeks were flushed, and she looked shell-shocked.

"Yeah." His voice was gravelly. He had so much to say to her and no words to say it.

She smoothed her hair with shaky fingers. "Let's get Phoebe cleaned up and take a walk down at the park. I want to soak in all the summer I can."

He wouldn't argue with that.

Between now and the festival next Saturday, he had to talk to Stu about staying. He also had to tell Gabby the truth about his money. And he'd better call his lawyer to find out the best way forward to purchase the inn.

And somewhere in there he had to tell her more… that he loved her.

Was the timing wrong, though?

He'd gotten Gabby to agree to a date, and he didn't

want to scare her off with the L-word. He'd talk to Stu and Ed this week, but Gabby?

He'd wait to confess his net worth and love for her until after the festival. One more week wouldn't hurt a thing.

This changed everything.

Gabby stood on her balcony later that night and touched her fingers to her lips for the thousandth time. Dylan had kissed her! And she'd wanted him to. Because he'd opened up to her about his guilt over Sam. And then, he'd shocked her by explaining his job at Stu's was exactly what he was meant to do. She'd expected him to spin wild dreams about owning a huge cattle ranch and what he'd buy after he'd made it big. Her daddy and Carl had always been chasing fantasies ending in riches.

Dylan wasn't like them.

And if he wasn't like them, there was no reason she shouldn't date him.

He'd been reliable, honest and trustworthy since he'd arrived in Rendezvous.

Babs was right—she could be open to the possibility of a future with Dylan. She certainly thought about him enough. Like all the time—at work, at home—and after that kiss, she doubted she'd get to sleep tonight.

The stars above twinkled, reminding her of last week when she'd met Eden out at the clearing. She'd checked on her a few times, and thankfully, Eden seemed to be back to herself.

Gabby took out her phone and texted her. Dylan kissed me today.

The reply was instant. What?

Yeah, and we're going to the Fourth of July Fest together. As a date.

No way! That's great!

She hesitated before texting what was on her mind.

Do you think I can trust him? What if he ends up being
a lying jerk?

A few moments passed before Eden replied. I think
you're strong enough to take the chance. If he's a lying
jerk, you'll deal with it. If not, you might have found your
dream man.

Tears pricked the backs of her eyes.

Thanks, Eden. I needed that.

A smiley emoji appeared.

She set the phone down and enjoyed the light breeze
on her face. As much as she'd tried to protect her heart,
she'd failed. Big-time. Eden was right. Whatever happened with Dylan, she'd deal with it—good or bad.

She'd already fallen in love with him.

It was hard to admit, but it was impossible to deny.

Chicken and biscuits, she'd fallen in love with a cowboy.

## Chapter Twelve

This had been the best week of his life.

Dylan held Gabby's hand as they strolled past food trucks and dodged children waving American flags. They'd already watched the Fourth of July parade with its line of fire trucks, floats, cowboys and cowgirls riding horseback and the Rendezvous high school marching band cranking out tunes. He was ready to make this town his permanent home.

"Let's get a picture before we eat." He tugged her to stand in front of a banner with the American flag, and they mugged for the camera on his phone before continuing on. "What are you hungry for?"

"Ribs sound good." Gabby pointed to a long line wrapping around a trailer advertising barbecue.

The red, white and blue theme was everywhere. Little flags had been stuck in the ground, patriotic banners were strung across the food trucks and even the picnic tables had red tablecloths.

"What time did you say the baseball game starts?" They'd decided to watch the local team play this afternoon. Later, when it got dark, they were joining the rest of the town to watch the fireworks display. "Do we have time?"

"Plenty of time." She held his hand as they walked. "It doesn't start for another hour."

He'd spent every evening except Tuesday this week with Gabby and Phoebe. They'd talked about their dreams and Phoebe's future. She wanted Phoebe to have a good education, lots of love and faith in the Lord, not in that order. He wanted the same.

He'd been tempted to blurt out the truth a few times, but until he had his plans lined up, he'd remain silent. He hoped Stu would still want to employ him when he told him who he really was. His wealthy background wouldn't matter, would it?

Acid chewed his stomach lining. He'd talked to his lawyer at length. Hopefully, when he told Gabby his real identity, the legal documents Ed had prepared would soften the shock.

Would she be mad? Hate him? She wouldn't hold a little thing like money against him, would she?

He was making mountains out of molehills. It wasn't as if he was a completely different person. So he had money. Lots of it. Big deal. There were worse things he could be—like a murderer or an embezzler.

But his conscience goaded him.

He had to tell her soon.

"Dylan?"

He and Gabby both turned at the high-pitched, feminine voice.

"Dylan Kingsley?" A petite blonde wearing a cowboy hat, sundress and cowboy boots rushed over. He froze. Amanda Bethel. Daughter of real-estate moguls James and Elizabeth Bethel. She'd been a key member in his group of college friends. Her smile lit her face. "It's been forever! How are you? I can't believe I'm bumping into you here."

Should he pretend he didn't know her? Of course not. He wasn't that immature.

"Amanda." He'd be polite, keep it short and nudge her on her way. "Good to see you."

"You, too. Oh, this is my husband, Jack." She twined her hand around the guy's arm. The tall, tanned man looked to be in his early thirties. "Dylan and I went to Texas A&M together. Bree, Charlotte and I used to hang out with him and his frat brothers all the time. We had so much fun. Remember skiing in Aspen over Christmas break sophomore year? And I will never forget the month in Paris and Rome with the crew. Do you ever talk to Travis and Dalton?"

"Uh, no, I don't." Too much information—Amanda was throwing out way too much information. He couldn't even look at Gabby for fear of what he'd see. "When did you get married? Have you been in town long? Did you see the old car show? You don't want to miss it." He pointed in the direction of the park.

"We're newlyweds! And no, we just arrived today. Hey, I'm sorry to hear your dad died." She frowned, then turned to her husband. "Jack, your mother probably worked with him. Kenneth Kingsley."

"Oh, right. King Energy," Jack said, looking bored. "Yes, I remember she did a few projects with your father over the years."

Did they have to spell out everything in his past? This was a disaster. A complete disaster.

"Are you getting in line?" Amanda asked. "We'll join

you. Then we can catch up." She flashed her perfect smile toward Gabby. "By the way, I'm Amanda. Are you and Dylan together?"

Gabby stared at the gorgeous woman who'd practically pranced over to them. For once she had no words. Who was this woman with her designer bag and expensive boots? And more importantly, who was the man Gabby had fallen in love with?

The Dylan Kingsley she knew was not the Dylan Kingsley Amanda was greeting.

Had he gone to Texas A&M? Was his father the owner of King Energy, one of the largest energy companies in the country? If he was, why had Dylan let her believe he was just any guy breezing into town?

Had Dylan been lying to her all this time?

Why?

Why would he do that?

"Amanda, this is Gabby Stover. Gabby, Amanda—" He frowned. "You're married now. What is your last name?"

Her laugh tinkled. "Turner. Amanda Turner. We got married last month, and we're working our way to Yellowstone as part of our honeymoon summer."

Gabby dug her fingernails into her palms. Honeymoon summer? Was this woman for real? Who had the money to take an entire summer off for their honeymoon? As the pit in her stomach grew to gaping proportions, Gabby tried to come up with a reasonable explanation for Dylan to be the person Amanda seemed to think he was.

She couldn't think of a single one.

"It was really good to run into you, but we have to go

or we'll be late. We have, ah, plans." Dylan took Gabby's arm and waved to the couple. "Have fun."

She let him lead her away as her head spun. This couldn't be happening—not after such an amazing week. Dylan had stopped by almost every night, and she'd let herself think of them as a couple—a real couple with a future. He'd been terrific with Phoebe, playing with her, changing her, holding her. And Gabby had loved every minute of it. They'd laughed and talked about the future. He'd helped her forget about her job and Allison being gone and Carl's betrayal and her dad's selfish ways.

She'd let herself trust him.

They were almost to the parking lot where Dylan had left his truck. When they reached the tailgate, he finally dropped her hand and stood in front of her. Every muscle in his body seemed to be locked in place, except for his facial muscles—his expression? Pure agony.

And still, she had no words. It might have been the first time in her life she couldn't form a sentence.

Guilt, regret, worry and a shimmer of hope flitted across his face, and it was the last one—the hope—that set her tongue in motion.

"Who was that woman?" She barely recognized her voice it was so calm.

"Amanda and I were in the same friend group in college."

"Texas A&M. I didn't even know you'd gone to college."

A white line rimmed his lips, and his eyes had lost all of their sparkle. "I did. I joined a fraternity, and that was how I met her and her friends—they were in a sorority."

"I see." Her heart started to split open then. "And your dad?"

"Is—was—Kenneth Kingsley, founder and previous owner of King Energy."

"You worked for him."

"I did. I was upper management."

Before her eyes Dylan morphed from traveling cowboy to rich, aimless liar. Rage flickered to life, flaming through her chest.

"The small inheritance wasn't so small." Her words held a bite to them.

"I'm a multimillionaire."

Multimillionaire. A vacuum hollowed out her stomach. She looked back and remembered all his vague replies when they'd met. "So when you said you'd been doing this and that for the past year, you really meant you were bored and traveled because you could."

"I told you I went overseas."

"And you let me believe you were poor."

"You decided that, not me."

"Obviously, you don't need money... Why did you work for Stu? You didn't need a job. You *don't* need a job." Every word she spoke came out harder, sharper, like flint on steel.

"You thought I was a deadbeat."

"You could have explained." Her voice had a strangled quality, kind of like her heart.

"I didn't want to." His jaw tightened.

"Why not?"

"Because I *did* need the job."

She squinted, trying to figure out what he was talking about. "I thought you just said you're a multimillionaire." An out-of-breath sensation had her head spinning.

"It wasn't about the money." He seemed to grow an

inch. "You made it clear I couldn't be around Phoebe unless I had a job."

"Don't give me that." Was he really trying to blame her for his dishonesty? "I didn't want her around a deadbeat. You obviously aren't one."

"I felt like one." His eyes flashed. "Maybe I needed a break from being the son of a mogul."

"And maybe I need a break from my entire life. Do you think I love having to carry on every day as if Allison didn't die? I've supported my sister, my grandma and now my baby—yes, I consider her *my* baby—and I never felt the need to lie to get out of any of it. You lied to me. Even after I told you…" She almost choked on the words. "I told you about my father and Carl. You knew how important honesty is to me, and you stood there and lied to my face."

His face crumpled. "I didn't mean to—"

"Yes, you did." She straightened to her tallest height. "You lied to me on purpose."

His lips drew together in a tight line.

"Why? Why would you do that?" The words flew out. "Why would you look me in the eye and let me believe you were an aimless, traveling cowboy? Was it funny to you? Did you have a good laugh?"

"It wasn't like that."

"Then what was it like? You came into town to meet your niece. Then, for whatever reason, you decide one night isn't enough. You're going to stay. So I told you to get a job." She grimaced as she tried to remember everything. What was she missing? Could anything explain this turn of events? "You could have told me right then, 'Actually, Gabby, I am not a deadbeat and don't need a job,' but you didn't. You went to the ranch." Her voice had risen. "Does Stu know? Does anyone else in town know?" His mouth had dropped open, and she jabbed her finger into his chest. "Am I the last person to know?"

"Know what?" He shook his head, his expression full of pain. "I'm the same guy who showed up a month ago."

"No, you're not." She had to get away from him. "You are not the same guy. Don't kid yourself that you are. You're Dylan Kingsley—spoiled rich kid who can do whatever he wants because of his daddy's money."

And with that, she pivoted to get away.

"Gabby, wait!" He blocked her path, and she shoved his arm to move past him, but he stood his ground. "You're right. I am a spoiled rich kid who can do whatever I want because of my dad's money. I won't argue with you about that."

"Then we're done here."

"No, we're not." He'd been stupid—so stupid—not to have told her all this when he'd arrived. She had every right to hate him, but he couldn't let her walk away. "I should have told you. I wanted to tell you."

"Oh, you *wanted* to tell me. That's great. Let's give the man a round of applause." She pretended to clap. He'd never seen her so angry...and hurt.

"Everything I told you was the truth." He needed to make her see he wasn't an ogre.

"Well, excuse me if I don't care. So your dad sold the company and didn't tell you. Boo-hoo. And your ex only wanted you because of your money. Join the club."

Her words hit him hard. She was right.

He raked his fingers through his hair. "I didn't tell you because I wanted to make sure you weren't like my mother or my ex. Then, I got to know you, and you were nothing like them. But I didn't know what to say. I didn't know how to tell you. And then… I fell in love with you. I love you, Gabby."

"Liar!" She gave him a final, deadly glare, then broke into a run. He tried to catch her, but she weaved through the crowd, and after several minutes, he dropped his hands to his knees to catch his breath.

He'd never hated himself more.

Letting down Gabby was the worst mistake of his life.

## Chapter Thirteen

"Eden—" Gabby gasped for air "—I have to talk to you."

"What's wrong?" Eden's face wrinkled in concern.

"Everything." She'd sprinted to the park where Eden had told her she was joining Mason, Brittany and Noah for the pet parade. Noah was clapping and pointing to a big dog wearing a red, white and blue handkerchief and star-shaped sunglasses. A chihuahua was right behind him.

"Come on, let's go somewhere we can talk." Eden hooked her arm in Gabby's and told Mason and Brittany she'd see them later.

Gabby's heart raced out of control as she tried to get her breathing back to normal. As they strode out of the park, Eden waved to people they knew until they'd reached her car. Gabby barely registered anything. All she was aware of was the aching pain in her heart.

"My house or yours?" Eden asked.

"Can we go to the ranch? I—I can't be home right now."

"Of course."

The first few miles Gabby stayed silent. She didn't know how to start or what to say. The humiliation of her breakup with Carl roared back. Why hadn't she learned her lesson? She'd tried so hard to steer clear of liars.

She hadn't tried hard enough with Dylan.

She'd reverted to stars-in-her-eyes Gabby—the dumb, gullible girl who knew better than to trust a cowboy. But she'd gone ahead and trusted one anyway.

Eden glanced her way, her forehead wrinkled in concern.

Gabby had to tell her. She might as well blurt it all out now. "Dylan is rich."

"That's great!" Eden's eyes lit up.

"It's not great. It's horrible." How could she explain? She stared out the window, not fully understanding why her pain cut so deep.

"Ok-a-ay. Why is it horrible?"

"It just is. I should never have let down my guard. I wish Dylan Kingsley had never come to Rendezvous. My life was fine until he showed up."

"What aren't you telling me?"

"He's a liar. I hate liars. I…I need to think for a minute." The miles rolled along. Gabby kept replaying the scene near the food truck. Was there something she could have done to have found out the truth sooner? Had she missed clues to Dylan's real identity—or purposely overlooked them to give him the benefit of the doubt?

What else had he lied about?

Eden turned down the gravel drive, and soon she'd parked in front of the house. Gabby got out and followed her to the front door. They made their way in silence to the screened-in porch. Sunshine spilled onto a table containing a ceramic pitcher full of fresh-cut pink roses. The sight unleashed Gabby's emotions.

Her life had been like that flower arrangement—simple, pretty, sweet-smelling—until the day Dylan arrived. And now it was shriveled, sour and ugly.

"He lied to me, Eden." She leaned back as she sat on her favorite couch. "He made me believe he was a drifter with no job or money. And he's really the heir to his father's energy empire. His dad owned King Energy. And Dylan inherited his millions."

"That can't be right." She shook her head. "Why would he take the job at Stu's then?"

"Exactly." She thumped her fist on the throw pillow next to her. "Why would he do that? Was he laughing at me? Pulling a prank on us all?"

"I don't know." Eden bit her lower lip. "He doesn't seem the type."

"What type is he?" She flashed her palms, fingers wide. "I thought I knew him, but I don't. Not at all."

"It doesn't change the fact he's Phoebe's uncle."

"It *does* change the fact I don't want her around him. I am not putting her through the mind games I went through as a kid. And I told him that from day one. She is too precious for me to let some lying jerk mess with her emotions."

"You don't have to get it all figured out today," she said quietly. "You're mad. When you cool down, you'll know what to do."

"I know what to do." Gabby nodded swiftly. "I'm done with him and so is Phoebe."

"Is that fair to her?" Eden sighed. "Why don't you tell me what happened?"

She took a deep breath. Maybe Eden could help her

connect the dots. It seemed like there was a giant piece of the puzzle missing, and as much as she tried to convince herself the piece was Dylan as the bad guy, something wasn't adding up.

"We were getting in line for ribs, and this perky blonde bounced over…" She told Eden everything—the college tales, the honeymoon summer and the argument by Dylan's car. "He claimed he got the job because I forced him to so he could be around Phoebe and that he's the same guy he was. Then he threw out 'I love you,' like it was supposed to make everything all right."

She still huffed over the last part. How dare he? How dare he pretend to love her to get his way?

"He told you he loves you?" Eden's eyes grew round. "What did you say?"

"I called him a liar and sprinted to the park to find you."

"Oh." She studied her nails. "Have you considered he might actually love you?"

"No, I haven't," she snapped. "Carl told me he loved me, too. And guess what? He was married. Married! To another woman. Using me, taking my money—so, no, I don't believe a liar who tells me he loves me."

"Married? Oh, Gabby. I had no idea. No wonder you hate cowboys." Eden pressed her hand to her chest. "I'm sorry."

"Yeah, well, so am I." Her anger ebbed and a knot formed in her throat. She'd never told anyone about Carl being married, and the embarrassment of it hit her fresh. "I never should have trusted Dylan. I knew better."

Eden stood. "Why don't I get us some iced tea?"

Gabby nodded, trying to will away the tears forming, but one dropped, then another. She swiped them away.

She'd been such a dummy. Hadn't she told herself not to trust him? That all cowboys were liars? But no, she'd opened her heart…and the worst part was?

She was in love with him.

She loved another lying loser.

Eden returned and handed her a glass.

"I have the worst taste in men."

"You couldn't have known Dylan would lie to you."

"Yes, I could." She took a sip, letting the ice-cold tea soothe her aching throat. "I knew. I knew the minute he walked into the inn that he was trouble. I blame myself."

Eden thought about it a minute. "You're assuming he's like Carl, though. That's not fair. Being rich and being married are two different things."

"Being a scumbag liar is the same thing."

"I've met Dylan, and he is not a scumbag. He seems genuine."

"It's an act." But was it?

"I don't think so, Gabby. I think he really likes you. You told me yourself he's wonderful with Phoebe. Reliable. Always shows up when he says he will."

She could feel her anger weakening. He had been dependable and reliable. But maybe it was all an act. "It really doesn't matter. He lied to me, and I'm done."

"No one is perfect." Eden's lips lifted in a brief, sad smile. "I'm not saying you're wrong. Maybe he is a terrible person. Maybe he's not. But given everything you've told me—he really might love you. And I know you have feelings for him. Shouldn't you at least consider giving him some grace?"

Grace.

What a loaded word.

Grace meant forgiving. And forgiving meant lying down and being a doormat—*Here, walk all over me!*

"I don't think so, Eden." She shook her head.

Eden nodded in understanding, but the strain around her mouth revealed her disappointment. "Pray about it. And I'll pray for you, too."

The last thing she wanted to do was pray. She wanted to crawl into her bed and never come out again.

He never should have stayed in Rendezvous. That night Dylan paced the length of his porch. Back and forth. Back and forth.

His heart was wrapped in barbed wire and getting squeezed tighter by the minute. He'd lost Gabby's trust, and he hadn't realized how important it was until she'd called him a liar.

He was a liar. A fraud.

And tomorrow, when he told Stu the truth—that he'd misled him, had zero ranching experience and didn't need the job or the money—he'd see the same disappointment and loathing from him that he had from Gabby.

Maybe he should sneak out of town tonight. Then he wouldn't have to confess to Stu or worry about bumping into Gabby again.

He paused, set his hand on the porch rail and gazed unseeing out at the stars. Pops from the fireworks in the distance filled the air. He should have been watching them with Gabby. If Amanda hadn't arrived and ruined everything, he'd be sitting there with Gabby now. Holding her hand. Planning how to tell her he wasn't the drifter she'd assumed.

He smacked the rail. It wouldn't have mattered. Either

way, he'd lied, and Gabby would hate him—did hate him. He didn't blame her. He hated himself.

Covering his face with his hands, he wiped his cheeks. How would this affect Phoebe? Would Gabby keep her from him? He couldn't bear not to see the baby's smiling face anymore.

Man, he'd blown it.

The humid air made his skin sticky, but he stayed outside.

What was he going to do now?

He thought of the documents his lawyer had drafted and emailed on Thursday. Dylan had the trust fund ready. He didn't have the child support documents drawn up, though—he'd foolishly believed they wouldn't be necessary. But a future with Gabby wasn't going to happen.

Still, the purchase agreement for the inn would ensure she had the freedom she wanted. He could feel good about that, he supposed.

Maybe the people closest to him were better off without him in their life.

He thought back to the night Sam died. How the paramedics found his little brother on the floor of some guy's apartment. He'd been dead for a few hours. He'd died alone in a stranger's house. His sensitive, caring, brilliant brother—gone. Just like that.

Dylan squeezed his eyes shut. Gabby was right—there was nothing he could have done to prevent his death.

The helplessness of it all crushed him.

He swallowed the lump in his throat. But there was something he could have done to prevent Gabby from hating him. Why hadn't he told her the truth? From the minute he'd met her, he'd been fascinated by her. She'd challenged him, pushed him and ultimately accepted him. He loved her more than he'd ever loved anyone.

Why had he been so stupid?

It had taken him less than two days to figure out Gabby was nothing like his mom or Robin. He should have told her he was rich then.

But he hadn't trusted her. Hadn't really trusted himself.

Did he now?

He peered at the outlines of the ranch before him. He hadn't just fallen in love with Gabby and Phoebe. He'd fallen in love with the cowboy life. This ranch. Helping Stu with the cattle, fishing, being one of the guys.

In some ways Stu was the dad he'd always wanted.

And he'd deceived him, too.

Tomorrow was going to be one of the toughest days of his life, but if he'd learned anything in Rendezvous, he'd learned he was strong enough to handle it.

Was he strong enough, though, to say goodbye to the first real home he'd had in years? To a job he was passionate about? To the woman he loved?

He went inside and closed the door.

It was going to be a long, sleepless night.

He'd do the right thing tomorrow. And after that? A long, empty future awaited him.

## Chapter Fourteen

She had a raging headache, a million questions and zero answers. Gabby padded into Phoebe's room a little after two in the morning. So much of her life had turned upside down in the past month. The only thing she knew for sure was she would do anything to protect and love her precious baby, and not just for Allison's sake—for her own.

*No one is perfect.* As much as she tried to drown out Eden's words from earlier, they kept repeating in her head.

What Dylan had done went beyond not perfect, though. Didn't Eden get it? And her whole grace suggestion—Gabby shook her head. No way. He didn't deserve it.

She kissed her index finger and gently touched Phoebe's forehead with it before heading to the living room. After dragging a soft blanket out of the closet, she settled on the couch, draping it across her legs.

Some offenses were too big to forgive.

Hiking the blanket to her chin, she recounted why she'd been right to cut ties with her dad and with Carl. And now with Dylan.

They'd put their own selfish needs above hers. She'd never asked for much. She hadn't held it against her dad when she and Allison had gone hungry and woken up during the winter months to see their own breath. She hadn't minded helping Carl out financially because she'd loved him. She'd loved both Dad and Carl, and she'd believed they'd loved her, too.

And Dylan… She'd opened up to him, shared the baby with him, introduced him to her friends…

He'd abused her trust.

The same as her father. The same as Carl.

*What he did wasn't as bad as Daddy or Carl.*

Where had that thought come from? Of course, it was as bad.

*I judged him the day he came to Rendezvous. I'm judging him now.*

It hadn't been judging… It had been forming an impression. And she had every right to judge him now.

She would never do to him what he'd done to her. She wouldn't have lied to him about anything. She was honest.

*No one is perfect.*

The secret shame she'd pushed deep inside threatened to burst out of her. She might not have lied to Dylan, but she'd been lying to herself for years.

Why couldn't she get real with herself about Carl? The signs had been there and she'd ignored them. Finding out he was married wasn't as big a shock as she pretended it was.

Her lungs tightened as if she'd been punched.

*I demand the truth, but if I value it so much, I need to be honest with myself.*

She swung her legs over the couch then buried her face

in her hands. It was true—she'd suspected Carl was married but hadn't wanted to believe it. The clues had been there—the odd hours they'd meet and his reluctance to spend time together out in public. One time she'd actually caught him taking off his ring and slipping it inside his pocket, and she'd never said a word.

*I'm not perfect. Eden's right. No one is.*

All the Tuesdays for the past couple of years with her friends came to mind. They prayed for each other and read from the Bible and supported each other. And it made her feel so virtuous. But she was a hypocrite. The biggest hypocrite imaginable.

She wasn't perfect. Never had been. Never would be.

*Lord, forgive me for expecting perfection and not extending grace. I'm not perfect, and yet, You give me grace all the time.*

It was time for her to forgive her father and Carl.

*Lord, I forgive Carl. I don't like him or ever want to see him again, but I forgive him. And I forgive my dad. Please give me peace about them.*

It hit her that forgiveness didn't always mean reconciliation, nor did it make her a doormat.

Maybe the real reason she didn't want to forgive Dylan was out of fear.

If she forgave him, allowed him back into her heart, he might hurt her again. She might wake up in a few months and realize she'd been right all along that he'd never cared about her the way she did him.

But if she didn't forgive…would she expect every man who came into her life to live up to a set of standards no one could reach?

The ticktock of the clock kept her company as she struggled with how to move forward.

He'd said he was the same guy who'd arrived a month ago, but could she believe him?

She didn't know.

Every man she'd let into the most special place in her heart had let her down. And now that she'd fallen for Dylan, she couldn't get the image of them together out of her mind. For years she'd wanted it all but had refused to admit it. She wanted a loving husband, a family of her own.

Gabby rubbed her temple. She didn't even know what a loving husband looked like.

She'd thought he looked like Dylan, but now? She had no clue.

"I need to talk to you." Dylan held his cowboy hat between his hands as he stood on Stu's porch the next morning. The sun was still low on the horizon, but he knew Stu would be up. Dylan hadn't gotten any sleep, and his stubble made his face as scratchy as his heart.

"What's going on? Something wrong with the horses? The cattle?" Stu shoved his stockinged feet into cowboy boots.

"No, nothing's wrong with the ranch." He sighed. "It's me."

Somehow Stu had managed to insert his toothpick between his teeth. He nodded, the toothpick moving up and down. "We'll talk better riding."

They strode in silence across the yard to the stables and tack room, and it didn't take long to saddle up and head down the trail toward the creek. The heat was already rising as they navigated familiar gullies and climbed hills. Dylan's nerves ratcheted the farther they went. At what point would Stu stop? And how was Dylan going to explain? He'd figured he'd tell Stu everything on his porch, sprint back to his cabin, load the truck, stop at Gabby's and…disappear.

"You see that clearing up ahead?" Stu pointed to a clump of trees with sunlight shining through them. "We'll stop there."

Soon they'd dismounted and were tying off the horses. Dylan marveled at the beautiful vista. They stood on a grassy hill with a panoramic view of the mountains. Smaller ridges lined the ground between them and the mountain range.

"Wow." He took it all in for a minute.

"This is where Josiah and I used to come every September. We'd talk about the ranch. What worked that year and what we'd do differently the next."

Now he felt even worse. He was going to ruin a special spot for Stu.

"Maybe we should ride somewhere else." He looked back at the horses.

"Nah. This is a good talking place. Have a seat." Stu gestured to a few stumps, and Dylan sat on one. His boss took the other. "What's on your mind?"

He didn't know where to begin. All night he'd tossed and turned, going over the same mistakes again and again. Maybe he'd be best off admitting he was rich right off the bat.

"I haven't been honest with you." Dylan stared down at his dirty cowboy boots, then met Stu's eyes. "I came here under false pretenses. I've never ranched. I don't need the money. I don't even need this job."

The toothpick bobbed slowly.

"I'm rich." He made the word sound like he'd told him he was a serial killer. "My dad owned King Energy. I used to work for him, but he sold the company. He didn't want me running it. Then he died about a month later. I inherited everything."

The toothpick paused. Was that a twinkle in Stu's eyes?

He pressed on. "My stepbrother died of a drug overdose a few weeks after Dad sold the company. And I didn't even take his call the week he died."

Why wasn't Stu saying anything?

He didn't know what else to say, so he sat there.

"Is that everything?" Stu asked.

He almost said yes, but it would be a lie, and Gabby hated liars—and he didn't want to be that guy anymore. "No, there's more. I love this job, and I'm in love with Gabby Stover. I lied to her, too. She hates me. I don't blame her."

"What'd you lie to her about?"

"The same as I did you. She thought I was some deadbeat cowboy for hire. She was the one who told me to work here, so I did."

"Why'd you do that?"

"I—" He raised his face to the sky. It was going to sound so stupid. But he owed Stu the truth. "I always wanted to be a cowboy."

Stu's face gave away nothing. "Was it the only reason?"

"No." He hung his head. "I'd spent the past year traveling around the world. And I had no purpose. No place to belong. I guess I wanted to see if I could belong here."

"And did you?"

"Yeah." Closing his eyes, he inhaled the fresh Wyoming air. Not a sound could be heard except birds singing in the trees and the gentle breeze against the leaves. "I did. I do. I belong here."

"So what's the problem?"

"What do you mean? I lied to you. I lied to her. I've got to go."

"Says who?"

"Says..." He hesitated. It wouldn't be fair to stay here if Gabby hated him. He wouldn't make her life miserable. "Me."

"Bah." He waved him off. "I don't care about any of that."

He didn't?

"I knew you weren't familiar with ranching, but you showed up at the right time. You're a hard worker, dependable, and you've got the heart for it. I've been struggling since Josiah died—even his horse, Jethro, was struggling—until you came along. You've given me a spring in my step to keep this place going."

The words wriggled into his heart, coated the raw spots with healing balm.

"I don't know what went on with your daddy, but it seems to me he missed out on a fine young man. As for your brother and the drugs, well, you can't compete with them. He was addicted, son. Nothing you could have done. Let it go."

A sudden burst of emotion pressed tears against his eyes.

Stu kicked at the ground. "I've hired a lot of cowboys over the years, and they weren't all living the right way. I tried to clean them up, too, and..." He turned away. "I couldn't. It takes time and prayer to realize there's only so much you can do when someone is fighting an addiction. It's their battle. Not yours."

Dylan clenched his jaw to keep his emotions under wraps.

"Listen," Stu said. "I've known Gabby Stover for years. She's a quality gal. A fine woman. And she's never met a cowboy she liked…until you came along. I don't know what all you two've got going, but if it's a matter of you not telling her you've got money, well, I think you'll be able to work it out."

Dylan wanted to believe it, but… "I don't think so. Honesty is very important to her."

"Well, then, I guess we'd better pray about it, huh? Cuz I want you to stay on as my right-hand man. Yes, you'll get a raise. No, you will not turn down the pay. You earn your money around here."

Wait. Stu wasn't disappointed in him? He was promoting him?

"I don't know what to say," Dylan said, shaking his head in wonder.

"Say yes."

He wanted to—oh, how he wanted to. "I have to talk to Gabby. I appreciate the offer, but I can't accept it unless… well, I probably won't be able to accept it." Stu had a forgiving nature, but he doubted Gabby had cooled down or would ever see him through compassionate eyes again.

"We'll see about that. Now, head back and get cleaned up. You want to look your best when you talk to her."

Stu didn't get it—Gabby wasn't just any girl. She'd let him into her life and allowed him to spend time with the baby. She'd trusted him. And he'd let her down.

They mounted the horses once more and headed back.

The urge to pray hit him hard.

*Thank You, God, for Stu's friendship. He may be the*

*first person who's ever accepted me for who I am. Well, that's not true. Gabby did, too. And that's why I love her.*

He didn't deserve Stu, either, but the man had brushed away his dishonesty as if it was nothing.

The same way God did.

*You're the One who's always accepted me, haven't You? How did I not see it?*

With each passing moment, his heart expanded. The realization hit him—whether he was worthy of Gabby or not, he finally felt worthy of himself.

He was finally comfortable in his own skin.

He was Dylan Kingsley, and he didn't need to define himself by his father, his money or his past.

He'd found himself in Rendezvous. He'd found home.

After three hours of sleep, two cups of coffee and a full hour of ruminating, Gabby was ready to think logically about Dylan.

She'd already gathered all of the details about his life that he'd shared with her, including Sam's death, his father's selling the family company, his traveling around the world, his mom using him as a pawn after the divorce and how his ex manipulated him for money, too.

She didn't think he'd lied about any of it.

The facts appeared in a different light when she'd thought he was an everyday Joe as opposed to a multimillionaire.

The only thing he'd really hidden from her—that she knew of—was the fact he was rich. And even she could concede he'd had good reasons for it.

Given what little she knew of his childhood and his ex, it made sense for him to not advertise he was wealthy.

She took a long drink of coffee number three. Plus

there was her own attitude. She cringed thinking of how she'd labeled Nolan as a rich kid who'd be nothing without his daddy's money. And then she'd slapped the same label on Dylan yesterday afternoon.

Not her finest moment.

Which left her…where? How was she supposed to move forward?

She still loved him. But she couldn't trust him. And deep down, she didn't believe he loved her. Why would he? They'd known each other for a month, spent time playing with the baby and gone on one date. Guys like him wouldn't fall in love that quickly, and especially not with her.

Tracing the rim of her mug, she sighed. Maybe that was the real problem. She still didn't believe a guy could love her.

If she was wrong about Dylan—if he *did* love her—what would she be throwing away?

Like a movie montage, she pictured him standing in her doorway with a pizza, then trying to diaper Phoebe for the first time, laughing at her tales from the inn, grinning as he explained how to vaccinate a calf. And then she saw him kissing her, how right it had felt to be in his arms, how good it had felt to be wanted, needed.

His kiss hadn't demanded—it had asked, it had given—just like Dylan himself.

Had he ever demanded anything from her?

She tapped the side of her mug. He'd accepted her conditions from day one. He'd followed her schedule, gotten a job on Stu's ranch, been there when she needed him. He'd spent the last year traveling alone. He'd lost both his dad and brother. He'd also lost his job—his place in the world.

Suddenly, his money seemed like the least important thing about him.

Her heart climbed to her throat. She'd been wrong about him. So wrong.

He really was the same guy who'd shown up last month.

Why else would he work long hours on a ranch and live in a tiny cabin with no air-conditioning? Yes, it was to be near Phoebe, but that couldn't be the only reason. He loved her—had to love her.

Was he still in town? Or had she driven him away?

Glancing down at her attire, she shuddered. Shower first. Call him later.

It was time to give him the benefit of the doubt.

It was time to take a chance—a real chance—on love.

## Chapter Fifteen

Dylan took a deep breath and went through his mental checklist. Bouquet of peonies from Gretchen Sable's flower garden. Check. Folder with legal documents. Check. Humble attitude. Check. Tell Gabby she was everything to him and he didn't want to live without her or Phoebe. Almost check.

After returning to his cabin earlier, he'd promptly showered and put on his Sunday best. Stu had taken it upon himself to call Gretchen to ask for the flowers, then texted Dylan that Gretchen would have them ready after church. Dylan had prayed for strength during the early service then picked up the flowers on his way to Gabby's place. He just hoped she would answer the door and hear him out.

He had so much to say.

With two sharp knocks, he stood his ground, clenching and unclenching his jaw as he strained to hear footsteps. He was preparing to knock again when the door opened. Gabby held Phoebe on her hip, and her eyes widened as she took him in.

"Can I come in?" He fully expected her to slam the

door in his face. She didn't say a word, simply moved to the side so he could enter. She wore a pretty sundress, and her hair flowed over her shoulders. His heart skipped a beat at how beautiful and vulnerable she looked. "These are for you."

She took them and set the paper-wrapped bouquet on the table.

This wasn't boding well. At least she'd let him inside. He held his finger out, and Phoebe wrapped her tiny hand around it, grinning and bouncing. "Hey, smiley."

Gabby still hadn't spoken, so he stood there awkwardly for a moment.

"Can we sit down?" he asked.

"Sure." They went to the living room. Gabby put Phoebe on her play mat, then sat on the chair with one leg crossed over the other, while he set his folder next to him and perched on the edge of the couch.

"First, I apologize for not being honest with you. I misled you about my financial situation." Her face became a plaster mask. He couldn't detect a single emotion. "And, yes, my dad owned King Energy and I worked for him. Everything else I told you was true. Sam died soon after Dad sold the company. I'd stupidly thought Dad and I would grow close and he'd make me his partner. Instead, he sold it and I found out from his administrative assistant. He died two weeks later. A week after that, my ex-girlfriend—who dumped me because in her words I was 'going nowhere'—came back into my life all sympathy and smiles. It was at that point I took off. Flew to Europe."

The expression in her eyes softened.

He continued. "You told me you didn't want Phoebe around a deadbeat—and you were right. I was a deadbeat when I showed up here. I hadn't had a job in over a year, and my position before then was a glorified token job given to me by my dad. I might as well have been a drifting cowboy looking for work—I had no purpose, no reason to live, really."

She shifted in her seat.

"So when I came here and saw Sam's eyes in the cutest baby I'd ever seen, something in me sprang to life. And the fact you weren't taking any nonsense anchored me. You even mistook me for a cowboy. As a teen, the only thing I aspired to be was a cowboy—I admired the tough, hardworking men I'd watched on my friend's ranch. And I thought, yeah, I don't have to travel anymore. I could be a cowboy for a while."

He rubbed his hand across his mouth. It was time to tell her the scary stuff. *God, give me courage.*

"Stu took a chance on me. Working with him makes me feel alive—and he's been patient with me, teaching me things my father didn't. And you—you took a chance on me. You let me spend time with you and Phoebe. Showed me how to take care of her. Introduced me to your friends. Made me feel like I could belong here."

Tears glistened in her eyes, and he wasn't sure if it was a good sign or a bad one.

"I knew I had to tell you the truth, but I was so afraid you'd reject me. This is the first place that's felt like home for me. I have a purpose here. Because of you." He reached for the file and opened it. He took out the first set of documents and handed them to her. She refused them, so he set them on the end table near her. "I always intended on providing for Sam's child. I've set up a trust fund for Phoebe. That's the paperwork for it."

Gabby stared unseeing up at the corner of the ceiling. A tear dropped on her cheek.

"I can see you're upset. I don't blame you. If I could do it over, I would have told you the truth the day after I arrived. It was unforgivable. You're right—I know how much you value honesty. And it may be late, but I'm being as real as I can possibly be right now. You gave me hope. You helped me find myself. And I love you. I love you so much. I will never stop loving you."

He pulled out the other sheaf of papers in his file.

"That's why I want you to have this." He handed her the papers. "You've given and given and given your entire life. Maybe it's time someone gave you something for a change."

Her lips were drawn together, and she still didn't speak. But she took the papers from him. She scanned the top sheet, her face paling.

He braced himself. Would she accept his gift?

"You can't be serious." Her voice held a spark of anger.

"I'm serious."

"You bought me Mountain View Inn?" She didn't sound happy.

"I did."

"It's bad enough you lied to me, but now you think you can buy my affection?" She threw the packet at him. The staple kept the papers from scattering. "I don't want your money. I don't want your inn."

Didn't he understand her at all? Gabby's heart couldn't take any more of this. Every word he'd said had pierced her in the most vulnerable places. His sincerity and the picture he'd painted of his life before Rendezvous had made her want to wrap him in her arms and never let him go. His money hadn't made him entitled. It had made him lonely, isolated and purposeless.

And then he had to go and buy her the inn.

"You can *never* buy my love." She sprang to her feet and crossed her arms over her chest. "I don't know how they do it down in Texas or in the circles you run in, but around here you don't give someone an expensive gift and think she'll fall into your arms."

"That's not what this is about." He stood, too, running his fingers through his hair.

"You know, I was ready to forgive you. And my heart hurts for you, for your life before you arrived. But I don't think I can forgive this." She waved her hand toward the packet of papers, which had landed on the couch.

"I'm not trying to buy your love. It never crossed my mind. I had my lawyer contact the listing agent last week. You deserve to own the inn. You don't need to worry about Nolan or anyone else coming in and making your life miserable. I don't want you to fear losing your job. You've been running the place for years. You have a vision for it. The only thing you don't have is the money to buy it. And it's the only thing I had to give you."

"It's not the only thing you can give me, Dylan." She lifted her chin. "It isn't even the best thing. You don't get it, do you?"

"Get what?" His eyes pleaded with her.

"Your money is the least attractive thing about you." She stared at him. Why did he have to say such nice things? Why did he have to be so generous? She couldn't hate him, no matter how much she wanted to. A sense of peace filled her body from her head to her toes.

She was ready to take a chance on him.

"You're humble. Undemanding. Generous. Kind. The

thing I admire most about you is your lack of ego. You're living in a tiny cabin without air-conditioning, working as a ranch hand, being considerate of my schedule, helping with the baby. You've shown me what real love—a partner—looks like."

His shoulders drew back, and his mouth dropped open.

"I don't like that you lied to me—"

"It was unforgivable." His chin dropped to his chest.

"No, Dylan, it wasn't." She took a step closer to him. "Nothing is unforgivable. And nothing should be. I forgive you."

He met her eyes, and his gleamed with wonder.

"As for those ridiculous papers—" she pursed her lips, shook her head and brought her fist to her mouth "—I don't even know what to say. So I guess it's time for me to be honest with you."

He inhaled and held it.

"I judged you from the minute I met you. Decided you were just like my daddy and my ex-boyfriend. Everything you did I saw through eyes colored by my past. And that wasn't fair to you. You confessed very private, personal things to me, and I'm going to do the same. Carl, my ex-boyfriend, didn't just use me for money. He also lied to me in the most terrible way. He was married, and I didn't know it. But as time wore on, I noticed signs. I suspected he had a wife, and I was so smitten, I pretended I hadn't."

"Gabby—"

"No, let me finish." She held her arm out. "Letting you into my life was hard not only because I didn't trust you, but because I didn't trust myself. You were patient with me. And I slowly began to think…"

He looked like he was going to speak. But she couldn't

let him, not yet, not when she still had the most important thing to say.

"Dylan—" her throat grew so tight she almost choked "—I love you. I'm scared. I'm terrified you're going to break my heart."

Wonder filled his eyes. In two steps he was directly in front of her, his arms wrapped around her back, and she sank into his embrace.

"Do you mean it? Do you really love me?" He leaned back to stare into her eyes.

She nodded, tears threatening to fall again.

"I'll never break your heart. It's the most precious gift I've ever been given. I'll do anything to earn your trust."

"It's hard for me," she admitted. "Do you think you have the patience to take it slow?"

"I have forever, Gabby." His grin spread across his face. "I love you. Nothing could change that."

When his lips pressed against hers, she knew taking a chance on him would be the best decision she ever made. A thrill rushed through her body. She'd found a man who valued her. She wanted those arms around her for the rest of her life.

He broke away and stroked her hair. "What do you want me to do about the inn? Shred the purchase agreement? I didn't buy it to win your love. I hope you know that."

For the first time it hit her. He truly had bought Mountain View Inn for her—not as a bribe, but as a gift.

"You really bought me the inn?" She couldn't wrap her brain around it.

He nodded. "No strings attached."

"There are always strings somewhere…" She narrowed her eyes.

"Not this time." His hands slid down to her waist. "Go ahead and read the purchase agreement if you don't believe me. It's in your name. My name is nowhere on it—I was the money behind it, nothing more."

He shifted toward the couch to get the papers, but she tugged him back to her. "I'll take your word for it, cowboy. Why don't you kiss me again?"

His lips curved into a wicked grin. "Anything you want. Just say you'll be mine."

"I'm yours."

As he lowered his mouth to hers, a loud "ba-ba-ba" interrupted them. Phoebe had pulled herself up and was standing next to the couch, holding on to it and bouncing.

Dylan met Gabby's eyes and laughed. "Someone's happy."

"That makes two of us." She stepped back. "What happens now? Does everything change?"

"Nothing's changing." He shook his head. "Stu wants me to stay on as his right-hand man. I'm getting a raise."

His face was so bright with joy, she couldn't help but laugh. "A raise, huh?"

"Yeah, it feels good to earn an honest day's wage."

She couldn't argue with that.

"I have a lot to learn—about ranching, raising a baby, Wyoming…" He tugged her close to him again.

"I'll be happy to help fill you in." She wound her arms around his neck.

"I need a lot of help." He dropped a kiss on her lips.

"Well, I'm good with the baby and Wyoming thing. But ranching? You're on your own."

His grin spread from ear to ear. "Thanks, Gabby."

"For what?"

"For giving me a place to belong. For giving me a purpose."

"You have it all wrong." She pressed her finger in the cleft of his chin. "You gave me a place to belong. In your arms. Thank you for buying me the inn. I…I can't believe you did it. No one has ever been so extravagant."

"Is it too much? I can sell it…"

"Don't you dare, Dylan Kingsley." She playfully slapped his chest. "I want it. Thank you. I don't know how I'll ever thank you enough."

"Why don't you start with a kiss?"

"Done."

# *Epilogue*

❦

"You can't trust just any cowboy." Gabby didn't look up from her computer at the front counter of Mountain View Inn. The late October sun streamed through the windows, landing on the new hardwood floors that had been laid as part of the hotel renovation. "You've got to make sure they have character—values."

"I'd give the one outside a shot if he had eyes for any girl other than you." Stella scanned the printout of the housekeeping checklist. She'd gotten more dependable in the past four months. There was hope for her yet.

"I wouldn't blame you." Gabby smiled at her.

Dylan walked inside carrying a bouquet of two dozen red roses. He wore dark jeans, cowboy boots and a button-down shirt open at the collar. His Stetson completed the picture of quintessential cowboy. She inwardly swooned. The man filled her heart.

"I'm looking for Gabrielle Stover." His brown eyes twinkled.

"You're looking at her." She bit her lower lip in anticipation. What was he doing? This wasn't the first time he'd brought her flowers, but something was different about him.

"Come with me." He held out his hand, and she exchanged a curious glance with Stella, who shrugged, before rounding the counter and taking his hand.

He led her to the lobby and stopped in front of the floor-to-ceiling stone fireplace complete with a crackling fire. He faced her then, standing inches from her.

"These are for you." He handed her the flowers. She inhaled their lovely scent.

"Thank you."

Then, keeping her hand in his, he lowered himself to one knee. Her heart began hammering so quickly, she thought it might explode. He was proposing!

"Gabrielle Stover, four months ago, I walked into this very inn, and my life changed forever. I found my niece. I found my calling. And I found myself. I couldn't have found any of it without you. You're the reason I wake up smiling. You're the reason I fall asleep anticipating another day. You're my everything. I want to spend forever with you. Will you marry me?"

He held a small, square box in his hand. He opened it, revealing an intricate diamond ring.

She blinked away the tears. "Yes, oh yes!"

He slid the ring on her finger, and she threw her arms around his neck and kissed him. He rose, not breaking their kiss. Then he tightened his grip and deepened the kiss. And she was lost. Lost in the safety of his arms and heart.

A round of applause interrupted them, and they both turned. The lobby had filled with friends and guests. Eden ran to her and hugged her, her eyes misting up.

"What did I tell you? You found your dream man." Eden beamed.

"You were right. It's time we found yours." She nudged her side.

"First things first. Let me get settled into my new apartment." Eden grinned.

Mason and Brittany approached.

"Couldn't be happier for you, Gabby." Mason hugged her then turned to Dylan. "You've got one of the best here, don't ever forget it."

"Trust me, I know." Dylan beamed, not taking his eyes off her.

Stu clapped Dylan on the shoulder. "I guess this means you're moving off-site."

"I'll still be on the ranch at the crack of dawn. Don't worry."

"I won't." Stu winked, his toothpick bobbing as he turned to congratulate Gabby.

"We have plenty of time to figure it out." She patted Dylan's chest. Then it hit her—Phoebe would finally have a daddy. A real daddy. The waterworks threatened behind her eyes again, and she had to close them tight for a moment.

"Say, have you two seen Gretchen around?" Stu asked.

"Um, I don't know." Dylan peered through the crowd. "Is that her over there?"

Stu turned and made a beeline to the group of church ladies in the corner.

"Sugar, you've found your Herb." Babs hugged Gabby and kissed both her cheeks. "I'm proud of you. You took a chance."

"Because of you." She squeezed Babs tightly. "I needed your tough love."

"You've got a fine cowboy, Gabby. Something tells me you two have a lifetime of adventures waiting."

"Babs?" She searched for the right words. "Thanks for being my mom away from mom."

"You're like a daughter to me." It was Babs's turn to get teary-eyed. "Oh, now look at me. I'll be right back. My mascara is running."

Stella came over. "Nicole wanted to come, but she's got her hands full with the triplets."

"You knew about this?" Gabby was surprised Stella had been so good about keeping the secret.

"Of course, I knew. Babs threatened to hack off my hair if I spilled a word."

Gabby laughed. "Well, I wouldn't expect Nicole to be here. Tell her I'll stop by to see the babies this weekend sometime."

After everyone congratulated them and dispersed, Gabby picked up the roses, inhaling their aroma again, and then admired her ring.

"I guess it's official." Dylan stared into her eyes.

"You're stuck with me, cowboy."

"I wouldn't have it any other way."

\* \* \* \* \*

# A RANCHER TO TRUST

Laurel Blount

For Leigh M. Hall, my wild and crazy sister—
and my first and truest friend.

Therefore if any man be in Christ, he is
a new creature: old things are passed away;
behold, all things are become new.
—*2 Corinthians* 5:17

# *Chapter One*

As Dan Whitlock pulled his pickup to a stop in the middle of the quiet Oklahoma cemetery, his cell phone buzzed against his chest for the third time. He fished it out of his shirt pocket and checked the screen. Sure enough, he had two missed calls and a text from rancher Colton McAllister.

Call me.

Dan looked out the truck window at the snowy cemetery and weighed his options. He'd planned to get this private errand over and done with before he touched base with Colt, but the new boss of the Bar M Ranch wasn't known for his patience. Might as well go ahead and call him back. Then maybe Dan could tend to his personal business in peace.

Colt answered the phone on the first ring. "About time."

"I was driving. Sorry, Colt, but my advice is pass on these heifers. They look a lot better on paper than they do in person. I know how bad you want to get in on the

Shadow Lady bloodline, but trust me, these aren't your girls."

Colt made an irritated noise. "I should have figured as much. Price was too good. I'll start looking in a higher dollar range and see what I can find."

The Bar M didn't have that kind of money to play around with right now. Dan started to argue but thought better of it.

*Not my call*, he reminded himself, *not anymore*. As the elderly Gordon McAllister's foreman, Dan had overseen the day-to-day ranch operations. But now that Colt's grandfather had passed on, Colt had shifted from being Dan's friend to being Dan's boss. The younger McAllister preferred to handle things on his own.

"Anyway," Colt said, "I appreciate you taking a look. You about ready to head home?"

Dan's gaze drifted back to the scattered gravestones, sparkling icily in the brittle January sunlight. "Yeah, shortly. I have something I need to do first."

"No rush on this end. Take your time."

Dan could barely hear his friend's muffled words over the whistle of the Wyoming wind and the sound of cattle lowing. Colt probably had his phone clenched between his chin and his shoulder, which meant his hands were busy with something else.

"You out choring? I thought you were supposed to be helping Angie take care of those new twins of yours."

"I'm fixing that section of fence in the south pasture. I was going stir-crazy in the house, so Angie finally shooed me outside. Oh yeah. She said you had a phone call yesterday."

"Who from?"

"Some girl, Angie said. She wanted to talk to you,

wouldn't say why. Angie thought it might be something important, though, because the number came up Pine Valley, Georgia. Isn't that your hometown?"

Dan tightened his grip on the phone. "This girl. She give Angie a name?"

"Yeah. Bailey somebody, I think it was."

*Bailey.* Dan's skin prickled in a way that had nothing to do with the sharp air finding its way into the truck cab. "Bailey Quinn?"

"That sounds right." Something in his tone must have alerted Colt, because his friend added, "You sound like you just took a punch in the gut. Who's this Bailey girl to you?"

Dan didn't answer. He stared through the fogged windshield at a nearby tombstone, darkened with age, the name barely visible.

Who was Bailey to him?

At one point in his life—everything.

Now? She was a memory so full of regret that the pain could reach across more than a decade of time and stop his heart cold. And she definitely wasn't somebody he wanted to talk about. Not with Colt.

Not with anyone.

After a second or two of silence, Colt went on, "Angie told her you weren't here, and she left a number. Said she needed to talk to you, please, as soon as possible. Nice-sounding girl, Angie said."

"Text me the number." He tried not to ask, but he couldn't help it. "Did Bailey say anything else?"

"Not that Angie mentioned. Is this girl one of your folks, Dan? Because if you want to go back to Georgia and see about her, you go ahead. You're not needed here, so there's no reason for you to hurry back."

"Well, that's never a good thing to hear from an employer."

Colt made a frustrated noise. "You know what I mean. And you also know I don't think of you as an employee. You're family to me and Angie, just like you were to Grandpa. Maybe your last name isn't McAllister, but you're one of us, just the same."

*You're one of us.* High praise from one of the most clannish families in all of Wyoming. "You going mushy on me, Colt?"

"If I am, it's not my fault. It's the twins. Nobody's sleeping around here, and there's way too much crying."

"They're cute little stinkers, though." That was an understatement. Dan's honorary niece and nephew were so adorable they could make any man hungry to have a couple kids of his own.

"Yeah, they're cute, all right. That's how they suck you in. Trust me, Dan. This parenting-twins stuff is harder than ranching any day. No wonder I'm going soft. It's enough to send any man around the bend. I'll get Angie to text you that number. And listen, if you've got some kind of trouble brewing back home, you head there without a second thought, okay? We can manage until you get back."

"Thanks, Colt." Dan disconnected the phone and shoved it back into his pocket. He sat in the chilling truck cab, thinking hard.

So after all these years, Bailey Quinn had called him.

Her face came into his mind as clearly as if he'd seen her yesterday. Eyes such a rich, dark shade of brown that you could only make out her pupils if you were close enough to kiss her. He recalled the soft curve of her cheek and the sassy way she'd tilt her head when she was teasing you—which, Bailey being Bailey, was most of the time.

Years back, not long after hiring on at the Bar M, Dan had been out checking a fence line on a June morning. A pretty, dark-feathered bird perched on a strand of barbed wire had cocked its head at him in just the same way. Pain had ricocheted out of nowhere with such force that his knees had almost buckled under him.

And that was just a dumb bird.

Even though the phone hadn't vibrated, he took it back out of his pocket and squinted at the screen. Nothing. Likely it would take Angie McAllister a while to get around to texting him Bailey's number. Colt's wife had her hands full wrangling their three-week-old babies, Josie and Finn.

In the meantime, Dan might as well do what he'd come here to do.

He turned the sound up on his phone so he wouldn't miss the text, got out of the truck and threaded his way through the graveyard, his boots crunching in the snow. It didn't take him long to find what he was looking for.

"Hey, there, Gordon." Dan removed his brown Stetson and then reached down and brushed the mounded snow from the top of his old boss's tombstone.

*Gordon Finnley McAllister.* The name was engraved deeply into solid gray granite Colt had chosen for his grandfather's memorial stone. It was one of the few decisions the new rancher had made that Dan hadn't privately second-guessed. Granite was a good fit for the stubborn old man he'd known.

Gordon McAllister's mind and body had been toughened by the wild land he loved, but the old rancher's heart had been shaped by the Lord he'd followed faithfully—

and gentled by the wife who lay slumbering beside him now. Josephine Andrews McAllister had always missed her Oklahoma home, so Gordon had buried her here, among her people. And when his time came, he'd asked to be laid beside her instead of in his beloved Wyoming. That request had shocked a lot of people back in Broken Bow, given how passionately the old man had loved the family ranch.

It hadn't shocked Dan at all. He knew Gordon had loved his Josephine more.

Dan cleared his throat. "Colt wanted me to take a look at some heifers a couple towns over, so I thought…while I was in the neighborhood." This felt awkward. But he forced himself to keep on going. "Colt's doing you proud, Gordon. He's got the makings of a solid rancher. Not as good as you, not yet. But one day he will be. I've stayed on to help get him started, like I promised you I would. But he's just about got his feet under him now, and I'm thinking…" Dan fought the lump that had risen up in his throat. This was hard. "I'm thinking maybe it's getting time for me to up stakes and move along. That's why I came by. To let you know. And to bring you something."

He fished a brass token from his coat pocket. It gleamed dully in the palm of his hand. "This is the chip I got from my support group when I was one year sober. You came to see me get it, eleven years ago this March. Getting through that first year without a drink was the first thing I'd done right in a long time, and one of the toughest. I'd never have managed it without you and that church you kept dragging me to. I've carried this thing with me ever since, but now I'm leaving it here with you." Dan gently placed the token on top of the grave marker. "I came here to thank you, Gordon McAllister, for taking me in and forgiving me when I didn't deserve it. I'll owe you a debt for the rest of my life, and me leaving the Bar M won't change that any. If Colt or Angie or those great-grandkids of yours ever need my help, I'll be there for them. No matter what. You've got my word on that."

He stood there for a long moment, his hand covering the token, the cold of the stone seeping into his fingers. Finally he lifted his hand and cleared his throat.

"That's all I needed to say, I guess. I'd best be getting along. Rest good, Gordon, here with your Josephine. You've earned it."

Then Dan settled his Stetson back on his head and started back toward the truck.

His phone chirped loudly just as he was settling into the seat. Angie had sent him a number, followed by, Colt says you go on to Georgia if you need to. Don't worry about us.

He wasn't worried about the McAllisters. Colt could run the Bar M just fine without Dan's help, even with a pair of brand-new babies thrown into the bargain.

But Dan had never planned to go back to Pine Valley, Georgia. He had his reasons for that, reasons that still tore him up when he allowed himself to think about them.

Which was why he didn't allow it.

Then again, if Bailey Quinn had reached out to him after what he'd done, after all these years…she must need something.

Something big.

He recalled something Gordon used to say when they'd hit a snag in their work. "Sometimes you gotta go back a few fence posts, son, and fix a crooked one before you can go forward. Ain't no fun, but it's the right thing to do. Every man makes his share of mistakes, but they ain't nothing to be ashamed of unless you leave 'em standing."

Dan had left some pretty busted-up fence posts standing back in Pine Valley. He should have done what he could to fix them a long time ago, but he'd kept putting it off. It was no easy thing, going back to the place where you'd behaved the worst, facing up to what you'd done before you found your feet and your faith.

He was at a turning point right now. He was about to strike out on his own again, away from the shelter of the Bar M and the McAllisters. He needed all his fence posts as straight as he could get them, and it looked like God had just handed Dan an opportunity to get that done.

Whether he liked it or not.

*Lord, what do You want me to do here?*

Dan knew the answer almost before he'd finished the question. The things he'd done and the people he'd hurt—like Bailey Quinn—deserved a lot more from him than a phone call. It was long past time for him to face up to them and make whatever amends he could.

Dan looked back down at his phone and slowly typed out a reply.

Headed to Georgia. Tell Colt to text me if he needs anything.

Then he hit Send, dropped the phone on the seat and shoved the truck into first gear.

"Lucy Ball, drop that right now!" Bailey Quinn jogged around the corner of her old clapboard farmhouse, trying to keep the mischievous Jersey calf in sight. "You'll choke!"

The long-legged red calf tossed her head and flexed her jaw, crackling the plastic of the stolen water bottle she held clenched in her teeth. She was having fun, and she was in no hurry for this game to be over.

The calf loped by the chicken coop, making the young Barred Rock pullets flutter and cluck, before slowing to a stop by the open barn door. Bailey halted, too, just at the corner of the back porch, her heart pounding.

"That's right," she murmured coaxingly. "Go in there, where I might have a shot at cornering you!"

The valuable calf had been a farm-warming present from her friends Abel and Emily Whitlock.

Abel had shaken his head ruefully when Bailey thanked him. "Let's see how you feel in a year or so. I know you've been wanting a milk cow, but they're a sight more work than most people realize. They've got to be milked rain or shine, whether you're sick or not, Christmas Day same as any other. Then there's the milk you'll have to deal with. A good milker will give you gallons a day. That's a lot for one person to deal with. And you can't sell raw milk at that store of yours, not unless you get state certified, and that's near about more trouble and expense than it's worth."

Bailey had only laughed. She didn't care if owning a milk cow was going to be a lot of work. In fact, she was counting on it.

Now that her organic grocery store was well established, she'd been hungry for a new challenge. She missed the invigorating struggle of building up a fledgling business. Working hard was what made her feel alive. And the tougher the work, the more Bailey liked it.

Given how this was going, that was a good thing. The minute she'd seen the calf's fluffy red topknot, Bailey had christened her Lucille Ball after the iconic redheaded television star, and Lucy seemed determined to live up to her name. A day didn't go by that the animal didn't find some kind of trouble to get into. She was cute as could be, but right now Bailey almost wished Emily and Abel had given her a toaster.

Lucy blinked her long-lashed brown eyes at the barn doorway for a second or two. She gave her head another sassy shake, making the water slosh noisily inside the bottle. Then to Bailey's dismay, the calf kicked her heels and started off again, heading back toward the front yard.

Bailey blew out a sigh. "I do not have time for this today," she informed her squawking chickens as she stalked past them.

She really didn't, but she fought a smile as she spoke. Yes, she had a lot to do, but she wasn't complaining. This crazy overload was exactly the tonic she'd needed.

It wasn't just the store. She'd been feeling restless for about a year now, ever since bookstore owner Anna Delaney had married Hoyt Bradley. Since then, Anna and Hoyt had welcomed their first baby together. Another friend, pastor's wife Natalie Stone, was expecting her second child in a few months. And Emily Whitlock had not one but two sets of twins to take care of, in addition to managing the local coffee shop.

Bailey was over-the-moon happy for them all, but lately she'd felt her usual zest for life ebbing a bit. Okay. A lot. It was just that, compared to all the exciting and meaningful stuff going on with her friends, Bailey's life had seemed a little...

Boring.

Well, not anymore. Not since she'd gone to that informational meeting about foster parenting hosted by Anna's bookstore, Turn the Page.

Bailey had only gone to help Anna with the refreshments and to support Jillian Marshall, the local social worker who was giving the presentation. Bailey had never expected to walk out of there with a packet of paperwork clutched in her hand and a new dream burning in her heart.

But she had. The pictures of those little faces had stirred up a dream she'd given up on a long time ago. As the "surprise" only child of older parents, Bailey had longed for brothers and sisters. She'd promised herself that someday she'd raise a big, rambunctious family of her own—preferably on a farm with plenty of animals and homegrown vegetables.

At the time, of course, she'd assumed she'd share that life with…somebody special.

That part hadn't worked out the way she'd hoped. But according to Jillian, single women could be foster moms. That nugget of information was a game changer. Bailey could build her dream family all by herself by giving a loving home to kids who needed one.

And since she couldn't do that in a cramped apartment, Bailey's first order of business had been sinking all her savings into a down payment on the biggest house with the largest acreage she could afford. Which also happened to be a really old house that needed an awful lot of work.

Jillian had shaken her head when Bailey had given her a tour. "Honey, I hate to tell you, but this place is going to have to be overhauled from top to bottom if you want to pass the home-study safety inspection."

Bailey hadn't flinched, even though her bank account

was anemic now. "No problem. Just tell me what I need to do, and I'll find a way to do it."

"Well, for starters, you're going to have to put a fence around that pond there. Bodies of water have to be fenced off. It's a rule."

When Abel had heard about that, he'd trucked over some extra fencing material he'd had on hand. Bailey had argued, but all she'd gotten was a lecture on looking gift horses in their mouths.

So fencing was today's project. Unfortunately, it wasn't going well, even without the impromptu calf chases. So far, she'd gotten exactly three fence posts in, and she'd been at it for an hour and a half. She definitely had her work cut out for her.

But first she had to catch that ridiculous calf. The question was, how?

As she walked by the barn, an idea struck her. She ducked inside and scooped a small amount of grain into a bucket.

When she rounded the side of the house, she saw Lucy standing in the front yard, nosing the water bottle along the ground. When the calf heard Bailey approaching, the animal picked up her stolen toy and tensed, ready to scamper off again.

"See what I have?" Bailey rattled the bucket.

The calf took three curious steps in her direction and halted. Bailey shook the grain again. That did it. Lucy dropped the bottle and trotted in Bailey's direction. Bailey backed up slowly, leading the calf toward the barn and jiggling her bucket enticingly with every step.

Five minutes later, Bailey was latching the big wooden doors behind her and dusting off her hands.

One problem solved, fifty bazillion to go. And she had no idea how she was going to manage most of them.

But, she reminded herself, Jacob Stone's last sermon had been all about how God often called ill-equipped people to do His work. "If you feel like what you're being called to do is impossible but is something the world needs, you're probably on the right track," the minister had said. "Just focus on doing what you can and trust Him for the rest of it. And always be prepared for Him to work things out differently than you might expect."

Well, Bailey couldn't wait to see what God was going to do with her situation, and if He wanted to tuck some surprises in along the way, that was fine by her. After a year of feeling purposeless and bored, this excitement was a welcome change.

On her way across the yard, she stooped and picked up Lucy's discarded plastic bottle. Returning to her fence, she stashed the slobbery container next to the last post she'd managed to get in and pulled on her work gloves. She hefted up her new post-hole diggers and focused on the spot she'd marked for the next post. Raising the heavy diggers as high as she could, she rammed them downward, biting into the soft brown soil.

She'd clamped out three more skimpy scoops of dirt when she heard the sound of a vehicle crunching up her rutted driveway. She turned to see a silver Ford pickup nosing its way toward her.

Just what she didn't need right now. Company. Oh well. Maybe it was a friend she could draft into helping her get this fence up while they visited.

Bailey's eyes narrowed as she got a better look at the truck. She knew pretty much everybody's vehicle around here, but she didn't recognize this one. It was a newer model, but it had the dings and scrapes of a work truck. She squinted, but the afternoon sun was glaring off the windshield. All she could tell about the driver was that he was wearing a cowboy hat.

Definitely not from around here, then.

Curious now, she studied the approaching vehicle, stripping off her canvas gloves and dropping them on the ground. Who could this cowboy be, and what was he doing way out here?

Only one way to find out. The truck rolled to a stop, and Bailey headed toward it. The driver unfolded himself from the cab when she was about half the way across the yard. He was tall and lean, but there was a muscular set to his shoulders. Too bad she *didn't* know him. This guy could probably set a fence post in no time.

"Hey, there," she called in a friendly voice. "You lost?"

The man had been scanning her place, but he turned his head toward her when she spoke. When he did, more than fifteen years of Bailey's life crumbled away, leaving her face-to-face with a part of her past she'd tried very hard to forget.

Dan Whitlock.

Bailey stumbled to a halt, not quite believing her eyes. But it was true. After all these years, Dan was standing in her driveway.

For the past couple of days, ever since she'd dialed the Wyoming number she'd found on the internet, Bailey had been jumping every time her phone rang. She'd wondered if Dan would even call her back—and how she'd handle it if he did.

But he hadn't called her back. He'd shown up in person.

She had absolutely no idea what to do right now.

He touched the brim of his hat. "Ma'am." The voice was definitely Dan's, but the gentle drawl of the deep South had been melded with something else, something stronger and brisker. "I'm sorry to trouble you, but a fellow back in town told me I might find a girl named Bailey Quinn up this way. Would you happen to know where she lives?"

Bailey had to swallow twice before she could speak. "It's me," she managed finally. "Dan, it's me."

*"Bailey?"* As Dan moved toward her, she saw that his voice wasn't the only thing that had changed. He walked with the rolling gait of a man accustomed to spending a good portion of his day on horseback, and he limped a little on his left leg.

As he came close, he pulled the hat off his head. Not everything about him had changed. His hair was still the same dark mahogany, its waves pressed flat against his head. The same greenish-brown eyes skimmed over her, head to toe, before meeting her own.

He looked every bit as dumbfounded as she felt.

"It *is* you! Man, I'm sorry. I didn't recognize you at first. You look so…different." His eyes dropped to the teeth that had endured five long years of belated braces to correct her overbite.

Now that he was standing right in front of her, the memories Dan had jarred loose felt even more overwhelming. Her heart was thudding so hard it actually hurt.

Bailey took a deep breath. *Settle down*, she told herself firmly. *You can handle this.*

She could. She didn't just look different. She *was* different. The night Dan had left her had marked the lowest point in her life. But after a few weeks of wallowing in self-pity, she'd washed her tear-splotched face and decided enough was enough.

Over the next few months, she'd toned up, given up sugar, ditched her glasses for contacts and straightened her crooked teeth. And while everybody else raved over how different she looked, Bailey knew the really important changes had happened on the inside.

She stood on her own two feet now, and she trusted her head a lot more than she trusted her heart. She'd learned those lessons the hard way, and she couldn't afford to forget them, no matter who pulled up in her driveway.

She forced a shrug. "It's been a long time, Dan. People change."

"Yeah." He nodded slowly. "I guess they do."

An awkward silence fell between them. Finally, Bailey raised an eyebrow. "Well, now that the pleasantries are out of the way, I guess we can move on to the main event. Why are you here, Dan?"

"You called me."

"I called you," Bailey repeated. He made it sound so simple, as if the two of them facing each other after all this time wasn't the most complicated thing that had ever happened in her entire life. Her jangled nerves found that ridiculously funny. She tried her best to swallow her laugh, but it just came out through her nose in a strangled snort. "And instead of—I don't know—calling me back, you decided to drive all the way here from Wyoming?"

"I wasn't in Wyoming. I was in Oklahoma tending to some business. Not that it would have mattered." He drew in a long breath. "I'd have driven here from Alaska, if that's where I'd been. You and I both know that I owe you that much. At least."

"Maybe you do." Bailey saw no point in skirting the

truth. "But I gave up on collecting that debt a long time ago."

He didn't flinch. "I figured. That's how I knew this had to be about something important. You'd never have called me otherwise. It's true, what you said a minute ago. People do change. I've changed. I don't expect you to take my word on that, but it's why I'm here. So just tell me what you need from me. If there's any way I can give it to you, it's yours. No questions asked."

Bailey's knees had started wobbling, and that irritated her. The unfairness of this whole situation irritated her. She wasn't supposed to be standing two feet away from Dan while they had this conversation. All of this was supposed to happen over the phone, and that would have been plenty tough enough, thank you very much.

She wasn't prepared for this.

But she should have been. She, of all people, should have known that Dan Whitlock had a knack for sending a person's well-crafted plans spinning sideways.

She clamped her hands together, digging her short fingernails into her palms. "I'm glad to hear you say that, Dan. Because the truth is, you're right. There *is* something I need from you."

"Okay." His eyes never left hers. "Name it."

"A divorce."

## Chapter Two

He couldn't have heard that right. "A *what*?"

"A divorce," Bailey repeated.

"But we're not still…" He stalled out, searching her face. "I mean, didn't you…?" He watched as a flush heated Bailey's cheeks. "Bailey, are you telling me we're still *married*?"

"Yes." There was a little muscle twitching in her cheek, but she held her ground. "I don't know why you're acting so surprised. You were there."

"But that was years ago." He stopped and shook his head. "I figured you'd have dealt with it, had it annulled or whatever people do. In fact, I was pretty sure that was the first thing you'd have done after I…left."

The flush in Bailey's cheeks deepened. "Better late than never."

Dan searched his mind for something to say, but he came up with nothing. "Maybe I was a little quick on the trigger with that no-questions-asked thing. Is there someplace we could sit down while we talk this over?"

Bailey hesitated then nodded reluctantly. "We can sit on the porch if you want, but there's really not much to talk about. The whole thing should be very straightforward."

*Straightforward* wasn't the word Dan would have picked. He'd been trampled by bulls and walked away feeling more clearheaded than he felt right now.

All these years, he'd been *married* to Bailey Quinn? It was more than he could take in. The feelings he'd kept corralled in the deepest part of his heart were stampeding in fifty different directions. The dust was going to have to settle some before he could make sense of all of this.

He hadn't even wrapped his mind around the fact that the woman standing in front of him was really Bailey. She looked so different from the girl he remembered.

Back in high school she'd carried a few extra pounds that softened her figure, and her front teeth had been a little crooked. She'd always worn a pair of dark-rimmed glasses that had slid to the end of her nose about every five minutes. She was forever pushing them back up with an impatient finger, and he was forever plucking them off so that he could steal a kiss.

All those things had just made Bailey cuter.

He could think of a lot of words to describe Bailey now, but *cute* wasn't one of them. This new Bailey was lean and fit, with perfectly straight teeth and a don't-mess-with-me way of looking straight at you.

She was beautiful, sure. No man alive would dispute that. But it was a whole different kind of beauty than he remembered.

Now this woman he barely recognized was telling him she was his *wife*?

The man he'd spoken to back in town had told him Bailey had just bought this place. The closer Dan and Bailey got to the farmhouse, the more he wondered why.

Bailey had her work cut out for her, all right. The house had good bones, but it needed lot of repairs.

There were no chairs on the porch, so he settled carefully on the splintered steps. After an awkward pause, Bailey joined him. She positioned herself against the sagging wooden handrail, leaving a generous space between them. The shadow of the overhanging roof blocked the thin warmth of the January sun, but the sudden chill Dan felt had little to do with the weather.

In the old days Bailey would have cuddled close to him, settling her head in the gap between his shoulder and his neck. He could still remember exactly how that had made him feel at nineteen. Fiercely protective and defiantly happy, at a time in his life when happiness had been pretty hard to come by.

Now the very same girl was treating him like a stranger. He'd earned the coolness in those beautiful brown eyes, every bit of it.

But, man, oh man. The pain of seeing it there was almost more than he could stand.

Dan cleared his throat. "Okay. First off, how is this even possible?"

Bailey cocked her eyebrows. "We eloped, Dan. To Tennessee, remember?"

Yeah, he remembered. He'd just gotten dinged by the county sheriff for underage drinking again, and Bailey's long-suffering parents had handed down an ultimatum. If he wanted to attend church with them, fine. That much they'd allow, although they didn't sound too enthusiastic about the idea. But they made it clear that their daughter wasn't to spend any more time alone with him. He wouldn't be allowed to drive Bailey anywhere or take her out to dinner. It was plain enough that Mr. and Mrs.

Quinn were more than ready to put a stop to a relationship they'd never really approved of in the first place.

The idea of being separated from Bailey had sent Dan into a tailspin. She was the one good thing in his out-of-control life, the only person in the whole town who hadn't heard his last name and shied away from him. But her parents, along with everybody else in Pine Valley, seemed sure that he and Abel would turn out to be drunks and thieves, just like their dad and uncles had been, and their granddad before that.

And deep down, he'd been scared that—in his case, anyway—they were dead right. At nineteen, his drinking was already starting to get away from him, and he'd tangled with the law a few times. Nothing big, not yet. But without Bailey in his life…well, he'd known exactly what that would mean for him.

He'd self-destruct fast.

The fear had made him desperate and angry—and selfish. So selfish that one moonlit June night, he'd sweet-talked the eighteen-year-old girl he loved into leaving her parents' tidy brick home and running away with him.

He'd never forgive himself for that.

Bailey was still waiting for his answer. He swallowed. "I know we *were* married. But we haven't laid eyes on each other in years."

Bailey gave a frustrated laugh. "A marriage certificate doesn't have an expiration date, Dan. It's not a jug of milk."

"Well, no. But after I…" He stopped short.

"Ran off and left me at that awful motel in Kentucky?" Bailey's eyes hardened as she finished his sentence. "You thought that made the marriage evaporate? Well, it didn't."

He winced. "You've got every right to be mad, Bailey. I deserve that for talking you into the whole elopement idea and then leaving you to clean up the mess all by yourself. I knew you'd have to do things. Fill out papers and all that. I'd always assumed that's what you did."

"Trust me, I wish I had taken care of it back then, but I didn't. So we have to deal with it now. Let's stay focused on that."

"Hold on a minute." He studied Bailey. That muscle was jumping in her cheek again, and there was a tenseness about her body that he recognized with the instinct of a man who'd spent most of his last decade moving cattle. She wanted to bolt. Something about this conversation was spooking her.

"Dan—" she started off again, but he interrupted, intent on circling back to the territory that was puzzling him.

"I'm sorry. I sure don't have any right to question how you handled things, but this just isn't making any sense to me. Your parents couldn't even stand the idea of me being your boyfriend. Me being your husband? That must have sent them straight into orbit. Mind you, looking back I can't say as I blame them. How come they didn't take you to file the paperwork five minutes after you got back home?" He couldn't think of a single reason they wouldn't have.

Bailey sighed, but she met his eyes squarely. "Because I never told them we got married."

Okay. Except for that.

"You didn't…what do you mean you never told them?"

"I didn't tell anybody." She looked away and continued in a rush, "Look, none of that really matters now, does it? We were young, and we made a mistake. I didn't call you to rehash the past. I called you because I'm ready to move on with my life, and there are certain things I can't do until we get this settled."

*Certain things.* The confused feelings swooping around in Dan's chest turned to stone and dropped heavily into the pit of his stomach.

So that's what this was about. Bailey had fallen in love with another guy—probably wanted to get married. But she couldn't, not while she was still legally bound to Dan.

When Dan didn't respond, Bailey glanced at him. His expression had changed. The sun creases in the corners of his eyes had deepened, and his jaw was set. He looked tired.

And a little sad.

He caught her eye. "I get what you're saying about leaving the past behind. No man who's made the kind of mistakes I've made would argue with you. But before we do, I'd like to give you an overdue apology. If you'll let me."

He was holding his hat in his hands, running the brim slowly around in a circle. He watched her face, waiting to see if she was willing to hear him out.

She wasn't. She was holding herself together by a thread, and this wasn't a road she wanted to go down right now.

"You don't need to apologize, Dan. I'll admit it hurt when you walked out on me, but in time I realized that even if you'd come back that night, things couldn't have worked out any differently in the long run. We never should have gotten married in the first place."

"And that's completely on me. I never should have talked you into it. But, Bailey, back then I was so in love with you. I was scared to death I was going to lose you, and—"

"Please. Just stop." Bailey stood. She'd had just about all she could take. "This isn't all on you, Dan. It's not like you kidnapped me. I *let* you talk me into eloping. And honestly, I was such a pushover, you could've talked me into just about anything. The way I see it, I'm just as much to blame as you are, and I take full responsibility for my own mistake. Now, I appreciate you driving all this way, but it really wasn't necessary. Once the divorce papers are drawn up, I'll just need your notarized signature, and it'll be a done deal."

"All right." He had stayed seated and was looking up at her, his expression carefully blank. "I'll make sure you get it."

"Thanks." Bailey reached into her shirt pocket and pulled out a crumpled scrap of paper and a pen. "Write down your email address, and I'll be in touch. Now, if you'll excuse me, I really need to get back to work." She hesitated awkwardly, unsure what she should say or do next. How exactly did you end a conversation like this with some kind of dignity? She had no idea.

Finally, she reached out a hand and laid it gently on his bicep. It felt like touching a sun-warmed rock. "Goodbye, Dan."

She turned away and headed across the yard to the unfinished fence. Leaning over, she snagged the work gloves she'd dropped on the ground…what? Twenty minutes ago, maybe?

It felt like a lifetime.

Her hands were shaking so much that she had a hard time getting her fingers into the right slots. When the gloves were finally on, she reached for the post-hole diggers. As she jammed them back into the hole she'd begun, she heard the boards of the porch steps creak.

Okay, good. Dan was leaving. She held her breath, waiting to hear his truck door open and close.

"Bailey." He spoke from so close behind her that she jumped like a startled deer. "Sorry. I didn't mean to spook you. But…what you said back there. You were wrong. I did come back."

She flashed him an irritated glance. "What are you talking about?"

"I drove around for a few hours. Did some drinking." His fingers were clenched down so hard on the weathered brim of his hat that his knuckles were white. "But then I came back to the motel room. It was about three thirty in the morning, and you were curled up asleep on the bed with wadded-up tissues all around you. You'd been crying—hard—and you almost never cried. I'd done that to you on our wedding day, because I'd fought with you about driving back to Pine Valley and facing up to your parents."

"Dan, like I said, there's no point in—"

He cut her off. "I told you I wanted to go west, start fresh someplace new, just the two of us. But the truth was, I was just a coward. I was scared if we went back to Georgia, your parents would talk you into getting out of the marriage. Why wouldn't they? I was a nineteen-year-old boy with a pretty serious drinking problem, a bad reputation and zero skills that would help me land a job. And standing there looking down at you, I knew they were right. I was going to ruin your life."

He stopped. When he spoke again, his voice was rough with conviction. "I don't think I ever sobered up as fast in my life as I did that night. And yeah, I left you there.

It was the hardest thing I ever did. I'm really sorry I hurt you, but when I think about some of the things that happened to me after that, some of the places I ended up before I finally got myself turned around… Well, I can only thank the good Lord that I didn't hurt you even worse."

Bailey stared at him, the post-hole diggers still clenched in her hands. What was she supposed to say to that?

After a second or two, he cleared his throat. "About this divorce thing. Lawyers can get pricey. I'd like to cover the cost."

"I'm not asking you to do that."

"I know you're not. But I want to, just the same. How long will it take get it all settled?"

Bailey blinked and swallowed hard. "I don't know. I'll have to meet with the lawyer and see how soon he can draw up the papers. Did you leave me your email?"

"I wrote it down." He offered her the scrap of paper she'd left behind on the porch step. She took it, careful not to brush his fingers with hers, and tucked it back into the breast pocket of her shirt.

"Okay. I'll be in touch once I know more."

"Would it speed things up any if I stayed in Pine Valley until the papers are ready?"

Bailey bit her lip. He wanted to stick around town? The idea made her uneasy. "That's not necessary. Besides, you've probably got things you need to tend to back home."

"Nothing more important than this. I came here to do whatever I could to set things right, Bailey. I can stay for as long as you need me to."

"Like I said, all I need is your signature, and we can handle that long-distance." She hesitated, but in the end she couldn't resist adding, "But if you're serious about setting things straight around here, you should stop by and make your peace with your brother before you leave."

Dan flinched. "Abel still lives around here?"

"He does, but not at the old cabin. He lives on Goose-feather Farm with his wife and kids now. He married Emily Elliott a few years ago."

"Is that so? He always was crazy about Emily, but he never figured she'd look twice at him. And he's ended up with Mrs. Sadie's farm to boot. He loved that place." Dan's wary expression softened. "Isn't that something? Well, I'm glad it all worked out for him."

Bailey hesitated, but the sadness in Dan's eyes and her long-standing friendship with Abel overrode her reluctance to meddle. "You should stop and see them, Dan. It would mean the world to Abel."

Dan shook his head absently, his eyes lingering on the semicircle of pines crowding the edge of the sparkling pond. "I doubt that. But maybe I will. I came here to face up to the messes I left behind. If Abel wants to take a swing at me, it's no more than I deserve."

"I think Abel might surprise you. But if you don't mind, could you keep our situation quiet? I wasn't kidding before when I said I didn't tell anybody about our marriage. Abel doesn't know, either, and since it's all about to be over and done with anyway, I don't see much point in telling him about it now."

"I don't imagine I'll be on Abel's property long enough to do a whole lot of talking, so don't worry yourself. He won't hear about it from me."

Bailey nodded. "Thanks. If there's nothing else, I really do need to get this fence up."

"Need some help? Because I could—"

"No." She cut off the offer quickly. "I'll manage. But thanks."

"All right, then. I'll leave you be." He settled his cowboy hat back on his head. His eyes were instantly shadowed, but she could feel them on her face, studying her. "I'll be seeing you, I reckon."

Her heart jolted at the idea. "Like I said, I'll be in touch once I've heard back from the lawyer." She stuck out her gloved hand. "I know things are—different between us now. But I'm glad to see you're doing so well, Dan. I truly am."

He took her hand and held it gently for a second or two. Even through the roughness of the glove, she could feel the strong warmth of his fingers. "It's good seeing you, too, Bailey. Doing so well."

Flustered, she nodded. She pulled her hand free and turned back toward the fence line.

"Be careful." He spoke quietly behind her just as she jammed the diggers into the dirt. "Set those posts in good and straight. Take it from me, it's a lot of trouble trying to fix up the crooked ones later."

Once Dan's pickup had rumbled out of the driveway, Bailey sucked in a long, deep breath and bent to rest her head on the wooden handles of the post-hole diggers. She stood that way for several long minutes until her heartbeat slowed back down to something closer to normal.

Then she straightened up, wiped her eyes briskly on her sleeve and went back to work.

## *Chapter Three*

Later that afternoon Dan clenched his jaw as he turned into the long gravel driveway leading to Goosefeather Farm. It was taking every ounce of his willpower to keep the truck pointed toward his brother's new home.

This probably wasn't a good idea, going out to see Abel right now. Dan was reeling from his talk with Bailey. Just seeing her again would've been hard enough, but discovering he was still married to her?

He hadn't been ready for that—or for finding out she'd fallen for some other guy.

That part probably shouldn't have hit him as hard as it had, given the circumstances. But it had thrown him some, and maybe he should've taken some time to lick his wounds before signing up for a third punch in the gut.

Still, he'd come to Pine Valley to mend what fences he could—not that his plan was working out all that well. Bailey had been polite enough, but it was plain that all she wanted was to see the back of him. He couldn't blame her for that.

His brother would likely feel the same. On the positive side, no matter what Abel said or did, it couldn't hurt him any worse than seeing Bailey had.

Dan reached the end of the winding driveway and studied the view through his windshield. Goosefeather Farm had prospered under Abel. The old white house looked snug and well kept, flanked by rolling pastures, green with a winter crop of rye grass. Even the big barn sported a fresh coat of dark red paint.

Dan wasn't surprised. Abel had always done his best to take good care of whatever ended up on his plate, including his ornery younger brother. As a young teenager, Dan hadn't much appreciated Abel's fumbling attempts to fill their drunken father's shoes. In fact, he'd fought Abel every inch of the way, and he'd followed that up by leaving town without so much as a goodbye.

Dan sat for a minute as the winter sun beat through his windshield. Abel had every reason to bear a grudge, and most likely this wasn't going to go well. It didn't matter. His brother was long overdue for this apology, whether he was willing to accept it or not.

One thing was for sure. Dan had better get what old Gordon used to call "prayed up" before getting out of this truck. He bowed his head and closed his eyes.

*God, help me face up to my brother and tell him I'm sorry for all the trouble I caused him. And no matter what he says or how mad he gets, help me to remember that he's got every right to feel that way. Amen.*

When Dan lifted his head, he saw movement out of the corner of his eye. Abel had stepped to the wide doorway of the barn and was looking in Dan's direction.

Unlike Bailey, Abel hadn't changed much. He was still lean and tall, a muscled scarecrow with a shock of black hair. He was wiping his fingers on a greasy rag as he squinted at the truck. Dan wasn't surprised that he'd caught his brother working. Abel had never been one to sit idle.

Abel tossed up a hand in a friendly greeting and started across the yard. Dan felt sweat break out under the brim of his hat, but he switched the truck off and pushed open the door. Drawing in a deep breath of air that smelled richly of cows and hay, he walked around the front of the truck and faced his brother for the first time in over fifteen years.

"Hey, there!" The familiarity of his brother's deep voice hit Dan hard in the pit of his stomach. "Don't usually see Wyoming plates around here. What can I do for you?"

Dan cleared his throat. "Abel, it's—"

Those two words were as far as he got. Abel froze. Then he flung the greasy rag to the side, and before Dan realized what was happening, he was tackled in a hug that made his ribs howl in protest. Abel's voice spoke roughly in his ear.

"Danny, it's really you! You're finally home! Thank You, God! Thank You!"

Abel must have been working on a piece of farm machinery, because the odor of diesel fuel was coming off him in waves so strong that Dan's eyes watered.

Although it could be that the fumes weren't the only reason for that.

Dan swallowed the lump in his throat, put his arms awkwardly around his brother and hugged him back. "It's good to see you, too, Abel."

"*Good*'s not even close to being a big enough word for this." Abel pulled back to look him in the eye, but his older brother kept a firm grip on Dan's upper arms, as if he were afraid to let go. "I've been praying for this for so long, I'd just about given up on God ever answering me. But here you are!"

Dan had been braced for a chewing out, maybe even for a punch in the nose. He deserved both of them for running off like he had, for sending no word back for so long.

He hadn't expected this kind of welcome, and he didn't know what to say. Except...

"Abel, I'm so sorry. I shouldn't have—"

"Nope." Abel grabbed him again in another bear hug, this time knocking the Stetson clean off Dan's head. "I'm not listening to any apologies. You're home, and that's all that matters to me."

"Abel?" A feminine voice called from the direction of the house. "Is everything all right?"

Dan looked over Abel's shoulder. A slender woman with masses of light hair falling around her shoulders was standing on the steps of the farmhouse. Twin toddlers with Abel's black hair peeked shyly from behind her skirt.

"Better than all right, Emily!" Abel's voice shook as he answered his wife. "Danny's come home!"

"Oh, Abel! That's wonderful! Well, don't keep him all to yourself! Come on into the kitchen, Danny! I just took some fresh bread out of the oven." She beckoned enthusiastically and then turned, taking her children's hands and leading them back into the house.

"I don't want to butt in—" Dan ducked down to rescue his hat, and when he straightened up, Abel flung one arm around his younger brother's shoulders and began herding him toward the house.

"'Course you're coming in! I've got kids for you to meet, Uncle Danny! I want to hear all about what you've been doing since you left town." Abel led the way across a screened side porch and opened a door, ushering Dan inside.

The farmhouse kitchen closed around him with as much warmth as his brother's unexpected hug. The room was clean and bright, with red-checkered curtains and flowers blooming cheerfully on a sunny windowsill. Two golden-brown loaves of bread were cooling on the counter, and children's toys littered the floor.

Before Dan knew what was happening, he was settled in a chair at the big oval table. A thick slice of bread sat in front of him, homemade butter melting into golden streams across its top. Emily set a steaming cup of coffee at his elbow before turning to pour cups of milk for the twins.

The toddlers were staring at him owlishly. The boy had Abel's blue eyes, but the girl had inherited her mother's green ones.

Keeping one wary eye fixed on Dan, the little girl flickered pleading fingers at her father, who immediately gathered her gently onto his knees. The boy stood his ground, watching the stranger closely, one thumb stuck in his mouth.

"That's your uncle Danny," Abel told them. "Dan, this little sweetheart is our Lily, and the fine-looking fellow over there is Luke. They just turned two back in December."

"Hi." The kids were cute as they could be. What must it be like, Dan wondered, to have a wife you loved and a home like this? Nice, he reckoned. "You've got yourself a fine family, Abel."

"And this isn't all of it." Abel grinned up at his wife. "There's two more of us. Paul and Phoebe are visiting their nana Lois for the afternoon. I sure hate they're miss-ing this, but I suppose you'll meet them soon enough."

"Four kids." Not only was Dan an uncle, he was an uncle four times over. It was a lot to take in, and he felt a twinge of envy. If things had been different, if he and Bailey had stayed together, maybe they'd have kids by now, too. "That's really something."

"Well, Phoebe and Paul came along with Emily when I married her, so I got a triple blessing there. You have any kids, Danny?"

"No. I'm not—" *Married*. That's what he'd started to say, but that wasn't true. "I'm not as blessed as you are," he finished awkwardly.

"Well now, don't give up hope. Sometimes God works things out slow, but He always gets the job done in His good time. The fact that you're sitting here at my table today is proof enough of that. I sure have a lot to thank Him for. You mind if I go ahead and get started on that now? We generally say grace before we eat, but if it both-ers you—"

"Nope." As off balance as he felt right now, Dan's an-swer came fast and sure. "The Lord's seen me through some hard times, Abel. I wouldn't be sitting here in front of you it hadn't been for Him and the good people He set in my path. So you go right ahead."

Joy sparkled in Abel's eyes. "That's real good to hear, Danny. Come on, kids, let's pray."

Dan closed his eyes and listened to his brother's deep voice. "Lord, I thank You for bringing my brother home to me. And please forgive me for all those times I got kinda short with You about how long it was taking. I should've known You were up to something bigger than I could think to ask You for. You've not only brought

Danny back, You've brought him back knowing You. That's a double gift, and now I'm grateful You took Your time. I surely am."

Dan felt a little hand come to rest on top of his. Startled, he opened his eyes. Luke had edged closer, and he was gripping Dan's thumb in one chubby fist. The toddler had his eyes squeezed tightly shut, his face puckered in concentration.

Dan quickly followed suit, doing his best to refocus his attention on his brother's brief prayer.

"Amen," Abel finished, and Luke's eyes popped open.

"Amen," the little boy echoed cheerfully. He loosened his grasp on Dan's finger and then reached out to cautiously touch the Stetson Dan had placed on the table.

Dan grinned as he studied his nephew. Cowboy hats drew little boys as sure as flowers drew honeybees.

What would it be like to have a son like this little fellow? Somebody to teach and love and look after? He'd probably never know, and most likely that was a good thing. Abel was prime father material, no doubt about it. Dan not so much.

Still. It might have been kind of nice.

"Let's not get Uncle Danny's hat all sticky, Lukey," his mother said. Emily flashed an apologetic smile at Dan. "He had that thumb in some jam just a second ago."

"That's all right." Dan picked the hat up and settled it on his nephew's head. It swallowed the little boy, making his parents chuckle. Luke poked the brim up with one hand and grinned from under it with such cheeky joy that Dan's heart gave another strangely painful twist.

"Now then," Abel said, reaching for the mason jar of homemade strawberry jam his wife had placed on the table. He scooted it in Dan's direction. "Spread some of this on that bread there and let's get ourselves all caught up."

An hour later, there were only crumbs on the plates, and Emily had refilled Dan's coffee cup for the third time. Abel leaned back in his chair and shook his head.

"So my baby brother's a rancher now. The Bar M. I sure would like to see that place. I'm such a homebody, I've never been farther west than Alabama myself."

"I'd love to have you come out west for a visit, Abel, but the truth is, I may not be at the Bar M much longer."

"Why not? You don't get along with this new Colt fellow?"

Dan shook his head. "It's not that. Colt McAllister's a good man, and we've been friends for years. But he doesn't need the same kind of foreman his grandpa did. Mr. Gordon was in his seventies when I hired on, and he'd had two heart attacks. It's different with Colt. Colt's young and healthy, and he likes to handle things himself instead of relying on an employee. Nothing wrong with that. I'd be that way myself, probably."

Abel nodded. "But it's tough to step back when you've been the one running the show. Is that it?"

"Something like that, I reckon. Colt will put in a good word for me, and folks trust the McAllisters. I shouldn't have much trouble hiring on someplace else, once I put out the word that I'm looking." Dan darted an uneasy look at his brother's face. "It's not pride, Abel. I've always known my place. It's just—"

"You don't have to explain," Abel interrupted him. "I can see for myself how it is. You've grown too big for the space this Colt fellow can give you. That's all. You need to find yourself a place where you can flex your muscles a little. A place of your own, maybe." His brother's eyes lit up. "I'd sure be happy if you settled down somewhere close to Pine Valley."

"Not likely. I never fit here the way you do, Abel. You know that."

"Seems to me you've changed a good bit since you've been away, Danny. Could be you'd fit in here better than you think. But I reckon that's something you'll need to find out for yourself. Either way, you won't be leaving right away, I hope. You can stay on a few days, at least, can't you?"

Dan hesitated, but then he nodded. "Yeah, I guess I could." He owed Abel that much, and maybe by then the divorce papers would be ready to sign. Then he could put Pine Valley in his rearview mirror with a clear conscience.

"Good! You can bunk up at the old cabin. I use the workshop behind it for my wood-carving business, but other than that the place has been standing empty since Emily and I got married."

The cabin? Dan shook his head quickly. "I don't want to put you to any bother."

"It's no bother, and that cabin's as much yours as it is mine, Danny."

Maybe so, but Dan would just as soon never lay eyes on that place again. The memories associated with the cabin where he'd grown up weren't good ones. But that's what this whole visit was about, wasn't it? Facing up to the past he'd been running away from.

All of it. Whether he liked it or not.

"All right, if you're sure I won't be troubling you any. Thanks." Dan shot a wary glance at the staircase. Emily had disappeared up that way a few minutes ago with the twins in tow, saying she was going to settle them down for a nap. It was quiet up there now, so Emily might be coming back down soon.

If Dan was going to ask the question burning a hole in his gut, now would probably be the best time. "Hey, Abel? How's Bailey Quinn doing these days?"

"Bailey? She's doing all right. She'll be happy to hear you're back in town. After you left, she nearly pestered the life out of me, wanting to know if I'd heard anything from you. She seemed to miss you something fierce. The two of you were pretty sweet on each other back in high school, weren't you?"

They were edging into the danger zone. "Yeah." There was no use for it. He had to know. "So who's Bailey sweet on these days?"

"Nobody." Abel's answer came instantly. "Hang on. I'll get a key to the cabin for you." Abel stood and went to rummage in a drawer.

"You sure about that? About Bailey, I mean?"

"Dead sure." Abel shot him a thoughtful glance. "Now that I come to think of it, she's never shown interest in any fellow since you two were hanging around together. Not once in all these years, at least as far as I can remember. You aren't looking to stir up the embers of that old campfire, are you?"

"No." Dan toyed with handle of his coffee cup. "Way too much water under the bridge for that. Just curious, is all." He spoke evenly, but it took some effort. "A smart, pretty woman like Bailey Quinn…seems strange that she hasn't settled on somebody."

"Not so strange. Bailey's got an independent streak a mile wide, and she keeps herself too busy for dating. She's never happy unless she's got herself neck-deep in some project. The more hopeless it is, the better she likes it. Come to think of it," Abel added with a wink, "that could explain why she took you on."

Probably more truth in that little joke than Abel realized. "What's she got going on nowadays?"

"For the past few years she's been all about that grocery store of hers. She's finally got it up and running, but now she's bought herself the Perrys' old farm to fix up. That place is in such bad shape, it's going to take a passel of time and hard work, so it's right up Bailey's alley." Abel shrugged and resumed shuffling items around in the drawer.

"What would a single woman want with a broken-down farm?"

"Well, Bailey's real softhearted about little ones, and she never got around to having a family of her own. Emily tells me that once Bailey gets the house fixed up, she's looking into being a foster mom. She's aiming to take in some kids who've had a hard time and give them a good home."

"Is that a fact?" Dan's heart stirred. That sounded like Bailey.

"Yes. It's going to take some doing. She told Emily they just about count the fillings in your teeth before they'll let you into the program. They check out your background and do a safety inspection, all that stuff. That farmhouse is going to need a lot of overhauling before it'll pass muster. I plan on helping her as much as I can, but between the twins, the farm and my carving business, I don't have much free time these days. Here it is!" Abel withdrew a key from the drawer and tossed it to Dan. "This'll open the front and back doors, and it's yours to keep. The cabin will be waiting for you to use whenever you feel like it."

"That's good of you, Abel." Dan weighed the key in his hand as he mulled over what Abel had told him.

So that's why Bailey had finally decided to deal with their situation. She needed a clear ending to their marriage so she could be approved to take in some foster kids.

Plenty of years had come and gone since Bailey had first caught his eye, but one thing hadn't changed. This woman he'd hurt so badly was still one of the nicest people he'd ever met.

Over the years, his regrets about Bailey had dogged him, aching off and on like the knee he'd busted during an ill-advised bull-riding experiment. He'd like to be shed of that pain and guilt. As he'd driven here, he'd found himself hoping Bailey needed a favor, something really big. Something he could do for her so he could leave Pine Valley feeling as if he'd made up for at least some of the pain he'd caused her.

Something a lot more than just a signature on divorce papers.

And from what Abel had just told him, Bailey *did* need help—a lot of it. She had no intention of asking Dan for it, but that didn't mean he couldn't make the offer.

"Dan?"

Belatedly he realized Abel had been talking to him. "Sorry. I zoned out there for a minute. What?"

"I was just saying, you should run by and see Bailey while you're in town. Tomorrow, maybe. She's always at that store of hers by eight thirty. You could surprise her."

"I might do that."

Abel chuckled. "That'll be something, won't it? You walking right in after all these years? Bailey's a hard girl to fluster, but that ought to do it. I can just see her face!"

Dan managed a tight smile. He could, too.

In fact, for the last few hours he hadn't been able to see much of anything else.

At eight o'clock the next morning, Bailey was in her store on her hands and knees chasing a rolling tangerine.

"Gotcha!" she muttered as her fingers closed around the runaway fruit. Then, *"Ow!"*

She'd absentmindedly lifted her head too soon, butting hard against the underside of the wooden table. She carefully backed the rest of the way out, before sitting up to massage her throbbing head.

This was getting ridiculous. Seeing Dan yesterday had really rattled her. So far this morning she'd broken a jar of spaghetti sauce, spilled her coffee on a stack of mail and dropped three pieces of fruit. She hadn't even opened the store yet, and she already wanted to go home.

"You okay?" a male voice called from her storeroom.

*Oh, brother.* "I'm fine!" Bailey answered quickly.

Lyle York, hands down her least favorite delivery man, poked his greasy head through the storeroom doorway.

"You sure? I could come help you if you want."

"No, thanks." Bailey spoke firmly as she got to her feet. "Everything's under control."

"Why don't you come help me unload this fruit then? It'd go a lot faster if we worked together." He winked suggestively. "It'd be a lot more fun, too."

*Ick.* Bailey suppressed a shudder. "Sorry. You'll have to handle it by yourself. I'm busy."

Lyle's eyes narrowed. "You don't look so busy to me, but fine. Be that way."

As the deliveryman sulked back into the storeroom, Bailey placed the rescued tangerine with the others in the tempting basket she'd angled on her front table. Just as she reached into the cardboard box for another one, a loud crash came from her storage room.

"Whoops," Lyle called, his voice heavy with sarcasm. "*Sorry.* That crate slipped right out of my hands."

Bailey ground her teeth and stayed silent. Lyle was a pain in the neck, and his efforts to flirt with her were getting more and more annoying. If he wasn't the grandson of the most reliable citrus supplier she'd ever found, she wouldn't have put up with him this long. The man just kept getting pushier, and soon she was going to have to set him back on his heels, no matter how that impacted her fruit deliveries.

But she wasn't feeling up to having that confrontation today. When Dan Whitlock had shown up yesterday afternoon, he'd thrown her so far off balance that she still felt unsteady.

After Dan had left, she'd tried to keep working on the fence, but after a frustrating hour, she'd abandoned the project. She couldn't focus. She couldn't do anything but think about Dan, replaying every snippet of their short conversation over and over again.

It was infuriating. This wasn't who she was, not anymore. The Bailey Quinn who'd been irresistibly drawn to creamy chocolate, greasy French fries and equally bad-for-you guys was long gone. The new and improved Bailey made smart decisions. She ate more kale, exercised faithfully three times a week and preferred do-it-yourself projects to guys with broody eyes, stubborn jaws… and cowboy hats.

It was just that Dan's visit had come at the worst possible time. She'd been feeling restless for a while now. For years she'd poured herself into Bailey's, and now the store was finally flourishing. She was proud of what she'd accomplished, but she needed a new challenge to tackle.

That shouldn't be a problem. According to Jillian, there were plenty of kids needing foster homes—kids who'd suck up every ounce of restless energy Bailey had. All Bailey had to do was get her mistake of a marriage taken care of and find some way to afford the necessary repairs around the farmhouse. Granted, that last part had her stymied, but she'd figure something out. She always did.

But she couldn't afford to get distracted.

Bailey pushed Dan to the back of her mind and returned her focus to the job at hand. Freshly in from Florida, these tangerines would add a nice splash of color to the front of her store. More importantly, they were organically grown and chock-full of vitamin C. In midwinter, these little gems were worth their weight in gold, but maybe she'd run a nice sale on them as a treat for her customers.

If so, she might need to make a bigger display, because they'd be likely to sell out quickly. She had several matching baskets in the storeroom, but she had no intention of venturing back there until after Lyle left. Maybe there was a stray basket stowed behind the checkout counter.

While she was rummaging, there was a knock on the door. Annoyed, Bailey glanced up at the old library clock ticking on the back wall. It wasn't time to open yet, but she'd go ahead and unlock the door. Folks frequently needed to zip in and grab a few things on their way to work, and she had to keep her customers happy.

Bailey took a deep breath and forced a smile—which lasted until the moment she saw who was waiting outside on the sidewalk.

What was Dan doing here? Her pulse sped up, and Bailey bit down sharply on the tender inside of her lower lip.

This couldn't be good.

She rounded the wooden counter, crossed briskly to the door and unlatched it. It took a minute—the lock was always tricky. Although she deliberately kept her eyes focused on the fussy mechanism, she was very aware of Dan standing just on the other side of the glass. In spite of her better judgment, she looked up and met his eyes as she slid the bolt free.

He was looking right at her, so close that his breath misted the glass between them. For a second, their eyes locked, and her heart gave a painful thump. She looked away and jerked the door open, too flustered to bother with courtesy.

"What are you doing here, Dan?"

He lifted an eyebrow at her tone. "Good morning to you, too."

"Sorry. It's just… I'm really busy right now."

He nodded. "Yeah, I heard you're doing really good with this place." As Dan's eyes left hers to skim the store, Bailey felt a little of her confidence return in spite of her skittering nerves.

Bailey's was as close to perfect as she could make it. The store's trademark decor was an eclectic mix of old and new, and she'd chosen each feature with care. She'd replaced the broken antique lights with retro recreations, and she'd splurged on the best heating and air unit she could afford. But she'd restored the wide pine floorboards, even though replacing them would have been cheaper. She'd even paid extra to have them refinished in a way that had showcased their interesting scarring.

She'd spent happy weekends combing estate sales and

antique stores for the primitive cabinets lining the walls. The jams and sauces displayed on their shelves were made using her own unique recipes, and she'd designed the brick-red logo on their labels herself. Everything in this space bore her personal touch—literally. She'd spent a few weeks three summers ago with oddly colored fingers after chalk painting the farmhouse tables she used to showcase baskets of fresh fruit and vegetables.

She missed those days. Fixing up a store was a lot more fun than running one.

"It looks like something out of a magazine." Dan had pulled his hat off his head and was running it around in his hands again. "Sorry, I don't mean to keep you from your work. I just wanted you to know that after I left your place, I went by to see Abel."

"Did you?" In spite of her irritation, Bailey was curious. "How'd that go?"

"Better than I deserved." Dan's surprisingly humble answer came back without hesitation. Like that cowboy hat he kept playing with, this humility was something new.

Which meant Bailey wasn't quite sure how to respond to it.

"Your brother's a good man."

"He is that. He invited me to stay in the old cabin for a few days. Spend some time getting to know his family and all. No—" Dan held up a hand when Bailey opened her mouth. "Don't worry. Abel thinks I've come back just to see him, and I haven't told him any different. I'm not planning to cause you any trouble. In fact, I think I've come up with a way I could be some help to you, if you'll let me."

"Help?" Bailey wrinkled her forehead. "What kind of help are you talking about?"

"That's going to take a little explaining, and I expect you'll have customers coming along shortly. Why don't you drive out to the cabin this evening for a few minutes? That way we can talk things over, just you and me."

*Just you and me.* The thrill she felt at Dan's words only made Bailey's inner alarm system clang louder. Bad idea, spending time alone with this man, any way you sliced it.

But oh, she wanted to. She wanted to go to that cabin so much it almost scared her. She wanted to sit down and listen to whatever Dan wanted to say. She wanted to *look* at him, to remind herself of past moments that she'd be far better off forgetting.

This wasn't good. The man had been in town less than twenty-four hours, and she was already flip-flopping like a hooked sunfish.

"Fruit's unloaded, Bailey." Lyle poked his head back through the doorway. "Now how about being a sweetheart and fixing me some coffee before I head out? I got more deliveries up around Atlanta. That traffic's killer, and I need to be alert."

Bailey threw him an irritated look. She'd offered Lyle a cup of coffee exactly once, when he'd used fatigue as an excuse for banging his truck into the concrete loading dock at the rear of the store. He'd taken the opportunity to sit too close to her and make skeevy comments about how great her hair smelled. She didn't have the time or energy for Lyle's nonsense this morning.

"Sorry. I don't have any coffee made. You could stop by the church coffee shop and get some if you want. They should be open by now. Drive safe, and give your grandpa my best."

Lyle's expression darkened. He darted a wary glance at Dan. "Before I leave, you better at least come back here and take a look at how I got this fruit stacked up. You know how picky you are about that, and besides, we haven't had any chance to talk since I got here."

Bailey frowned, but before she could reply, Dan cut in.

"I believe the lady said you could go." His voice was calm, but there was a steely undertone in it that made the hairs on the back of Bailey's neck tickle, the way they did when lightning was about to strike.

Lyle opened his mouth to protest, but then his narrowed eyes scanned Dan from head to toe. The pace of the delivery man's gum chewing picked up nervously, and he held up both hands in a conciliatory gesture. "Hold your horses there, Tex. I don't see how this is any of your business, but fine. Have it your way, Bailey, but you better not go complaining to Pops if you end up having to move those heavy crates around by yourself. I'll stop back by on my way home in a couple of days and see if you got any additions to your order. Maybe by then you'll be in a better mood."

Bailey ignored him. She waited until she heard Lyle slam the loading door before she spoke again. "Dan—"

Dan interrupted her, his eyes still focused on the back of the store. "That guy's trouble, Bailey. You should make sure you have somebody else in the store with you when he comes back by."

"*Lyle?* He's annoying, sure, and I obviously need to set him straight about a couple things. But, trust me, he's harmless."

"I don't think so. I've worked with a lot of different kinds of men on the ranch, and I've run across a few like him. A man like that's going to try something, sooner or later."

"I doubt that, but if he does, I'll handle it. I'm not the same girl you knew back in high school, Dan. I've gotten pretty good at looking after myself." Bailey let the pointed words settle between them for a second. Then she opened her mouth to nix the whole cabin conversation idea in no uncertain terms. Whatever Dan had to say to her, he could say right here and right now or not at all. "Look, I'm sorry, but—"

But before she got any farther, the shop bell chimed. Bailey's heart dropped as Jillian Marshall came into the store.

The sharp-eyed redhead was the last person Bailey wanted to see right now. She and Jillian were friendly enough, but Jillian was also Pine Valley's senior social worker. When it came to her job, she was a professional all the way down to her cute ankle-high boots. Bailey didn't have a clue what Dan wanted to talk to her about, and she didn't want to jeopardize her foster parent application by having that conversation in front of Jillian.

"I'm so glad you're open early, Bailey! You've saved my life. One of the social workers in the office has a birthday today, and I totally forgot it was my turn to bring the goodies."

As Jillian headed for the baked goods, Bailey turned back to Dan and spoke in a low voice. "All right. I'll stop by the cabin after work. Say around seven? But I won't be able to stay long."

"That'll be fine. I'll see you then." He flashed an easy smile that effectively stopped her heart. Then he settled his hat back on his head and started for the door. Bailey watched him go.

No man who was as much trouble as Dan Whitlock should be that good-looking. It wasn't fair.

"Bailey?" She jumped and turned to see Jillian holding up two packages of cookies with a confused expression. "I think you'd better come help me. I left my reading glasses at home, and I've been making a mess of everything all morning."

Bailey sneaked another glance at Dan's retreating shoulders and sighed. "You're not the only one," she muttered.

A few minutes before seven that evening, Bailey nosed her protesting truck up the driveway to the old Whitlock cabin. She hadn't been up this way in a while, and she'd forgotten how steep this driveway was.

"I know how you feel, Maude," she said, patting the sputtering pickup on its faded dashboard. "But we'll survive this, both of us."

At least she hoped so.

As she pulled the keys from the ignition, Dan stepped out onto the cabin's high front porch. "I heard you coming from the time you turned off the county road," he called as she got out. "You might need to get that engine checked over."

"No worries. Maude likes to kick up a fuss, but she never lets me down." Bailey climbed the wooden porch steps. Determined to act cool, collected and perfectly normal, she held out a polite hand as soon as she was within arm's length.

Dan swiped his own hand on his jeans before accepting hers. "Sorry, my hand's pretty sweaty. Being back here at this cabin's making me squirrelly."

Small wonder. Bailey squeezed his hand a little more

warmly than she'd originally intended. It couldn't be easy for Dan, coming back to this house. He'd been miserable here.

"The cabin's different, though," she pointed out gently. This property had been an unkempt, trash-littered wreck back in the day. Dan and Abel's father had spent what little money he managed to cadge or steal on liquor, not home maintenance. When Abel had inherited the cabin, he'd set about transforming it in his slow and steady way. "Anybody would be proud to call this place home now."

"Not me. If I were Abel, I'd have bulldozed it to the ground." Dan looked around, his lips tight, then shrugged and pushed open the door. "But you're right. It does look a lot better than it used to. Come on in and see for yourself."

Actually, Bailey had visited the restored cabin before, but now, a new homeowner herself, she looked around with a sharpened interest. She was always prospecting for ideas, and this living room had exactly the feel she loved best. Welcoming, simple and warm.

The knotty pine floor gleamed. The fireplace, made of smooth river stones, sheltered a small, crackling fire, and the oversize furniture angled around the hearth was comfortable and unpretentious. The room had a masculine feel leftover from Abel's bachelor days, but Emily had added a few feminine touches here and there. An old-fashioned braided oval rug brought red and turquoise notes to the room. The attractive colors were echoed by some throw pillows and a snuggly looking afghan tossed over the back of the leather sofa. Some of Abel's wood carvings were displayed on the built-in bookshelves, with small lights carefully angled to showcase their delicate details.

That would be Emily's doing, too. She was fiercely proud of her husband's incredible talent, while he tended to downplay it.

Bailey crossed the room under the pretext of warming her hands at the fire, but really she just needed to put a buffering distance between herself and Dan. Whenever he was close by, Bailey caught a whiff of seasoned leather mixed with fresh cedar. That particular smell was something she'd always associated with Dan, and it was making it really hard for her to think.

And way too easy for her to remember.

Bailey never allowed herself to dwell on the weekend they'd run away together. Some scars were best left unpoked. But being here with Dan, inhaling his scent, brought it all flooding back.

She'd been so excited that Friday night, riding in the middle of his truck's bench seat, cuddled against him as he drove north under the stars. When they'd rolled past the Tennessee state line, she remembered, he'd looked down at her.

"You're not scared, are you, Bailey?"

"Not a bit," she'd assured him. "Not while I'm with you."

But of course she'd been scared. With strict parents like hers, running away was no joke. And getting married at eighteen…well, that brought up plenty of other things to feel nervous about.

When Dan had taken her hands in the secluded corner of her parents' backyard and asked her to elope, he'd seen her hesitation. And she'd seen the surprised hurt on his face, seen the defiant way he'd set his jaw. He was leaving town with her or without her, he'd said. He loved her, and if she wanted to stay here with her parents, he understood. But she was going to have to make her choice.

And so she'd agreed to his plan, confident that once they were married, she'd be able to talk him into coming back and making peace with her parents. Dan always did what she asked sooner or later. And as his wife, she'd have even more leverage.

Turned out she hadn't known Dan nearly as well as she'd thought.

After their quickie wedding, she'd broached the subject of returning home and facing her family, and he'd stared at her as if she'd lost her mind.

"I'm your husband now, Bailey. We're a family, just the two of us. Aren't we? That means our home can be anywhere we want it to be. Just as long as we're together." They'd argued for hours, and then he'd stormed out.

Waiting alone in the shabby motel room, she'd studied the cheap gold band on her finger through her frustrated tears and finally realized the full gravity of the choice she'd made.

Things had only gotten worse from there. When Dan hadn't reappeared by the next morning, she'd taken all the money in her purse and hired a taxi back home, told her worried parents a lie and waited for him to show up. Surely he'd come back for her. After all, they were married.

But weeks, then months had ticked by, and Dan had never come back.

Until now.

That brokenhearted girl who'd peered so hopefully through her mother's living room curtains had learned a few things since then, and Bailey had enough sense to know that she was revisiting some dangerous territory.

"I can make a pot of coffee if you want," Dan was saying.

Bailey shook her head. "No, thanks. I really can't stay long. In fact, you'd best just go on and say whatever it is that you wanted to say to me."

He looked uneasy, but he nodded. "All right. Abel told me you're working to get your place fixed up so that you can take in some kids who need homes. I thought while I was here maybe I could help you out with that. Working on a ranch for the last ten years has taught me how to fix pretty much anything. I run a good, straight fence line, too." He offered her that slow smile that always made her stomach shift. "Judging by what I saw yesterday, you could use some help that department."

Bailey shot him a narrow look. "For crying out loud, Dan, I wasn't doing *that* bad."

"Not for a newbie, I'll give you that. Anyhow, I've got a little time to spare, and Abel wants me to get to know the kids and all. But he won't want me underfoot all the time, and I sure don't want to hang around this cabin. Seems like a no-brainer to me."

Bailey stared at him. She knew perfectly well this was a crazy idea, but he made it sound so sensible. And free skilled labor? Wasn't that just what she'd been praying for?

But still.

*Lord, I'm honestly not sure what to do here. Is this really Your answer? Dan Whitlock?*

"So?" Dan prodded. "What do you say?" When she didn't respond, he went on earnestly, "I know you've got your reasons for wanting to keep your distance, and I don't blame you. But just from what I saw out at your place, you've got a lot of work to do. I came back here with an eye toward making things right between us, so I'd really like to help you out. Besides, you know the kind of home I grew up in, how bad it was. If you're trying to take kids out of places like that, I'd consider it an honor to be a part of what you're doing." He waited a second and then added gruffly, "I know we're over, Bailey. But let me end things right this time. Please."

That half-shamed *please* did her in. She sighed. "If you really want to help, I guess… I guess we could give it a try."

Dan's eyes lit up. "Great! I know you're in a hurry, but how about we sit down for just a minute so you can tell me what all you're looking to do? Abel's sure to have some paper stashed around her someplace. I'll find it, and we'll make a list of everything you need done. It won't take a minute." As he disappeared in search of the paper, he called over his shoulder, "You won't be sorry, Bailey, I give you my word. Anyway, what have you got to lose?"

"The same thing I lost last time you gave me your word," Bailey mumbled when she was sure he was well out of earshot. "Everything."

# *Chapter Four*

Bailey pulled back the edge of her living room curtain. The dawn had barely begun to turn the edges of the sky pink, but Dan was already pulling up in her driveway. She cupped her hands around her mug of steaming coffee and watched as he got out of the truck, retrieved a box of tools from the bed and headed toward the house.

He was wearing a sheepskin-lined vest over a plaid shirt and jeans today. And that ever-present cowboy hat, a constant reminder that Dan didn't belong in Pine Valley, Georgia, anymore.

Not that he ever had, no matter how much she'd wanted him to.

She opened the door just as he reached her porch. "You're here early."

He set the toolbox beside the door and gestured toward the brightening light behind him. "Sun's up. Back on the ranch, that means it's time to get to work. Besides, I hoped if I came over early enough, you'd have time to walk the fence line with me and show me exactly where you want it run." He skimmed a glance around her shabby living room and raised an eyebrow. "You sure you want me to start with the fencing? No offense, but this house needs a good bit of work."

"I know, but the fence is a priority. I have to block off the pond for the safety inspection, and I'd like to get it done while the weather's cooperating." Besides, having Dan work outside felt a lot less intimate than letting him work inside her home.

"You're the boss." He glanced down at her feet. "Do you have time to show me where you want the posts set or not? If you do, you'll need to ditch those heels."

He had a point. She'd dressed for work and for the visit to the lawyer's office afterward. The shoes she'd chosen weren't made for trekking through damp pastures. "I think so. The area I want fenced isn't very big, so it won't take long. Go help yourself to some coffee while I swap shoes."

"That sounds good. Thanks." He smiled his slow smile, and Bailey's pulse thumped its standard response.

As she headed up the creaking staircase, she practiced taking deep, calming breaths. If Dan was going to be hanging around, she couldn't keep going all jittery every time the man looked at her.

She switched to a pair of scuffed leather hiking boots and clumped back down the stairs to find Dan waiting in the living room, holding a coffee mug.

"You good to go?"

When she nodded, he opened the door with his free hand, gesturing for her to step through. She walked into the bracing January air.

"Chilly today," she remarked as they headed for the garden area.

His laugh puffed into a coffee-scented mist. "If you say so."

"I do." Bailey made a face at him. "But I guess you're all toughened up from living in the frozen north."

"Not so north and not so frozen, just a lot colder than this. More open, too." He glanced at the pines around them. "I forgot how many trees there are around here. And the smell of them—of these particular pines, I mean—takes me back."

Judging by the tone of his voice, the place that piney scent took him wasn't someplace he wanted to go. Bailey felt a little stung. "Your time in Georgia wasn't all bad, Dan. Was it?"

He glanced at her, and their eyes met. And for a second there, the memories that glimmered between them in the frosty air seemed almost as visible as the clouds of their breath.

"No," he finally said, softly. "Not all bad."

Bailey felt her lips tipping upward, and her internal alarm system pinged. What was she doing? They hadn't even made it to the fence line yet, and she was already bringing up the past, dabbling her toes in dangerous waters. It was going to take them at least fifteen minutes to walk around the little area she needed enclosed. Who knew what they'd end up talking about?

She needed a distraction.

Abruptly she broke away and headed for the barn. "Wait here a second," she called over her shoulder.

Once in the barn, she went for Lucy Ball's stall. The gate leading into the small back pasture was open, but the long-legged calf was still inside finishing her breakfast. She looked up curiously as Bailey approached, crumbs of grain clinging to her damp black nose.

"Feel like a walk, Lucy?" It was a rhetorical question. Lucy always felt like a walk when it meant she got to kick up her hooves on the wrong side of her fence. Bailey un-latched the gate, and the calf gamboled past her and out into the sunshine.

Dan was drinking his coffee, his head angled toward the sun peeking through the fringes of the dark green pine needles. When he saw the calf trotting in his direction, he lifted an eyebrow.

"Got an escapee?"

"This is Lucy Ball. She likes to go for walks."

"You mean, like a dog?" Dan shook his head ruefully. He held out one hand, and the inquisitive calf came up slowly. He wiggled a finger, and she licked it with her wide pink tongue. "She's a nice-looking calf. One of Abel's?"

"Yes, she was a farm-warming gift. Did they tell you?"

Dan laughed. "I've been working on a ranch for ten years, Bailey. I may not know much else, but cattle I know. This one has the same lines as that old milk cow out at Goosefeather."

Lucy pranced off toward the pond, and Bailey and Dan fell in step behind her. "This ranch you keep talking about. You like working there?"

Dan hesitated before answering. "I like the work. It's simple. Clear cut." He chuckled. "Hard. I came to it when I needed that kind of life, and it made a big difference for me. Well, that and the people I met there. Gordon McAl-lister owned the ranch, and his grandson, Colt, worked on it during the summers. They got to be like family to me."

"Oh?" Bailey kicked at a small stone. It skittered through the frosted grass, making Lucy Ball shy to the side. So Dan had found himself a new family out west. As if he hadn't had anybody back home waiting for him. Worrying about what might have happened to him. "How'd you meet them?"

"I hired on as a seasonal hand when I was at a pretty low point. My drinking was out of control by then, and it wasn't long before it caught up with me. I totaled one of the ranch trucks driving drunk. Instead of firing me like I expected, Gordon bailed me out on his own dime. He gave me a chewing out I deserved and a second chance I didn't. It came with conditions, like going to AA and attending church with him every Sunday. I slipped up a couple more times, but Gordon never gave up on me. He believed I had the makings of a decent human being, and finally I decided maybe he was right."

His use of the past tense and the sadness in his voice clued Bailey in. "He's not…with you anymore?"

"Gordon passed on about a year ago." Dan inhaled deeply. "Colt and his wife, Angie, run the Bar M now."

"I'm sorry, Dan. Both my parents are gone now, too. When you lose people who've meant that much to you, it's really hard."

"Yeah. It is."

"But you still work on the ranch?"

He shot her a quick sideways glance. "For now. So, you'll want the fence to turn here and cut in front of the tree line?"

"Yes." She waited as Dan broke off a branch and rammed it into the ground. For the next few minutes, they crunched along on the fragrant pine needles without talking.

When they reached the third turn, Dan stuck in another branch one-handed. Then he took a last swallow of coffee before dumping the dregs out on the ground.

He stood for a minute, looking over the scene in front of them.

The small round pond glittered under the blue sky, and in the distance the dilapidated farmhouse nestled among its overgrown azalea bushes. Those were still winter bare, but an optimistic forsythia bush was putting out tiny glowing buds of bright yellow beside the front porch. If it didn't freeze in the next cold snap, at least she'd have one pretty thing to look at until spring got here.

Bailey darted a quick look up into Dan's face. "Go ahead and say it. The place looks awful."

He shrugged. "It needs fixing, that's all. Other than that, it's nice. Some houses just look like houses. But this place looks like it could be a home."

Funny. That was exactly what she'd said when the real estate agent had brought her here. *It looks like home.* "Yeah, but it'll take a lot of work."

"Anything worth having takes work." He met her eyes and winked. "Another thing ranching taught me, I guess."

"How big is the ranch you work on?" she asked as they resumed their trek around the fence line.

"The Bar M? A shade over twelve hundred acres."

Bailey's mouth dropped open. "I thought this place was huge, and it's only twenty-six acres including the house lot!" She shook her head slowly. "Twelve hundred acres!"

"Size isn't everything. I'm just the foreman at the Bar M, but this place is all yours, Bailey. That counts for a lot. Besides—" his greenish-brown eyes twinkled "—you wouldn't want to buy fencing for a twelve-hundred-acre spread, would you?"

"No, I guess not. Speaking of fencing—" Bailey gestured toward the heap of fencing materials piled close to the house. "That's what I have to work with. Abel had some leftover wire and posts, and he let me have them. You'll have to set the wire close enough that a child couldn't slip through. I hope it'll be enough to go around."

Dan's eyes skimmed the stack. "Should be. You know, it's a really great thing you're doing, Bailey, taking in kids who need a home. Not that I'm surprised. You're a good person. Even back in high school, you were always looking for somebody to help."

Her heart swelled at his praise, and she tried to hide her reaction by taking a sip of her cold coffee before replying. "You're the one helping me right now, Dan, and I appreciate it. I want you to know that."

"I'm glad to do it." Dan looked down at her, and the gentleness in his eyes hit her with the forceful jolt of a bittersweet memory. He'd always looked at her like that. But only her. He'd viewed pretty much everybody else with a chilly suspicion that had come across as a sullen defiance. But whenever he'd turned those hard eyes in her direction, they had instantly softened. It had made her feel… "Special," he was saying, and for a second, she was afraid she'd spoken her thoughts aloud.

"Wh-what?"

"You're special to me. I know our past has its black marks, believe me, but I just want you to know, even after the divorce is final—if you ever need me, all you have to do is call."

"That's nice of you."

Their eyes held, and the moment stretched out a fraction of a second too long.

Bailey could feel the heat rising into her cheeks. She dropped her gaze and looked at her watch.

"I'd better get to work. I'm leaving the house unlocked for you. Bathroom's the third door on the left down the hall, and there's a water dispenser in the fridge."

"All right." He nodded at Lucy, who was licking one of the wooden fence posts. "I'll put your calf-puppy back in her pasture, and I'll see you when you get back."

"Thanks!" Bailey started toward the house. She needed to grab her keys and her purse and get on the road. "But you'll probably be gone by the time I get home. I have that appointment with the lawyer after work, so I'll be late."

"I'll be here," he called after her. "Until the light goes, anyway."

Bailey nodded. She glanced down at her wristwatch again as she went up the steps, but the late hour wasn't actually her biggest problem anymore.

That unmistakable little thrill of joy she'd felt at Dan's words was way more worrisome.

*I'll be here.*

At half past twelve, Dan set down the post-hole diggers and stretched his back. He was just over midway around the perimeter of the fence line. It had been a while since he'd set fence by hand, and he'd forgotten what hard, sweaty work it was.

And Bailey had figured on doing this job all on her own. He had a lot more upper-body strength and experience, and it was still tough going. He didn't see how she could have managed it, but he was impressed by her gumption.

He fished a slightly squashed sandwich out of his toolbox and glanced toward the house. Bailey had said she'd left it open. He could go inside. It would give him a chance to sit down for a few minutes, maybe drink a cold glass of water.

It would also give him a chance to take a closer look at the nest Bailey was making for herself—and get a better idea of the repairs that needed doing.

Dan shed his dirty boots on the front porch and padded sock-footed into the empty house. The place was shabby enough to be an eyesore, but he kind of liked it anyway. It felt peaceful. Something tightly wound inside him uncurled a little.

In a strange way, it reminded him of the ranch house at the Bar M, although the two looked nothing alike. The McAllister home was a sprawling place, well kept and built to handle all the extremes the Wyoming weather would throw at it. And this…well, this place was about two steps up from a dump. But somehow the houses had a similar feel. Maybe because they were both old enough to have their own personalities, like a pair of jeans that were worn enough to fit you just right.

This one needed a ton of work, but that didn't scare him any more than it had scared Bailey. In fact, if things had been different, if he and Bailey had been house hunting together like a regular married couple, he'd have been completely on board with buying this place, warts and all.

He wouldn't have told her that at first, though. He'd have teased her about the place's flaws while she praised its good points. He'd have drawn the argument out, just for the sheer fun of it, but in the end he'd have laughed and picked her up and twirled her right through that big, heavy old front door and—

He broke off the daydream midtwirl. No point going any farther. Might-have-beens were dead ends.

He looked around. The living room was furnished

with a comfortable rust-red love seat and an overstuffed chair with a chubby footstool in front of it. The colors had some spark, and nothing looked too spindly to actually sit on. Really pretty but not persnickety.

Just like Bailey. No wonder he liked it.

It had some major issues, though. The walls were horizontal unplastered boards layered with peeling paint, and there was a drop cloth in one corner where Bailey had scraped through at least five colors. There was a suspicious dark splotch on the ceiling that probably led to a leaky spot in the roof, while the second window down the side of the room had a spiderwebbing crack in it.

Making mental notes about the material he'd need to make the repairs, Dan carried his sandwich into the kitchen.

This room needed even more work. The cabinets and flooring were throwbacks to another age. The appliances were new, though. The stove that hunkered in one corner was every bit as massive as the one at the Bar M, but from the look of its control panel, it sported even more bells and whistles.

Bailey had always loved to cook, and she'd always done a bang-up job of it, too. He had a sudden image of her busy at that stove, her face flushed with warmth. He'd be standing by with the intention of helping her out, but he'd probably just get in her way—and get swatted when he tried to sneak a taste too soon.

He shook his head to clear the appealing picture. He shouldn't have come inside. This place was getting to him. He saw Bailey everywhere he looked.

Maybe she hadn't lived here very long, but her touches were all over the place. The little streaks of paint she'd dabbed onto the old cabinets, testing out the colors. The pot of narcissus blooming in the window, shaking its fist at the winter. They all said *Bailey* to him.

But he hadn't come in here to moon around dreaming silly daydreams. He needed to eat his lunch and get back to work.

He opened one of the sagging cabinets and discovered a cache of clean glasses, neatly upended on clean paper. He grabbed one and headed for the ice dispenser on the fridge.

He stuck it in the little niche, pressing the lever, and as the ice clanked into the glass, his eye was caught by an index card stuck on the front of the appliance.

He squinted and read the words aloud. "'I will lift up mine eyes to the hills, from whence cometh my help. My help comes from the Lord, the maker of heaven and earth.'"

The verse echoed in the stillness of the kitchen. Underneath it she'd written, "The Lord will send me the help I need. Nothing is impossible with God."

A sudden clattering sound woke him up. "Whoa!" He'd forgotten about the ice and his glass had overflowed, bits of ice hitting the peeling linoleum and skittering around. He spent the next minute collecting the frozen shards and tossing them into the chipped porcelain sink, thinking hard.

When he'd cleaned up the mess, he filled his glass carefully with water and settled down at the table with his sandwich in front of him.

He hesitated. He'd come a long way in his faith over the past years, but praying was something that he still found hard sometimes. Finally, he glanced up toward the old-fashioned, grooved board ceiling.

"God? I figured You brought me back here for a reason, but that verse there just clinched it. Looks like Bailey's been praying for some help, and if it's all the same to You, I'd like to ask for the job. The whole job. Not just the fencing." He paused, looking around the shabby room. "Doing the work won't be much of a problem, but talking Bailey into it is going to be a whole different ball game. I'd sure appreciate Your help with that part. Thank You, and amen."

Then he unwrapped his sandwich and took a big bite. He needed to make a trip to town, and he didn't have any time to waste.

# *Chapter Five*

At Banks Building Supply, Dan waited while Myron Banks, the elderly owner, totaled up the cost of the supplies on a chittering adding machine.

"This is a passel of stuff," the old man mumbled, punching keys with gnarled fingers. "Gonna come up to a fair amount." He shot Dan a look from under his bushy white eyebrows. "You sure you got the green to pay for all this, son?"

"Yeah, I can cover it." Dan pulled his wallet out of his jeans pocket. Thumbing through, he lifted out his personal credit card.

Bailey wasn't going to be too happy about him paying for the stuff he needed to get started on the house repairs. But according to the deal he'd just struck, that fell on God's end of things. Dan would focus on doing his part, which meant getting Bailey's place fixed up as best he could in the time he had.

"There." Myron ripped off a strip of curling paper and pushed in Dan's direction. "Told you it was going to be steep, but I gave you a discount 'cause you're buying so much."

"I appreciate that." When Dan offered his credit card, an alarmed look spread over the old man's face.

"Sorry, I got a policy. I don't do no credit cards." He indicated a hand-lettered sign on the back wall—No Credit or Debit Cards. "I don't fool with all that computerized stuff. Folks'll steal you blind, you go putting your money on the internet."

"No problem." Smothering a smile, Dan tucked the card back into his wallet. "I'll write you a check. You got any policies against those?"

The old man looked cautious. "Well now, that depends. What's your name, son?"

Dan pulled out the blank check he always kept in his wallet for emergencies and picked up a pen from the chipped mug on the counter. "Dan Whitlock."

"Whitlock, did you say?"

The change in the man's voice made Dan's spine stiffen. He looked up. Then he dropped the pen back into the mug. He wouldn't be writing any checks in this store.

"That's right."

"Kin to the Whitlocks here, are you?"

"Abel's my brother."

"*He's* a good man." There was the faintest emphasis on *he*. "You'd be the younger of Elton's boys, I'm reckoning?" When Dan nodded, the man went on. "You buying this stuff for Abel?"

"No, just helping out a friend while I'm in town."

The old man studied the steep figure circled on the adding machine paper. "Out-of-town checks are too chancy for a small operator like me. Cash would do better. You can take your check right over to the bank downtown. They'll cash it for you." *If it's any good.* The unspoken words hung in the air. The elderly man straightened his thin shoulders resolutely. "I'll hold this material for you until five o'clock this evening. That'll give you time to see to getting a check cashed. After that I'll have to put it back in the stock. That's the best I can do."

"I understand." Dan chewed on the inside of his cheek, but he kept his voice civil. "I'll be back." He picked up his hat from the counter and clapped it on his head.

"No offense meant, son," Myron called after Dan as he left the office area. "Just trying to stay out of trouble, that's all."

"So am I," Dan muttered.

He fumed the entire brief ride to the bank, but he aimed most of the anger at himself. He should've seen this coming a mile off. He'd forgotten where he was—and who he was when he was in Pine Valley. Myron's refusal to accept his check had nothing to do with it being from out of town…and everything to do with the name on it.

Whitlock.

Once he'd been used to the suspicions that clung to that name, but he'd gone away and nearly forgotten. Here in Pine Valley, Whitlock stood for thievery and double dealings. Even Abel's straight-arrow way of doing business couldn't entirely erase the stink of generations of cheats, especially not for an old-timer like Myron Banks.

Especially not when Dan had cheated people more than once himself, back in the day.

Funny. Back in Wyoming, Dan didn't even have to go down to the building supply in person. He just called in what he needed, and they had it delivered. Promptly. As the trusted foreman of the sprawling Bar M and a close friend of the well-respected McAllisters, Dan's name tended to open doors rather than shut them.

But back here in his hometown, a man was too suspicious of him to take his check.

That stung, but it fell into the category of things Dan couldn't change, and he'd learned a long time ago to leave that alone. It was another thing Gordon McAllister had drilled into Dan's brain. A man couldn't control what happened to him, but if he could control himself, well, that went a long way.

Fortunately, it didn't take the bank long to verify that he had the necessary funds in his account. Within fifteen minutes, he was walking out, his wallet thick with bills. As he stepped off the curb beside his parked truck, his eye caught on fluttering green-and-white-striped awnings down the street.

Bailey's store. He paused.

She'd be working now. But since he was already in town, he could stop in and see her. That'd be a natural enough thing to do, wouldn't it? He could buy a soda and talk to her for a minute. He could tell her about how that silly Jersey calf of hers had stolen his second-best hammer and run off with it. That'd be sure to make her laugh.

He loved to hear Bailey laugh.

He hesitated another long minute, and then shrugged, impatient with himself. What was he acting so squirrelly about? He'd stop in the store for a second then go back to the building supply and pick up the materials.

This decided, he left the truck and headed down the narrow sidewalk.

He'd never felt at home in this town, but he had to admit, it was pretty. A lot of these one-horse places were dying out—especially downtown—their old-fashioned town squares abandoned in favor of sprawling shopping centers on the outskirts of town.

But Pine Valley was holding her own. Every one of the stores facing the rosy brick courthouse was occupied, and most seemed to be doing a brisk trade. The businesses all looked neat and attractive, the sidewalks were swept, and the traffic was orderly.

All in all, this was a hardworking, honest little town, a fine place to live and raise a family.

If your last name didn't happen to be Whitlock.

"Danny?"

Emily hurried out of a building with big coffee cups painted on its windows. She was wearing an apron, and she had her hair clubbed up into a sleek bun. To Dan's astonishment, she skipped to him and gave him a warm hug.

"I figured that was you! Hard to miss that hat around here! Are you headed to Bailey's?"

"Yeah, for a minute." He smiled at her. After his wake-up call down at the building supply, Emily's kindness was a welcome change.

"I'm headed there in a few minutes myself." Emily glanced at her watch. "Sometimes she closes up for a few minutes around this time of day so she can grab some lunch and putter around in the storeroom. If her sign's up on the door, just slip through the alley and go in the back. That's what I always do. Listen—I want the two of you to come to dinner Friday night. Nothing fancy—just a beef stew—but we're anxious to spend as much time with you as we can while you're in town. Seven o'clock. Tell Bailey I'm not taking no for an answer! Okay?"

When he nodded, she gave his forearm a quick squeeze. "Wonderful! Now I'd better get back inside. I've got a tray of lemon squares almost ready to come out of the oven. Tell Bailey I'll see her in a bit."

With another friendly smile, Emily vanished into the café. Dan stared after her for a second or two before resuming his walk in the direction of Bailey's store.

His welcome in this town sure went from one extreme to the other. Abel and Emily seemed overjoyed to see him. Bailey was kind but wary, and people like Myron Banks were downright suspicious.

It sort of threw a man off his feet.

He pressed the brass lever on Bailey's door, but it didn't budge. Sure enough, when he glanced up, he saw a small square sign posted in the window.

Temporarily Closed. Will Reopen In… The little adjustable clock was showing a time twenty minutes in the future.

He couldn't wait around out here for twenty minutes. He needed to get back out to the building supply and pick up that material. He hesitated, remembering Emily's breezy instructions.

He wasn't sure it was a good idea for him to go around to the back. He was going to be treading on some pretty thin ice with the house repairs. He didn't need to make matters any worse by bugging Bailey while she was having her lunch.

It was too bad, though. He'd really liked the idea of dropping in on her. He thought for a minute, then he walked a short way down the sidewalk.

Just as Emily had said, there was a narrow alleyway leading to the loading area behind the stores. Couldn't do any harm to walk through and see if maybe Bailey happened to be out back.

He emerged from the damp, shaded alley into an asphalt parking lot and frowned. A delivery truck emblazoned with a huge orange was butted up to the concrete loading pad at the back of Bailey's store.

Had to be that Lyle fellow stopping by on his return run. The back of Dan's neck crinkled uneasily, and he picked up his pace. Just as he mounted the block steps going up to the deck, he heard Bailey's voice drifting through the half-opened door.

"Lyle, I'm not telling you again. The answer is no."

"Aw, come on. You don't really mean that."

"Yes, I do." Bailey spoke firmly, but her voice shook on the last word, just a little.

Whatever was going on in there had her nervous. Dan's heart turned hard and cold at the same time, and his hands fisted against his jeans.

From somewhere inside a man snickered, but there was no smile on Dan's face as he barreled through the doorway.

It happened so fast, Bailey's brain couldn't catch up. One minute, a smirking Lyle had her cornered against a stack of boxes, pestering her to agree to go out with him. Then in a blink he'd been yanked backward by the collar of his shirt.

Dan backed Lyle flat against the brick wall, his forearm pressing against Lyle's neck. Lyle's eyes were wide, and his mouth flexed open and shut like a landed fish.

"Dan!" Bailey choked out. "What are you doing?"

"Teaching this fellow a vocabulary lesson." Dan spoke quietly, but she could see the taut muscle under the sleeve of his shirt as he kept the other man pinned against the wall. "He seems to have some trouble understanding the word *no*."

"I was just playing around—" Lyle protested, but he choked back into silence as Dan adjusted his hold slightly.

"It's not playing unless both people want to play. Maybe you'd better say it out loud so I'm sure you've got that, Lyle."

"You're crazy! Look, Tex, this is none of your business—" Dan shifted his position again, and the delivery man's argument ended in a wheeze.

"Dan!" Bailey called out worriedly. "Be careful."

"It's all right, Bailey. Almost done here. Go ahead, Lyle. Say it."

"It's not playing unless both people want to play," Lyle mumbled grudgingly.

Instantly Dan released him. Lyle sagged down, massaging his throat, his eyes filled with outrage.

"I could have you arrested for that!"

"Go for it," Dan answered evenly. "Now get, before I think up a few more lessons you need to learn."

Alarm kindled in Lyle's eyes, and he edged farther away. Once he was safely out of Dan's reach, he began to bluster. "Don't worry, I'm going. And I won't be back, either. Just you wait until Pops hears about this, Bailey! You won't be getting any more special treatment, that's for sure!"

"If this is your idea of special treatment, I'm not interested," Bailey retorted. "And trust me, I'll be having a word with your grandfather myself."

Lyle's face darkened. He started to speak, but he darted another look at Dan and headed out the door at a trot. A second later, she heard the truck's engine roar to life.

The knot in her stomach loosened at the sound, and

her knees began to shake. She reached out and grabbed a metal shelf to support herself.

"Bailey? Are you okay?"

She swallowed hard. "I'm all right. I don't know why I'm shaking. It wasn't… Lyle was just being obnoxious. He called me back here, and then he kept badgering me about going out with him." She flushed. It sounded silly when you said it out loud, but it hadn't felt silly. When he'd cornered her in the storeroom, there had been something in his eyes… She'd gotten truly spooked there for a minute. She forced herself to take a deep breath. "I'm fine."

"You don't look fine." Dan crossed the room in one stride. Maybe it was because all her nerves were already on high alert, but as he neared, her whole body went into a convulsive shiver. "You need to sit." He dragged a wooden stool over. Taking both her upper arms gently in his hands, he lowered her onto the seat. "Try taking a few deep breaths. It's just adrenaline. You'll settle down in a minute."

"What's going on, Bailey?" Emily stood framed in the large open loading door. Her friend hurried over and draped a protective arm over Bailey's shoulders. "Danny, what happened? Is she hurt?"

"She's had a scare," Dan said quietly.

"What kind of scare?" Emily frowned and glanced over her shoulder. "Does this have anything to do with that truck that just squealed out of here? The driver jumped the curb and almost ran over Trisha Saunders's new Pekingese."

"The fruit delivery guy needed a little lesson in manners, that's all," Dan said. "I don't think he's going to be a problem anymore."

Emily looked from Dan to Bailey. "He scared you?"

"I'm not scared. I'm fine," Bailey stood, frustrated to find that her knees still wobbled under her. She couldn't believe she was acting like such a fragile flower...over *Lyle*. "Thanks, Dan. I appreciate you stepping in, but I'm really okay. Now, did you need something from the store, Emily? You must have, or you wouldn't be here."

"Walnuts," Emily admitted after a second. "I need some walnuts."

"Okay." Bailey's voice was already almost back to normal. Good. "No problem. Come out front with me then, and I'll get you fixed up. I need to grab some water anyway. Dan, you wait here, okay? I imagine you had a reason to stop by, too. I mean, apart from setting Lyle straight. Let me take care of Emily. Then I'll be right back, and we'll talk."

Dan nodded. "Take your time. I'm in no particular hurry."

When she and Emily were in the front area of the store, Emily planted herself in front of Bailey.

"Okay, we're alone. Now, Bailey Quinn, you tell me what happened back there! And don't say *nothing*, because you're as white as a sheet. Honey, did that delivery guy put his hands on you?"

"No. Lyle was being..." Bailey struggled to find the right word. "Inappropriate," she finished finally. In spite of herself, she laughed. "Wow. I sound like somebody's old maid aunt, don't I?"

"Tell me exactly what happened," Emily insisted. As they picked out the nuts Emily needed, Bailey described the incident in the storeroom.

Somehow talking about it helped. By the time she'd

finished, her breathing had slowed back down to its usual pace, and her knees had stopped jiggling like jelly.

Unfortunately, the story seemed to have the opposite effect on Emily. Her friend's cheeks were a hot pink, and she was shaking her head.

"That's just awful! When I think what could have happened… What a blessing Danny stopped by when he did!"

Bailey threw a quick look back toward the doorway leading to the storeroom and lowered her voice. "He had Lyle up against the wall before I knew what was happening."

"Good. Abel would have done the same thing," Emily said. "He and Danny must be more alike than I thought."

"Alike?" Nerves made Bailey's laugh a little shaky. "Dan and Abel? Hardly. You wouldn't say that if you'd seen him in that storeroom, Emily. For a second there, I was afraid he was going to hurt more than Lyle's pride."

"But he didn't, did he?" Emily shuddered. "When I was a waitress in Atlanta, I had some run-ins with men like that. I'm glad Danny set that guy straight. And I sure hope it'll change the way people around here see Danny. You wouldn't believe some of the mean-spirited comments folks have made since they've heard he's back in town!"

"Oh, I'd believe. Trust me."

"That's right." Emily looked at her and lifted her brows. "Abel told me you guys dated for a while back in high school. In fact—" she paused for a second "—he wonders if maybe you're why Danny finally came back to town."

"Oh?" Bailey felt a fresh wave of nervousness. "Why

would he think that?" She busied herself weighing out the nuts.

"Just an idea he got from a conversation they had. He hopes there's some truth to it. He'd love for Danny to stick around, and Abel already thinks of you as a sister. If you and Danny got back together—"

Bailey interrupted her. "That's not going to happen, Emily. Will a pound of nuts do you?"

"Better make it two. I'm baking apple-walnut muffins. So you really don't care for Danny anymore? That's a shame. Abel's convinced that Danny still has some pretty strong feelings for you."

Bailey bit her lip as she tipped more shelled walnuts onto her vintage scale. Then she glanced up and met her friend's worried eyes. "I'll always care about Dan, Emily. But it won't go any farther than that. I won't let it."

"But, honey, why not?" Emily's eyes narrowed as she scanned Bailey's face. "Danny's my brother-in-law, Bailey, but you're my best friend. If there's something I need to know about him—"

"There isn't. At least, not now, as near as I can tell." Bailey twisted the top of the full cellophane bag and fastened it with a tie. "But I learned my lesson a long time ago where Dan was concerned."

Emily frowned. "You're the last person I'd expect to hold a person's past against them. Dan's really changed, Bailey. Abel's sure of it."

"I hope so. I really do. But I'm still keeping my distance. You know all that gossip you're hearing? I used to be just as outraged about how people talked about Dan as you are now. But here's what I learned—where there's that much smoke, there's usually fire. I ignored everybody's warnings, and I got burned. Badly. If Dan's turned his life around, I'm truly glad, and I wish him every happiness. But for me, that's as far as it goes. I'm not letting him get close enough to hurt me that much again."

A soft cough from the back of the store made both women stiffen. Bailey turned to see Dan standing in the doorway. One look at his face told her that he'd overheard what she'd said.

Bailey's face flushed. She hadn't meant to hurt his feelings. She was just trying to be as honest with Emily as she could be. But after what had happened in the back room, how Dan had come to her rescue, it must seem pretty ungrateful of her to be talking this way to his sister-in-law.

"I'd best be getting on back, Bailey," he said quietly. "I've got work to do. I'll see you this evening, most likely."

"And I'll see both of you at supper on Friday," Emily inserted quickly. Then she turned to Bailey with a pleading expression. "Abel's just so happy Danny's home, and we're celebrating. We really want you to be there, Bailey. Please. For Abel."

Bailey's heart fell, but she recognized the look on Emily's face. Her friend wasn't going to take no for an answer.

"All right. I guess I'll see you then."

## Chapter Six

"Redheads," Dan observed aloud, "sure can be troublesome creatures."

Lucy Ball snorted and tossed her curly topknot. She pranced out of reach, his pliers clenched in her mouth. The calf had been stealing tools for the past half hour, and the contents of his toolbox now littered Bailey's pasture.

Lucy was making a nuisance of herself and slowing him down. He should never have let her out of her stall in the first place. But he figured Bailey would be driving up any minute, and he hoped dealing with a mischievous calf would buy him some time while he figured out how to say what he needed to say.

Or if he should say it at all.

Because, for Dan, at least, everything was different now.

The instant he'd charged through that doorway and seen Bailey backed into a corner, he'd known. The feelings he'd kept tied down and hidden for years had been tugging at their tethers ever since he'd heard about Bailey's phone call, but in that moment, they'd surged up with an unstoppable strength. His whole world had shifted and reformed like one of those little gizmos with the colored bits of glass that made different patterns with every turn. The truth had shone out so clearly it had staggered him.

He didn't want a divorce. He wanted to win Bailey back. She was different now, but she was still the woman he wanted, the only woman he'd ever want.

And he wanted it all. He wanted all those sweet little scenes he'd imagined in her house. He wanted to love this woman, protect her, laugh with her. Raise a family with her. Grow old with her.

Hours had passed since then, but his deep certainty hadn't faded a bit, not even when he'd overheard Bailey telling Emily how she didn't trust him and never would. She had every right to feel that way, and he had no clue how to go about changing her mind. But he knew he had to try.

One thing was for sure. He didn't want to talk about any of this with Bailey until he'd thought it through a little better. He'd be sure to say the wrong thing, and there was way too much at stake for that. So he'd let a calf pester the life out of him for the last hour and a half, just so there'd be something to distract Bailey when she got home.

Apparently, he needn't have bothered. Bailey was running late, and the sun was setting, throwing streamers of orange and pink into the sky behind the dark bristles of the pines. Time to pack up, he realized with a sense of relief. He'd spend some time tonight praying and trying to find some kind of answer in the dog-eared Bible Gordon had given him years ago. Maybe by tomorrow he'd be ready to talk to Bailey.

"Come on, girl." Lucy danced sideways playfully, batting her brown eyes and daring him to chase her. Dan didn't bite. He ignored her and started ambling toward the barn by himself. Just as he'd expected, the calf's curiosity got the better of her. He heard the sound of hooves behind him, and sure enough, she followed him right into the stall, where he gave her a bit of grain and plenty of good, clean hay.

"That'll taste better than those rubber tool handles," he murmured, tousling her red mop of hair. Lucy snorted at him, but she swiped his hand with her grain-encrusted tongue.

Dan left the barn, wiping his sticky hand on the leg of his jeans. He sure wished folks were as easy to understand as animals.

He gathered up the scattered tools as fast as he could, but he wasn't quite quick enough. He was cleaning calf slobber off his pliers when he saw the headlights of Bailey's old truck bouncing up the driveway.

His mouth went dry, but he squared his shoulders and stood by the fence line to wait. If he hadn't been watching for it, he'd have missed Bailey's brief hesitation before she headed in his direction. For the first time, it occurred to him that she might have run late on purpose, that maybe he wasn't the only one nervous about this.

Bailey scanned his work in the dimming light and gave him a tense smile.

"Well, you were right. You can run a better fence line than I can. Quicker, too. I can't believe how much you got done in just one day." The admiration in her voice made his sore muscles worth it.

"I've had plenty of practice." Together they surveyed the long row of fence posts marching into the trees. "Light's gone now, though. I was just about to leave."

Bailey kept her gaze focused on the fence. "I figured you'd already be gone. I had to wait nearly an hour at the lawyer's office. Mr. Monroe's going to draw up the papers for us, but he's got a lot going on right now. It's going to take him a while—he said maybe a couple of weeks. Are you planning to stay in town that long?"

Dan's heart thumped painfully. "About that," he started.

"Dan?" She broke in, her voice puzzled. "What's all that stuff on the porch?" He winced. Her eye had caught on the large stack of Sheetrock and other materials he'd unloaded a few hours earlier.

"I stopped by the building supply in town." He wished he hadn't jumped the gun and put Lucy Ball back in her stall. "By the way, I let that calf of yours out to run a little while. You're going to have your work cut out when you start training her to milk, I'll tell you that much. She's got a personality the size of Texas, and she's already spoiled rotten."

"Dan." There was a dangerous tone in Bailey's voice. "You were just supposed to help me with the fence, remember?" She squinted at the porch. "I see a couple of windows and some siding and a bunch of other stuff up there."

"We said I'd *start* with the fence. The house repairs have to be done, and it's a lot easier to have everything on site so I don't waste time running back and forth to town."

Even in the fading light, he could see the worried creases on her forehead. "I understand, but I'm on a tight budget, Dan. You really shouldn't have bought all that without checking with me first."

"Don't worry about that. It's on me." He saw her face

change, and he rushed on, "Look, I heard what you said to Emily. I get that you've got good reasons for keeping your distance, and I don't blame you. But I'd really like to take care of this for you, and I hope you'll let me."

Bailey chewed on her lip for a second. Then she sighed. "I guess we'd better have a talk. When you're done getting your tools together, please come on inside." She turned away and walked toward the house.

Dan watched her go with a sinking feeling. Looked like they were having this conversation now, ready or not. He hoped he wouldn't blow it.

By the time Dan had gathered his tools and stowed the toolbox in the bed of his truck, it was almost fully dark. Bailey had flipped on the living room lamp, and a warm square of bright yellow lit up the front porch. The welcoming golden light made the gathering darkness surrounding him seem even colder and blacker.

It put him in mind of his first few months on the ranch. He and the other hands would work until dark. They'd all come riding up, tired to the bone, and they'd see the ranch house lights glimmering over the hill. At the time, that light had meant food and a safe place to sleep. Those had been pretty valuable commodities for him back then, and he'd been thankful for them. For a long time, the ranch had been the closest thing to a home he'd ever known.

But even back then he'd never felt the same pull he felt now, and he knew why. Bailey hadn't been there, waiting inside. And he was starting to understand that home for him was wherever Bailey Quinn happened to be.

Even when she was ready to chew off a strip of his hide.

Bailey met him at the door. She wasn't smiling, but she held out a mug of steaming coffee. "Here. I figured you might be chilly. It's decaf, so it won't keep you from sleeping."

"Thanks." He accepted the mug, cupping his hands around the warmth. Back in Wyoming he drank fully leaded coffee around the clock, and it had never stopped him from sleeping whenever he had the chance. Caffeine was no match for long hours of ranch work. But at least Bailey cared about whether or not he slept. That was encouraging.

"Let's sit down. I have a couple of things I'd like to say to you."

"Sure." Dan lowered himself onto the overstuffed chair. Bailey settled on the sofa, tucking one leg under herself.

She drew in a breath and looked him in the eye. "First off, I want to thank you again for helping me out with Lyle today. Apparently I misjudged him, and I'm really grateful you came in when you did."

"You're welcome. And don't beat yourself up for not taking Lyle's measure right off. I've been fooled by a few like him myself."

Bailey's fingernails tapped the side of her mug. "I'm sorry about what I said to Emily. I was…flustered. But that's no excuse. You've gone out of your way to be kind and helpful ever since I called you. It wasn't tactful of me to say all that, especially not to your brother's wife."

It wasn't *tactful* of her to say she didn't trust him. Not it wasn't *true*.

"You were just being honest." He took a breath. "More honest than you've been with me. You keep saying you've gotten past what happened between us, but it's pretty clear you haven't, not really."

"I've forgiven you." Bailey looked exasperated, and

there was a tired vertical line between her dark brows. "But that doesn't change the fact that you still scare the life out of me."

He could actually feel the color draining out of his cheeks. "Bailey, you have to know that I'd never hurt you." Belatedly he realized how stupid that statement must sound to the woman he'd already hurt so badly. He opened his mouth to explain, but she shook her head.

"That's not what I meant. Look, you seem to have turned your life around, and I give you a lot of credit for that. But it's just—for me, you're like chocolate. Remember how much I always loved chocolate? I've been eating healthy for years, but if you put a box of chocolates in front of me right this minute, I'd struggle not to eat them all. Even though I've worked really hard to shed those extra pounds. Even though I know better. Do you understand?"

He understood, all right. She was saying that he was bad for her.

"Yeah. I do."

"Good." Bailey looked relieved. "Anyway, like I said, the divorce papers will be ready before long, and then you'll be going back to Wyoming."

The words came out before he could stop them. "Maybe not."

"What do you mean?"

Dan hesitated, but it was too late to back off now. "I may not be going back to Wyoming. I'm considering staying on in Pine Valley, maybe for good."

*"What?"* Bailey's mouth dropped open. "But why? Because Abel's here?"

For a second he considered letting her think that. It

wasn't the whole truth, but it would be so much easier. Smarter, too, probably.

But then he shook his head and looked her in the eye. This might be stupid. It most likely was. But he wasn't going to start this out with a lie. "No. Because you are."

Bailey stared. "Dan…"

He couldn't hold the words back. They rushed out of him like the waters of a stream after a heavy rain. "I want another shot with you, Bailey. I know I don't deserve one, and I know you've got plenty of reasons not to give me one. But I'm going to be up-front with you. You're still my wife, for the next two weeks, anyhow, and I still—" he stopped short of using the word *love*, as that would scare her off faster than anything else "—care about you. And I'd like to use that time to prove to you that I've changed. If you'll give me an honest opportunity to do that, then if you tell me no, I'll believe you. I'll sign those papers, and we can both get on with our lives."

"There's no way you could change my mind about us, Dan." Bailey sounded sure. "You'd just be wasting your time."

"Well, it's my time to waste. Just think it over, Bailey. That's all I'm asking. We're both having supper at Abel's on Friday night." He set down his coffee and stood up, settling his hat back on his head. He'd better leave before he dug this hole any deeper. "Think on it until then, and we'll talk again after. In the meantime, I'd best be getting along. I'll be back around sunrise tomorrow to work on the fence. I should be able to get the rest of the posts in tomorrow so I can start running the wire. Then I'll see what I can do about the house repairs, if that's all right by you."

Bailey stood, too. She looked alarmed, and she didn't

seem to know what to say. He laid a gentle hand on her arm and felt her tense at his touch. He was making her uneasy.

"I'd just like one fair shot at changing your mind before we make our goodbyes permanent. I know our marriage isn't…real, exactly. But we did say vows to each other, and I think we should be sure before we sign those papers. Don't you?"

She didn't answer. She just looked at him, her brown eyes wide.

She sure made a pretty picture, standing there in the middle of this simple room. If things were different, if she was really and truly his wife, this home would belong to the both of them. And their babies. Surely they'd have had children—sons, maybe—with his muscles and her eyes. Or little girls who'd smile up at him and tilt their heads like their mother did.

Something broke loose in his heart and rose up to clog his throat. He needed to get out of here. "I'll see you on Friday," he managed. He headed for the door.

"I'm not going to change my mind, Dan." Bailey spoke quietly behind him.

He hesitated with his hand resting on the old brass doorknob. Then he opened the door and walked out without arguing. He'd said what he needed to say, and most likely he'd blown it. Just like he'd figured.

Outside he flipped up his collar and shivered as he headed across the dark yard to his truck. Winter in Georgia had more of a bite than he'd remembered. Right now the chill seemed to be settling right down into his bones.

On Friday evening Bailey gloomily considered the welcoming lights of Abel and Emily's farmhouse through the smudged windshield of her truck. She loved the Whitlock family dearly, and Emily's cooking was always a treat. But given her seesawing emotions about Dan, Bailey wasn't looking forward to this supper. Or to the talk Dan likely wanted to have afterward.

She'd been replaying their last conversation over and over again, seeing Dan's face as he looked at her and asked her to think about giving him another chance.

She'd thought about it, all right. In fact, she hadn't been able to think about anything else. And the more she thought about it, the more conflicted she became. Right now her heart seemed to be split right down the middle.

That was going to make it awfully hard to do the smart thing and tell him *no* tonight. But that's exactly what she was going to do. The whole point of this reunion was to bring their impulsive marriage to a long-overdue end so she could move on with her life. It was a good plan and a sensible one. And she was sticking to it.

But it wasn't going to be easy.

Dan was already here. His truck was parked by the barn. And there was a silver sedan close to the house that gave Bailey another reason to want to turn tail and run.

Lois Gordon was here, too.

Bailey didn't dislike Lois. As the doting grandmother of Emily Whitlock's older twins, Lois could be a very pleasant woman. And the elderly widow had suffered more than her share of tragedy, losing her only son, the twins' father, when he was barely out of his teens. But she was also the biggest gossip in Pine Valley, and that was saying something. She had an inconvenient talent for ferreting out people's secrets.

Bailey sighed and opened her truck door. Leaning over, she retrieved the basket of jams and jellies she'd packed up back at the store. Well, she was here now. She'd just have to watch what she said and hope for the best.

Glory, Goosefeather Farm's resident goose, watched her from the yard. When Bailey shut the truck door, the bird cocked her head and honked loudly.

"Oh, hush up," Bailey scolded.

"I haven't said anything yet."

Bailey jumped, and the jars in her basket clattered together as she fumbled to keep her grip on the gift. Dan emerged from the darkened barn.

"You scared the life out of me! What are you doing hanging around out here?"

"Same thing you were doing sitting in that truck. Stalling." As he drew closer, she caught the usual whiff of cedar, mingled now with hay. The butterflies that seemed to be ever present in her stomach these days woke up and flexed their wings. "I'm not exactly looking forward to seeing Lois Gordon again. She's hated me ever since I picked roses off her prize bush back when we were in high school."

Bailey was grateful for the dimness of the twilight. She could feel her cheeks heating up. "That was a long time ago. She's probably forgotten all about it by now, but I'm sure she'll find something else to fuss about. Come on. I guess we'd better go in."

Lois might have forgotten about those roses, but Bailey hadn't. Dan had picked them for her, and the fragrant pink blossoms had been the first flowers a boy had ever given her. For years she'd kept one dried, papery bloom pressed between the pages of her Bible.

"Before we do—" Dan reached out and caught her arm gently. "Have you thought any more about what I asked you?"

Bailey swallowed. "Please let's not talk about this right now." She glanced at the farmhouse. "If Lois overheard us, our secret would be all over town before breakfast tomorrow."

"Maybe that wouldn't be such a bad thing." When Bailey made a disbelieving noise, Dan went on. "Sorry. It's just that I'm getting pretty uncomfortable keeping all this a secret from Abel. No," he went on, when she started to protest. "I won't say anything tonight, so don't worry. I'll wait until we figure out what we're going to do. But after that, either way, I'm going to want to my brother to know the truth. Abel's been really kind, welcoming me back like he has. I don't deserve it, and I don't take it lightly. If you decide...if we end up going through with the divorce, I'll ask him to keep all this to himself, of course, but you know Abel."

Bailey did know Abel. The man had a heart of gold— and a real gift for sticking his foot in his mouth. Abel always meant well, but if he knew their secret, he was likely to blurt it out at the worst possible time.

On the other hand, Bailey knew it wasn't fair for her to ask Dan to be less than honest with his brother.

"I'm sorry," Dan added. "I don't mean to make any more trouble for you."

She shook her head. "If I'd been honest years ago, none of this would even be an issue now. I'm the one who's sorry. When I asked you not to tell Abel, I didn't really think about the unfair position I was putting you in."

"Whoa." Dan reached out and curved a finger under her chin, tilting her face up toward his. "This is on me, Bailey. All of it. I don't want you blaming yourself. I just never expected Abel to take me back in like he has. If he'd thrown me off the farm like I expected him to this would never have been an issue. Like I said, I can wait on telling him until things are decided one way or the other. Our secret's kept this long—it can keep a little while longer."

"Thanks." She darted a grateful glance up at him. As their gazes caught, she saw his expression shift from concern into something else. Suddenly the air between them seemed oddly charged. He leaned toward her, and the barnyard around them blurred and softened.

"You're both here! Wonderful! Come on in!" Emily called from the back porch. "Supper's almost ready!"

Bailey felt as if she'd been dunked in cold water— and just in time, too. Giving Dan a flustered smile, she pulled away. Then she scurried up the steps and into the warm safety of the Whitlocks' kitchen.

"Oh, goodie! Some of your jams! Thanks, Bailey!" Emily hurried back to her stove, which was covered with gleaming pots. Her cheeks were flushed, and her hair straggled down the back of her neck, but the table was set with a pretty checkered cloth and the air smelled delicious. "I've just got to get these biscuits out of the oven, and we'll be good to go."

"Anything I can do to help?" Dan hesitated in the kitchen doorway. Bailey kept her eyes on the bubbling food, but she could feel his gaze on her.

"Why don't you go get Abel? He's in the living room playing a board game with Paul and Phoebe. Luke and Lily are over at Natalie Stone's for the evening, bless her sweet heart. I don't know how I'd have managed with two toddlers underfoot today."

Dan vanished, and Bailey stepped over to her friend's side and began peeking under pot lids. A scrumptious-looking stew bubbled in the biggest pot, and cinnamon apples steamed in another.

"This all looks great, Emily. Need me to taste test anything for you?"

Emily laughed wearily. "If you really want to help, you could go upstairs and fetch Nana Lois. She wanted to lie down for a few minutes before dinner. Phoebe and Paul spent the afternoon with her, and as much as she adores them, I think they wore her out."

"Sure." Bailey agreed readily, but she mounted the stairs with a sinking heart. As she stepped into the upstairs hall, Lois cracked opened the door of the spare bedroom, not a silver hair out of place.

*Nap, my foot*, thought Bailey.

"Bailey, dear, I'm so glad to have a moment alone with you. Is he here? Abel's brother?"

"Dan's downstairs with Abel and the kids. Emily says dinner is just about—"

Before she could finish her sentence, Lois reached out and drew Bailey inside the spare room, closing the heavy door behind them.

"With Paul and Phoebe? Oh my." The older woman clucked her tongue. "That's what I was afraid of. Such a bad influence! Can you believe he's turned back up after all this time? Just like a bad penny, that's what!"

Bailey frowned. "Dan's changed a lot since he's been away, Miss Lois. And I know it means the world to Abel to have him back home."

"Dear Abel has such a trusting heart. And naturally he'd like to believe the best about his family. But, Abel, I told him, when a man like Daniel Whitlock shows back up out of the blue, you know he's up to something!" Lois shook her head sadly. "I don't think Abel can bring himself to see that." She shot Bailey a sharp glance. "I do hope *you* will be more careful this time, my dear."

"Careful about what?"

"Well, I don't mean to bring up a sensitive subject, but that young man did manage to turn your head years ago. Most unsuitable, of course, and so distressing for your dear mother, rest her soul."

Bailey felt a surge of annoyance. All right. That was enough of *that*. She should put an end to this little conversation before she lost her grip on her temper. "We'd better go downstairs now, Miss Lois. Dinner is ready."

The other woman wasn't listening. "No good ever came of associating with a Whitlock. Everybody in town knows that. Abel is the one and only exception. As for Daniel? Well, once a troublemaker, always a troublemaker. That's what I told Emily, not that she thanked me for pointing it out."

"Nana Lois? Bailey?" Emily called up from the kitchen, sounding worried. "Supper's on the table."

"We should go downstairs." Bailey pulled her arm free and opened the door.

"I'm just so concerned about dear Paul and Phoebe," Lois murmured as she followed Bailey into the hall. "Children are very easily influenced."

Bailey didn't answer. She stayed silent all the way down the stairs, devoutly relieved when they made it back into the kitchen. Lois couldn't very well keep up her fussing in front of Abel and Dan.

And that was a good thing. Bailey might have a few doubts of her own about Dan, but it still irritated her to hear Lois Gordon's pessimistic fretting. People in Pine Valley had never been willing to see the good in Dan. And there was good in him—there always had been, even back when he'd been at his lowest point. Maybe if people had spent a little more time focusing on that goodness—

and a little less time spotlighting Dan's problems—things could've turned out better for everybody.

"Come with me, Nana Lois." Paul, Emily's eight-year-old son, offered his grandmother an arm. "Let me help you to your seat."

The worried creases on Lois's forehead relaxed as she beamed at her grandson. "What a gentleman you are, Paul! You take after your grandfather. He had the loveliest manners." She allowed herself to be led toward the table.

"I put Paul up to that." A basket of steaming biscuits cradled against her apron, Emily paused close to Bailey and whispered into her ear. "I wanted a chance to apologize for sending you into the lion's den. I wasn't thinking. Lois has had a bee in her bonnet all day about Danny being back home. She's part of our family, and we love her dearly, but she isn't always the easiest person to reason with when she gets on one of her rampages. I imagine she gave you an earful. I'm so sorry."

Bailey managed a smile. "Don't worry. I can hold my own with Lois Gordon. Now, something smells wonderful, and I'm starving! Let's eat."

"Sit here next to me, Miss Bailey! Please?" Phoebe, Paul's twin sister, patted the chair beside her own.

"Sure!" As Bailey settled into her seat, she glanced up to see Dan looking uneasily at the only empty chair left at the crowded table. It was right next to Lois. Dan looked as if he'd rather sit next to a rattlesnake.

He wasn't the only one less than thrilled. As he sat, Lois made a show of picking up her black suitcase of a purse and stowing it carefully on the opposite side of her own chair.

"You're the guest of honor tonight, Danny." Abel

beamed from his position at the head of the table. "How about you say grace?"

"Humph." Lois's skeptical murmur was barely audible, but Bailey saw a muscle flicker in Dan's cheek. He'd heard her, as no doubt he'd been meant to.

Bailey's heartbeat sped back up indignantly, and she bit down on her tongue. Okay, so Dan didn't have the most squeaky-clean past. But Lois Gordon had plenty of her own faults, just like everybody else.

As they clasped hands and bowed their heads, Bailey heard Dan clear his throat.

"Thank You, Lord, for this food and this family and these…friends." Bailey felt a little tickle run up her spine. Had that slight hesitation had been because of her or because of Lois? "Bless this food to our body's use and us to Your service. In Jesus's name, amen."

Bailey lifted her head in time to see Lois snatch her fingers away from Dan's. She picked up her spoon and stirred the stew in her bowl.

"My late husband was sought after for his lovely table blessings. I've always believed you can tell a real Christian by the grace he offers at a table."

"Have a biscuit, Nana Lois." Emily sounded desperate as she poked the basket in Lois's direction. "Have two."

Lois accepted the basket, but it was going to take more than biscuits to slow her down. "So, Daniel, it's my understanding that you're involved in some sort of farming enterprise out west? If that's so, I'm surprised you were able to get away for such an—extended time."

"Danny manages a ranch, Nana Lois," Abel explained proudly. "But now the rancher's grandson's taken over, so Danny isn't as needed. I'm doing my best to talk him into coming back to Georgia permanently. He says he's thinking it over."

Bailey stiffened. She glanced at Dan, and their eyes met.

"Permanently?" Lois sounded alarmed. "Are you seriously considering that, Daniel?"

"I haven't made my mind up yet. Could you pass the butter, please, Paul? These biscuits are really good, Emily."

"Of course they're good. She bakes professionally." Lois spoke impatiently. "Well, if you're considering moving here, I'd think you'd be behaving yourself a bit better. You've barely been in town any time, and you've already tried to pass a bad check to Myron Banks. You needn't all gasp at me like that! This is a small town, and word gets around. In the future you'd do well to remember that, Daniel. You won't be getting away with any of your dishonest shenanigans around here!"

Bailey saw Dan shoot a concerned glance at his brother. "The check was good. Myron just didn't want to take it because…" He trailed off. "I took it to the bank, and they cashed it with no trouble."

Bailey frowned at Lois, but the older woman was buttering her biscuit with a self-righteous expression. Bailey set her own biscuit back down on the plate. She'd lost her appetite.

It wasn't right for Dan to have to defend himself when he'd done nothing wrong. It wasn't right, and it felt all too familiar.

Caution was one thing. Caution was sensible. This was just…mean.

"You don't have to explain anything to me, Dan." Abel's lean cheeks had gone ruddy with frustration. "I can guess the truth of it. But I reckon it's a blessing you did have to go to the bank. If you hadn't, you wouldn't have been around to help Bailey when that delivery guy got fresh with her."

"Abel—" Dan and Bailey spoke at the same time, but it was too late. Lois straightened up and peered at Abel, the biscuit in her hand unbitten.

"I hadn't heard a thing about that." She sounded a little insulted. "What happened?"

Well, at least it was a distraction. "There's not much to tell," Bailey interjected quickly. "Dan stepped in before things got out of hand."

"So you see? It was a good thing he had to go to the bank after all," Abel pointed out triumphantly.

Lois's eyes narrowed. "But *why* was he hanging around Bailey's store at all? That's my question. The bank's a good little walk from there."

"Dan's doing some repairs at my new farm. For free. Isn't that kind of him?" The explanation didn't help much. Lois arched her eyebrows.

"Why would he do that? For that matter, why's he come back to town at all? I'm sorry, but somebody has to speak up here! Nobody understands the importance of family better than I do, but every family has its black sheep. Of course," Lois amended, "in the case of the Whitlocks, it's more like they had one white sheep. And that's you, Abel, dear. Daniel here has never been anything but trouble. And he wouldn't have come back to Pine Valley if he didn't want something, I promise you that. Money, most likely. I was talking about that very thing upstairs just now with Bailey."

Dan glanced at Bailey, and then back down at his plate. A muscle jumped in his jaw, and the expression on his face made her feel sick to her stomach. Her lips moved, but she couldn't seem to get any words out.

Abruptly, Dan pushed back his chair and stood. "Maybe I'd better go."

"Danny, please don't—"

Emily's protest was interrupted by the trill of Dan's cell phone. He fished it out of his pocket, looking relieved.

"It's the ranch. Colt wouldn't be calling me without a good reason, so I'll need to call him back. I'll head on back to the cabin. Abel, Emily, I'm sorry. I…" He seemed not to know what to say next. Finally, he just nodded, snagged his hat from the counter and started toward the door.

Bailey looked desperately around the table. She hated seeing that grim, defeated look on Dan's face, and she was partly responsible for it. He couldn't tell people the truth about why he was really back in town because she'd asked him not to.

Dan had his hand on the doorknob. Abel rose and exchanged a horrified glance with his wife. Neither of them seemed to know what to do.

Lois's wrinkled cheeks were a defiant pink. "Good riddance is what I say. Whatever trouble this scoundrel has come back here to cause we can certainly do well without."

That did it. Bailey stood. "Dan didn't come back here to cause trouble. He came back because I called him."

Everybody froze. Dan turned to look at her, the door open, one boot already on the back porch.

"Bailey," he said. Just the one quiet word, but she knew what he was telling her. *You don't have to do this. I can take care of myself.*

"*You* called him?" Emily looked up at Abel. "Did you know—?"

He shook his head. "No. Danny never said why he came back, and I never asked."

"You *called* him?" Lois shook her head. "Bailey Quinn! Why on earth would you do a foolish thing like that?"

"Because—" Bailey locked eyes with Dan and raised her chin a defiant notch. "He's my husband."

## Chapter Seven

Three hours later, Dan stood in front of the fireplace in the cabin watching Bailey pace. She muttered to herself as she stalked from one end of the small room to the other.

"Why did I *do* that?"

Dan didn't try to answer her. Right now Bailey wasn't looking for answers from anybody other than herself.

It had taken them two full hours to pull themselves away from the chaos at Goosefeather Farm, and they were both still a little shell-shocked. There had been long explanations and apologies to work through, and he had a feeling they'd only gotten started.

He was relieved Bailey had agreed to come to the cabin, even if all she'd done so far was try to wear a hole in Abel's braided rug. He wasn't being much help, but at least she wasn't working through all this on her own.

Bailey stopped at one end of the room, staring out the darkened window, the first time she'd been still in half an hour.

Maybe it was time for him to step in.

"Bailey? Come on. Why don't we sit down and talk this over?"

She glanced at him, and his heart stuttered. Her face was so pale that her eyes looked even darker than usual.

"I've made a huge mess, haven't I?" she murmured.

Dan crossed the room and took her gently by the elbow. She allowed herself to be led to the sofa, and as Dan settled himself next to her, he prayed he'd have the ability to say the right thing.

"Look, Bailey, you have nothing to feel bad about. All you did was tell the truth, okay? And I'm glad you did."

"You can't be serious." She swallowed. "I know you were planning to tell Abel eventually, but spilling it out like that with no warning was a terrible thing for me to do. Did you see their faces? Emily and Abel were just… floored, especially Abel. I never really thought before about he'd feel, finding out I'd kept this from him all these years."

"He just needs a little time. He'll get past it. You know he will. And I don't know Emily all that well yet, but I'm thinking she's cut from the same cloth."

"Maybe, but Lois Gordon is a different story." Bailey groaned and dropped her head in her hand. "I can't believe I blurted this out in front of her. There's no putting the cat back in the bag now. It'll be all over town tomorrow. If it isn't already. Why did I *do* that?"

"You were sticking up for me." He was trying to keep a lid on his own feelings, but a crazy hope expanded in his chest as he pointed that out. "Thanks for that, by the way."

"Save it, because I don't think I did you any favors. After Lois gets through spinning this, you're not going to come out looking very good. And neither am I." Bailey groaned. "That woman knows everybody in town, and I gave her the exclusive on a nugget of gossip beyond her wildest dreams. I just made her whole year, I'll tell you that." She stared distractedly at the small fire he'd kindled. "And I ruined mine."

Bailey's knee was jiggling up and down, and she was twisting her fingers together nervously. Impulsively he reached out and captured her hands. "I'm sorry. I know it's embarrassing to you, having everybody know you're married to somebody like me. I can't do much about that, but—"

Her hands, which had gone limp in his, suddenly clenched his fingers in a grip so tight that he winced. "Wait a minute. Dan, do you think I kept our marriage secret all this time because I was ashamed of you?"

Well, sure. He had thought that. Kind of. "I'm not saying I blame you."

Her eyes narrowed. "You'd better not be saying that, because it's not true! I was never ashamed to be married to you. I was humiliated that you dumped me, sure. Any bride who gets jilted before the ink on the marriage certificate is dry is going to feel pretty embarrassed. And it was even worse for me. I'd stood up for you to my parents and to everybody else in town. I believed in you, Dan, and then you dropped me after one fight. I felt like such a fool. When I finally got back home, I was too humiliated to admit what had happened, so I just…didn't."

There was something in Bailey's expression as she spoke, something vulnerable and sad that made his breath hitch in his chest. He felt an overwhelming urge to punch the man who'd put that pain on her face.

Which was a little unfortunate, given the circumstances.

"I'm sorry," he muttered raggedly. "I'm so sorry, Bailey. I honestly never thought about that side of it."

Bailey laughed shortly. "Right."

"I didn't. You were so beautiful. So smart and funny, and so special. Everybody said you were way out of my league, and down deep I knew it was true. I knew you'd be upset that I left the way I did. But later on, after your parents got the marriage annulled and you'd had time to think things over, I figured you'd be relieved."

There was a short silence, punctuated by the quiet crackling of the fire. Dan was very aware of Bailey's slim, strong hands resting in his. He should probably let them go, but he didn't want to. So far she wasn't pulling away, so he stayed still.

"I loved you back then, Dan, with all my heart. I had to deal with a lot of feelings after you left me, but I promise you, I never once felt relieved."

Dan's heart had expanded to the point that he could barely take a breath. She'd loved him. *Back then.* He felt both the joy and the sadness of that all the way to the toes of his boots. "Bailey," he said gruffly.

Something of what he was feeling must have come out in his voice, because she gently slipped her fingers free from his and scooted a few inches away. When she spoke, she kept her eyes fixed on the fire.

"Maybe it would have been easier for me if I'd understood why we even had that argument in the first place. All I wanted was for us to come back here and face up to my parents as a married couple. I didn't agree with them about you, Dan. But I still loved them, and I was their only child. I needed them in my life. I was *eighteen*, Dan."

"I know." He swallowed.

"But you wouldn't listen to reason. You told me we were going out west, period, and we were never coming back. When I argued with you, you yelled at me and stormed out."

He remembered.

"I'm sorry. I was scared, Bailey. I was sure if we came back to Pine Valley your parents would manage to break us apart. They'd been trying the whole time we'd been dating, and I knew they'd never forgive me for talking you into eloping. I was terrified they'd talk to you, and you'd wise up and realize what a mistake you'd made. Then I'd lose you for good."

She studied him for a minute. "You should have told me that."

"No man worth his salt wants his brand new wife to know he's a coward, Bailey. Maybe I should have told you. But the truth is, even if I had, I don't know that it could have worked out any better for us, not back then. You loved your parents, so you needed to come back. But my situation was totally different. If I hadn't gotten away from this place, I probably would've turned into the man everybody around here expected me to be. I needed the fresh start. But now—"

"Now you've turned that fresh start into a whole new life out in Wyoming. And I've sunk my roots even deeper into Pine Valley." Bailey shook her head slowly. "Nothing's different, Dan."

"*I'm* different, Bailey. You want to stay here in Pine Valley? Then I'll stay here with you. Forever, if you want me to."

He saw the hope dawning in her expression, and his heart sped up. But there was doubt there, too. He held her eyes with his, willing her to believe him.

*Yes, Bailey. I'm dead serious.*

She pulled her gaze away, and he saw her throat pulse as she swallowed.

"What about the ranch? Your phone's been buzzing ever since we left Goosefeather Farm. You love that place, and you have friends there who obviously need you."

"Colt likes to run things by me, that's all. He doesn't really need me. And how I feel about the ranch is nothing compared to how I feel about you. If you tell me I have a chance with you, any chance at all, I'll call him this minute and put in my notice." He paused, his heart lodged so tightly in his throat he could barely breathe. "Are you going to give me that chance, Bailey?"

"Dan, I honestly don't know…"

"I'm not asking you for any promises, Bailey. Not yet. But I'm making you one. If you tell me I have any hope of winning you back, I'll put Wyoming in my rearview mirror for good. You have my word on it." He waited, watching her face. "So do I make that call or not?"

She chewed on her lip. Finally, she sucked in a quick, broken breath and nodded. "Make the call."

The breath he'd been holding whooshed out of his lungs in a huge sigh of relief. He wanted to kiss her, hug her, pick her up and spin her around.

But he also didn't want to spook her into changing her mind, so he just took his phone out of his pocket and tapped the screen.

He'd missed half a dozen calls from the ranch. Colt probably had some new scheme about buying into the Shadow Lady bloodline he was so excited about. Well, whatever it was, he was going to have to pull it off without Dan.

Leaving Bailey sitting on the sofa, Dan started for the

bedroom. Colt might not need him, but his boss wasn't going to let him go without an explanation, and he didn't want Bailey to hear that. He'd made it to the doorway when he heard the line connect. He hurried to speak before Colt could. "Hey, Colt. Listen, man. I've got something to—"

It wasn't Colt.

Dan stopped short, listening to the frantic ranch hand on the other end of the line. "I'm on my way," he said finally.

He turned. Bailey was watching him from the couch. "Dan? What's wrong?"

"There's been an accident. Colt…my boss…my friend…he's in the hospital. They don't know if he's going to make it." The awful words sounded like they were coming from someplace far away. "His wife is hurt bad, too. I have to go back to the ranch right now. Tonight."

"I see."

"I'm sorry, Bailey. I just told you I'd stay…and now…"

"It's all right." She stood up and crossed the room. And for the first time in years, she put her arms around him and hugged him tight.

The embrace was brief, but somehow it cut through the swirling confusion in his brain and steadied him.

She stepped back and looked up at him. "Now go. No," she added when he started to speak, "please don't worry about me. You go help your friends."

"I don't know how long this is going to take, but once it's over with, I'll be back. And this time I'm coming back to stay." She nodded so quickly that if he hadn't been looking for it, he'd have missed the flicker of doubt in her eyes. "You have my word on that, Bailey."

She didn't answer. She only nodded again and pressed her lips together into a sad attempt at a smile. "Take care of yourself, Danny" was all she said.

*Danny.* She hadn't called him by his old nickname since he'd come back, not once. It had been *Dan*.

And that's when he knew.

For Bailey, history was repeating itself. He was leaving her behind, and she wasn't sure she'd ever see him again.

And no matter how many promises he made right now, nothing was going to make her believe any different.

Three weeks later, as she drove home from the store after work, Bailey listened to Jillian Marshall's voice coming over the Bluetooth speaker she'd mounted on the dash of her truck.

"What are you going to do, Bailey?"

Bailey lifted one hand from the steering wheel and massaged her throbbing temples. The headache was no surprise. Neither was Jillian's question. Ever since she'd outed her marriage at that dinner, her life had been nothing but one big pain.

The backlash of that little bombshell, coupled with Dan's abrupt departure, had caused a gossip storm of hurricane proportions. Her store had been mobbed on a daily basis, but nobody really wanted to buy anything. They just wanted to hear all the juicy details firsthand.

They also wanted to express their opinions. Bailey had bitten her tongue so often it was sore. And as much as she liked Jillian, she suspected that this phone call was just more of the same. Jillian was more interested in getting the scoop on what was going on than she was about the status of Bailey's foster parent plans.

Well, she couldn't really blame Jillian—or anybody else. Bailey had lived in a small town her whole life, and she knew how folks reacted to things like this. Naturally people were going to be curious.

It was her own fault for blurting out her long-kept secret like she had. She should have remembered—impulsive decisions didn't usually work out all that well for her.

Especially not when they involved Dan Whitlock.

"Bailey?" Jillian's voice came over the speaker. "Do you really believe he'll come back? I mean, I know he's supposedly dealing with some emergency, but if he hasn't even called you..."

*Supposedly.* Lois Gordon had done her work well. Apart from Abel's staunch belief that Danny would be back as soon as he could, that was the common theme Bailey kept hearing. Dan Whitlock had proved once again that he couldn't be trusted.

And poor Bailey Quinn had been taken in for a second time.

Unfortunately, she didn't have a whole lot of evidence to contradict either of those things. It wasn't the first time she'd found herself clinging too long to promises Dan had made.

Well, there was no point beating around the bush. Jillian was right. Dan hadn't been in touch since the day he'd left town, and that really left only one reasonable option. "The lawyer finished with the divorce paperwork last week. It just needs our signatures. If I don't hear from him by tomorrow, I'll forward it to Wyoming. Hopefully he'll sign, and that'll be the end of it."

"And if he doesn't?"

"According to the lawyer, there are some other options. But we have to try this one first."

"I'm sorry, Bailey. But don't you think this is for the best, really?"

She didn't want to talk about this anymore. "I've got to go, Jillian. I'll be back in touch once I've got the divorce papers signed, and we'll get the foster care process started."

She disconnected the call with a firm tap. She'd had enough of nosy people for one day. Now she was going to go back to her tiny little farm, love on Lucy Ball and get her animals all settled in for the night. She'd brew herself a nice cup of chamomile tea and spend the evening cuddled up with some seed catalogs.

Maybe she'd even pull out that informational packet she'd picked up at the foster care seminar. She'd take another look at those cute faces and try to rekindle the dream she'd been all too willing to set aside the minute Dan had looked into her eyes and asked her for a second chance.

If he'd really meant all those things he'd said, why hadn't he called? At first, she'd assumed he was busy seeing about his friends. He'd call when he could. But now that Dan's silence had stretched into weeks, that excuse had worn thin.

She wasn't going to make the same mistake she'd made last time. She was older and wiser now, and she knew better. She was going to accept the reality of her situation and deal with it. Tomorrow she'd sign the divorce papers and overnight them to Wyoming. And she'd close out the Dan Whitlock chapter of her life once and for all.

"Better late than never," she said aloud as she turned into her driveway.

And then she saw his truck.

Her heart pounded as she parked, her eyes fixed on

the figure slumped over the steering wheel. Dan's truck was still running, and he seemed to be asleep, his forehead resting on his hands. For once the cowboy hat was nowhere in evidence.

She walked slowly across the yard, battling her emotions at every step. Relief, joy, aggravation.

Hurt.

Well, he'd come back, just like he'd promised. But why on earth hadn't he called in all this time?

She was close enough to touch the door handle before he lifted his head. And when he did, she drew in a quick, hard breath.

The raw pain in his face made all the doubts she'd been fighting fall to the side. She yanked open the truck door and put one hand on his shoulder.

"Dan, what is it? What's happened?"

At the sound of her voice, a thin wail came from the back of the cab, joined almost immediately by a second one. Stunned, Bailey tiptoed and saw two rear-facing infant car seats installed in the back seat. One had a pink blanket trailing out of it, the other a blue one. Both blankets were wiggling.

She turned her astonished gaze back to Dan, her heart melting at the anguish in his eyes. *"Dan?"*

It took him a minute to answer her. When he did, his voice was hoarse and broken. "The accident was bad, Bailey. They're gone. Both of them. First Angie. Then Colt."

"Oh no." She tightened her grip on his shoulder. "Oh, Dan. I'm so sorry. Are these…are these their babies?"

He nodded slowly. He drew in a ragged breath and covered her hand with one of his. "Yeah. Their twins. Finn and Josie McAllister."

"But I don't understand. Why…why did you bring them here?"

"I had to. They're mine now, Bailey. Colt wrote it all down in his will. I don't know why. Well, I mean, he left a letter. The lawyer showed me. It said I was like a…a brother to him. Closest thing to family he had. And he knew I'd take care of the twins, make sure they grew up understanding what it meant to be McAllisters. He never thought this would really happen, you know? He and Angie were young and healthy. He just needed a name, I guess. So he put mine down. He left me everything, Bailey. The ranch. All of it."

He pulled his hand away from hers and covered his eyes. It took her a minute to realize what was going on.

Dan Whitlock had always taken life's blows with a set jaw and an uptilted chin. He wasn't the kind of man who cried. He never had been, not even as a gangly teen, not even when his dad had beaten the daylights out of him.

But he was crying now.

# Chapter Eight

❧

Dan sat on Bailey's sofa, holding Josie, who was sound asleep. Bailey was sitting cross-legged on the floor, sorting through the suitcases of baby supplies he'd hauled in. She had Finn in her arms, so she sorted one-handed as the exhausted baby slept against her.

The babies ought to be worn out, the both of them. He sure was. The twins had cried off and on through most of the long drive. He'd stopped frequently, done everything he could think of to make them comfortable, but they'd still seemed miserable. He'd hated the feeling of helplessness that had given him, and he'd had to fight the urge to press the gas pedal all the way to the floor in order to get back here faster.

For the last couple of weeks, it had been all he could think about. Getting back to Bailey.

"You did a good job, Dan." Bailey surveyed the huge array of formula cans, baby medicines, diapers and bottles spread across her living room floor. "I think you have everything here they could possibly need."

"Angie's friends packed it up for me," Dan admitted. "Angie didn't have any family to speak of. It was something she and Colt had in common. But she had some really good friends."

"So did Colt," Bailey spoke softly. "You must have been an awfully good friend to him, Dan. I don't think there's a higher compliment one man could pay another one than to trust him with something as precious as these two."

The knife that had been resting in Dan's heart shifted deeper, and pain that had just started to scab over broke through again. "Like I said before, he didn't know anything like this really was going to happen, Bailey."

"But he knew that if it did, he wanted you to take care of what he loved best in the world. That says a lot, Dan. In fact, that says everything." She looked down at the tiny boy sleeping in her arms, and her face softened. "What a mercy that the babies weren't hurt in the accident."

"They weren't in the car." Dan swallowed hard. "Angie and Colt hadn't been out anywhere just the two of them since the twins came along, and it was their anniversary. So they left the babies with Angie's best friend, Mallory, so they could go out to dinner. Mallory took care of the twins for me while I was at the hospital. And later, while I was dealing with the funerals. It was nice of her because she has a two-year-old of her own to look after. She tried to teach me how to take care of them, too." He still remembered Mallory's worried, tearstained face as she showed him how to change a diaper, how to burp a wiggling baby midbottle.

She'd been as nice and helpful as she could possibly be, but Dan had seen the alarm in her eyes when he'd told her he'd be taking the twins to Georgia for a while. Not that he blamed her. The only thing he knew about babies was that he really didn't know anything about babies.

That reminded him. He fished in his shirt pocket and brought out a folded sheet of notebook paper. "She wrote down for me what to do, when to feed them. How much, and all that. I've been trying to do what she said." *Exactly* what she said, measuring formula powder out three times before he was satisfied he had it right, checking the temperature of the special sterilized water he'd bought so carefully that more than once he'd had to reheat it.

The twins hadn't been too happy about that. *Don't make hungry babies wait for food.* That was one of the first things he'd learned the hard way.

It hadn't been the last, and he was barely getting started.

"Let me see." Bailey reached for the paper, and he surrendered it with a feeling of guilty relief. She scanned the handwritten instructions quickly, her dark brows furrowed. "Okay. Nothing here looks too complicated. Just the usual baby stuff. We can manage this."

*We.* Dan had to fight the urge to reach over and hug Bailey fiercely with his free arm. Ever since he'd found out he was the sole guardian named for the twins in Colt's will, he'd been reeling. Finding himself entrusted with the Bar M would have been tough enough. He'd been the ranch foreman, sure, but he'd never been solely responsible for all the top-level decisions.

He'd come close, though, when Gordon's health had failed him. Dan knew most of the ropes there, and what he didn't know he could figure out. Yeah, he could manage the ranch, although taking sole charge of Gordon McAllister's beloved spread was a heavy responsibility.

But the babies? Being entrusted with the twins took everything to a whole different level. He was in way over his head, and Bailey's quiet assumption that she was in this with him, that they were going to figure it out together?

That brought such a tidal wave of relief over him that if he hadn't already been sitting down, he'd have fallen to his knees.

But he wasn't sure exactly what that *we* meant, and he was afraid to ask. His heart already felt like it had been chewed up by a wolf. He really didn't think he could handle any more pain right now.

But if it was coming, he might as well meet it head-on. "Bailey? We kind of left things hanging between us before. I guess we need to figure out where we stand now, you and me."

Bailey looked up from the can of formula she was examining, her expression wary. "Yes, I guess we do." She set the can on the floor and struggled to her feet, still holding Finn. She retrieved a large brown envelope from a table and handed it to him before sitting back down. "The lawyer finished the divorce papers."

His heart fell hard. "Is that what you want?"

She didn't answer him at first. She looked down at the infant cradled in her arms, then back at him. "I haven't signed them yet," she said quietly. "But I was planning to. I was going to send them to Wyoming. When you didn't call for so long, I figured that was what *you* wanted."

"I'm sorry about that. I just…things were happening so fast. The hospital wouldn't let me use the cell phone in intensive care, and then my battery died. I'd forgotten the charger at the cabin, and it took me a couple days to buy a new one. By that time, I was just surviving, trying to figure stuff out. And I couldn't see any way I could explain all this—" he gestured at the jumble of baby stuff all over Bailey's living room "—when I didn't even understand it myself. I figured it would be better for us to talk about it in person."

He was telling her the truth, just not all of it. Partly he'd been scared to call. He'd been afraid when she heard about the ranch, heard about how his situation had shifted, she'd back away, and he'd lose her. He hadn't been able to stand the thought of that. So he'd set his mind on getting back here as fast as he could, hoping he'd have a better chance of convincing her if they talked face-to-face.

"It's okay. I understand how hectic things get when you're in the middle of a crisis." She wasn't telling him the whole truth, either. He could see the hurt in her eyes, hear it in her voice. His silence for the past three weeks had done some serious damage.

He wanted to kick himself.

"I should have called. I'm sorry, Bailey."

"It's all right, Dan." One corner of her mouth tipped up in a smile. "At least you came back this time. That counts for a lot."

He drew in a slow breath. "I did. But I've brought along a good many responsibilities that I didn't have when we talked before."

Bailey's gaze drifted back to the slumbering baby in her arms. "You sure have. And they're beautiful, Dan. Just beautiful."

True, but the twins were only part of what he'd been talking about—and honestly, not the part that worried him, at least not where Bailey was concerned. He'd known Bailey wouldn't blink about taking on a pair of orphaned twins. She was that kind of woman—the best kind, strong and sure and good.

But the rest of it was going to be a much tougher sell,

and before he tried, he needed to make sure she understood something.

"Everything's different now except for one thing. I still care about you, Bailey. I still want to see if we can work things out." He paused. "You say you were going to sign these papers because you thought that's what I wanted. It isn't, not by a long shot. But the question is, what do you want?"

He waited for her answer with his heart hammering. She took her time giving it.

"I don't know yet." Her dark eyes reminded him of a doe's, cautious and careful. "But I think I'd like the opportunity to find out."

That was exactly the answer he'd been praying for. After three weeks of grief and worry and confusion, the relief that crashed over him felt as crazy and wonderful as a thunderstorm breaking a long summer drought. But mingled in with his joy was a splinter of doubt. There were some important things about his new situation that he needed to make very clear.

Before they went any further, he had to make sure Bailey understood exactly what she was getting herself into—and exactly what he'd be forced to ask her to give up if she decided to remain his wife.

He didn't like it. But it was what it was, and she needed to know.

"Bailey," he started, but she interrupted him firmly.

"No, Dan. Please don't press me for anything more than that right now. We both need some time to process everything that's happened, don't you think? Besides, you rushed me into marrying you the first time, and that didn't work out all that well. We're going to have to take things slowly. One step at a time. And we'll see how it goes. That's the best I can do."

He stopped short. If he kept talking right now while everything between them was so fragile, he'd likely ruin the last chance he had with this woman. If he waited a few more days, let things settle a bit, maybe the connection growing between them would be strong enough to handle the weight he had to lay on it.

Bailey wanted some time, and he needed it. But that was part of the problem. Time was the one thing he didn't have to spare. And soon—very soon—he was going to have to explain that to Bailey.

The next Sunday after the eleven o'clock service, Bailey learned an important lesson: when a couple shows up at church with a pair of unexpected twins in tow, they're going to get mobbed.

Bailey stood on the side lawn of Pine Valley Community Church, surrounded by women who were exclaiming over the twins and asking all kinds of questions. She didn't mind. For the past few weeks, she'd been fielding questions about her marriage. This was a welcome change.

Besides, who could blame them? The babies were adorable, even if she did say so herself. She'd insisted on coming over to Dan's cabin early this morning and helping him get them ready for church. She knew Dan could've handled it alone. He was so careful and gentle with the twins that Bailey's heart melted every time she watched him tending to them. But she'd wanted the fun of dressing the babies herself.

And it had been pure joy. She'd loved every second of the process, even when Josie had spit up all over her pretty pink dress. Bailey hadn't minded a bit—there was a precious yellow dress she'd almost chosen, and this gave her an excuse to pull it back out. Josie looked every bit as beautiful in it, and Finn looked equally sweet in his little green romper. Bailey had taken so many pictures with her phone that they'd arrived five minutes late.

Bailey usually fretted over running late, but today she didn't care a bit. It was a beautiful, perfect Sabbath day. Spring had decided to visit Georgia early. The late-February day was unusually balmy, and the pear tree in the churchyard had already budded out in multitudes of white blossoms. The slim sapling looked like a bride, all decked out in a frothy white dress, waiting for her groom.

That image gave Bailey's insides an exciting little stir. She looked through the crowd of women to where Dan was standing in the big arched doorway of the church, talking with Pastor Stone and Abel. Jacob Stone and Dan's brother were nice-looking men, but Bailey privately thought Dan put them both to shame today. He was dressed in khaki slacks and a crisp green shirt that strained a little across his muscled shoulders. It was the first time she'd seen him in anything other than jeans, and she had to say, the man sure cleaned up well.

As if he felt her glance, he turned his head in her direction. He didn't smile. Smiles hadn't come easily for Dan just lately. But the sun creases in the corners of his eyes deepened slightly as their gazes caught. Bailey's heart flipped over, and she had to force herself to focus her attention on the cooing women around her.

"They're so precious." Emily had Josie nestled under her chin, the skirt of the yellow dress fluffed out over her supporting arm. "Of course, you know how partial I am to twins," she added with a chuckle. "And a good thing, too, since I don't seem to be able to have anything else!" Then she sighed. "It just breaks my heart, though. About their parents, I mean."

"I know." Bailey bounced Finn, who'd begun to squirm in a way that meant he was about to start fussing. "The accident was a horrible tragedy."

She kissed the top of Finn's fuzzy head. The McAllister twins had stolen Bailey's heart from the first moment she laid eyes on them, and the attachment was only growing deeper. If things worked out with Dan, Bailey would instantly have the family she'd dreamed about for years.

But the joyful hope budding in her heart brought some guilt along with it. The twins would never have come to Georgia if it hadn't been for that terrible accident. She'd never met the McAllisters, but from everything Dan said, they'd been wonderful people.

"Yes, it *was* a tragedy." Natalie Stone reached out a finger and touched the frill of lace on Josie's tiny sock. "But our God specializes in bringing great good out of even the worst situations." The pastor's gentle wife smoothed the fabric of her simple dress over a baby bump that was just beginning to show and smiled. "I know that firsthand. I think that's what we need to focus on now— our confidence in the blessings the Lord will bring about for these little ones. I expect you're going to be a big part of that, Bailey."

"I hope so." Bailey threw a grateful look at her friend, who was living proof of God's goodness in tough situations. As a brand-new Christian, Natalie had been jilted at the altar by her irresponsible fiancé—and she'd been eight months pregnant with her son, Ethan, at the time. But God had turned that disaster into a blessing beyond imagining, and now Natalie was happily married to Pastor Jacob Stone.

Natalie's quiet words helped. Bailey felt the lingering guilt ebbing away. She couldn't change the past. But maybe, just maybe, like Natalie had said, she could be a joyful part of the twins' future.

Alongside Dan.

She drew in a deep breath of air scented with the sweetness of spring blossoms and baby shampoo and felt tears pricking at the back of her eyes. She blinked hard and smiled brightly. "Isn't this weather amazing? You'd never know it's February."

"It *is* February, though." Arlene Marvin, the church's elderly secretary, edged her way through the crowd. "No matter what that foolish pear tree happens to think. Winter's not done with us yet, and those blossoms are going to get frost nipped, you mark my words. And Cora Larkey told me to tell you those blueberries you're so fond of are blooming out, too, more's the pity."

Bailey frowned. "So early?" She loved the heritage blueberries that grew on Lark Hill Farm. They were always a huge hit at the store, and she had contracts to provide them to several area restaurants, as well.

"Yes. Our next frost'll get them for sure, but like this silly tree, they couldn't resist a false spring."

"You never know. Maybe spring's truly come early this year, Arlene," Bailey said. She realized she didn't much care either way. Blueberries and pear blossoms were small losses compared to the sweet hopes that had started to nestle in her heart.

"I doubt that. We're bound to get one more hard freeze before warm weather sets in for good. We always do. Now, Natalie, you need to get out of this sunshine and go sit down. You've been on your feet long enough. You know what Doc Peterson said."

"All right, Arlene. I'm going." Natalie gave Bailey and Finn a hug. "I'm praying for you and Dan and these sweet, sweet babies," she murmured. "Every single day."

Lois Gordon, who'd been lingering on the outskirts of the group, snorted. "Somebody'd better be praying," she grumbled. When the other women shot warning looks in her direction, Lois squared her shoulders. "Stop glaring at me. Nearly everybody in town's thinking it. Somebody might as well say it to her face. We're worried about you, Bailey. You're a good person, and we all care about you. But Daniel Whitlock is a cat of a different stripe. I know that's probably not what you want to hear right now, but it's the truth. And if you can't speak the truth in the churchyard, where can you?"

Emily lifted her chin, a sure sign that she was gearing up for battle. "I'd say if you can't show a little Christian mercy and forgiveness in a churchyard, where can you?"

Lois tightened her lips, and tears glimmered in the older woman's eyes. "I'm sorry, Emily. I know he's Abel's brother, but they're nothing alike, never have been. Daniel took after their skunk of a father. You and Abel mean the world to me, but I'm worried about having a bad influence like Daniel around my grandchildren."

"Dan had his issues in the past, but people can change, Mrs. Lois. Dan's wonderful with the twins, and he's been nothing but honest and kind to all of us since he's been back in town." Bailey spoke firmly, pitching her voice so that everybody nearby could hear. Lois was right about one thing. She was only saying what a lot of people were thinking. Bailey had heard plenty of those opinions while Dan had been gone.

It was really frustrating and very unfair to Dan. Given what he was going through right now, the last thing he needed was more of this kind of thing.

Bailey was getting pretty sick of it herself.

"I suppose people do change sometimes, but it's very risky to stake your future on it lasting for very long. Time will tell, that's what. In the meantime, the less time he spends around my grandchildren, the happier I'll be. And I certainly wouldn't rush to toss out those divorce papers if I were you, Bailey, no matter how cute these little babies are."

"Don't you worry about Bailey," Anna Bradley said firmly. "She's not rushing into anything. She's far too smart for that. She'll take her time and make the wisest possible choice."

A murmur of agreement came from many of the women. But not all of them. Bailey couldn't help noticing the worried looks some of the ladies shared.

She straightened her shoulders. So what? She couldn't blame them for having the same doubts she'd struggled with herself.

Although ever since Dan had come back with the twins, those doubts seemed to be getting scarcer. It wasn't hard to see why. There was something so endearing about watching Dan push his own grief aside as he tried to learn how to take care of the orphaned babies. Like yesterday at the cabin, when she'd caught him scrubbing at his wet eyes with one shoulder while he struggled to dress Finn in a Daddy's Little Rancher onesie.

She'd come alongside and showed him how to roll up the tiny outfit before pulling it over the squirming baby's head. Standing so close to him, seeing the soft warmth in his eyes as he thanked her for helping…well. She wasn't quite ready yet to name what she'd felt at that moment, but one thing was for sure.

It hadn't been doubt.

"Hello, ladies." A deep voice spoke suddenly, and she looked up to see that Dan was edging gently through the women. "Hi, Emily." He nodded at his sister-in-law, who offered him a warm smile over Josie's head.

Everybody wasn't as welcoming. An uneasy silence fell, and several of the women backed away from the group and began to make embarrassed goodbye noises.

Dan's friendly expression faded into a determined politeness. "I'm sorry. I didn't mean to interrupt. I was just wondering if you were ready to go, Bailey. The twins will be kicking up a fuss to eat soon."

"Yes, I'm ready." She couldn't tell if Dan had overheard any of the women's remarks, but from that look on his face, it didn't matter. He'd clearly picked up on the guilty glances the women were tossing around.

Bailey's heart sank. So far Dan had quietly accepted everything this town had thrown at him, but Pine Valley's lingering suspicions had to bother him. He'd come back to his hometown grieving and trying his very best to parent two orphaned babies, but people were still giving him sideways glances.

He deserved so much better. From all of them.

Dan had come up in front of her and was reaching for Finn. Before she thought better of it, Bailey went up on her tiptoes.

And for the first time in well over a decade, her lips met Dan Whitlock's.

She heard the swift intakes of breath around her, but the women weren't the only ones caught by surprise. She felt Dan startle, for just a second. Then the arms that had been reaching for the restless baby went around her waist instead and pulled her into the warmth of his kiss.

The feel of his lips on hers was at once sweetly familiar and unsettlingly new. Her heart hammered furiously as emotions she'd kept dammed up for years broke free and washed over her like a waterfall.

It was all over in a few sweet seconds, but that didn't matter. Bailey felt the impact of Dan's kiss all the way to the tips of her toes. When she went back down on her heels, she had to brace her knees to keep them from buckling.

Maybe she should have thought this through a little better. Unfortunately, right now her brain couldn't have come up with a rational thought if her life had depended on it. She was barely able to stay upright.

Dan must have seen something in her face, because he quickly scooped the warm bundle of baby out of her arms. Then he cupped her elbow with one hand, steadying her.

Her heart hammering with a frantic mixture of joy and daring, Bailey looked up into his face. His greenish-brown eyes locked onto hers, but instead of the joy she'd expected, she saw shock mingled with something else, something that made uneasy goose bumps pop up on her arms.

When Dan finally spoke, his words came out in a guilty rush. "Bailey, I think we need to talk."

# Chapter Nine

When Bailey's face changed, Dan knew he'd messed up.

As they walked toward his truck, each of them holding a squirming twin, he cut worried sidelong glances at her. She kept her eyes away from his, her jaw clenched. She didn't speak, but he didn't need her to. It was plain enough to see that he'd embarrassed her—and probably made her mad to boot.

He hadn't meant to. That kiss had just thrown him for a loop, coming out of nowhere like it had. He felt like kicking himself. He'd been hoping and praying for something like this for so long—and when it had finally come, he'd blown it.

What he'd said was true. They did need to talk. But he shouldn't have blurted that out in front of all those ladies. Apparently, Abel wasn't the only Whitlock with a talent for sticking his foot in his mouth.

When they pulled out of the church parking lot, he glanced at Bailey. "I thought we'd go to the cabin. We can feed the twins and put them down for their naps. And then we can talk."

"All right." That was all she said, but he saw the tense

furrows deepen on her forehead. Bailey already suspected she wasn't going to like what he had to tell her.

He didn't like it, either. Gordon McAllister hadn't only shown him the ropes of ranch work—the old man had also given him some no-nonsense lessons about honor. One of the main things the rancher had stressed was the fact that a decent man never went back on his word.

But that's just what Dan was about to do.

They pulled up into the cabin driveway and began the process of getting the twins out of their car seats and into the house. They worked together to warm up tiny bottles of formula, change diapers and settle the sleepy twins into the cribs Dan had arranged against the wall of his bedroom.

For the first time since he'd become responsible for the babies, he wished they'd take some extra time to settle down. He needed some time to think through what he was going to say. But once their bellies were full, the little traitors dozed off. Both of them. At the same time. That almost never happened.

Go figure.

Dan glanced at Bailey, who was tucking a giraffe-printed blanket around Finn. Her face was relaxed and unguarded as she hovered over the sleeping infant, and Dan's heart tightened in his chest. He really didn't want to have this conversation right now. He wanted more time, but that sweet, unexpected kiss had forced his hand.

If he wanted more of those kisses—and he definitely did—he had to be completely honest with Bailey. There was no way around it.

"They're down," he whispered. "Let's go." He backed up against the full-size bed to allow her to pass by him.

He noticed she pressed herself tightly against the crib rails in order to squeeze by without brushing against him.

So they were back to that.

Once in the living room, Dan paused to pull the bedroom door closed. Bailey frowned.

"Shouldn't we leave it open so we'll hear them if they wake up?"

Dan laughed wryly. "Don't worry. In this little cabin, you'll hear every squeak. Trust me on that."

Bailey nibbled on her lower lip as she sank down on the sofa. "Maybe we should alternate nights, so I can help out more. I could stay here with the twins every other night, and you could bunk out at my place. You're having to miss a lot of sleep trying to take care of them all by yourself."

That was kind of her, but it wasn't what he was shooting for. He wanted all four of them together in one house, living like a real family. But at least her offer gave him a flicker of hope that he hadn't messed things up too badly.

Not yet, at least.

He sat beside her, leaving a careful gap between them. "I appreciate that, Bailey, but until you and I work things out, the twins are my responsibility. Don't get me wrong, I'm really thankful for all your help, but I'll handle the night shifts solo for now. I still don't have a clue what I'm doing, but I don't think I'm messing up too bad."

Some of the color returned to Bailey's face. "You're not giving yourself enough credit. You're wonderful with the twins, Dan." Her expression softened. "You're going to be a great dad."

She sounded like she truly believed that. His eyes met hers, and his breath got caught someplace midway between his chest and his throat. Suddenly all he wanted in the world was to take this woman in his arms and kiss her again.

He'd better get this over with before he lost what little self-control he had left.

He cleared his throat. "Like I said back at the church, Bailey, we need to talk."

"Because I kissed you." Bailey was watching him closely. "I'm sorry, Dan."

"Don't be." The words burst out of him. "I'm not a bit sorry you kissed me, Bailey."

"Okay." A shadow of a smile drifted across her lips as she studied him. "I'm glad to hear it. But I shouldn't have surprised you like that, right there in front of everybody."

He drew in a long slow breath. He shouldn't ask her. He should go right ahead with what he needed to say.

But he couldn't help it. He had to know. "Why, Bailey?"

"You're actually going to make me spell it out?" Bailey made a rueful face, but she nodded. "Okay." She tilted her head and looked at him steadily. "I've been asking God to help me build a family, and I thought I knew how He was going to do that. But now I'm wondering if maybe He has a different idea. I don't have everything figured out yet, Dan. But I think, maybe, I'd like to see if you and I can make this marriage work."

And there it was. Everything he wanted, there for him to take, like a rosy ripe apple hanging temptingly on the lowest branch of a tree.

As she waited for him to answer, her lips were trembling just the tiniest bit, so slightly that most folks wouldn't even have noticed. But he noticed everything about Bailey, and he knew that she'd just put her heart out on the line for him. Again.

And he knew what that was costing her.

It was costing him, too. Costing him everything he had not to take her into his arms, kiss her senseless and tell her she'd just made him the happiest man on the planet. Not too long ago, that's exactly what he would have done.

Now he couldn't—not until he made sure Bailey understood exactly what she was getting herself into. But first he had one last question of his own.

"Please don't take this the wrong way, but I have to ask you. Is this…" He trailed off. This was hard. "Is this just because of the twins?"

*Or does it have anything to do with me? With us?* He left that part unsaid, but it hung in the air between them all the same.

"No." She paused. "At least, not entirely. I won't lie to you. I'm so in love with those sweet babies already that I can hardly stand to be away from them. But I also care about you, Dan. Or I'm beginning to. Watching you navigate your way through this crisis, as bad and tragic as it's been…well, it's been beautiful. You've been so faithful, so determined to take care of the twins, even though I know you're way out of your comfort zone. It's changing the way I see you, how I feel about you. It's as simple as that."

She was *so in love* with the twins, but she *cared* about him. He wished those two expressions had been reversed. But still, given their past, even those words coming from Bailey felt like seeing spring flowers poke their heads through the dirty mush of leftover winter snow.

But she was wrong about the *simple* part. Nothing about this was simple.

"I'm not saying we should rush into anything," Bailey went on. "That's what got us into trouble the last time.

This time we should take things nice and slow. We have a lot of details to work out. You'll need to find a job, and we'll need to get the house fixed up. By that time, people around here will have realized how much you've changed, and all this silly gossip will have died down. And maybe, when we're ready, we can have a little vows-renewal ceremony. Nothing fancy. Just something to mark our fresh start in front of our friends and neighbors, you know? If Finn and Josie are going to grow up here, I think it might be important to do that. Don't you?"

He had to tell her. Now.

"Bailey, if you want a ceremony, I'm all for it. We'll do whatever you want to do. But Finn and Josie won't be growing up in Pine Valley. I'm sorry, but I have to take them back to Wyoming."

*"What?"* She couldn't believe what she was hearing. "But I thought that part was already settled. If I…if we decided to try to work things out, you were staying here. You gave me your word, Dan."

"I know what I said." His face had gone pale. "And at the time I meant it. I'm sorrier to break that promise to you than I've ever been about anything, Bailey. But please understand, my whole life has changed since then. Colt didn't just trust me with the twins, he trusted me with the Bar M, too. I can't let him down."

*But you can let me down.* "I see."

"I hope—I hope with all my heart—that you do see. Because I said my whole life had changed, but really that's not true. One thing hasn't. I still want you to be my wife, Bailey. I want us to make a life together, be a family together, you and me and the twins. And just now you told me it's what you want, too. That's what really matters, isn't it? Where we live is just geography."

"So where we live doesn't matter, but we have to live in Wyoming? That's the decision you've made for both of us. Without even discussing it with me first." She couldn't keep the bitterness out of her voice—not that she tried all that hard. "This is starting to feel really familiar, Dan."

There was a short, pained silence before he answered her. "But I'm not making a decision, Bailey. Not this time. I'm just stating a fact. As the owner of the Bar M, I have to live in Wyoming."

"Why? Couldn't you sell it?"

Shock tightened his face, followed by a swift, definite shake of his head. "You don't understand how things are. We're talking about a family legacy. That ranch is the twins' birthright. Generations of McAllisters have poured their blood, sweat and tears into the Bar M. It's not something I'd feel right about selling."

"Maybe that's true, but the problem is I own a business, Dan. Here, in Georgia. And I just bought a farm. I've got a mortgage to pay. I can't just dump all that and follow you out to Wyoming. It would mean giving up everything I've built, everything I've worked for."

Dan nodded slowly, his eyes intent on hers. "I understand. You've got a lot on the line here, and you have every right to be upset. I know it's a big thing to ask. But I think you'd love Wyoming, Bailey. It's beautiful there—a different kind of beautiful than here, that's true. And living on a ranch can be hard sometimes, but you've never been afraid of tackling tough things." One corner of his mouth tilted up slightly. "You took me on."

"I did. And I'm not really sure bringing that up helps

your argument." She shook her head. "I don't know, Dan. I just don't see any way we could make this work."

"I know this is coming out of nowhere, Bailey. But you said a minute ago that you thought you saw God's hand in this. Right? And you and I both know that sometimes the Lord chooses to take us down roads we'd never have picked out on our own. Maybe this is one of those times. Would you at least pray about this before you make a decision? Please?"

She didn't answer him right away. Her emotions were swooping around like the swallows she'd had to evict from her farmhouse's old chimney.

One thing was for sure. History really did repeat itself, just like people said.

If you let it.

A muffled whimper came from the bedroom. Bailey stood, grateful for the interruption. "That sounds like Josie. I couldn't get her to burp after her bottle, so she's probably got a tummy ache. I'd better go get her before she wakes Finn up, too."

Dan had risen, too, and he put a gentle hand on her arm. "Bailey. Please."

"I'll pray about it, Dan." It wasn't so much a promise as a statement of fact. Of course she'd pray about this. What else could she do? This was too big to handle without God's help. But no matter what choice He led her to, one thing was for sure.

She was going to end up losing something important.

"Thanks, Bailey." Dan spoke with a quiet gratitude as he followed her toward the bedroom, where Josie's whimper was escalating into a full-fledged fuss. Before Bailey made it to the doorway, a second angry wail started.

They hadn't been quick enough, and Finn was joining forces with his cranky sister.

So much for naptime, but Bailey didn't blame the babies a bit.

Right now, she felt like crying, too.

# Chapter Ten

❧

"So? What are you going to do?" Trisha Saunders leaned over the counter at Bailey's, her beady eyes alight with excitement.

Bailey gritted her teeth behind a bright smile as she finished ringing up the local florist's half pound of dried apricots. She'd never cared much for Trisha. "I haven't made a decision yet."

That was at least the twentieth time she'd said those words this morning. Trisha's reaction was the same as everyone else's.

"Oh?" Trisha looked disappointed. She'd obviously hoped to leave Bailey's with some juicy gossip to add to her apricots. "Really? Well, if you ask me, I wouldn't consider it for a minute. No sense throwing your life away for a man like Dan Whitlock."

"Nobody's asked you that I heard. And who says she'd be throwing anything away?" Arlene Marvin was next in line, holding a packet of loose-leaf herbal tea that Bailey knew perfectly well the caffeine-addicted church secretary would never drink. Trisha wasn't the only one here under false pretenses this morning.

Being caught in the middle of a gossip storm might be good for business, but that was the only silver lining Bailey saw in it. She was so sick of this—she wanted to go home, lock the door and hide.

But she couldn't do that. She had a store to run whether she felt like it or not.

"Your receipt is in the bag. Have a great day!" *And don't let the door hit you on the way out.* Bailey held out the apricots, but Trisha was too busy glaring at Arlene to notice.

"Of course that's what she'd be doing, Arlene! Giving up a successful business and moving all the way to the middle of nowhere to raise somebody else's kids? For a man who's already dumped her once?" Trisha shook her head. "I don't see how any woman with half a brain could do a thing like that."

Arlene snorted. "I don't see how any woman with half a heart could do anything else. Those poor, orphaned babies need a mother. What's a grocery store compared to that?"

Bailey gave up and set Trisha's bag on the counter. "Excuse me." She attempted to reach past Trisha to get to Arlene's tea. Neither woman glanced in her direction.

"You don't know what you're talking about, Arlene. You're from a different generation, and you haven't built a business from the ground up like Bailey and I have. No matter how much she cares about the twins, Bailey has to look after herself. She needs to be sensible."

"Well, I may not know much about running a business, but I do know there's nothing sensible about love," Arlene announced solemnly. "And I don't believe for a minute that those twins are the only ones Bailey cares about. Bailey kissed Dan Whitlock in the churchyard right in front of God and everybody. She wouldn't have done that if she didn't trust him, and if she trusts him, maybe we should, too!"

Bailey felt her cheeks flushing as she finally managed to snag the packet of tea from Arlene's gesturing hand. How could these women talk about her personal life as if she weren't standing right here? "Arlene, you do realize this is decaf, right?"

"That's fine, dear," Arlene said absently, proving once and for all in Bailey's mind that this little visit had nothing to do with buying tea—or anything else.

"That was before all that stuff on the internet came to light." Trisha turned to Bailey. "She didn't have all the information then. Isn't that right, Bailey?"

Bailey had no idea what Trisha was talking about. "What—" She stopped the question short. If she asked, she'd be throwing fuel on this fire, and that was the last thing she wanted to do right now. She needed to get these ladies out her door, and not only because she had half a dozen other customers milling around.

Dan was bringing the twins by in a few minutes so that he could spend the day working on the farmhouse. She definitely didn't want him walking into the middle of this.

"That will be five dollars and thirty-five cents, Arlene," Bailey said.

"Pooh!" Arlene said dismissively. She was rummaging around in her large black purse, and for a second Bailey thought she was fussing about the price of the tea. "You shouldn't pay attention to the nonsense people post on the internet, Trisha. You'd be better off paying attention to what the pastor has to say about gossip."

"*You're* fussing at *me* about gossiping, Arlene Marvin?

Maybe you should pay attention to Pastor Stone yourself! You're the biggest gossip in this whole town!"

Arlene's face flushed a mottled magenta, and Bailey winced. This was rapidly getting out of hand, and her other customers were beginning to take notice.

"Ladies, please," she began, but the women ignored her and continued to speak over each other, punctuating their fuss with plenty of *I never*s and *of all the nerve*s.

Bailey felt a reassuring squeeze on her forearm. Natalie Stone had slipped beside her.

The pastor's wife cleared her throat. "Arlene?" No response. The other two women were intensely focused on each other, and their discussion had grown so loud it was starting to echo. Natalie tried again. *"Arlene!"*

Arlene turned her eyes to Natalie and blinked. Natalie smiled her gentle smile, but Bailey saw a glint of steel in it. "Jacob is looking for you. Apparently the choir robes arrived, and they seem to be the wrong color."

"What?" Arlene's eyebrows, which were already at a dangerous level, rose up into her hairline. "Wait a minute. Are they maroon? Don't even answer me. I'm sure they are. That Mavis Jones! The committee made it perfectly clear that the robes were to be a lovely pale blue, but she was dead set on that horrible maroon. Kept saying we'd all change our minds if we could just see them. Not likely! The only taste Mavis has is in her mouth. You tell Jacob not to worry. I'll get those things returned for the right ones." Arlene hurried toward the door, muttering. "Maroon, my foot! If I don't give Mavis a piece of my mind."

"I think maroon is a lovely color," Trisha said irritably. "I honestly don't see how Jacob puts up with that woman, Natalie. She's so opinionated!"

Natalie made a noise that could have been a laugh, but she disguised it deftly with a cough. "Trisha, wasn't your Pekingese outside tied to the bike rack?"

"Yes. Why?" The florist squinted through the window. The bike rack was empty. "Oh no!" She ran out of the door, leaving her apricots behind on the counter, calling her dog.

Bailey watched her go with a feeling of relief. "Well, I hope she finds her dog safe and sound, but I also hope it takes her a while."

"I imagine it will. Her husband was the one who untied him, so they're probably at home by now." Natalie blinked innocently. "Maybe I should have mentioned that, but she ran out of here so fast I didn't have a chance."

"Thanks," Bailey shook her head admiringly. "You pulled that off like a champ. I owe you one."

Natalie chuckled. "No, you don't. I'm a minister's wife, and I know what it's like to be the star goldfish in the town's fishbowl. This will all blow over, Bailey. Just hang on until it does. And don't pay any attention to what people say. Things get so exaggerated, particularly on the internet. People will post things online they'd never say in person. Well," Natalie added with a second wink, "except for Trisha and Arlene. Those two will say pretty much anything right to your face."

There was that internet thing again. Bailey frowned. "What are people posting on—" Before she could finish, a car honked from outside. A silver sedan had pulled up to the curb.

"There's Cora. She's coming with me to my ultrasound appointment today. She's so excited about being an honorary grandmother to this new baby, she can hardly stand it! I'd better scoot on out before she comes inside.

The last thing you need is Cora weighing in on your personal business, and I know she wouldn't be able to resist." Natalie gave Bailey a quick hug. "Jacob and I are praying for you. All of you. God will work this out for the best. Just trust Him."

With one last squeeze, Natalie was gone. Just as she reached the door, Dan walked up.

He set both of the twins' carriers on the sidewalk to open the door for Natalie. She paused briefly to exclaim over the babies before climbing in the passenger side of Cora's car.

Bailey hurried to the door and held it wide so that Dan could bring in both twins at once. "Thanks," he murmured, and a tiny smile ticked up his lips. As Bailey stared up at him, all rational thought left her brain, and her heart sped up into what she privately called "Dan gear."

One thing was for sure. She was never going to be able to make a sensible decision if this kept up.

"Where do you want me to set them down?" Dan asked.

Bailey took hold of the handle of Finn's carrier. "I cleared off some space on the table behind my counter. That way I can keep an eye on them while I'm working. I've got a playpen folded up in the back. I'll bring it out when they wake up."

As they got the babies settled in the middle of the wide wooden table, Bailey fussed over the blankets. She couldn't resist trailing a finger over Josie's plump cheek. The infant girl stirred in her sleep, poking a tiny foot out from under her blanket.

The dainty sock Dan had put on her was half-off, and

Bailey gently readjusted it. "How long have they been asleep?"

"They zonked out on the ride over. I fed them right before I left, and I've got a couple of bottles already made up in their bag. We'll need to stick those in your fridge. I changed them right before I put 'em in their car seats, so they hopefully should be good for a little while." He glanced around the busy store. "Maybe they'll let you get a little work done before they wake up. Once they do, though, it's a whole different ball game. Could be this wasn't such a good idea, my bringing them over."

"Don't be silly. I'll love having them here." She smoothed Finn's blanket and glanced up at Dan. "Don't worry about them for a minute. I'll keep them the rest of the afternoon and bring them home after work."

Bailey glanced around the store. Her remaining customers were keeping a wary distance now, shooting curious glances toward them, but not venturing close. She knew that the minute Dan stepped back out the door, they'd be making a fuss over the twins and asking more nosy questions.

She wasn't in any particular hurry for that. "What are you planning to work on today?"

"I'm done with the fence, so I'll be working inside. I've noticed a couple more repairs that I'd like to get done, and I need to pick up some things from the building supply. Then I'll be heading over to your place."

"More repairs?" Bailey frowned, noting the tired lines in the corners of his eyes. "You look exhausted already. With the twins keeping you up most of the night, you sure don't need to be working yourself into the ground over at the farmhouse all day."

He drew in a slow breath. "Got to. I had a call from

the ranch this morning. One of the top hands is dealing with everything for me while I'm here. He's doing his best, but he's in over his head. Looks like I'm going to have to get back even sooner than I'd thought."

Bailey's heart fell. "When?"

He paused. She saw in his eyes that he didn't really want to tell her. But he did. "Soon, Bailey. Within a week. I'm sorry. I know this is rushing you, but I don't have much choice, not if I want to keep the ranch afloat."

Bailey managed a jerky nod. "I see. Well, even more reason not to worry too much over the repairs, Dan. You can't possibly get much done in that amount of time, and there's no point wearing yourself out trying."

"I want to do as much as I can, though, Bailey. I promised I'd see to this for you."

He had. But then, he'd promised her a lot of things. "I really wish you wouldn't worry about this, Dan. You've got enough on your plate right now."

"I want to do what I can," Dan repeated stubbornly. He had his cowboy hat in his hands again, running it around and around like he did when he was uneasy. She felt a sudden urge to snatch it and fling it across the store. That out-of-place hat was a stark reminder that Dan was out of place here, too.

He waited a second or two then clapped the hat back on his head. "I'd best be getting on with it. If the twins get to be too much, just call me. And we'll…" He hesitated. "We'll talk more this evening. Okay?"

She knew what that meant. He wanted her answer about Wyoming. And she still didn't have one.

"Sure." She managed a quick smile, but her heart wasn't in it.

He nodded, his eyes searching hers. His gaze slid over

to the dozing babies for a second, and his jaw tightened. Then he turned and headed for the door.

Just as she'd suspected, the instant he was out on the sidewalk, her customers flocked to the twins. Bailey smiled wearily as the handful of women exclaimed over the babies.

She made a sudden, highly unusual decision. She couldn't take much more of this, not today. Sidling past them, she went to the door and flipped the store sign to Closed.

Once she waited on these people, she'd take a break. She'd sit down for a few minutes while the twins were still asleep, do some more praying and try her best to figure out what answer she was going to give Dan.

The customers were in no particular hurry to leave, but finally only Anna Bradley was left.

The bookstore owner pushed her weekly supply of cookies across the table with a sympathetic smile. "You've got your hands full, don't you? In more ways than one. I felt bad coming in here this morning when I saw how swamped you are, but you were totally right when you suggested these cookies. If I don't keep a plate of them out by my coffeemaker, my customers will riot."

"Believe me, Anna, I don't mind seeing you, not one bit. How's the baby?"

Anna's face lit up. "He's wonderful! Oh, that reminds me." She rummaged in the cloth shopping bag swinging on her elbow and produced a book with a smiling baby on the cover. "I brought this for you. I've read just about every baby book out there, and this one is definitely my favorite. No," she added as Bailey reached for her purse, "it's a gift. Trying to keep Turn the Page up and running with a baby on my hip is a real challenge. I don't see how Emily manages twins and the coffee shop, but she does. You're so blessed to have her as your sister-in-law. She can give you lots of tips about balancing twins and a business, I'm sure."

Bailey slipped the cookies into a bag. "Well, it doesn't look like I'll be dealing with the twins *and* a business. It seems like it's either-or."

Anna nodded seriously, twining one long strand of her curly hair around her finger. "Yes, I'd heard Dan was planning to move back to the ranch. But I'd thought maybe, you know, given what people out there are saying about him on the internet, he might be reconsidering staying in Pine Valley."

There it was again. This time she was getting to the bottom of it. "Anna, what are you talking about? What's on the internet?"

Anna's eyes widened. "You don't know? Oh, Bailey. I'm sorry—I assumed you'd heard all about it. The bookstore's been buzzing with it this morning."

Bailey shook her head. "I haven't heard a word about it. What's going on?"

Anna hesitated, but when she caught Bailey's eye, she reluctantly explained. "Trisha Saunders found a newspaper website for Broken Bow, Wyoming. There was an article posted there about the twins' parents. And there was a comment option, you know, so people from the town could express condolences or…whatever."

"And people were saying negative things? About Dan?"

Anna nodded slowly. "Some were. About half of the comments were about the McAllisters: what a wonderful couple they were, and what a tragedy the accident was. But the rest of them were all about Dan." Anna bit her lip. "But I'm not sure you can put a whole lot of stock in that, Bailey. You know how people are. They say all kinds of things that aren't strictly true. Especially online."

Bailey glanced back at the twins. Finn had his mouth open and was snoring gently, and Josie had her head cocked sideways.

They were so incredibly beautiful. She couldn't imagine giving them up.

And Dan. If she let him go back to Wyoming without her, she knew she'd likely never see him again. The very idea made her feel sick to her stomach.

She believed Dan had changed. She did. But she'd blindly followed her feelings for Dan into trouble before. She couldn't make that mistake again.

Probably Anna was right, and whatever was being posted on the internet wasn't anything worth paying attention to. But given the circumstances, Bailey needed to be sure. She was going to have to find that website and read those comments for herself.

"Anna? I hate to rush you, but I think I might head home for a little while."

"Of course, Bailey. And I hope… I really do hope things work out for the very best. For all of you."

"I do, too, Anna," Bailey said quietly. "I do, too."

At the building supply, Dan took his time flipping through the book showing windows that could be ordered. He'd already found the one he needed for Bailey's spare bedroom. That had taken him all of five minutes. Now he was just biding his time until Myron Banks finished waiting on the only other customer in the store.

Dan had taken the precaution of going by the bank and cashing a check, and his wallet was stuffed with hundreds. But he wasn't in the mood to have Myron's sorry-I-can't-take-your-check-son conversation in front of anybody else. There was enough gossip going around this town already without adding more to it.

Dan shut the window book and opened the book on doors. That back door of Bailey's needed to be replaced. He'd noticed some splits around its base, so he figured he might as well add a door to the order.

Of course, Bailey was right. There was a limit to how much he was going to be able to get done in a week, and he couldn't stay longer. In fact, given the conversation he'd had with Jimmy this morning, a week was stretching it.

Jimmy had sounded stressed. "Guy came rolling up with a trailer this morning, had three heifers on it. Said Colt paid him half up-front for 'em and was supposed to pay him the rest on delivery. It was a lot of money, Dan. I didn't see as I had much choice but to write him a check, but there ain't much left in the account now. I don't mind overseeing the cattle and the hands while you're gone, but this finance stuff is more than I feel comfortable with. You got to tie up whatever loose ends you've got hanging down there and get on back."

After promising to come back as quick as he could, Dan had sighed, closed his eyes and pressed the hot phone against his forehead. So Colt had finally found some Shadow Lady heifers somewhere—and apparently he'd paid a pretty penny for them. Jimmy wasn't kidding, either—the ranch wasn't flush with cash right now. Dan needed to get back there and get down to the business of sorting everything out.

As best he could, anyway.

The truth was, he didn't know much more about the

financial side of things than Jimmy did. A little, thanks to helping out Gordon all those years, but not a lot. He was going to have plenty of learning to do—and he'd be doing it with the twins in tow.

And maybe without Bailey beside him. Her reaction this morning when he'd told her about the deadline had twisted his stomach into a leaden knot.

It was written plainly on her face. She still wasn't any too sure about the idea of relocating to Wyoming— or about trusting him with her future. He'd had to fight himself to keep from getting down on his knees and begging her to give him a chance.

Right now, the hope that he and Bailey could set things right between them was the only sliver of good that he saw left in the world. Well, that and the twins. If he could keep the babies safe and if he had Bailey by his side, then he could handle anything life threw at him. He knew that. But if he had to go back to the Bar M without her...

*Please, Lord. Don't make me face that.*

"You done hanging around back there, son? You may have the day to waste, but I don't."

Myron's gruff voice startled Dan out of his thoughts. "No, sir. Truth is, I don't, either." He walked up to the rough wooden counter and pushed a handwritten slip of paper across it. "This is what I need."

Myron scooted his reading glasses down on the end of his nose and peered at the list. "Passel of stuff again." The man lifted his rheumy blue eyes and studied Dan over the half-moons of his lenses.

"How much?"

"Hold your horses," Myron grumbled, pulling his adding machine across the counter. "Gonna take me a minute. All this for Bailey Quinn's place?"

Dan didn't bother to hide his sigh. Pine Valley gossip even made it into the building supply, apparently. "Yes, sir, it is."

"That's who you was doing that fencing for, too, so I heard."

"That's so." He looked pointedly at the gnarled fingers resting idly on top of the adding machine. "You mind getting this totaled up for me? Like you said, I don't have a lot of time to spend waiting around."

"From the look of this list here, you got no choice but to do some waiting." The man glanced back down the items. "I got some of this in stock, but I'll have to order the rest."

This wasn't good news. "How long will it take to get here?"

"Delivery truck just ran yesterday, and it won't be back for a couple of weeks."

Dan's heart fell. He'd be long gone by then. He'd have to figure out a plan B. "Okay. Just get it ordered, please."

Myron nodded, and the keys of the adding machine began to chitter. Dan stood there breathing in the scent of sawdust and studying the calendar tacked crookedly on the wall behind Myron. It was a month behind.

Dan wished the calendar was right. A month ago, things had been so different. A month ago, he could have kept his promises to Bailey, and the twins would have been safe and happy with Colt and Angie.

Now it seemed like the whole world had been flipped upside down, shaken hard and handed to Dan to fix. He didn't know what he was going to do, but he knew he couldn't afford to mess up. And he sure couldn't afford to put his personal hopes and dreams ahead of what he knew was right.

No matter how desperately he wanted to.

When Myron finally announced a total, Dan lifted an eyebrow. "That's lower than I thought it would be. You sure you added it right?"

The old man shot him a hard look. "I been doing this since before you were born, so don't you go questioning my work. The total's right. I gave you a discount. It's a big order, and it's for Bailey." Myron jutted out his chin. "I'm right fond of that little lady. She always gets a discount here."

In spite of everything, Dan felt his mouth twitching upward. "She's worth being fond of."

"Ain't she, though? Spunky, too. Don't take nothing from nobody and can outwork a man most any day. Not that outworking a man's much to brag about these days. Men ain't what they were back in my day, that's for sure." The old man shot him a look. "I hear you're a pretty good worker, though."

Surprised by the compliment, Dan froze, his wallet halfway out of his jeans pocket. "Thanks," he said finally. "I try to be."

"You planning on writing a check, are you? No, now, don't go all hotheaded on me. I was just going to say, it's fine by me if you want to. I'd have taken your check the last time if I'd known you was working for Bailey."

"As it happens, I've got the cash handy. But I appreciate it, just the same." Dan counted out the bills, and Myron began fussing with making change.

"Well, next time, you don't worry about it. Your check's fine here. Bailey Quinn wouldn't put up with any shady dealings, not from you nor from anybody else. She's a smart girl. But I reckon you know that much already. Heard you married her back when the two of you was just wet behind the ears."

"I did."

"Well, more power to you. I don't care a bit what those old women say with their wagging tongues. I don't blame you. A man finds a woman like Bailey Quinn, of course he's going to marry up with her if he can. Parting company with her, that's a horse of a different color. That there seems mighty stupid to me."

"I won't argue with you."

"But then I don't imagine you'll be making that same mistake again. Will you?"

"I don't want to." Dan accepted his change. "But some of that's up to Bailey."

Myron nodded. "If I were a younger man, maybe I'd have given you a run for your money. But as it is, I'll just give you a little advice. First off, you hang on to Bailey if you can, and don't you hurt her or you'll be answering to me." The other man thumped his bony chest with one finger.

Dan kept his lips straight. "I hear you. Anything else?"

"Yeah. Don't you pay any mind to all the stuff they're saying on those internets. Nobody in their right mind pays any attention to that kind of nonsense." Myron scrawled out a receipt. "I'll get everything I got in stock delivered in an hour or so."

"That'll work." Dan folded up his receipt, puzzled. What did Myron mean about the internet?

"That all you needed, son?" Myron asked. Suddenly there was something so fatherly about the old man that Dan found himself grinning.

"For now." Dan stuck out his hand. "Thanks."

"You're welcome enough, I reckon," Myron said

gruffly. His hand felt papery dry in Dan's. "You be sure to give Bailey my best, now."

"I'll do that."

Out in the parking lot, Hoyt Bradley was getting out of a hulking work truck. The building contractor caught Dan's eye and nodded. "Danny."

"Hoyt, it's good to see you." Dan stuck out a hand, wondering if Hoyt would take it.

Hoyt had been the quarterback of the football team back in high school, and Dan had been a running back who made more trouble than he was worth. Hoyt had taken plenty of heat for Dan back in the day, and they hadn't parted on the best of terms.

But Hoyt hesitated only a second before giving Dan's hand a hearty shake. "Good to see you, too."

"Listen, Hoyt, I need a word with you. You got a minute?"

"Right now? No, I'm sorry, I don't. I got my guys waiting on some stuff out at the job site." The other man hesitated a second then fished in his pocket and produced a business card. "Here. My number's on there. You can call me tonight, if you want." Hoyt waited a second before asking, "You needing some help, Danny?"

"'Fraid so. I'm in kind of a jam right now."

"Yeah. I heard about that. You ask me, people ought to be ashamed, writing stuff like that online instead of saying it straight to a man's face. Don't know what I could do to help you out with that, though." Hoyt glanced quickly at his watch. "Computers aren't really my thing. And I really do have to get back to work."

Computer stuff? Dan's mind flashed back to Myron's remark about the internet. What were they talking about? "No. This has nothing to do with…that." Whatever it was.

"The help I need is more up your alley. And I'll be paying you for your time, too."

Hoyt nodded, looking relieved. "Call me, then, and we'll hash out the details tonight. See you, Danny."

Dan spent the rest of the drive to Bailey's place mulling over Myron's and Hoyt's comments, but when he parked beside Bailey's truck in the driveway, he wasn't any closer to figuring things out.

In fact, now he had another question. What was Bailey doing home at this hour? Had the twins been too much trouble for her to keep them at the store?

If so, he owed her an apology. He took the porch steps two at a time and pushed open the door. Finn and Josie were lying on a red-and-white quilt folded thickly on the floor, kicking their feet and making soft grunting noises. Bailey was on the sofa, intent on the laptop she had propped on her knees.

"Bailey?" When she heard his voice, she jumped and snapped the laptop closed. She looked up at him, her face stricken, almost guilty, and Dan suddenly felt a rush of weariness so profound that he wanted to lie down and sleep for a month.

Maybe longer.

Something fishy was going on for sure. And he honestly didn't think he could cope with any more trouble at the moment.

But as usual, he didn't have a choice.

"I guess you'd better tell me what's on the internet that has everybody around here talking, Bailey."

"Dan, I don't think—"

"I need to know."

Bailey hesitated a second. Then she reopened the laptop and tapped a few keys. She set it beside her on the couch and rose to her feet.

"Here. See for yourself. Watch Finn, won't you? I think Josie needs a diaper change." She leaned over to scoop up the baby and hurried out of the room.

## Chapter Eleven

Fifteen minutes later Bailey came back down the steps, Josie cradled in her arms. As she turned to go into the living room, the baby stirred against her. Bailey nestled the tiny girl closer, settling her cheek against the infant's downy head and breathing in the sweet baby scent. A quivering thrill ran through her, fierce and unmistakable.

It might be wrong of her to feel so hopeful after reading the remarks on the webpage she'd found, but she couldn't help it. Now maybe Dan would change his mind.

*Lord, please. Use all that mean-spirited sniping on the internet for good. Let it show Dan that Wyoming's not as good an option for us as Georgia. Let him decide to stay here with the twins, because I really don't think I can stand to let him go.*

She kissed Josie on the top of her head and walked across the sagging floorboards into the living room. It was empty. Her laptop was resting on the sofa, closed, but Dan and Finn were nowhere to be seen.

She hurried toward the window. When she saw Dan's truck was still in the driveway, she exhaled the nervous breath she'd been holding.

He was still here, but where was he? She was about to check the kitchen when she saw Lucy Ball trotting around the corner of the house. The calf had picked up a fallen pecan branch and was carrying it carefully in her mouth.

Dan must have let her out. That meant he and Finn were outside. Snatching up Josie's rose-colored blanket, Bailey headed out to find them.

She didn't have to look long. Dan was standing in the side yard, Finn cradled in his arms, squinting up at the farmhouse. He seemed to be deep in thought, but when Finn squeaked and flailed a tiny fist, Dan gently raised the baby up and kissed the wiggling hand.

"It's okay, buster. I've got you."

"Dan?"

He turned at the sound of her voice, and his slow smile warmed his face. It didn't quite reach his eyes, though, and she could see the tired worry there. "That calf of yours was bawling, so I let her out for a minute." Dan shook his head and chuckled softly. "You're rubbing off on me, Bailey. Now I'm treating that little Jersey like a puppy, too." He nodded back at the farmhouse wall. "You've got some rotten siding there that'll have to be replaced. Not much, but some. I ordered some at the building supply today, and Myron should be delivering it pretty soon. But I didn't think to get a ladder. You don't happen to have one lying around someplace, do you?"

"Not one that's tall enough for that." Bailey watched Dan closely. "Are you okay?"

"Me? Yeah. Finn here is a different story." Dan glanced down at the baby in his arms. "I'm thinking he may need a diaper change. I'll take him inside and see to that before the delivery truck gets here."

He started toward the side steps leading up to the

porch, but Bailey caught his shirtsleeve as he passed her. "Dan, don't you think we should to talk about it?"

"Talk about what?" He raised an eyebrow. "All that junk on the internet? Not really. It doesn't matter, Bailey."

Bailey had been braced to see Dan angry and hurt, maybe even bitter. But Dan seemed none of those things. If anything, he seemed indifferent.

Which, given how passionately he'd spoken to her about the Bar M and his friendships there, didn't make a lick of sense.

"Why didn't you tell me about it?"

He frowned. "I didn't know about it, Bailey."

She waited, but he didn't add anything else. She hated to rub salt in a wound, but he was going to have to spell this out for her. "You didn't know any of it? You didn't know people were saying you conned the McAllisters into leaving you the ranch? That you'd cheated the twins out of their inheritance?"

He was looking down at her, his eyes shaded by the brim of his hat. A tiny muscle in the corner of his mouth pulsed.

"People don't generally say things like that to a man's face." He paused. "I got a feeling something was going on when I was back in Broken Bow, but it was nothing specific. It was more of a…whiff of trouble. Kind of like Finn's diaper right now." He smiled, but there was no humor in it.

"Why didn't you mention that to me?"

"I don't know." The smile faded as he studied her. "Like I said, I didn't think it mattered that much. Does it, Bailey? Do you need me to tell you that none of the things people are saying are true?"

Something in his expression made her flush. "I don't

believe you conned anybody, Dan. But are you telling me it doesn't bother you that people think you did?"

Dan shrugged. "One thing I've learned, Bailey. People are going to think what they want to think." One corner of his mouth lifted a little. "I guess when you've been on the ugly side of public opinion as often as I have, you get kind of philosophical about it. Changing people's opinions is a dicey business, and it's not something you have a whole lot of control over. I do my best, and I try not to worry too much about what folks say."

He waited a second or two, then added. "If you have questions, Bailey, you don't have to go looking stuff up online. If you want to know something, just ask me. I won't lie to you."

There it was—the first little note of hurt she'd heard in Dan's voice. And it was there because she'd gone online rather than come to him with her questions.

Fine. She'd ask him, then.

"Is it true that the ranch is bankrupt?"

"No." Dan's response came instantly. "There's no denying that we've had some tough years, and money's pretty tight. Before Gordon passed on, we'd gotten the ranch back in the black, but then Colt took over, and…" Dan trailed off and cleared his throat. "Colt was one of the best men I ever knew, but he wasn't that good with money. He had big ideas, and he hadn't spent enough time in the past couple of years actually working the ranch to know where the soft spots were. So from what I can tell, he dug himself into a hole."

"I see." Bailey felt nerves start to form a lump in her stomach. Leaving Georgia to take charge of a ranch with money problems. It sure didn't sound very…sensible.

Dan crooked a finger under her chin and lifted her

face so that they were looking into each other's eyes. "It's nothing I can't fix, Bailey."

She nodded and managed a weak smile back. "Right."

"I saw Gordon build the place back up, and I know a little bit about how to go about that. I'm not saying I won't make my share of mistakes while I figure stuff out, but we're probably looking at only two or three more lean years before the ranch is turning a solid profit again."

Josie whimpered, and Bailey resettled the infant, patting her freshly diapered bottom gently.

It was so hard to think with Dan's hand under her cheek. His thumb was tracing her chin. The touch was gentle, but it was so...*there*. She couldn't afford to get distracted. She needed to see this through. "Is it true that one of the neighboring ranchers wants to buy the ranch?"

Dan removed his finger, but he held her gaze as he nodded slowly. "I haven't had an offer, but probably so. The Jensens own the spread next to us, and they'd love to get their hands on the Bar M. I wouldn't be surprised if I heard from Neal Jensen shortly." Dan blew out a short, frustrated breath. "He's a skinflint, so he'll offer me half what the place is worth and get hot when I don't take it. But he'll come around in time, and so will the rest of them. The ranchers need each other too much to stay mad for long."

"How can you be sure? Some of those remarks seemed so mean-spirited. I'm sorry, I don't mean to make this worse. I just...don't see how you can be so determined to go back to a place full of people like that."

To her astonishment, Dan gave such a belly laugh that Lucy Ball, who'd been stealthily approaching them, dropped her stick and bolted back toward the barn.

Neither of the twins was too happy with the sudden

noise, either. They set up fussy protests, and Bailey and Dan spent the next few minutes shushing and soothing.

When they had the babies calmed, Bailey spoke in a whisper, "I don't get why that's so funny! It's a legitimate question."

"Bailey, maybe you don't know because you haven't ever lived anywhere but here, but every place is like that. Pine Valley is like that. Not for you, maybe. But for some of us, it is. People are people the world over. Folks are saying some mean stuff, sure. It's what people do when they're grieving. They talk out of their hurt, and they look around for somebody to be mad at. But underneath all that, most of these people are good folks. I know that about them, even if they're not so sure about me right now."

That reminded her. "What about the other thing they said. About your drinking?"

The world really didn't get any quieter after she asked that question. The babies still snuffled, and Lucy Ball loped back by chasing a gray-striped hen who'd escaped the coop and was squawking for all she was worth.

But the silence from Dan was so loud that it was all Bailey heard as she waited for his answer.

"I've been sober for over ten years. I saw that remark about me hanging out at the bars. That was wrong, or at least," he amended, "it's wrong now. I'm telling you the truth, Bailey."

She believed him, but— "You're not worried that all this stress—the twins, the ranch and all the rest of it— won't tempt you to—"

"No. I fought that battle, Bailey, and with God's help, I won it. My drinking days are behind me. So, no. I'm not worried." He waited a second or two before speaking again. "Are you?"

She started to tell him no, of course she wasn't worried. But then she stopped herself.

Because it just wasn't true. "Yeah, Dan. I'm worried. Not necessarily about you drinking, but you've got a ranch that's struggling and twins to cope with and a community that sure isn't coming across as supportive as you made them out to be. And then—" She hesitated. She didn't even like to bring this up, but— "Somebody mentioned that there was some question about the twins' guardianship."

"There isn't."

"Are you absolutely sure?" Of all the snarky comments, that one had struck the most fear in her. "Maybe we should have a lawyer here look over the papers. Do you have them with you?"

"The papers are all in order, Bailey. Both Colt and Angie were only children. They didn't have any close family to take their babies. I'm not saying they couldn't have chosen somebody else, but they definitely made the twins my responsibility. They're my son and daughter now, and I'm going to do the best I can by them." He looked down into Finn's face, and Dan's expression shifted in a way that made her heart clench tight and warm up all at the same time.

Dan Whitlock was a fine-looking man no matter what he was doing. But when he was looking down at his new son with his heart in his eyes... Well, then he was so drop-dead gorgeous that when he lifted his head and looked at her, all starch went right out of her knees.

"I really want the four of us to be a family, Bailey. I

know that comes with a steep price tag for you, and I'm sorry. But there's not much I can do about it."

"Maybe there is, though, Dan." She rushed forward, desperately. "I still don't see why you couldn't stay here. There's somebody who wants to buy the ranch, and you said yourself the place is struggling. Wouldn't selling it be the most sensible thing to do?"

Dan shook his head. "We've talked about this already, Bailey. Selling the ranch isn't an option. The Bar M has been in the McAllister family for generations."

"But you're not a McAllister, Dan. And neither am I."

"Finn and Josie are. As far as I'm concerned, the Bar M is theirs, no matter what the legal papers say."

"They're only babies, Dan. They don't have any emotional attachment to the ranch. You don't even know for sure if they'll want to be ranchers when they grow up. If you sell the place, you could put the money into a trust for their educations. That way they could choose their own paths."

"I'll make sure they get whatever kind of education they need, but I'll find a way to do it without selling their birthright. I'm sorry, Bailey, but like I've said before, I don't have a choice here. Colt knew that I'd see this the way he and his grandpa did. He trusted me to do the right thing."

"But is it more important to do the right thing for the McAllisters or for *us*, Dan? My business is turning a solid profit. You keep talking about the importance of family? Well, your family, your real family, is in Pine Valley. Abel and Emily are just a few miles down the road, and the twins could grow up knowing their cousins. Do we really want to give all that up for a ranch that could very well go belly up and leave us with nothing?"

Dan studied her, a muscle jumping in his cheek. "You really think I'd let that happen, Bailey? That I'd ever see you and these babies left with nothing? You don't believe that I'd make sure the three of you had everything you needed?"

"Dan—"

Just then a horn blew behind them. A large truck with Banks Building Supply in script on its sides was pulling into the driveway.

"The material's here." Dan looked down at Finn. "I'll go get him changed real quick. Then can you watch the twins while I help get the stuff unloaded?"

"Sure." There was something stiff about the way he asked, like he was asking a stranger for a favor. It hurt her heart. She snagged his sleeve as he passed her. "Dan, I care about you, all of you. I do."

He halted, but he kept his eyes fixed on the approaching truck. "I believe you care, Bailey. I just don't think you trust me all that much. And that's where we get mired up, you and me. Every single time."

And with that, he left her and headed into the house.

The next afternoon, Dan stepped back from the tractor and wiped his greasy hands on a rag. "Try her now, Abel."

Abel obliged by turning the key, and the tractor sputtered before choking down again. "Still not quite there."

"At least she's turning over. I'll do some more adjusting, and we'll see where we are."

"All right. But before you get back into it, there's something else I'd like you to have a look at. Wait here a minute."

Abel climbed off the tractor and disappeared out the barn door. For a few seconds, the only sounds were the

contented clucking of the Goosefeather Farm hens in their
enclosure and an occasional honk from Glory the goose,
who was strolling around the yard. Dan finished wiping
off his fingers, a waste of time since they were just going
to get greasy again, and waited uneasily.

Looked like Abel was finally getting around to the
real topic he'd wanted to discuss when he'd summoned
Dan over here. Dan had known this wasn't really about
a broken-down tractor. It had taken Abel long enough.
They'd been working in the barn for the better part of
two hours.

Not that Dan was complaining. Abel probably wanted
to talk about all the sniping plastered across the *Broken
Bow Tribune*'s website, and Dan wasn't particularly anxious to have that conversation. Focusing on the ailing
tractor had been a welcome distraction.

Abel came back in with a folded-up paper in his hands.
"Here," he said, thrusting at Dan. "This is for you."

Dan unfolded the paper and scanned it. It was some
kind of legal document. Dan didn't speak lawyer all that
fluently, so it took him a minute to figure it out. "This is
the deed to the cabin."

Abel nodded. "And the ten acres around it. Emily and
I have talked it over, and we're agreed. We want you to
have it."

Dan shook his head and held the paper out. "I can't
accept this, Abel."

Abel made no move to take it. "Sure you can."

"I guess this means you've heard about the stuff on the
internet. So what, now you're going to try to talk me into
living at the cabin instead of going back to Wyoming?"

"Nope. The cabin's yours free and clear. You can sell

it if you want. Use the money for whatever you might need back at that ranch of yours."

"Thanks, but I don't need a handout, Abel."

"Good, because I'm not giving you one. I'm just splitting things up fair, that's all. I kept the fifteen acres that adjoin Goosefeather, and I've been thinking ever since the twins were born that I needed to move my woodcarving shed closer to home. So this makes sense."

Dan shook his head and set the deed on the worn seat of the tractor. "You're not fooling me. You saw that comment about the ranch being underwater financially, and you're trying to help me out. I appreciate it, but there's no need, Abel. I'll have the Bar M back where it ought to be soon enough, and I'll do it on my own."

"I don't doubt it."

"Then you're the only one that doesn't." Dan reached back into the engine. This conversation had gone about far enough. "Let me tweak this a little more and we'll see how she does. I think we've just about got her straightened out."

That was Abel's cue to climb back up on the tractor, but he stayed where he was.

"You're talking about Bailey, aren't you? 'Course you are. She's the only person whose opinion you've ever cared much about apart from your own. Danny, I don't have much business giving anybody advice, but I'm going to give you some anyhow. You've got to stop pushing Bailey. If you don't, you're likely to lose her for good."

"Seems like that's going to happen anyhow." Dan weighed the wrench in his hand.

"And that's scaring you to death and making you stupid. You know better, Dan. You have to. You've worked around animals, and people aren't that different. You push 'em, they just dig in their heels and fight you harder. 'Specially if they've been hurt in the past. Trust takes its own sweet time, Danny. You can't rush it."

"Then there's no hope, I guess." Dan's heart sank to the bottom of his boots, and he flung the wrench onto a nearby hay bale. "Bailey still doesn't trust me as far as she can throw me, and I'm leaving at the end of the week."

"As long as we've got the Lord in our corner, there's always hope. Sometimes He likes to show off by waiting until the last minute, and sometimes He doesn't answer our prayers the way we want Him to. Could be Bailey's not the only one who's got to learn how to trust. Leave it in His hands, Danny, and see what happens." Abel hoisted himself back up onto the tractor. He plucked the folded deed off the seat and held it out wordlessly in Dan's direction.

Dan hesitated, then he took the deed from his brother's hand and stuffed it in his pocket. "All right. Let's get this tractor running. I guess I'd better go have a talk with Bailey."

## Chapter Twelve

Bailey grabbed the lowest plank of rotten siding with both hands and gave a mighty tug. Nope. It still wasn't loose enough to come away. She looked down for the crowbar she'd dropped on the ground a few seconds ago, but it had disappeared.

"Lucy!" Bailey spotted the calf a few yards away. She'd dropped the metal tool on the ground and was nosing it curiously. "I need that!"

She'd known better than to let the calf out when she was trying to work on a project, but nowadays the house just seemed so empty whenever Dan and the twins weren't here. When a person was miserable and lonesome, even the company of a mischievous calf was better than nothing.

Bailey was determined to stop mooning around and worrying. Even if Dan did go back to Wyoming, it wasn't the end of the world. She'd had a perfectly good life all planned out here before Dan had come back, before he'd brought the twins into her life. If Dan was determined not to listen to reason, she could go back to that plan and be perfectly happy.

Eventually.

That's what she was telling herself, anyway. If it seemed a little hard to believe right now, that just meant that she had to try harder. She needed to start handling things on her own again, like she'd been doing before Dan's truck had rolled up in her driveway.

To start with, she could rip down some of this rotten siding Dan had pointed out. But she needed her crowbar.

Lucy watched Bailey's approach cautiously. "I need that, Lucy." Bailey took another step, and Lucy rolled her big brown eyes and nudged the crowbar an inch or two on the grass. "They're rotten enough to need to be replaced, but not rotten enough that they come off easy. Although," Bailey added in a mutter, "I don't know why on earth I expected anything about this house would be easy. Everything has been a challenge right from the start, and things just keep ballooning. Wyoming's starting to look not so bad."

She was joking. Sort of. Sure, homeownership was turning out to be tougher—and more expensive—than she'd expected, but so what? She'd gone through the same sort of stuff when she'd opened Bailey's, and she'd made it through that. Now the store was doing great.

Well, more or less. Not only was she coping with an endless flow of customers who really just wanted to chat about her personal life, but yesterday she'd received the official word that Lyle's grandfather was taking her off his delivery route. She'd spent most of the afternoon trying to find another organic citrus supplier, but her options didn't look good.

That plus the house problems plus the whole dilemma with Dan was pushing her stress level into the danger zone. But, she reminded herself, pretty much anything worth doing had its tough moments. That came with the territory.

She just wished all the hard stuff wasn't happening at once. It was chipping away at her resolve to stand her ground.

"You don't want to move to Wyoming, do you, Lucy Ball? Probably not. You wouldn't be the star of the show. Lots of other pretty cows out there."

Lucy Ball huffed at her and shifted her weight. Then the calf leaned down, nimbly picked up the crowbar in her mouth and dragged it farther away.

Bailey sighed. She knew the drill. Lucy Ball's interest in that crowbar would last about as long as Bailey's did. If Bailey left her alone, Lucy would probably abandon the tool in search of something else.

"It's a good thing you're so cute." Bailey shot the calf a dirty look before turning back to the house. She'd give that siding another mighty pull and see if she could get it to give way with just her hands.

She'd succeeded in loosening it a little more when she heard Dan's pickup crunching up her gravel driveway. Her heart immediately leaped up and wedged itself in her throat.

Bailey tiptoed and tried to see into the truck cab. Had he brought the twins with him? She darted a quick look at the watch on her arm. Nearly time for a bottle. She'd knock off work and feed Josie for him. The baby girl always lost interest in her bottle before Finn lost interest in his, and she was so much tinier than her brother. Bailey had discovered that if she burped Josie a little more frequently, the baby would take an ounce or two more formula.

Bailey started toward the truck, but she only made it a few steps before Dan climbed out of the cab. Alone.

"Where are the twins?" she called, not quite able to keep her disappointment out of her voice.

"I asked Emily to watch them for me for a little while so we could talk."

Bailey shivered suddenly, and she rubbed her hands up and down her arms. Three guesses what he wanted to talk about. He needed a definite answer, and she didn't have one. Whenever she tried to pray about it, she just ended up having imaginary arguments with Dan about staying in Pine Valley. If he pressed her now, she was going to have to say no. It was the only sensible thing to do. Her brain knew that. Her heart was arguing with her, the same way she'd argued passionately with her mother back when she was eighteen.

*You can't throw just your future away for the sake of that Whitlock boy, Bailey! You're smarter than that!*

*But I love him, Mom!*

Dan walked over and squinted up at the siding. "You're trying to take this off by yourself?"

"Yes, but I'm not getting very far. I can't pull it loose with just my hands, and Lucy stole the crowbar."

"Of course she did." Dan grabbed hold of the piece she'd been fighting with and pulled it free in one quick move. He tossed it on the ground.

"Show-off." She wrinkled her nose at him. "And just so you know, I loosened that up for you."

"Yeah, I noticed. I was planning to get these boards down for you, Bailey. I just got tied up over at Abel's."

Bailey shrugged. "Don't worry about it. I know you don't have much time. I can manage."

Dan sighed deeply, but he didn't argue. "Look, I'll put

this board someplace Lucy can't get hold of it, and then we need to talk. Okay?"

Bailey nodded. They'd talk. But if he wanted an answer from her today, he probably wasn't going to like what she had to say.

They settled on the porch rockers. Dan looked out over the budding forsythia. "I forget how early spring sets in around here. Hard to believe it's only February, with things already blooming."

"It's nearly March. The forecast is calling for a freeze tonight, though." Bailey pointed at the fruit trees, frothing white beside the house. "Bad news for those. I was excited when I saw all the blooms, but Arlene was right. I doubt there'll be any apples or pears this year. *Early springs bring false hopes.* That's what the farmers around here say."

Dan nodded. "After a long winter, a nice warm spell is mighty welcome. But then when the cold comes back, it feels even sharper."

Bailey was watching him closely. "Sometimes it causes a lot of damage, too."

He didn't think they were talking about the weather anymore.

Dan looked down at the hat he was holding in his lap. "Bailey, listen. I know you don't understand why I'm so set on going back to Wyoming, but I want you to know that it's not because I don't care enough about you to stay. The truth is—" He halted, his heart pounding so hard he could hear its pulse against his eardrums as he struggled to find the right words to go on with. "The truth isn't just that I love you, Bailey. It's that I don't think I ever stopped loving you. In all the years we've been apart, there's never been anybody else for me. The other guys used to rag me about that some." One side of his mouth tilted up as he remembered. "Called me Brokeheart. Kept introducing me to girls. I even went out with a few. I didn't know we were still married. I thought for sure we weren't. But even so, I never asked anybody out a second time. It didn't matter how pretty they were or how sweet. They weren't you, and I couldn't get past that."

To his surprise, Bailey reached over and took his hand in her own. "If you really feel that way, then don't go, Dan. Sell the ranch and stay here with me. Let's build a new life together with the twins."

"I can't do that, Bailey. It's killing me. But I can't." He took a minute to get hold of himself before he went on. "And I can't keep asking you to give up your life to come with me, either. I did that before. I was wrong to do it then, and it's just as wrong of me to do it now. And just like last time, I've made this all about me, whether you cared about me enough, whether you believed what I said or what other people said about me. I'm sorry for that. Wyoming taught me a lot of things, Bailey. And one thing was that a man doesn't ask for anything that he hasn't earned, fair and square. I haven't had the time to earn your trust back like I'd hoped to. So I'm not asking you to trust me, not anymore."

Bailey's lips went pale, but she squeezed his hand gently. "I wish—I really wish—it could be different, Dan."

"So do I." He looked down at their entwined fingers. "It's funny. Your hand always felt like it fit so perfect in mine. It still feels that way to me. Our lives, though. They never did seem to fit together like that."

"No. I guess not."

There was just one last thing he needed to do, and he'd stalled long enough. "Wait here a minute. Okay?"

Bailey rose, watching as Dan walked to the truck. Part of her mind was noticing that there was something grim about the set of his shoulders. The other part was trying to memorize everything about him before he disappeared from her life again.

Because from what he'd just said, it sure sounded like that's what he was about to do.

She felt a flutter of panic. She wanted to call after him, tell him she'd changed her mind. That she would go with him after all.

She bit her lip and stayed silent, her pulse pounding. It was a painful place to be, caught here between her breaking heart and her hard-earned good sense. But she couldn't let that pain push her into making another mistake.

Dan fished around inside the truck cab for a minute. When he headed back toward the porch, he held a large brown envelope in his hand. Bailey knew what it was even before he handed it to her. Her heart went ice-cold.

"You signed the divorce papers?"

He nodded. "They're notarized, so everything's in order. You be sure to look them over, but I think you'll find everything you're going to need is in there. All you have to do is sign them, and it's a done deal."

Bailey looked up from the envelope. "This is what you want?"

"No." His answer was swift and sure. "It's not. But if it's what you need, I want you to have it." He looked away from her, off to the new fence standing strong and straight around her little pond. "I'm sorry, Bailey. I came back here to try to make things right between us, but all I ended up doing was making more promises to you that I couldn't keep." He darted an apologetic look back at her. "Seems I've got a habit of that where you're concerned, and I know I'm causing you even more hurt this time. You've gotten attached to the twins."

"Very." She wasn't sure about much right now, but there was no doubt about that.

Dan didn't smile, but the crinkles in the corners of his eyes deepened as he looked at her. "I don't know much about mothers. I never knew mine very well, but I'd say you've got the makings of a great one. I didn't bring the twins with me today because I figured we needed to have this one talk without any pint-size distractions. But if you want to see them again, to say goodbye, I'll bring them over before I leave town."

Bailey shook her head. *To say goodbye.* If she saw the twins again, if she had to kiss them knowing it was for the last time, she'd fall apart into a million pieces.

"No, Dan. I appreciate the offer, but I don't think I could handle that. It's not that I don't care about Finn and Josie, I want you to know that. I care too much, I guess. I hope you understand."

"Yeah, I do."

"But I'll be praying for them and for you every day." Bailey cleared her throat, trying her best to cling to the scraps of strength she had left. "You should probably get the twins' things to take with you. I've got the portable cribs, and some outfits…"

"You keep those things. You'll likely be needing them for some foster babies soon."

Bailey's stomach twisted painfully. Maybe that idea

should have brought her some comfort, but it didn't. "I bought them for Finn and Josie."

"I know. I appreciate how kind you've been. But Bailey, this isn't easy for me, either. I just don't think I could stand looking at all the cute things you bought for them. Seeing those reminders every day would just keep me wishing things were different. Know what I mean?"

Bailey nodded. She knew.

But it was what it was, and the sooner they got this over with, the sooner they could both move on with their lives.

"All right. I'll keep the things. And if I don't manage to pull everything together to be a foster mom, I'll just give them to Jillian. I'm sure she can find somebody who can use them."

"You'll be able to pull things together. I'm sure of it." Dan's eyes zeroed in on hers. "But no matter what happens from here on out, remember this. You're always going to own a big chunk of my heart, Bailey. That's never going to change. If there's ever anything you need me to do for you, anything at all, you know where to find me."

"At the Bar M." She couldn't quite keep the sadness out of her voice.

"Yeah." He held out his hand for her to shake, and she took it in her own. But then she tiptoed up and kissed him on his stubble-roughened cheek, just a little southwest of his lips.

For a second she thought he would turn his head and turn it into a real kiss, but he didn't. Instead, as she drew away, he looked down into her eyes and gave her hand a gentle squeeze.

"I'll be—" He stopped. "I was going to say I'd be seeing you. But I reckon I won't be, most likely. But I'll be thinking about you, Bailey, you can count on that." One corner of his mouth tipped up. "Same as always."

He gave her hand one last squeeze, then he released it and went down the steps.

One of the saddest things in the world, Bailey thought, was watching somebody you care about drive away. But she watched until Dan's pickup had vanished behind the pines.

Then she sank back down on the rocking chair. Just a few minutes ago, the air had seemed almost balmy. Now she felt chilled.

She stared into space for a few minutes, watching Lucy Ball. The calf had finally abandoned her crowbar in favor of a bright pink watering can. Bailey had snagged it at the dollar store, and she'd absentmindedly left it in the yard after watering the daffodil bulbs she'd planted along the front of the house.

It was made of plastic, and Lucy would destroy it in no time flat. Bailey would have to figure out some way to take it away from her.

But first… Bracing herself, Bailey bent up the metal tabs securing the flap of the envelope and pulled out the sheaf of papers. Flipping through them, she saw Dan's scrawled signature everywhere it needed to be. But when she got to the end of the documents she'd given him, there seemed to be a few extra sheets tacked on. Bailey scanned then, frowning.

It took her a minute or two to absorb what she was reading, but when she understood what she was looking at, she was still confused. This didn't make any sense.

Dan had enclosed the deed to Abel's cabin, along with

the paperwork necessary to transfer it into Bailey's name. There was a sticky note stuck on the last page.

*Abel gave me the cabin free and clear. I didn't want to accept it, but you know Abel. He was too stubborn to take it back. You understand how I feel about this place, so I'm giving it to you. You're probably shaking your head right now.*

Bailey gave a surprised, tear-clogged laugh. She was, actually.

*But don't feel bad about taking this. The time I spent at this cabin was the worst part of my life in Pine Valley. But the time I spent with you, Bailey Quinn, that was the best. I want you to sell it and use the money to make your dreams come true. God bless you. Dan*

It was a lot to take in. So Bailey sat on the porch until the afternoon faded while tears streaked down her chilly cheeks, watching Lucy Ball break the watering can into half a dozen pieces.

# *Chapter Thirteen*

Early the following Saturday morning, Bailey stood barefoot in her kitchen having a fight with her sink.

She hadn't intended to get up this early. The ache she'd felt in her chest watching Dan drive away hadn't eased off any. Sleep was the only relief she got, but last night she'd dreamed nonstop about Dan and the twins. She'd woken up with tears on her face, and the pain had been almost unbearable. She'd finally thrown back the covers, even though it was still dark and she wasn't supposed to open the store until ten.

She'd get some coffee, spend some time praying and reading the Bible, then start making lists of all the home repairs she needed to get done for the foster care home study. Once she got that process rolling, she'd get her energy and her enthusiasm back.

Of course she would.

Unfortunately, her morning plan had hit a snag when her sink decided to be a brat. The old faucet handle was stuck and wouldn't turn. It was offering only the tiniest trickle of water, and this was interfering with the all-important production of her first cup of coffee.

This was not okay. She definitely needed coffee— probably a lot of coffee. Otherwise she didn't know how she could possibly face another long, miserable day of minding her store when all she could think about was how much she missed Dan and the twins.

She hated feeling like this. It wasn't like her. She loved her little store. She'd loved it since the day she'd held her grand opening, but now she dreaded going in every day. The idea of standing behind that counter for another eight hours made her feel sick to her stomach.

Of course her only other option was stay home, and that didn't sound any more appealing. Everywhere she looked, she saw something else that needed fixing. Once seeing the projects all around her had felt energizing. Now it just felt exhausting.

And at least at the store there was coffee.

Bailey sighed. She had to stop moping around and take charge of her life again. She'd start by dealing with this stupid faucet.

"Come *on*," Bailey muttered. She took hold of the handle and wrenched it wide-open, hoping to get a better flow.

Instead, the handle broke off in her hand. The frustrating trickle stayed exactly the same.

For a second or two, Bailey just glared at the metal and porcelain handle lying on her palm, willing herself not to fling it across the room.

"This is only temporary." She spoke aloud, her words echoing in the empty kitchen. "I'll get back to the way I used to be sooner or later, and things will be fine."

In spite of the encouraging words, Bailey found herself blinking back tears. Her new tendency to start crying at any moment was getting out of hand. Like last night when she'd found one of Finn's little blue socks wedged behind the couch cushion. She'd sank down with the soft scrap of cotton in her hand and boo-hooed like an idiot.

Well, she *wasn't* an idiot, and she *was* going to get past this. But she wasn't going to do it without some help. Bailey squeezed her eyes closed.

*Dear God, help me get myself back on an even keel, because I honestly don't know how much more of this I can take.* She waited, but she didn't sense any answer. *Please,* she added desperately.

Then she stiffened. Somebody was knocking on her front door. She swept a quick glance at the fitness tracker on her wrist and frowned. It was way too early for visitors. The only person she knew who'd be likely to show up at this crazy hour was...

*Dan.*

The broken handle still clenched in her fingers, Bailey jogged through the living room, finger-combing her hair with her free hand as she went. Breathlessly, she pulled open the door.

Abel stood on her porch, his lean face worried. Hoyt Bradley stood behind him, and he didn't look much happier than Abel did.

Bailey's hope tanked into disappointment, followed quickly by a little stab of fear. Abel wouldn't just show up like this without a good reason. "What are you guys doing out here so early? Has something happened to Dan?"

To her relief, Abel shook his head. "Far as I know, Dan's fine. I sent you an email saying that Hoyt and I'd be coming out and to let us know if it wasn't convenient. Didn't you get it?"

"I'm behind on my email." She'd seen Abel's message

in her inbox, but she hadn't opened it. She'd been feeling a little too raw for that. "Why'd you need to come by?"

"Well." Abel looked at Hoyt, who only shrugged uncomfortably. "Look, it's kind of chilly out here. Do you think we could talk about this inside?"

"Sorry. Sure." She stood aside to let them come in. As Hoyt edged past her, she noticed the large metal toolbox he was holding. She frowned as she shut the door behind them.

"All right, Abel. Spill it. What's going on?"

"I told you she wasn't going to like this," Hoyt muttered to Abel. "And I know I don't like getting in the middle of it."

Bailey's eyes narrowed. "In the middle of what?"

Abel held up a hand. "Now, don't get all ruffled up. It's simple enough. Before he left town, Dan hired Hoyt to finish up your repairs. He said what with the twins and having to head back to Wyoming quicker than he'd thought he would, he wasn't able to finish them. He didn't want to leave you in the lurch."

Dan had done *what*? Bailey fisted her hands on her hips as her emotions went into overdrive. She hadn't known a person could be so annoyed and so utterly touched at the same time. She turned her gaze to Hoyt, who set his toolbox down with a clank and held up his hands in surrender.

"Look, Bailey. None of this was my idea. Danny came asking me for a favor. We go way back, and I didn't like to say no, that's all."

"He didn't say anything to me about this. Not one word."

"You'd never have given him the go-ahead," Abel answered easily, his eyes skimming the house as he spoke.

"Like they say, it's easier to ask forgiveness than to get permission sometimes. I don't see what the problem is, Bailey. You've got plenty to do around here if you want to get ready for that foster care inspection. And you already agreed to let Danny help you. He's just doing it long-distance, is all."

"Danny's put the money down for this job before he left town," Hoyt added. "So I hope you're not going to make a fuss. But the bottom line is, this is all up to you. I told Danny I couldn't work on your property without your permission."

Bailey listened silently, then looked at Abel. "Let me guess. That's why you came along, isn't it? Dan asked you to talk me into accepting the help. He figured I'd listen to you."

Abel shifted his weight from one boot to the other. "I reckon he thought maybe I could help you see the good in this plan of his, yeah. Look, Bailey, Danny just feels bad about leaving you in a fix, and he wanted to make sure these repairs got done as fast as possible."

"It's going to be weekends, though," Hoyt put in quickly. "Weekends and evenings. I'm snowed under at work. And just from what Danny told me and what I've seen so far, you've got a lot that needs doing. But I'll get it done—and done right."

"See?" Abel said encouragingly, "That's just what you need, isn't it? And I'll come out and help when I can, too. Don't let your pride get in the way of your common sense, Bailey. You've got a passel of work to do out here. You've got siding that needs replacing and a couple of windows, and from the sound of that dripping coming from your kitchen there, you've got plumbing problems to boot."

Bailey looked down at the faucet handle still clutched

in her hand. "The kitchen sink blew up on me this morning. Sorry I can't offer you guys coffee, by the way."

Abel plucked the handle out of Bailey's fingers and tossed to Hoyt. "I reckon you'd best start by taking a look at that sink, Hoyt. And put a rush on it. Bailey without her morning coffee is nothing to play around with."

Hoyt disappeared into the kitchen. Abel shut the door behind the contractor and then turned back to Bailey, his face serious.

"You don't look so good," he said.

"I wasn't exactly expecting company at six thirty on a Saturday morning, Abel."

"That wasn't what I was getting at. Your eyes are all red, and you've got dark circles under them. You look like the raccoon I caught raiding the chicken coop last week. Only not as cheerful. What's wrong?"

"Nothing. Or at least nothing I can't get over."

Abel stood silently, his expression unreadable. "Danny told me he'd signed those divorce papers, and I was right sorry to hear it. I'd have been proud to keep you as my sister-in-law, Bailey."

Her heart constricted. "I appreciate that. But this was really the best choice, Abel. For me and for Dan."

Abel nodded slowly. "I reckon you're right. If you don't love him, then it's better you let him go."

The careful restraint in Abel's voice made Bailey feel sick. She and Abel had been good friends for years, but this mess she'd gotten into with Dan was pulling Abel's loyal heart in two different directions.

She swallowed. "It wasn't that."

The lanky farmer's blue eyes sharpened. "Are you saying you do love my brother, Bailey? Because if you do—"

She cut him off. "It's more complicated than that."

"No, it's not, Bailey. If you two love each other, it's simple enough. It's just not easy."

"Abel, I don't want this to ruin our friendship, but you don't understand how things stand with Dan and me."

"I understand enough to know that it gutted my brother to leave you behind. I told him he needed to stop pushing you so hard, but when I saw the look in his eyes when he came to say his goodbyes to me and Emily… And now you're standing here looking like something the cat spit up." He shook his head. "I should have kept my big mouth shut."

"This isn't your fault, Abel."

"Maybe I should call Danny. If he knew how bad you're hurting, he'd—"

"Do what? Come back to me? He's not going to do that, Abel. And I wouldn't want him to. He made his choice."

"And you made yours."

"Yes, I have. And I won't apologize for it. I've thought long and hard about this, Abel. Staying in Pine Valley is the smart decision. I wish with all my heart Dan could have seen that, but he couldn't—or wouldn't. I can't help that, but I'm not going to ignore my own common sense to go along with him. Not this time." She was preaching to herself as much as to Abel.

Abel looked unconvinced. "For a person making such a smart decision, you don't look too happy about it."

"Maybe I'm not too happy, but I'm not sure that matters."

"Of course it does."

"Really? You know the happiest I've ever been in my life, Abel? I was eighteen, and I'd just kissed your brother in a county clerk's office in Tennessee, right after the man told us we were man and wife. We both know how that turned out. Sometimes the things that make us happy aren't the smart choice. Like chocolate, for instance. It might make me happy, but that doesn't mean it's good for me."

Abel sighed. "Maybe not. But then again, what's life without a little sweetness in it?" Her friend ran one hand through his shock of black hair. "You know, before he left, Danny said something to me about how he didn't have the right to ask you to trust him enough to chuck everything you've got here to follow him out to the ranch. But now I'm not so sure that you trusting Danny is really the problem here. Sounds to me like the real trouble is you don't trust yourself very much."

"Maybe there's a reason for that. I don't exactly have the best judgment where your brother is concerned. If I did, I wouldn't be feeling so bad right now because I know good and well that I can't afford to keep making the same mistakes. This isn't about losing my store, Abel, or this house. There's a lot more at stake than that. It's about losing *me*, the person I became after Dan left. I'm a lot smarter now. I'm a lot stronger. I've built a good life here in Pine Valley, a life that I'm proud of. I belong here. If I throw all that away just because your brother asks me to… Well, then I go right back to square one, don't I? I can't risk that."

Abel shook his head. "I admire you, Bailey. Always have. And you're right about one thing. You're one of the strongest people I know. Strong enough to bend a little for the people you love without breaking, I'm thinking. Of course you belong here, but a woman like you can make a place for herself anywhere she chooses to go. That's why I don't think you should stick with a life you've out-grown just because you're determined to play it safe."

Bailey made a wry face at her friend. "You're a fine one to lecture me about playing it safe, Abel Whitlock! You're still living a mile from the cabin you grew up in."

Abel didn't hesitate. "That's true enough. I never wandered far, but that doesn't mean I haven't taken more than my share of risks. I fell for my Emily the moment I laid eyes on her. You want to talk about losing yourself? It happened to me in a split second. I might as well have handed her my heart in a box with a bow on it, because it belonged to her just as sure as if I had. I had to wait years for her to feel the same way about me, but in God's good time, she did, and I married her. There are days when I still can't quite believe it really happened, when I wake up and think for a minute there it was all just a dream. There's nothing safe about loving somebody like that. You take it from me, Bailey Quinn. Falling in love is the riskiest adventure there is." He offered her a lop-sided smile. "And the best."

Suddenly Bailey found herself blinking back tears. "You're blessed to have found love so close to home, Abel."

Abel shook his head. "You've got it all inside out. I'd lived in Pine Valley all my life, but it was never truly my home, not until Emily came back with her two little ones in tow. Love's what makes this town my home, Bailey. Without it—" he shrugged "—this place is nothing to me but another dot on the map."

Suddenly a loud clatter came from the kitchen followed by a sound of gushing water. "Abel! Bailey! I need a hand in here. And a bucket! These pipes are old as dirt. The whole plumbing system's going to have to be replaced."

"Coming, Hoyt!" Abel ran toward the kitchen, but Bailey didn't budge.

She stood there quietly in the middle of the room, thinking hard about what Abel had said. Shouts, bangs and other frantic noises came from her kitchen, but she ignored them.

She was lost in a swirl of memories so vivid it seemed as if Dan was standing right in front of her.

Dan at nineteen, scarcely an hour after they'd gotten married, his face taut with hurt when she'd demanded he take her back home to her family. *"But I'm your husband now, Bailey. We're a family, just the two of us. Aren't we? That means our home can be anywhere we want it to be. Just as long as we're together."*

That very same pain had glimmered in his eyes when she'd argued with him about moving to Wyoming. *"I still want you to be my wife, Bailey. I want us to make a life together, be a family together, you and me and the twins. That's what really matters, isn't it? Where we live is just geography."*

Just geography.

And what was it that Abel had said? Something about love making a place a home.

She looked around the living room. This house had thrilled her the first time she'd walked through it. She'd seen all its flaws; of course she had. But none of that had mattered. The run-down farmhouse had caught at her heart because she'd felt confident that with a little work, she could turn it into a real home.

But it couldn't, she realized. No matter how hard she

worked here, this place would never be a home. Not for her, not now.

Not without Dan and the twins.

Without the three people she loved best in the world, this endearingly ramshackle farmhouse, her trendy, successful little store…in fact, the whole of Pine Valley, Georgia, were nothing but…what was that expression Abel had used?

Nothing but dots on a map.

And somehow Dan Whitlock, the guy who'd grown up with the worst home situation she'd ever seen up close, had figured all that out before she had.

She'd been so worried about losing herself by reuniting with Dan and so determined not to surrender her hard won independence that she'd missed something big. She'd missed out on the fact that her feelings for Dan and the twins had become a huge part of who she was now—and of who she wanted to be. By letting them go to Wyoming without her, she'd lost not just them, but a lot of herself, as well.

That's why she was feeling so miserable and unsettled. Because most of her wasn't even here anymore. The heart she'd been so afraid to risk had simply packed up and moved to Wyoming without her.

Playing it safe had turned out to be the riskiest plan of all.

*Oh, Lord*, Bailey prayed sadly. *Please help me. I think I've made a really big mistake.*

Ten minutes later, a drenched Abel and Hoyt walked into her living room and told her sheepishly that they'd had to shut off all the water to the house and had no idea when it could be turned back on.

Bailey looked at the dripping men. "You know what?

Leave it off." She reached for the hook on the wall and took down her key chain. "Hoyt, here's a key. Do whatever repairs need doing, okay?"

Hoyt took the key and nodded, looking relieved. "You got it. I'm going to start off by cleaning up the mess we just made in your kitchen. I'll be right back."

"Abel," Bailey said as soon as the contractor had squelched out onto her porch, "I need to buy a livestock trailer fast. Can you help me with that?"

"No need to buy one. I've got one you can use."

"I appreciate the offer, but I don't know when I'll be able to get it back to you." She met his eyes squarely. "Could be quite a while."

"I see." There was a short beat of silence as Abel studied her. "Going somewhere, are you?"

"You know what? I think maybe I am."

For a second, she thought she saw tears glimmering in the tall man's eyes, but he only shook his head and grinned. "Then you're welcome to the trailer and anything else I've got. After all—" he flung one wet arm over her shoulders, pulling her close and soaking her in the process "—you're family, Bailey Quinn. Or—" He leaned closer and muttered in her ear, "Is it Bailey Whitlock now?"

"I'm not sure," she answered honestly. "But I'm ready to find out."


"Shh, buddy. It's okay!" In the ranch house nursery, Dan flexed his knees, bouncing a wailing Finn against his shoulder while he tried to change Josie's diaper one-handed. "Just let me get your sister fixed up, and we'll go downstairs and have breakfast."

Finn's fussing only got louder, and Dan winced. It

was like the kid knew that once they all managed to get downstairs, there was still going to be some lag time as Dan heated up bottles and traded off feeding the twins.

Finn had an appetite like a horse, and he didn't like to wait for his food. And the problem was, the two little ones seemed to be connected. If Finn screamed, it always freaked out Josie, too.

"I can handle all things through Christ Who gives me strength," Dan muttered as he struggled to get the sticky tapes on Josie's disposable diaper in the appropriate spots. He hoped this one actually stayed on. He had about a fifty-fifty track record in that area lately, and there were a lot of tiny pink bloomers waiting in the laundry hamper.

He shot a quick glance at his scratched wristwatch. The vet was going to be here any minute to do those pregnancy checks, and Dan hadn't even started with the bottles yet. Finn was going to lose his mind.

What a day for the new sitter to cancel on him. Although he hadn't been all that surprised, really. The look on the older woman's face when he'd said "twins" had been a pretty clear warning.

He'd start a new babysitter search this afternoon, but for right now he'd just have to find a way to manage on his own.

"Come on, munchkins. Let's go downstairs and get some grub." He gently picked up both twins and started picking his way down the wide wooden stairs toward the kitchen. Sometimes movement calmed the twins down— Dan had spent half of last night pacing the floor with one twin or the other. But right now, nothing seemed to do the trick. Finn's crying had stirred Josie up, and both babies howled the whole way down the steps.

Dan's eye snagged on a photograph of Colt and Angie,

and he sighed. He felt so strange living in the McAllisters' huge, echoing house. He knew it belonged to him now, at least until the twins were grown. He'd stowed away the McAllisters' personal belongings, rearranged the bedroom he'd picked out, trying to make it feel more like his own. It hadn't helped much. He still felt like a trespasser, like he'd overstepped his bounds somehow. If it wasn't for the babies, he'd have bunked out with the hands, but he'd figured the twins needed to be in their familiar nursery.

He'd hoped that once they were back on their home turf, the babies would settle down, but that hadn't happened. They were miserable, and so was he.

He was missing Bailey like crazy.

Even though he'd known that was coming, he hadn't been prepared for how the pain of leaving her had ramped up mile after mile. It had taken every bit of determination he'd had not to turn that truck around and head back to Georgia, take Bailey in his arms and promise her anything he could think of if she'd just throw out those stupid divorce papers.

But he'd driven on, bleary-eyed and exhausted, until he'd made it to the Bar M. The hope that his mood would improve once he was back on the ranch had flopped. If anything, he felt worse. It was like being away from Bailey was cutting off his air supply—he was slowly suffocating without her.

But the ranch needed him. He hadn't been back five minutes before he'd found out one of the prize bulls was limping, two of the ranch hands were in Broken Bow's county lockup, the tractor had a flat tire and the pregnancy checks were two weeks overdue.

It was a no-win situation, all right. The ranch needed him. And he needed Bailey.

He fumbled through the bottle routine in record time. At least he was getting a little better with the mechanical side of this childcare gig. Settling into a wide armchair, he tried his hand at feeding both twins at the same time. He had to steady Josie's bottle with his chin, but it worked, sort of. And that was a good thing, because just as he managed to get Josie to finish the last of her formula, he heard a truck pulling up outside.

The vet was here. Dan carefully laid Josie down next to Finn, who was already stretching and kicking on the quilt Dan had folded up on the floor.

On to the next problem—how to manage two babies while he briefed the vet about the bull and the pregnancy checks. In a situation like this, a man had to do whatever it took.

No matter how stupid it made him look.

Dan snatched up the pink flowered sling thing that he'd found stashed in the nursery, still in its plastic wrapper. Going by the picture on the front, you fastened this around your middle and you could carry one baby swaddled up in it. If he could do that, then he could carry the other twin in his arms while he walked the vet out to the barn.

Unfortunately, fastening the thing wasn't as straightforward as he'd thought. Dan buckled the belt of the gizmo around his middle and started trying to sort out its folds. Meanwhile the twins scrunched up their faces and began to fuss.

"Just give me a minute here, guys. I've almost got this." He looped the thing over his arm. This couldn't be right. The baby-holding part was on his back now.

Frustrated, Dan pulled his arm back out and snatched the crumpled directions back off the couch for another look.

A brisk knock sounded on the door. He'd better go answer it. Doc Andrews was the only vet in the county, and he was overworked and not particularly patient. If somebody didn't make it to the door fast enough, the vet would be backing up his truck in a split second, heading off to his next call.

"Hold on! I'm coming!" Dan shouted over the twins' fussy cries. He scooped them up and headed toward the door.

Then he stared at the doorknob, stymied. He had no free hand. "It's open!" he called finally. "Come on in!"

The door edged open. Dan found himself looking straight into Bailey Quinn's dark eyes, and the bottom fell right out of his heart.

In the back of his mind, he knew he should be saying something—probably a whole lot of very important stuff. But he couldn't manage a single word. All he could do was stare at her, like a starving man would stare at a buffet table.

She looked tired, but she had that determined, you-can't-tell-me-what-to-do look on her face. She tilted her head as the babies increased their wails.

"Well, you seem to have your hands full, don't you? Here. Gimme." She reached forward and scooped Finn out of his arms.

Her fingers barely brushed Dan's chest, but the touch felt like an electric shock. His brain stuttered back into action.

"What are you doing here?" Then he shook his head. "You know what? Don't answer that—not yet, anyway. Come in."

Bailey walked into the sprawling living room, and Dan used one boot to kick the door shut behind her.

She turned, and her eyes met his, searching them over the top of Finn's head. They were bouncing the squirming babies in perfect rhythm, which would have been funny if Dan hadn't known that everything that really mattered in his world was hanging on what happened in the next few minutes.

Dan tried to read Bailey's expression, but before he could make much headway, Bailey pulled her gaze away. She scanned the disheveled room, and when she looked back at him, she lifted an eyebrow. "It looks like a baby store exploded in here." She nodded at the frilly pink strap dangling off his shoulder. "And what's that about? Getting in touch with your feminine side?"

"I love you, Bailey." He hadn't meant to blurt that out, but he couldn't help it. "Before you tell me why you're here, I need to say my piece. I've been dying here without you. No," he added, as her eyes dipped to the twins. "This has nothing to do with the babies. Well, okay, yeah, they're helping kill me, but that's not what I'm talking about. I can figure out how to be a single dad if I need to. But I can't figure out how to live without you."

"Dan—"

He cut in. He had to say this. "I'll do whatever it takes to make this work for you, Bailey. I've never begged anybody for anything in my life, but I'm begging you right now." He reached out with his free hand and traced her cheek. Her eyes went misty at his touch, and a tear skimmed down and puddled above his thumb. He leaned close and kissed it away, whispering against her skin, "Stay with me, Bailey. Please. Marry me. Or I guess I should say—marry me all over again. Make a family with me. And I give you my word that I'll spend the rest of my life making sure you never regret it."

When Dan's lips brushed her cheek, a waterfall of feelings cascaded over Bailey, and she felt her knees trembling. "Dan," she began huskily, looking up into his eyes.

Before she could get any farther, the squirming baby in her arms went stiff and produced an impressively loud burp. Bailey and Dan locked eyes. All the crazy emotions clogging Bailey's throat got tangled up with her laugh and came out her nose in a snort.

Dan made a face at Finn, who was wide-eyed with surprise at the noise he'd just created. "Real romantic. You're not exactly helping me out here, buddy. Although—" Dan looked back at Bailey "—you might as well be clear on what you're getting yourself into, I guess."

"Danny Whitlock, you know perfectly well that I loved these babies from the first minute I laid eyes on them, so you can knock that off. Besides," she added, "Lucy Ball's outside in a trailer along with a bunch of really annoyed chickens. I think that evens up the score pretty well."

"What?" Dan leaned over and flicked a curtain aside to peer out the window. Sure enough Bailey's truck was attached to a livestock trailer, and he could see Lucy Ball's pink tongue flicking through, licking the rails. "You brought your animals with you?"

"Of course I did. I wasn't leaving them behind."

"But, then…you're staying?" The unabashed joy that broke over his face made her grin right back at him.

"That's the plan. If you'll have me."

"What about your store?"

"Well, I've been doing some thinking while you've been gone. I built that store from the ground up. What's to stop me from doing that again? People in Wyoming need to eat, too, don't they?"

"Yeah." A pained look crossed his face. "But then there's your house. You'll be giving that up, too."

"That doesn't matter. Turns out what I really want is a home, and no place feels like home to me without you. This one will suit me just fine." She glanced around at the expansive, wood-paneled room littered liberally with twin debris, and smiled. "It's got a lot of space. I like that—plenty of room for a nice, big family."

Dan shifted Josie in his arms and bent his head so he could search Bailey's eyes. "You really mean that, Bailey?"

She met his questioning gaze squarely. "I do." She laughed softly. "That's the second time I've said those particular words to you, I believe."

"And this time's no more romantic than the first, is it? I'm sorry, Bailey. You deserve better."

She shook her head. "I sure didn't drive all the way out here for anything as flimsy as romance. I came here for love, a real love that won't fade out, and a real marriage with the man I can't live without. And that's you, in case you're wondering." She dropped a kiss on Finn's head. "Getting to mother these babies just sweetens the deal even more. Now do you think you could make this official and kiss me?"

"I do." He looked at her for a minute, his eyes gentle. Then he nodded slowly. "I surely do."

Dan leaned forward, angling so that Finn and Josie settled next to each other between them. And even though Bailey had already closed her eyes in anticipation of his kiss, she felt the warmth of his smile even before it met her own.

# *Epilogue*

"Hold still." In the parking lot of the Broken Bow Community Center, Bailey Whitlock adjusted her husband's tie then stood back and tilted her head as she gave it a critical look. "Perfect. You clean up pretty well when you put your mind to it."

"I shouldn't be cleaning up at all. It's calving season. I should be in the barn. I don't see why they can't just mail me this plaque."

"For the twentieth time, because this is a big deal. You're the cattleman of the year. It's an honor." Bailey sneaked a look at her watch. It was nearly time for the ceremony to start. She scanned the parking lot. If her special guests didn't show up soon, she and Dan would have to go in without them. "Now behave. I didn't buy a new dress and put on these silly heels to listen to you fuss all night."

Dan's eyes flicked over her, and he smiled in that way that still made Bailey's heartbeat stutter, even though it had been over a year since they'd renewed their wedding vows. "If I didn't happen to mention it before now, you look beautiful, Bailey."

Bailey laughed. "I think you mentioned it twice before we got out of the driveway."

"Yeah, well. It's a long driveway." Dan leaned down and kissed her. "You're always beautiful to me anyhow, heels or not, but they do put you in closer kissing range, so that's a plus. You sure you don't want to forget about this and just go back home?"

"Nice try, but absolutely not. You're accepting this award, and I'm going to stand up and clap like crazy. If you're not proud of yourself for this, at least I'm proud of you. Remember when people were posting all that negative stuff about you online? And now look at you. The ranch is already turning a tidy profit and you're raking in awards. God's been good to us, and I think we should take time out to celebrate. You'll get back to work tomorrow, but tonight let's enjoy ourselves, okay?"

"I always enjoy myself when I'm with you. Okay, we'll do this your way, but we're not staying out too late."

A pickup turned into the parking lot, and Bailey's heart jumped happily. They were here! "Don't start, Dan. The guys can handle the cows for one night, and Finn and Josie are perfectly happy with Carla. She's their favorite babysitter, and she brought her stuff so she could stay overnight. This is a special night."

And it was about to get a lot more special.

"I'm not worried about the twins or the cows, Bailey. But I am a little worried about you. You've been looking tired lately. I think you're working too hard at the new store. Ever since you landed that big spread in the cooking magazine, you've been swamped. I know you don't want to hear this, but I think you're going to need to hire more help."

"Okay. I'll set up some interviews next week."

Dan frowned suspiciously. "That was way too easy. What's going on, Bailey?"

"Excuse us. We're looking for the cattleman of the year. You got any idea where we might find him?"

Dan jerked around. "Abel!" He grabbed his brother in a fierce hug as Bailey embraced Emily.

"Thank you for coming," she whispered.

"Are you kidding?" Emily whispered back. "We're thrilled you invited us. We wouldn't have missed this for the world."

"I can't believe you came all this way just to see some-body hand me a piece of wood with my name on it," Dan was saying.

Abel coughed and shot Bailey a look. "Yeah, well. Bailey seemed to think it was important."

"It *is* important," Emily put in quickly. "They even did a story about it in the *Pine Valley Herald*. I have it posted up on the bulletin board in the coffee shop. How are Finn and Josie? I can't wait to see them!"

Dan kissed his sister-in-law on the cheek. "They're doing great. Maybe you can help me talk Bailey into cut-ting out of this thing early. Then we can make it back to the ranch before they go to sleep."

Bailey made a face. "Don't let him fool you. He has two Shadow Lady heifers about to deliver, and he just wants to get home to supervise."

"We passed your new store on the way in. It looks wonderful, Bailey, and your store back home is doing well, too. We all miss you, of course, but Johanna is doing a great job managing it. You'll see for yourself next time you guys come back to stay at the cabin. I can't believe you're a franchise now! Before long you'll have yourself a whole chain!"

"Don't give her any ideas. She's wearing herself out with just the two stores. Last night she fell asleep with her head on the kitchen table."

"Don't worry yourself, little brother. That's just the first trimester. Emily was the same. In a couple of months, Bailey will have more energy than she knows what to do with." Abel held open the door to the hall. "Is that steak I smell? Good. Last time I had to go to one of these award dinners, they served chicken. It tasted like plastic." Dan, Emily and Bailey all stood frozen on the steps. Abel looked at them. "What? What'd I say?" Then his eyes locked with Emily's, and his face fell. "Uh-oh."

"Bailey." Dan had to try three times, but he finally managed to get out his question. "Are you *pregnant*?"

"Abel, you ruined the surprise!" Emily turned stricken eyes to Bailey. "Oh, honey. I'm so sorry."

Bailey only laughed. Her eyes were fixed on Dan's face, watching his expression shift from astonishment to wonder.

And then to hope. He took a step toward her. "Is it true, Bailey?"

She nodded, and he swept her up into his arms. For a few seconds, the rest of the world disappeared.

When they finally drew away from each other, Abel cleared his throat uncomfortably. "I'm real sorry about that, Bailey."

She gave his arm a playful swat. "Don't be silly. Why do you think I told you in the first place? You've never kept a secret in your life. I knew you'd forget and say something sooner or later. Part of my fun was going to be waiting to see how you'd end up doing it. I have to say, though, I thought we'd at least make it out of the parking lot. Now come on, let's get inside. We can talk about all this after the ceremony."

"Careful, now," Dan worried aloud as they started up the steps. "Maybe those heels weren't such a great idea after all."

"Oh no, you don't, cowboy. I'm not about to let you wrap me up in cotton wool for the next seven months." Bailey sighed happily. "Having a baby is a perfectly natural thing, and I'm planning to enjoy every single minute of it."

"I can tell you from personal experience that every single minute of pregnancy isn't all that enjoyable," Emily said wryly from behind them. "But you hang on to that thought, Bailey."

"No," Dan said quietly. He tucked Bailey's arm in his and bent down to kiss her on the nose. "You hang on to me, sweetheart. You hang on tight."

Bailey laughed and gave his arm a squeeze as they walked into the banquet hall. "That," she said, "is exactly what I'm planning to do."

\* \* \* \* \*

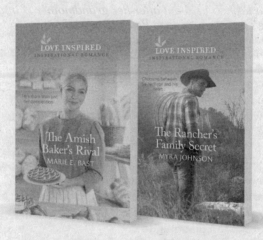

"Time to get back to work," Marshall ordered, and the other men pushed their chairs back and started filing out the door.

"But, *Groossdaadi*, Peter's not done with his pie yet," Susannah pointed out. "And that's practically the main course of this meal."

Marshall glowered, but as he put his hat on, he told Peter, "We'll be in the north field."

"I'll be right out," Peter said, shoveling another bite into his mouth and triggering a coughing spasm.

"Take your time," Lydia told him once Marshall exited the house. "Sweet things are meant to be savored."

Susannah was still seated beside him and Peter thought he noticed her shake her head at her stepgrandmother, but maybe he'd imagined it. "This does taste *gut*," he agreed.

"*Jah*. But it's not as gut as the pies your *mamm* used to make," Susannah commented. "I mean, I really appreciate that Almeda made pies for us. But your *mamm*'s were extraordinarily *appenditlich*. Especially her *blohbier* pies."

"*Jah*. I remember that time you traded me your entire lunch for a second piece of her pie." Peter hadn't considered what he was disclosing until Susannah knocked her knee against his beneath the table. It was too late. Lydia's ears had already perked up.

"When was that?" she asked.

"It was on a *Sunndaag* last summer when some of us went on a picnic after *kurrich*," Susannah immediately said. Which was true, although "some of us" really meant "the two of us." Peter and Susannah had never picnicked with anyone else when they were courting; Sundays had been the only chance they had to be alone. Dorcas, the only person they'd told about their courtship, had frequently dropped off Susannah at the gorge, where Peter would be waiting for her.

"Ah, that's right. You and Dorcas loved going out to the gorge on *Sunndaag*," Lydia recalled. "I didn't realize you'd gone with a group."

Susannah started coughing into her napkin. Or was she trying not to laugh? Peter couldn't tell. *How could I have been so* dumm *as to blurt out something like that?* he lamented.

After Lydia excused herself, Peter mumbled quietly to Susannah, "Sorry about that. It just slipped out."

"It's okay. Sometimes things spring to my mind, too, and I say them without really thinking them through."

It felt strange to be sitting side by side with her, with no one else on the other side of the table. No one else in the room. It reminded Peter of when they'd sit on a rock by the creek in the gorge, dangling their feet into the water and chatting as they ate their sandwiches. And instead of pushing the romantic memory from his mind, Peter deliberately indulged it, lingering over his pie even though he knew Marshall would have something to say about his delay when he returned to the fields.

Susannah didn't seem in any hurry to get up, either. She was silent while he whittled his pie down to the last two bites. Then she asked, "How is your *mamm*? At the frolic, someone mentioned she's been…under the weather."

*I'm sure they did*, Peter thought, and instantly the nostalgic connection he felt with Susannah was replaced by insecurity about whatever rumors she'd heard about his mother. Peter could bear it if Marshall thought ill of him, but he didn't want Susannah to think his mother was lazy. "She's okay," he said and abruptly stood up, even as he was scooping the last bite of pie into his mouth. "I'd better get going or your *groossdaddi* won't let me take any more lunch breaks after this."

He'd only been half joking about Marshall, but Susannah replied, "Don't worry. Lydia would never let that happen." Standing, she caught his eye and added, "And neither would I."

Peering into her earnest golden-brown eyes, Peter was overcome with affection. *"Denki,"* he said and then forced himself to leave the house while his legs could still carry him out to the fields.

*Don't miss*
An Unexpected Amish Harvest *by Carrie Lighte,*
*available September 2021 wherever*
Love Inspired *books and ebooks are sold.*

LoveInspired.com

LIEXP0821

# LOVE INSPIRED

## INSPIRATIONAL ROMANCE

### UPLIFTING STORIES OF FAITH, FORGIVENESS AND HOPE.

---

Join our social communities to connect with other readers who share your love!

Sign up for the Love Inspired newsletter at **LoveInspired.com** to be the first to find out about upcoming titles, special promotions and exclusive content.

---

### CONNECT WITH US AT:

Facebook.com/LoveInspiredBooks

Twitter.com/LoveInspiredBks

Facebook.com/groups/HarlequinConnection

**HARLEQUIN**

*Heartfelt or thrilling, passionate or uplifting—Harlequin is more than just happily-ever-after.*

With twelve different series to choose from and new books available every month, you are sure to find stories that will move you, uplift you, inspire and delight you.